THE

CAVALIERS OF VIRGINIA,

OR THE

RECLUSE OF JAMESTOWN.

AN HISTORICAL ROMANCE OF THE OLD DOMINION.

WILLIAM A. CARUTHERS

BY THE AUTHOR OF

"THE KENTUCKIAN IN NEW-YORK."

IN TWO VOLUMES.

VOL. I.

NEW-YORK:
PUBLISHED BY HARPER & BROTHERS,
NO. 82 CLIFF-STREET,
AND SOLD BY THE PRINCIPAL BOOKSELLERS THROUGHOUT
THE UNITED STATES.

1834.

Reprinted by
THE GREGG PRESS/RIDGEWOOD, N. J.

First published in 1834 by Harper & Bros.
Republished in 1968 by
The Gregg Press Incorporated
171 East Ridgewood Avenue
Ridgewood, New Jersey U.S.A.

Library of Congress Catalog Card Number: 68-23715

Reprinted from a copy in the collections of
The New York Public Library
Astor, Lenox, and Tilden Foundations

Printed in United States of America

AMERICANS IN FICTION

In the domain of literature the play may once have been the chief abstract and chronicle of the times, but during the nineteenth and twentieth centuries the novel has usurped the chief place in holding the mirror up to the homely face of society. On this account, if for no other, the Gregg Press series of reprints of American fiction merits the attention of all students of Americana and of librarians interested in building up adequate collections dealing with the social and literary history of the United States. Most of the three score and ten novels or volumes of short stories included in the series enjoyed considerable fame in their day but have been so long out of print as to be virtually unobtainable in the original editions.

Included in the list are works by writers not presently fashionable in critical circles—but nevertheless well known to literary historians—among them Joel Chandler Harris, Harriet Beecher Stowe, Thomas Bailey Aldrich, and William Gilmore Simms. A substantial element in the list consists of authors who are known especially for their graphic portrayal of a particular American setting, such as Gertrude Atherton (California), Arlo Bates (Boston), Alice Brown (New England), Edward Eggleston (Indiana), Mary Wilkins Freeman (New England), Henry B. Fuller (Chicago), Richard M. Johnston (Georgia), James Lane Allen (Kentucky), Mary N. Murfree (Tennessee), and Thomas Nelson Page (Virginia). There is even a novel by Frederic Remington, one of the most popular painters of the Western cowboy and Indian—and another, and impressive minor classic on the early mining region of Colorado, from the pen of Mary Hallock Foote. The professional student of American literature will rejoice in the opportunity afforded by the collection to extend his reading of fiction belonging to what is called the "local-color movement"—a major current in the development of the national belles-lettres.

Among the titles in the series are also a number of famous historical novels. Silas Weir Mitchell's *Hugh Wynne* is one of the very best fictional treatments of the American Revolution. John Esten Cooke is the foremost Southern writer of his day who dealt with the Civil War. The two books by Thomas Dixon are among the most famous novels on the Reconstruction Era, with sensational disclosures of the original Ku Klux Klan in action. They supplied the grist for the first great movie "spectacular"—*The Birth of a Nation* (1915).

Paul Leicester Ford's *The Honorable Peter Stirling* is justly ranked among the top American novels which portray American politics in action—a subject illuminated by other novelists in the Gregg list—A. H. Lewis, Frances H. Burnett, and Alice Brown, for example. Economic problems are forcefully put before the reader in works by Aldrich, Mrs. Freeman, and John Hay, whose novels illustrate the ominous concern over the early battles between labor and capital. From the sweatshops of Eastern cities in which newly arrived immigrants toiled for pittances, to the Western mining camps where the laborers packed revolvers, the working class of the times enters into various other stories in the Gregg list. The capitalist class, also, comes in for attention, with an account of a struggle for the ownership of a railroad in Samuel Merwin's *The Short-Line War* and with the devastating documentation of the foibles of the newly rich and their wives in the narratives of David Graham Phillips. It was Phillips whose annoying talent for the exposure of abuses led Theodore Roosevelt to put the term "muck-raker" into currency.

While it is apparent that local-color stories, the historical novel, and the economic novel have all been borne in mind in choosing the titles for this important series of reprints, it is evident that careful consideration has also been given to treatments of various minority elements in the American population. The Negro, especially, but also the Indian, the half-breed, Creoles, Cajuns—and even the West Coast Japanese—appear as characters in various of these novels or volumes of short stories and sketches. Joel Chandler Harris's *Free Joe* will open the eyes of readers who know that author solely as the creator of humorous old Uncle Remus. And there is a revelatory volume of dialect tales, written by a Negro author, *The Conjure Woman* by Charles W. Chesnutt.

In literary conventions and the dominating attitudes toward life, the works in the Gregg series range from the adventurous romance illustrated so well by Mayne Reid or the polite urbanity of Owen Wister to the mordant irony of Kate Chopin and the grimmer realism of Joseph Kirkland's own experiences on bloody Civil War battlefields or the depressing display of New York farm life by Harold Frederic. In short, the series admirably illustrates the general qualities of the fiction produced in the United States during the era covered, just as it generously mirrors the geographical regions, the people, and the problems of the times.

PROFESSOR CLARENCE GOHDES
Duke University
Durham, North Carolina

December, 1967

WILLIAM ALEXANDER CARUTHERS

William A. Caruthers was born in Lexington, Virginia in 1802, the second son in a family of ten children. His ancestors came from one of the oldest clans in Scotland, and it was said that the Carruthers (note the different spelling) fought for Mary Stuart. The first Caruthers arrived in America during the wave of Scottish emigration which occurred in the early 18th century, and the family followed the common pattern of movement: Scotland, Ireland, Pennsylvania, Canada, and then the southern United States. William Caruthers, Sr. was a successful merchant, a gentleman farmer and a highly respected member of society. Like most of the Scotch, he was avid for education.

William Jr. studied the classics at Washington College (now Washington and Lee), which at that time had only forty-four students. In 1818 he wrote a delightful account of the climbing of the National Bridge in Virginia. From 1821-1823 he studied medicine in Philadelphia, returning to Lexington in 1823 to marry Louisa Gibson, a beautiful heiress who belonged to the Tidewater aristocracy. The couple bought an elegant home, in which they were able to entertain with the hospitality and graciousness typical of their class and of the old South.

In 1829, because of financial difficulties, William and his family went to New York, where he practiced medicine, arriving just in time to combat a cholera epidemic which was decimating the filth-ridden city. Here, he got acquainted with many literary men, and wrote a short biography of Daniel Boone, and a witty, sophisticated sketch called "A Musical Soiree." *The Kentuckian in New-York* appeared in 1834, a year of great literary activity. In that epoch, unlike ours, Southern writers were not well regarded—"there is evidently a current in American Literature, the fountain-head of which lies north of the Potomac, and in which a southern is compelled to navigate up the stream if he jumps in too far south," wrote Caruthers. *The Kentuckian in New-York* was nevertheless quite successful, both with the critics and the public. In 1835 *The Cavaliers of Virginia* was published, also by Harper and Brothers. Two years later the family moved to Savannah, where William became a member of the Georgia Historical Society. His third and last book, the *Knights of the Golden Horse-Shoe,* appeared in monthly instalments in *Magnolia.* Never in good health, Caruthers succumbed to tuberculosis in 1846.

Though a cosmopolitan who knew the great cities of the eastern United States, Caruthers glorified and possibly sentimentalized his first love, the colonial Virginia gentry: "Oh may that day soon come, when Virginians will learn to venerate more and more the land where the bones of their sires lie; that land consecrated as the burial place of a whole generation of high-hearted patriots, and where yet breathes the purest spirit of enlightened freedom that ever refreshed and purified the earth; that land in which was exhibited that rarest combination of social aristocracy and public equality — where virtue, and talents, and worth alone were consecrated to reverence, through hereditary lines of descent." (From *The Knights of the Golden Horse-Shoe.*)

F. C. S.

THE

CAVALIERS OF VIRGINIA.

CHAPTER I.

The romance of history pertains to no human annals more strikingly than to the early settlement of Virginia. The mind of the reader at once reverts to the names of Raleigh, Smith, and Pocahontas. The traveller's, memory pictures in a moment the ivy-mantled ruin of old Jamestown.

About the year 16—, the city of Jamestown, then the capital of Virginia, was by no means an unapt representation of the British metropolis; both being torn by contending factions, and alternately subjected to the sway of the Roundheads and Royalists.

First came the Cavaliers who fled hither after the decapitation of their royal master and the dispersion of his army, many of whom became permanent settlers in the town or colony, and ever afterwards influenced the character of the state.

These were the first founders of the aristocracy which prevails in Virginia to this day; these were the immediate ancestors of that generous, fox-hunting, wine-drinking, duelling and reckless race of men, which gives so distinct a character to Virginians wherever they may be found.

A whole generation of these Cavaliers had grown up in the colony during the interregnum, and, throughout that long period, were tolerated by those in authority as a class of probationers. The Restoration was no sooner announced, however, than they changed places with their late superiors in authority That stout old Cavalier and former governor, Sir William Berkley (who had retired to the shades of Accomack,) was now called by the unanimous voice of the people, to reascend the vice-regal chair.

Soon after his second installation came another class of refugees, in the persons of Cromwell's veteran soldiers themselves, a few of whom fled hither on account of the distance from the court and the magnitude of their offences against the reigning powers. It will readily be perceived even by those not conversant with the primitive history of the Ancient Dominion, that these heterogeneous materials of Roundheads and Cavaliers were not the best calculated in the world to amalgamate in the social circles.

Our story commences a short time after the death of Cromwell and his son, and the restoration of Charles the Second to the throne of his fathers.

The city of Jamestown was situated upon an island in the Powhatan, about twenty leagues from where that noble river empties its waters into those of the Chesapeake Bay.

This island is long, flat on its surface, and presents a semicircular margin to the view of one approaching from the southeast ; indeed it can scarcely be seen that it is an island from the side facing the river—the little branch which separates it from the main land having doubtless worn its way around by a long and gradual process.

At the period of which we write, the city presented a very imposing and romantic appearance, the landscape on that side of the river being shaded in the back ground by the deep green foliage of impenetrable forests standing in bold relief for many a mile against the sky. Near the centre of the stream, and nearly opposite the one just mentioned, stands another piece of land surrounded by water, known to this day by the very unromantic name of Hog Island, and looking for all the world like a nest for pirates, so impenetrable are the trees, undergrowth, and shrubbery with which it is thickly covered.

To prevent the sudden incursions of the treacherous savage, the city was surrounded with a wall or palisade, from the outside of which, at the northwestern end, was thrown a wooden bridge, so as to connect the first mentioned island with the main land. A single street ran nearly parallel with the river, extending over the upper half of the isl-and and divided in the centre by the public square. On this were situated the Governor's mansion, state house, church, and other public buildings. Near where the line was broken by the space just mentioned, stood two spacious tenements, facing each other from opposite sides of the street. These were the rival hotels of the ancient city; and, after the fashion of that day, both had towering signposts erected before their respective doors, shaped something like a gibbet, upon which swung monotonously in the wind two huge painted sign-boards. These stood confronting each other like two angry rivals—one bearing the insignia of the Berkley arms, by which name it was designated,—and the other the Cross Keys, from which it also received its cognomen. The Berkley Arms was the rendezvous of all the Cavaliers of the colony, both old and young, and but a short time preceding the date of our story, was honoured as the place of assembly for the House of Burgesses.

The opposite and rival establishment received its patronage from the independent or republican faction.

It was late in the month of May, and towards the hour of twilight; the sun was just sinking behind the long line of blue hills which form the southwestern bank of the Powhatan, and the red horizontal rays fell along the rich volume of swelling waters dividing the city of Jamestown from the hills beyond with a line of dazzling yet not oppressive brilliance.

As the rich tints upon the water gradually faded away, their place was supplied in some small degree from large lanterns which now might be seen running half way up the signposts of the two hotels before mentioned, together with many lights of less magnitude visible in the windows of the same establishments and the various other houses within reflecting distance of the scene. The melancholy monotony of the rippling and murmuring waters against the long graduated beach now also began to give place to louder and more turbulent sounds, as the negroes collected from their work to gossip in the streets—Indians put off from the shore in their canoes, or the young Cavaliers collected in the Berkley Arms to discuss the news of the day or perhaps a few bottles of the landlord's best. On this occasion the long, well-scrubbed oaken table in the centre of the "News Room" was graced by the presence of some half dozen of the principal youths of the city. In the centre of the table stood the half-emptied bottle, and by each guest a full bumper of wine, and all were eager to be heard as the wine brightened their ideas and the company received fresh accessions from without.

"Oh, here comes one who can give us some news from the Governor's," said the speaker *pro tempore*, as a handsome and high-born youth of twenty-one entered the room with a proud step and haughty mien, and seated himself at the table as a matter of course, calling for and filling up a wine glass, and leisurely and carelessly throwing his cap upon the seat and his arm over the back of the next vacant chair, as he replied—" No, I bring no news from the Governor's, but I mistake the signs of the times if we do not soon hear news in this quarter."

All eyes were now turned upon the youth as he tossed off his wine. He was generally known among his companions by the familiar name of Frank Beverly, and was a distant kinsman and adopted son of the Governor, Sir William Berkley. News was no sooner mentioned than our host, turning a chair upon its balance, and resting his chin upon his hand, was all attention.

" What is it, Frank?" inquired Philip Ludwell, his most intimate friend and companion.

" Some mischief is brewing at the Cross Keys to-night," replied Frank, as the landlord moved up his chair nearer to the table, more than ever on the *qui vive*, when the Cross Keys became the subject of discussion.

" There is no one in the Tap of the Keys, as I can see from here," said another of the party, " and there is no light in any other portion of the house except the apartments of the family."

" They hide their lights under a bushel," continued Frank, with an affected nasal twang and a smile of contempt. Taking his nearest companion by the lappel of his doublet, and drawing him gently to where the rival establishment was visible through the door—"Do you not see a line of light just perceptible along the margin of the upper window? and if you will observe steadily for a moment, you will see numerous dim shadows of moving figures upon the almost impenetrable curtain which is drawn over it."

"Master Beverly is right, by old Noll's nose," said the landlord, as they all grouped together to catch a glimpse of the objects mentioned.

"You may well swear by Noll's nose in this case," returned Frank, "for unless I am much mistaken, those motions and gestures proceed from some of his late followers; indeed I know it. I was accidentally coming up the alley-way between the Keys and the next house, when I saw four or five of them cross the fence into the yard, and from thence enter the house by the back door."

"That's true, I'll swear," said the host, "for there they are, some dozen of them at least, and I'm a Rumper if a soul has darkened his front door this night. But couldn't you, Master Beverly, or one of the other young gentry, just step to the stout Sir William's, and make an affidavy to the facts? My word for it, he'd soon be down upon 'em with a fiery facias or a capias, or some such or another invention of the law."

The youths all burst into a loud cachinnation at the zeal of the landlord to unmask his rival, and reseating themselves, called for another bottle, which our friend of the Arms was not slow to produce, by way of covering his retreat and hiding his disinterested zeal. As they all refilled their glasses, Frank waved his hand for silence. "Has any gentleman here seen Mr. Nathaniel Bacon very lately?"

"I have not—I have not," replied each of the party, and the interrogator then continued, "I would give the best pair of spurs that ever graced a Cavalier's heels to know whether his long absence has had any thing to do with the getting up of yonder dark conclave?"

Whether any of the party were Bacon's immediate friends, or whether they suspected Frank's motives in the case, we shall not undertake to determine at present; but certain it is they were all silent on the point except his intimate friend Ludwell, who replied—"By St. George, Beverly, I believe you are jealous of Bacon on account of the favourable light in which he is said to stand in the eyes of your fair little mistress."

"If I thought that Virginia Fairfax would entertain a moment's consideration for a person of such doubtful parentage and more doubtful principles as Mr. Nathaniel Bacon, the ill-advised protegé of her father, I would forswear her for ever, and dash this glass against the floor, with which I now invite you all to join me in pledging her,—What say you? Will you join me, one and all? All rose at the invitation, and while standing with glasses suspended midway to their lips, Ludwell added the name of "the pretty Harriet Harrison." It was drunk with three times three, and then the landlord was brought up by the collar of his jerken between two of the liveliest of the party, and made to tell the reckoning upon the table with his well-worn chalk. Having settled the score, they proceeded to decant full half the remaining bottle into one of his own pint flagons, seized from his shelves for that purpose. "Mine host" made sundry equivocal contortions of the countenance, and practised by anticipation several downward motions of the muscles of deglutition, and then swallowed the enormous potation without a groan.

"There now," said Ludwell, "bear it always in your remembrance that a like fate awaits you, whenever your wine bears evidence of having passed rather far into the state of acetous fermentation." As the party were now leaving the room in pairs, linked arm in arm, "Stop! stop!" cried Beverly; "I have one proposition to make before we separate. It is this. You know that there is to be a grand celebration the day after to-morrow, which is the anniversary of the restoration. The whole to conclude with a ball at the Governor's, to which I feel myself authorized to say that you will all be invited. Now I propose that we all go at different hours to-morrow and engage the hand of the fair Virginia for the first, second, third, fourth, fifth, and sixth sets. So that when Mr. Nathaniel Bacon returns, as he assuredly will, to claim her hand, to which he seems to think he has a prescriptive right, he will find no less than six different successful competitors. What say you, gentlemen?"

The proposition was instantly acceded to by all the party, and then the landlord of the Arms was left to digest the pint of his own sour wine in solitude, as he leaned his overgrown person against the casings of the door and watched the youths as they departed one by one in different directions to their respective places of abode.

"Natty Bacon is a goodly youth, however," he muttered in soliloquy; "ha, ha, ha; but he shall know of the plot if I can only clap eyes on him before they see the young lady. Let me see; can it be possible that Natty can have any thing to do with yonder dark meeting of Noll's men? I'll not believe it; he is too good a youth to meddle with such a canting, snivelling set as are congregated there. He always pays his reckoning like any gentleman's son of them all; and a gentleman's son I'll warrant he is, for all that no one knows his father but Mr. Gideon Fairfax."

The Cromwellians alluded to, who were supposed by the youths to be assembled at the Cross Keys, were a few of the late Protector's veteran soldiers, and were the most desperate, reckless and restless of the republicans who, as has been already mentioned, had fled to Jamestown after the restoration. These soldiers were unfitted for any kind of business, and generally lived upon the precarious hospitality of those of their own party who had settled themselves as industrious citizens of the new community.

The names of the leaders of these veteran soldiers and furious bigots were Berkinhead, Worley, Goodenough and Proudfit; and of these the reader will hear more anon.

CHAPTER II.

Late in the afternoon of the day succeeding the one designated in the last chapter, towards the southwestern extremity of the beach and outside of the palisade, a young and gentle creature, of most surpassing loveliness, moved thoughtfully along the sandy shore, every now and then casting a wistful glance over the water, and as often heaving a gentle sigh, as a shade of girlish disappointment settled upon her blooming face. Her dress was simple, tasteful, and exquisitely appropriate to her style of beauty. She had apparently scarce passed her sixteenth birthday; and of course her figure was not yet rounded out to its full perfection of female loveliness. So much of her neck as was visible above a rather high and close cut dress, was of that pure, chaste and lovely white which gives such an air of heavenly innocence to the budding girl of that delightful age. The face although exceeding the neck in the height, variety and richness of its colouring, was not disfigured by a single freckle, scar or blemish. The features were generally well proportioned and suited to each other, the lips full and gently pouting, with a margin of as luxurious tinting as that with which nature ever adorned the first budding rose of spring, and when parted, as they often were, by the most gentle and *naïve* laughter, displayed a set of teeth beautifully white and regular. Yet one could scarcely fasten the eye upon them for the admiration excited by the exquisite expression of the dimpled mouth, ever varying, and as it seemed, more lovely with each succeeding change. The motion of her eyes was so rapid that it was difficult to ascertain their colour; but certain it is they were soft and brilliant, the latter effect produced in no small degree by long fair dewy lashes which rose and fell over the picture, as lights and shadows fall from the pencil of an inspired painter.

The fair flaxen ringlets fell beneath the small gipsey hat in short thick curls, and were clustered around her brow, so as to form the most natural and appropriate shade imaginable to a forehead of polished ivory. She was about the medium height, symmetrically proportioned, with an exquisitely turned ankle and little foot, which *now* bounded over the beach with an impatience only surpassed by her own impetuous thoughts, as her eyes became intently riveted upon a moving speck upon the distant waters. The wild and startled expression, excited in the first moment of surprise, might now be seen merging into one of perfect satisfaction, as the distant object began to grow into distinct outlines at every plunge of the buoyant waves; her heart heaving its own little current to her face in perfect unison with their boisterous movements.

A beautifully painted canoe soon ran its curled and fantastic head right under the bank upon which she stood, and in the next moment a gallant and manly youth leaped upon the shore by her side, and taking her unresisting hand, gently removed the gipsey hat so as to bring into view a certain crimsoning of the neck and half averted face. Nathaniel Bacon, the youth just landed, was about twenty-one, and altogether presented an appearance of the most attractive and commanding character. He wore a green hunting jerken, buttoned close up to his throat so as to show off to the best advantage a broad and manly chest. Upon his head was a broad brimmed unstiffened castor, falling over his shoulders behind, and looped up in front by a curiously wrought broach. A small brass hunting horn swung beneath one shoulder, while to the other was suspended a short cut and thrust sword. In his hand he bore a fishing rod and tackle.

Few as evidently were his years, much painful thought had already shadowed his handsome and commanding features with a somewhat precocious maturity. It was obviously, however, not the natural temperament of the man which now shone out in his features, after the subsiding of the first glow of delighted feeling visible for an instant as he watched the heightened bloom on the countenance of the maiden.

"You were not irreconcilably offended then at my rash and disrespectful behaviour to your father at our last meeting?"

"Certainly not irreconcilably so, Nathaniel, if

offended at all; but I will confess to you candidly, that I was hurt and mortified, as much on your own, as on my father's account."

"You are always kind, considerate and forgiving, Virginia, and it behooves me in presence of so much gentleness, to ease my conscience in some measure by a confession. You have sometimes, but I have never, forgotten that I was thrown upon your father's hospitality an orphan and an outcast. This fact constantly dwells upon my mind, and sometimes harrows up my feelings to such a degree that I am scarcely conscious of my words or actions. It was so on the occasion alluded to. I forgot your presence, the respect due to your father and my benefactor, as well as what was due to myself. I had been endeavouring to revive some of the drunken reminiscences of that eccentric fellow who sits in the canoe there, but they tended only to inflame my ardent desire to know something more of myself. Certainly some allowances must be made for me, Virginia, under the mortifying circumstances in which I am placed. I thought your father could and ought to relieve this cruel suspense."

"He will if he can, Nathaniel; and that he does not do so immediately, is the best evidence to my mind either that he knows nothing on the subject, or that some powerful reason exists why he should not disclose his knowledge at present. Come, then, return with me to our house; my father will take no notice of your absence or its cause, unless to jest with you upon your want of success in your fishing expedition, which it seems was the ostensible motive of your absence."

"It was my purpose to return, but I had not so amiably settled the how and the when; indeed the objects I had in view were so urgent that I determined to brave even your father's continued anger in order to obtain an interview with you."

"With me, Nathaniel!"

"Ay, with you, Virginia! You know that there are on the island some restless and turbulent spirits—late soldiers of the Protector. They have some dangerous project brewing I am well satisfied, from circumstances which accidentally fell under my own observation. You know too that the Recluse is said to have unbounded influence with these desperate men, and to be familiar with all their designs and movements. And notwithstanding your childish dread of him, you know that he loves you more than any living creature."

"I know all the things you speak of, except the last, and for that I suspect I am indebted to your imagination; but to what does all this lead?"

"I have just returned from a visit to that strange and mysterious old man, and as I have already hinted, hastened hither for the purpose of seeking an interview with you, which fortune has so opportunely thrown in my way."

"But I am yet in the dark. Why did you hasten from the Recluse to me, after discovering the things you speak of?"

"I will tell you; but you must be cool, calm and considerate while I do so, because I have that to tell and that to propose which will astound you!"

"Oh do tell it at once then, and not play upon my feelings thus."

"Your father's and your uncle's life is in danger, Virginia! Heaven, what have I done?" he continued, as he saw his companion turn deadly pale and lean against the palisade for support. But instantly recovering herself she asked.—

"Whence does this danger come?"

"That I do not know exactly; but the Recluse knows, and I have been vainly endeavouring to learn it from him; and this brings me to the proposition which I have to make. You must visit him this night! Ay, Virginia! start not, you must do it for your father's and your uncle's sake!"

"Visit the Recluse, and at night! What will my parents say to it, think you?"

"They must not know one word of it."

"Then it is absolutely out of the question."

"Do not say so, Virginia, till you hear me out. As I have already said, the Recluse loves you better than he does any creature in the colony. He knows all the plots and counterplots that are going on, and if you will surprise him with a visit to-night, he will divulge the whole affair to you."

"Why must it be to-night?"

"Because there is no time to be lost. To-morrow is the anniversary of the Restoration. There is to be a grand celebration during the day, and a ball at night; this opportunity is to be taken advantage of in some way or other by the desperate men alluded to. If we wait till to-morrow, and make our visit publicly, these men will all know of it, and its very object be counteracted by that circumstance."

"Your reasons are plausible I confess, Nathaniel, and secret enemies are at all times dreadful, but your alternative is scarcely less so."

"I will pledge my life for your safety. You have the keys of your father's house at command, you can go and return through the servants' hall when they are all asleep. No sentinels are placed on the walls since the general peace with the confederated tribes of Indians. My canoe lies under the first abutment of the bridge. I will watch you from your father's door till you arrive there. We can then cross the creek in the canoe, so that no one will see us at the bridge. Brian O'Reily shall wait on the opposite shore with my horse and pillion for you, and another for himself. What then is there so much to be dreaded in this simple nocturnal excursion to a retired old man, who, to say the worst of him, is nothing more than fanatical on religious subjects, and certainly he is very wise and learned upon all others."

"It is the clandestine nature of the expedition that I object to, Nathaniel; it is so hurried—at such a strange hour too. At all events I must have a little time to consider of the propriety of the step."

"Certainly, you shall have as much time as the nature of the case will admit of. But see, the long shadows of the trees are already extending across the river and the birds are seeking their resting places for the night."

"Oh, happy little songsters! would to Heaven that my rest could be as sweet and tranquil as theirs this night? But Nathaniel, at what hour shall I meet you at the bridge, provided I determine upon the step you propose?"

"As the clock from the tower of the church strikes eleven I will be at my post." And as he stepped into his canoe, he continued, "Remember, Virginia, that it is your own peace and your father's safety that I am endeavouring to secure in the course I urge you to adopt."

As the little vessel rose and sunk over the swelling waves in its passage round the town, Virginia stood on the brink of the river and gazed upon the scene in a deeply meditative mood, very new to her young and hitherto careless heart. At length when her late companion had long disappeared from her sight, and the sombre shadows of evening were fast closing around the ancient city, she slowly passed into the gates of the palisade and sought her father's dwelling.

CHAPTER III.

VIOLENT was the struggle of contending emotions within the bosom of Virginia Fairfax, when she had gained her own apartment, and strove to form her determination in the matter proposed by Nathaniel Bacon. On such occasions feeling usurps the place of reason, and the longer we deliberate, the more perplexing seem to grow our doubts and difficulties. If, however, there were powerful feelings contending against the enterprise, there were equally if not more powerful ones operating in its favour. Not the least among these was the estimation in which she held both him who proposed the nocturnal expedition and him whose advice and aid were expected to be gained. Bacon himself, it was generally believed, had acquired most of his knowledge of books from the mysterious personage alluded to, and he in his turn had been the instructer of his fair young associate and playmate. It is true that these relations of the several parties had somewhat changed of late years, as the two younger ones approached the age at which their continuance might be deemed improper, to say nothing of any little misgivings of which, they might themselves be conscious, as to the nature of many strange and novel impressions, the growth of years and intimacy, perhaps, but not suspected until with advancing years came change of relative situation and prospect for the future.

All the various relations of our heroine to the other parties presented themselves in successive aspects to her view, as she endeavoured honestly to decide the matter according to the dictates of duty. While she was thus deliberating, the usual evening meal was announced. As she entered the apartment, and beheld her father and mother waiting for her to assume the head of the table, which on account of the latter's delicate health had been her custom of late, all the contending emotions which had so lately occupied her mind were renewed with increasing force by the sight of the beloved objects in whose behalf she was solicited to undertake the strange adventure.

Gideon Fairfax, the father of Virginia, was one of the Cavaliers, before alluded to, who fled to Jamestown during the interregnum. He was brother-in-law to the Governor of the colony, and was, at the time of which we write, a member of the council. He was one of that remarkable race of men which has so powerfully influenced the destinies of the Ancient Dominion from that day to the present. He was rather above the medium height, with light hair and eyes, and although he had considerably passed the prime of life, there was a sparkling of boyish vivacity in his eyes, and a cheerful expression always hovering about his mouth, which instantly dispelled any thing like formality in his intercourse with others. Yet withal there was a bold, reckless daring in his look, together with an open-hearted sincerity which served to give a manly dignity to the lighter expressions already mentioned. To his only daughter he was most devotedly attached.

Mrs. Emily Fairfax seemed about the same age as her husband, and though she still preserved some evidence of former beauty, her countenance was now mostly indebted for any charm that it possessed to a mild, lady-like and placid serenity, which was occasionally shadowed by an air of melancholy so profound, that more than once her friends were alarmed for her reason. As Virginia assumed her place at the board, the conflict in her mind was in nowise subdued by observing that one of these melancholy visitations was just settling upon her mother's countenance; indeed there seemed to be a mutual discovery on the part of mother and daughter, that each had some secret cause of uneasiness; but the effect was by far the most painful to the mother's heart, as it was the first time that she had ever seen her daughter's gay and happy temperament seriously disturbed. The parting hour for the night arrived, without making either of them wiser as to the cause of the other's pre-occupation and evident anxiety; the mother having sought an explanation in vain, and the daughter being too much accustomed to her present state of mind to intrude farther upon her sorrows, whatever might be their cause or nature. Bacon's arguments prevailed, and long before the hour appointed, Virginia was sitting at the window, her light extinguished, mantle drawn close around her to exclude the damp air from the river, and her hat tied on in readiness for the expedition.

At length the town clock began to send its slow and solemn sounds across the water. The house was still and dark, and the inmates apparently wrapped in profound slumber. Her own clandestine movements, so new to her, seemed like the trampling of armed heels rather than the footfalls of her own slight figure. More than once she was on the point of retracing her steps, so tumultuous and painful were her emotions in prosecuting an adventure which still appeared to her of such questionable propriety. The servants' hall, garden, and postern gate were all passed without the slightest interruption, save an occasional start at her own shadow, or the impetuous beating of her agitated heart. The moon was at her zenith, and the clouds coursing high in the heavens, so as every now and then to obscure her reflected beams, and present alternate and fantastic contrasts of light and shade upon the surrounding objects. The river for one moment looked like a dark abyss, and the next a mirror of light as the silver rays fell sparkling upon the rippling waters beneath the bridge. The interminable forest beyond was at one moment dark as Erebus, and the next as light as fairy land. There is no appearance of the heavens, perhaps, which produces a greater tendency in the mind to undefined and superstitious terror than that which we have attempted to describe. Our own shadow, visible as it is only for an instant, will startle us ; and the ill-omened birds of night acquire huge and unnatural proportions as they flit swiftly by on noiseless wings in this rapid alternation of light and gloom. The wolves and other beasts of prey might be heard at long intervals, as their wild and savage howls broke upon the ear, reverberating from cliff to cliff as they fell upon and were borne across the water. Under these circumstances it may be readily imagined that our heroine was not a little relieved at the sight of Bacon leaning against the nearest abutment of the bridge, anxiously watching for her approach. In a few moments he had seated his companion in the boat, upon a cushion formed of his cloak, and was rapidly approaching the opposite shore. When they arrived at the appointed rendezvous, a very unexpected source of uneasiness was speedily discovered. As has been already intimated, Bacon had early in the evening despatched his usual attendant, Brian O'Reily, across the bridge to wait their arrival. The horses were indeed there—and O'Reily was there, but so intoxicated as to be apparently in no condition to guide the motions of a horse, even should he be able to keep the saddle. Bacon lost all patience at this discovery, and would perhaps have taken summary and not very agreeable means to sober his attendant, had he not been reminded by his gentle companion of the peculiar and privileged position which Brian had from time immemorial enjoyed in his service, as well as that of their own family. "How comes it, sir," said the young man, "that I find you in this predicament when I gave you such strict injunctions to keep yourself sober? Now of all other times!—when I had taken so much trouble to instruct you whom you were to guard, and upon what expedition?"

"By the five crasses but you've hit the very nail upon the head. By the contints of the book but that's the very rason I took a dhrop of the crathur!"

"What is the reason, you drunken old fool?"

"The business were an to be sure! you wouldn't be after axing a sinner like Brian O'Reily to ixpose himself to sich a timptation widout taking a dhrop, and may be your haner would do that same for all your spaking aginst it so immedely."

"And what may the nature of the temptation be of which you speak?"

"And is it Brian you're after axin? O be gorra, but that's runnin away wid the story intirely, so it is; sure it's me should be axin your haner after that same!"

"None of your subterfuges, sir! I am determined to know your ideas of this dreadful temptation."

"By my purty an is it Brian's idaas you're axin after, divil a miny o' them he's got any way, barrin a small bit of a smotherin about the heart whenever I think of the business we're on, and the gintleman we're goin to see, savin your prisence and the beauty o' the world by your side."

"What gentleman—speak out and I will forgive your drunkenness, provided you give me up that bottle I see peeping from the pouch of your jerkin."

"An is'nt it the man widout the shadow you're after making a tay party wid?"

"And who is the man without a shadow, Brian?" inquired Virginia, willing to forget her own misgivings in the more ludicrous superstition of the son of the Emerald Isle, whose countrymen, it may be remarked, formed no inconsiderable part of the inferior population of the city at that day.

"Oh bad cess to me, but I'm as glad to see you as two tin pinnies, you beauty o' the world; but it bates all the love I had for you and ever had these ten years past to see where you'r going."

"Well, where is it, Brian?"

"Hav'nt I tould your ladyship it was to a tay party wid the inimy himself."

"Come, see if you can assist Virginia to the pillion," said Bacon, as he sprang into the saddle.

"By my purty and I'll do that same;" kneeling upon one knee and taking one foot in his hand, and then seating her as easily and gracefully as if he had been a stranger to the bottle for a month.

"I had no idea that you were such a coward, Brian," continued his master.

"Sorra a dhrop o' coward's blood runs in Brian O'Reily's heart, iny way. It's one thing to trate the grate inimy with dacent respect, and its another to fight the yellow nagres that go dodgin from tree to tree like so many frogs; the devil fly away wid the one and the t'other o' them for me, I say."

"And who is the great enemy?"

"Sure hav'nt I tould your haner and the beauty o' the world by your side, it was the man widout a shadow what lives in the stone house widout windows, as well he may, seein the light o' his own counthenance may be seen across the river the darkest night any day."

"Sit your horse straight, you drunken piece of stupidity, or you will break your neck."

"Oh! an if Brian never breaks his neck till he falls from a horse, sure he'll live to take many a dhrop of the crathur yet before he dies. Sure I was only crassin myself, divil a word o' lie's in that, iny way."

"There, I have broken one of your necks at least," said Bacon, as with the butt of his riding whip he struck the neck from a bottle which every now and then peeped from Brian's pocket as the motions of the horse raised him in the saddle.

"Oh! murther all out, but you'll come to want yet before you die. Oh sure, but the crathur's safe after all. Wo, ye divil of a baste, don't you hear the crathur all runnin down the wrang side o' me. Wo, I say! Oh but the bottle sticks as tight to the pouch as if it growed there. Oh murther all out, I'm ruined, I'm ruined intirely."

"Draw your arm from your jerken, Brian, and then you can drink out of your pocket," said Virginia, suppressing a laugh.

"Oh you beauty o' the world, see what it is to have the larnin," replied the Irishman, immediately adopting the expedient ; but here a new difficulty presented itself. "Oh murther, but the gable end's all knocked off and fax the chimney went along with it. Oh, but the crokery sticks up all round like pike staffs. Wo you murthur'n baste ; Now I've got it, now I've got it, you beauty ; sorra one of the lane cows at Jamestown gives sich milk as that, fax if they did, I'd be head dairyman to the Governor any way."

Thus our adventurers beguiled the way through a dreary and trackless forest of some miles, until they approached a spot where Bacon signified to the party that they had accomplished so much of their journey as was to be performed on horseback. What farther befell them will be described in the ensuing chapter.

CHAPTER IV.

Bacon and his companion having left O'Reily with the horses, now commenced descending an immense hill which formed one side of a dark and dismal looking glen. The tall pine trees with which the higher grounds were covered seemed to reach half way to the clouds. A cold midnight breeze swept through the damp and dewy foliage of the trees and shrubbery. The birds of night chimed mournfully and dismally in unison with the monotonous rustling of the leaves, and the rippling of a little brook just before them. When they had stepped across the stream, and cast their eyes up the face of the opposite hill, the rays of the moon suddenly broke through a fissure of the clouds, revealing to them rather the darkness around than any distinct traces of the path which they were to pursue. Bacon stood for an instant, and gazed intently upon a little spot of partially cleared ground half way to the summit, then gently drawing his companion to the same place where he stood, and pointing upwards, he said "Do you not perceive something moving yonder? It is he! you must now proceed alone!"

"Alone, Nathaniel? Impossible!"

"You must, Virginia; he will not admit more than one person at a time within his cell. Fear not there is no earthly danger; I will be within call. Rouse your drooping courage! the worst half of your undertaking is now accomplished."

"By far the worst half is yet to come, Nathaniel; you can form no conception of the awe with which I look upon that being! You forget that I have never seen more of him than I see now, notwithstanding you say that he is so much attached to me."

"It is strange, I confess, Virginia, but it is nevertheless true."

"His affection, if it exists, must be the fruit of your representations as to some imaginary proficiency in my studies."

"Not at all; he seems to know every one in Jamestown, and all the circumstances connected with their history: but come, Virginia, we are losing precious time. Move on and fear nothing."

Clasping her hands, and internally summoning up all her resolution, she advanced with a sort of desperate determination. Having arrived within some forty yards of the spot before alluded to, the outlines of a gigantic figure could easily be discerned as his footfalls were distinctly heard moving restlessly to and fro on a sort of platform or level space, left by nature or formed by art, in the side of the hill. His head towered far above the stunted undergrowth, interspersed among the rugged outlines of the scene. And as he impatiently measured the narrow limits of this outer court to his castle, he seemed not unlike a chafed and hungry monarch of the forest when making the narrow rounds of his iron bound limits. Having gone thus far, she was sensible that it was nearly as bad to recede as go forward, and that if she retreated now upon the very eve of the fulfilment of all that Bacon had promised, her past anxieties would have been endured for nothing: she braced her nerves therefore, and endeavoured to subdue the overpowering terror which the distant view of this strange and mysterious man had excited. Summoning all her resolution for one desperate effort, she threw herself forward and fell at the feet of the huge mortal, who stood apparently astounded at the abrupt appearance of his unwonted and untimely visiter. When Virginia found courage enough to raise her lately closed eyes, she was not a little astonished to see him leaning against the stone walls of his cell, no less agitated than herself. He was apparently about sixty years of age, his hair slightly silvered, and his features worn and weatherbeaten, yet eminently handsome. His person was very remarkable, being about six feet and a half in height and perfectly proportioned. His dress conformed in some degree to the military fashions of the day, having however rather the appearance of undress than full uniform. The expression of his countenance was decidedly intellectual; and about the lower part of his face there were some indications of a disposition to sensuality, but tempered and controlled in no ordinary degree by some other fierce and controlling passion.

His eye was wild and unsettled at times, and again assumed the mild serenity of the profound student. Altogether, his presence was intellectual and commanding in the highest degree.

As he stood against the wall of his cell quaking like an aspen, an indifferent observer would have been at a loss to determine which was the most agitated, he or his gentle visiter. Virginia noted with more than one furtive glance his strange and unexpected embarrassment, still however, preserving her humble and supplicating posture. At length, struggling with the emotions which unmanned him, muttering all the while broken sentences which fell strangely upon her ear, and among which she could distinguish repeated allusions to herself, and to events of long passed years, recalled as it appeared by some fancied resemblance traced by his excited imagination in her form and features. He approached the kneeling maiden, and taking her hand, he raised her from the ground, and said in a tone of kindness, "My wayward fancies frighten thee, my child ; be not alarmed, however—there is nothing here to harm thee. My house is poor and cheerless, but such as it is, thou art welcome to its shelter, and to any services which I can render to thee. Come, my daughter, let us in from the damps of the night."

The cell of the Recluse was formed on three sides by stone walls without windows, as O'Reily had described them, the fourth being furnished by the side of the hill, and the roof an arch of masonry overgrown with moss, grass and weeds.* Pressing open the rude door, he entered, followed by Virginia. Near one corner of the room stood a common deal table, on which was placed a small iron lamp, and near to it a three legged stool of the rudest construction. These were the only articles of furniture of which the apartment could boast. The floor, which consisted of the earth, as nature had made it, was overgrown with weeds and bushes. "This," said he, with a bitter smile upon his countenance, "is my hall of audience! Here I receive my guests, with one solitary exception; thou shalt be another." Having thus spoken, he took the lamp from the table, and drawing aside some dried bushes which were piled against the side formed by the hill in apparent carelessness, he exhibited to her view the mouth of a cavern, not sufficient in height by several feet to admit his person in the erect position. "This," said he, as he stooped to enter, "is not a house made with hands, and it is built upon a rock of ages. The rains may descend, floods may come, winds blow and beat upon it, but it falleth not. It is proper that thou shouldst see it, and such has long been my intention. I have much to say to thee, and doubtless thou hast something to communicate to me, or thou wouldst not have made this visit. But not a whisper of what thou mayst see or hear must ever pass thy

* A house very similar to that we have described stands to this day near the Ancient City. Its former objects and uses are entirely unknown.

lips, save to those I shall authorize thee to make partakers of thy knowledge. This is a condition which thou must impress upon thy mind." Stepping in a bent position within the mouth of the cavern, he moved forward and downward, motioning her to follow. They descended many rude and natural steps, which were imperfectly seen by the light of the lamp borne by her singular guide, the rays being often obscured by the bulk and great height of his person in the narrow passages of the cave, so that she was more than once compelled to grope her way by sliding her hand along the cold damp and dripping walls, and by slipping her feet over the uneven ground, without raising them in the act of stepping. Having completed the descent, she found herself in a long natural vestibule to the inner apartments. Her guide had gained rapidly upon her, so that when once more upon level ground, some thirty feet below the outer surface of the earth, he was almost out of sight. She would have cried out, had she not been restrained by a counteracting feeling, which placed her in a grievous dilemma between horror at the dismal place, and fear of the singular being who had undertaken to guide her through its recesses. Commending herself however to her Maker in mental prayer, and trusting in his protection the more confidently on account of the motive for her undertaking, she hastened forward so as with great exertions to keep within sight of the rising and sinking light of the lamp, and the devious windings of the cavern. The footfalls of her Herculean guide reëchoed along the damp and gloomy tunnels with an awful and dismal effect, amidst the grave-like stillness of the place. Occasionally flickering shadows were reflected against the walls, when the light turned suddenly round a projecting rock, affording to her imagination the most startling and frightful images. While her mind was combatting these unreal terrors, she was surprised by the tone of a deep hoarse voice abruptly rumbling through the high dark arches far above her head, with that reverberating sound peculiar to these secret places of the earth. But her amazement was still greater, when lifting her eyes in the direction of the lamp she beheld the Recluse standing upon a lofty but narrow ledge of rock, the lamp flickering and sinking every now and then so as to threaten total darkness. He was pointing with his finger, and directing her to a projecting and winding pathway by which she must ascend to the platform upon which he stood. This once gained, she had a complete view of the resting place of her mysterious guide.

Immediately fronting the platform was a natural doorway, about as high as her own head, leading into the inner chamber. From the high and vaulted arches hung thousands of the fantastic creations of hoary time, and from the centre of these a cord swung into the middle of the area, to which was suspended a burning lamp, the rays of which were brilliantly reflected from a thousand shining mirrors of nature's forming. In one corner she discovered, as they entered, several pieces of fire-arms, and against the wall on one side hung huge swords, long enough for two-handed weapons to ordinary mortals, together with Indian war clubs, moccasins, wampum, pipes, tomahawks, spears, arrows, and other implements of savage warfare. In another corner stood a rude bedstead, evidently constructed by the hands of its nightly occupant, a small table, two or three chairs, and a few culinary articles,—some the manufacture of the savages, and others the product of civilized ingenuity. By far the largest part of one side of the room was occupied by coarsely constructed shelves, bearing many volumes of the most venerable appearance. One of these was lying open upon the table, a pair of horn spectacles upon the page to mark the place where the owner had last been engaged. The very letters in which it was printed were entire strangers to the eyes of our heroine. Some thirty yards distant, in the remotest part of the room, a little furnace diffused a narrow circle of glowing light through its otherwise gloomy precincts. These completed the establishment, so far as the eye could discover its arrangement.

When he had led Virginia into the habitable part of this area, he placed a chair, and motioned for her to be seated, drawing a stool near the table at the same time for himself, and resting his head upon the palm of his hand. "I will not affect ignorance of thy name and person, my daughter, nor yet of thy errand here. The first I should most certainly have known, if I had not surmised the last. Alas ! my child, thou wilt think no doubt that I speak in riddles when I tell thee that those features have been engraven upon the heart of one who has forsworn the world for many a long and irksome year. Thou mayest well look amazed, my poor bewildered child, but it is true ! I cannot explain it to thee now, however ; some day perhaps thou mayest know all. Oh, if thou couldst imagine what events must take place in this little isolated world around Jamestown, before the mysteries of which I speak can rightfully be made clear to thee, thou wouldst fall upon thy knees and pray that such disastrous knowledge might never come to thy understanding !"

As his eye rested from time to time, while he spoke, upon the features of the beautiful girl, he covered his face with his hands, and seemed for an instant to give way to an agitation similar to that which unnerved him at her first appearance on the platform. Occasionally too, when not speaking himself, he became profoundly abstracted for a moment, and his eye was wild and restless, and not a little alarming to his gentle visiter, as it ever and anon fell upon herself, and seemed to gather in her face the solution of some subtle doubt of his troubled mind. But observing that his glances, wild as they were, always became humanized and softened as they rested upon her face, she seized the first opportunity to complete the object of her journey, not well knowing how it might terminate, being herself ignorant of its especial object, and indeed of the very nature of the threatened danger.

"Father, I came here to seek your aid and protection for those who are near and dear to me; My honoured parents—my mother"—she would have proceeded, but at the mention of her mother's name he was seized with such a convulsive shudder that she paused in astonishment. It seemed as if the hand of death was already laying its cold grasp upon his vitals. His eye gleamed wildly—his lips trembled, and his hands shook as one stricken with the palsy, or overwhelmed by some sudden stroke of calamity. By a desperate effort of resolution, he speedily resumed his attention to the discourse, and she proceeded: "I have been advised and urged in my resort to this step by one not unknown to you, under the vain hope, I fear, that you were cognizant of some threatened danger to my dear parents and kindred, and that you would communicate the knowledge to me rather than to him."

"As I have already said, my daughter, I surmised that something of this nature was the object of thy visit, and I will now confess to thee that this appeal places me in an embarrassing position between some friends of former and better days and my desire to grant thy request." Pausing and apparently soliloquizing, he continued: "But have they not acted against my advice? Did I not tell them, that we had had enough of that already? Did I not warn them against this very result ? I cannot betray them, however; no, no, my old comrades, I will give you another warning, and then your blood, if it must flow, be upon your own heads." He was about to resume his discourse to his visiter, but stopping suddenly and raising his finger in the attitude of one listening in the profoundest attention, he seized the small lamp, rushed past the little furnace in the direction of the cave through the hill opposite the entrance, at one time rising and anon descending, until Virginia (who had followed, fearing to be left alone) supposed they must be again near the surface of the earth. He paused once more to listen, motioning her at the same time to be silent. He had scarcely done so, when the distant sound of running water struck upon her ear,—sometimes distinct, and again as if buried in the bowels of the earth. Then came the noise as of a stone splashing in the water. The eye of the Recluse sparkled as he turned with a quick and expressive glance towards his companion. He hastily applied his ear to the rocky side of the cavern and listened for a second, then hurried back, taking Virginia by the hand in his return, and leading her to her former seat. He then busied himself for a few moments in exchanging the short cutlass by his side for one of the huge weapons hanging on the wall, and placed a pair of large and richly inlaid petronels in his belt, as if about to march on some secret and desperate expedition.

Whether these were really for such a purpose, or were his usual preparations for repose, Virginia was entirely at a loss to determine. Meantime she had an opportunity to survey the features and expression of his countenance, as he from time to time faced towards her, intently engaged with his occupation, and muttering all the while words to her altogether inexplicable at the time.

His large and light blue eye had an expression of forced resignation and calmness, drops of cold perspiration stood upon his brow, lip, and bald head, which was now uncovered. His features were large and striking, but well proportioned, the lips protuberant, the teeth large, white and regular, and as a smile, indicative more of wretchedness than mirth, played upon his face, the impression was irresistible that the wrinkles which marked his features were the impress of suffering rather than of age. In his personal as well as mental attributes he was eminently gifted, though there seemed to be a settled design, as much to clothe the one in the garb of age, as to exhibit the other, if at all, in meekness and humility.

"It is not consistent with my duty to all parties in this business, my daughter, to enlighten thee as to the nature of the danger which threatens thy friends, or as to the means of preventing it. I owe it to myself, first to warn those from whom it comes, yet once more against their undertaking, as I have already done—but thus far in vain. If they are still deaf to my admonition and entreaes, rest assured that I will leave no power or influence within my control unexerted to thwart their purposes. Thou mayest therefore direct him who must have conducted thee hither, to see me early on the morrow, and I will inform him as to the result of my endeavours and the best means to pursue in case they are unsuccessful. Rest thou contented yet a little while ; I see thou art impatient, but I have some things to say to thee concerning other matters than those which brought thee hither. I see thou art studying these evidences of years in my features as the forester examines the rings in the fallen tree to estimate its age, but these (pointing to the wrinkles) are records which years alone could not have wrought. Few of us, my daughter, can read these marks of time and destiny, and trace through them one by one, the disappointed hopes, the cruel mishaps, the hair-breadth adventures, their failure, sealed perhaps in the blood of those who had basked together with us in the sunshine of youth and hope, without a sinking of the heart within us, and a deep sense of the utter worthlessness of all those gay illusions which beam so brightly on thy own youthful features.

"I allude to this subject now, my daughter, because there seems to be some connexion between it and the one upon which I have been so anxious to commune with thee. Although we have never met before, it is not the first time I have seen thee, nor is this, which thou hast given me, the first information I have received concerning thee and thine. I have taken some pains to learn even the minutest circumstances connected with thy past history, present occupation and future prospects. I see thy surprise, but it was not done in idle gossip thou mayest be well assured. My motives will all be made plain enough to thee some day. In the mean time I must approach a subject which I fear will give thee pain, but my duty is imperative, I mean the state of thy mind and feelings."

"Alas, father, I fear you will find them but too deeply engrossed with the cares and pleasures of this world."

"Thy mistake is a natural one," said he, (one of those smiles of wretchedness passing over his pale countenance, as a flash of electricity darting along the horizon sometimes shows us the extent and depth of the darkness beyond) "my situation and past misfortunes would indeed seem to fit me for a teacher of holy things, but my present business is with thy worldly affections. Start not, my daughter; I have the most urgent reasons which a mortal can have for thus endeavouring to intrude myself into thy feminine secrets; believe me, no trifling cause could impel me thus to startle thy maidenly delicacy, nor indeed needest thou be startled on one account which I see agitates thee. Thou very naturally supposest me to have some charge to bring against thee for want of proper spirit and maidenly reserve; I see it by thy blushes; but there is no such thought within my breast; thou mayest have been even more guarded than is customary with females of thy age. My business is with facts, and facts of such a nature that however stubborn they may be, I fear that thou art unconscious of them, though they relate to thyself and one other person only. However, without bringing thee to confessional, I think I can sufficiently put thee upon thy guard without wounding thy delicacy. The only question in my own mind is, whether the time to speak has not already passed."

"I am at a loss to comprehend you, father."

"I will speak more plainly then. Thou hast been associating for some years with a youth of little more than thine own age. He is noble and gifted with every manly and generous attribute; well instructed too for his time and country. To thee I will give credit for corresponding qualities suitable to thy own sex, and I have no doubt that thou possessest them. Thinkest thou then that two such persons could grow up together constantly within the influence of each other's expanding personal attractions, besides the nobler ones of mind and heart, without feeling more towards each other than two ordinary mortals of the same sex? Oh, I see the crimson tell-tale mounting in thy cheeks; thou hangest thy head too in tacit acknowledgement, that I have surmised no more than the truth."

His visiter for some time made a vain effort to speak, and at length overcoming her confusion and surprise, in broken sentences exclaimed, "Indeed, indeed, father, you wrong me! indeed you wrong us both ! such a subject was never mentioned between us to this hour ! Nay more, it never entered our,"—as she looked up and perceived his searching glance riveted upon her countenance, her head again sunk in embarrassment, and the words died upon her lips.

"Cease, cease, my daughter, to punish thyself. I will give thee credit for all thou wouldst say. I am willing to believe that neither of you has ever mentioned this subject, and perhaps that neither has ever been conscious of more than a brotherly affection towards the other. Nevertheless, the last half hour has fully convinced me that self-examination, some sudden prospect of separation, or some untoward circumstance in the ordinary current of your intercourse was only necessary to awaken both to the perception of the truth. But my business now is of a far more painful nature than the mere finding of the facts. I am bound in duty to warn thee ! solemnly warn thee that this passion must be subdued in its inception. I beg of thee not to suppose for one moment, that my warning has reference merely to obstacles which commonly obstruct the current of young and mutual affection ! They are absolutely insurmountable,—far more so than any that could arise from difference of rank, or faith, or country ! Nay, if death itself had put its seal upon one or both, the gulf could not have been more impassable !" His language began gradually to grow more impassioned, his eye shot forth a continued instead of occasional gleam of wildness—he rose upon his feet, and as he pronounced the barrier to be impassable, he took down a large and ancient manuscript volume, bound in leather, threw it open upon the table, and to her astonishment a bloody hand was all that was visible upon the page which seemed to have been accidentally turned up. He pointed to this singular sign-manual—his finger trembling with emotion—"See there," said he—"see what it is to neglect a solemn warning. There is the diary of my eventful life—the transactions of every day for more than twenty-seven years are there written, save one! There is the only record of that day! Its history is written in blood! The seal of Cain is stamped upon all the events of the succeeding pages. Since that bloody token was placed there, its author has been a wanderer and an outcast. I was born among the haughty and the proud of a proud land—there is my coat of arms," said he, with a horrid laugh which sent the blood coursing back to the heart of our heroine chilled and horrified. "These are not or should not be uninteresting records to thee!—had that crimson attestation never been imprinted there, thou wouldst never have been born! but this will suffice for the first lesson," (and he closed the book and replaced it upon the shelf;) "at some more convenient season I will reveal another page of the history of one with whom henceforth thou wilt be more connected than thou now imaginest. Now, my daughter, before thou takest leave, let me entreat thee to remember and ponder well upon what I have said to thee. Shouldst thou ever be in any sudden strait of danger or difficulty send to me a memento of the bloody seal and I will come to thee, if within the compass of mortal means; and remember likewise, should I ever send such an emblem to thee—pause well upon what thou art about to do. Now thou mayest depart in peace, but say nothing of what thou hast seen or heard farther than I have directed thee to do." And thus speaking he took the lamp and conducted her out by the same opening at which they had entered.

They stood upon the platform overlooking the shadowy mazes of moonlit foliage down the glen; all nature was as silent as when it first came from the hands of its Creator. Looking towards heaven, and placing his hand upon her flaxen ringlets, now wafted about in the richest reflections and deepest contrasts of light and shadow, as a cold breeze from the valley beneath sought an opening to the plains beyond, he said, "May God Almighty bless and preserve thee, my daughter!" And then led her some distance down the hill—bade her adieu, and left her to seek her more youthful guide, and to ponder upon some novel and not very pleasing passages in the diary of her own experience.

Her ideas were any thing but clear and definite. The whole scene of her late interview was so new—the subject so startling to her young and innate delicacy. Taking it for granted, however, that all the surmises of the Recluse were true with regard to herself, that person has studied human nature to little purpose, who supposes that she, after all that had been so solemnly announced, admitted the undefined obstacles mentioned to be as insuperable as the person who suggested them seemed to imagine. Nevertheless an injunction so grave and authoritative had its minor effects—the first of which were visited upon the head of our hero, who impatiently awaited her approach at the foot of the hill.

CHAPTER V.

When Virginia arrived at the foot of the hill, and looked back, she could see the Herculean figure of the Recluse, throwing its tall shadow far down the face of the cliff, as he paced his narrow court exactly as she had found him doing.

The surrounding scenery now looked doubly brilliant to her confused senses, after the gloomy contrasts of her late subterranean journey. The fleeting clouds were entirely dispersed, and the moonbeams shone clearly forth in undimmed splendour, tipping with silver light each tree and shrub, on the hill side and in the dale, and sparkling like gems along the rippling current of the purling brook on the banks of which Bacon waited her approach.

Although the language of the Recluse was somewhat dark and oracular, it was sufficiently explicit to produce a very sensible effect upon the mind of Virginia, which our hero was not long in discovering; for as he extended his hand to assist her across the brook, she tacitly declined the proffered aid, as if unobservant of his intention, and leaped the streamlet unassisted. He was the more astonished, that in the whole of their long intercourse he could not recollect such a whim or freak occurring towards himself. She seemed reserved and formal too, as they moved up the opposite hill; but without remarking on her altered mood, he sought to draw from her the result of her expedition. Barely communicating so much as she had been directed to do, however, she remained to him inexplicably silent.

While he was revolving these things in his mind his companion, silently and moodily walking at his side, without availing herself of his offered arm, they met Brian O'Reily somewhat farther down the hill than the spot where they had left him—the bridle of a horse slung upon each arm—a handkerchief tied round his waist, into which were stuck two pertronels from his own saddlebow; and in his hand his master's, ready for use.

"In the name of all the saints in Ireland, what is the matter, Brian ?" exclaimed Bacon.

"Oh ! an be the Holy Father at Rome, is it there ye are ? Sure as death, but I'm the boy that thought ye were clane murthered iny way."

"Murdered! why who was to murder us ?"

"Faix, an there's enough iv them to do that same in *this* bloody place. Barrin the tay party wid the great inimy in the side iv the hill yonther, a'int there enough iv the bloody nagurs (the savages,) ranting about like so many wild bastes, ready to peale the tap iv your heads like a pair of onions or murpheys—divil a word a lie's in that iny way."

"Are there any of the savages abroad to-night?"

"Be the contints iv the book, but there is five

yallow rascals gone over the hill towards the city half an hour since. Oh, by my purty, but I was as near putting a key note to one of their whistles, as two tin pinnies, only, that I was jalous iv your own safety, and the beauty by your side at that same reckning."

"I commend your discretion in not shooting—and I wonder at your sobriety, considering the condition in which we left you."

"Oh, is it Brian O'Reily's discretion your haner's after namin?—an is'nt it me that's a pathern o' sobriety? Oh, by the five crasses, but it all comes iv the dhrap o' the crathur I got by the larnin iv you, ye beauty; divil a word a lie's in that."

"Gone towards the town have they?" said Bacon, musing—and then examining the priming of his petronels, he took them—placed them in their holsters, and mounted his horse, motioning to his attendant at the same time, to assist Virginia to the pillion. She being mounted, he continued his discourse to her. "Keep up your courage my brave pupil; no danger shall molest you unencountered."

"Strange as it may appear," replied she, for the first time uttering something more than a monosyllable. "The real danger in which we seem placed, has few terrors, after my late subterranean visit." This last part of the sentence was said in an under tone, as they cantered over the hill.

"You have done bravely, Virginia, and now

Brian it is our turn. Do you ride foremost—but on no account pull trigger, or draw your sword, without my orders. We are at peace with the confederated tribes of the peninsula:—should the party therefore prove to be any of these, bloodshed will be unnecessary. Remember, and be watchful!"

"Oh! be the powers iv mud and darkness, but there's no more profit in watchin these skulking nagurs, than there is in spakin to the fish to make them take the bate; both the one and the tother o' them bites when you laste expect it. Oh! would'nt it be a fine thing to have a praste to walk along afore ye wid the contints of the book spread out before him?"

"Get along O'Reily with your nonsense; one would suppose, to hear you talk, that you were the greatest coward in Christendom."

The conversation of the Hibernian was at all times amusing to our adventurers, and was enjoyed with more zest, doubtless, on account of the many excellent qualities which they knew him to possess, being as they knew, brave, devotedly attached to them both, and of unvarying good humour. On the present occasion, Bacon encouraged his volubility in order to divert his companion's attention from dwelling upon the danger which he but too clearly saw might await them on their passage to the city; and thus was the time beguiled, until they arrived at the top of the hill commanding the town and river, without encountering a single foe, or meeting with any adventure worth recording. As they descended towards the river, and O'Reily was just felicitating himself "that there was a clane path intirely across the stream." A sudden exclamation of surprise from Bacon, induced him to rein up his steed, in order to ascertain the cause. This however was clearly seen before the retrograde movement was completed.

"Oh! the murtherin thaves iv the world," said O'Reily, "there they are in our boat too, as sure as my name's Brian O'Reily. Your haner's a good shot across that same little river, any way, and by these pair o' beauties that never lie nor chate" he continued, unslinging his arms, "but I'll be bound for a couple or three more iv them. By the vestments but we'll put some o' them to slape, wid a tune that'll ring in their ears to the day o' their deaths."

"Softly! softly, O'Reily" said Bacon, "you are as far on the one extreme now as I thought you on the other a while ago. Don't you see that two watch on this side, besides the three in the boat? And as I live, they are preparing to push off. Quick, Brian, dismount and follow me behind these bushes! we must despatch these two, at least, without the use of firearms. And you, my gentle pupil, must remain with the horses. If we fall, remain quiet until they have carried off whatever it is they are endeavouring to steal, and then leave the horses and seek a passage by the bridge

I know your situation is a trying one, but it is the best we can do under the circumstances."

"Oh! no, no, Nathaniel!" said Virginia, suddenly recovering her feelings as well as her voice. "It is not the best we can do. Stay here yourself, and I can slip round, unperceived, to the gate of the bridge, and from thence alarm the city. Do, Nathaniel, suffer me to go."

"Not for worlds!" answered Bacon; "do you not perceive that it would be impossible for you to pass the two on this side unnoticed? Besides, were you even to gain the gate, they would tomahawk you before you could arouse one person in the town. No, no, you must remain. Seat yourself on the sward and hide your eyes, if you will, until we despatch these two, and then we can hold the others at bay."

"But what is the necessity of attacking them at all, Nathaniel?"

"Do you not see that they have been committing some depredation?—perhaps worse, and would be sure to make fight were we to show ourselves in so small force. But come, O'Reily, we are losing precious time; follow me, and for your life do not shoot."

This short and earnest dialogue was held in whispers, and in much less time than we have taken to record it.

The precaution against using firearms was doubtless given for fear of betraying to the inhabitants of the town the delicate and apparently equivocal position in which Virginia was placed. "We must be upon these two with our good swords, O' Reily," said Bacon, "before the others can join them, and if possible before they perceive us."

"Devil burn me but my hand itches to get acquainted wid the taste o' their skulls any way. Oh! if we can only smash these two but we'll keep the others to see their own funerals iny way."

In a few moments, Bacon and his trusty follower were silently gliding through the bushes on the banks of the river, and advanced to within a few rods of the savages, unperceived either by the party on the beach or those loading the boat on the opposite shore. But as they were just emerging from the last bush which protected their movements, a characteristic and startling exclamation "hugh!" from the watch stationed in the boat, at once precipitated their movements, and put the two on their guard whom they were about to attack.

There was at that day no male inhabitant of Jamestown or the surrounding Colony, arrived at the years and vigour of manhood, who was entirely unacquainted with the mode and usual end of Indian warfare. Of course, on such occasions as the present, the contest was for life or death.

Bacon, notwithstanding his youth, had already acquired some renown as a warrior in these desperate single-handed conflicts, which doubtless gave him and his companion more assurance of success on this occasion, notwithstanding the fearful odds which it was possible might be brought against them. Springing upon their adversaries, who, as has been seen, were on their guard, the conflict at once became desperate, while those in the boat made the utmost efforts to join their companions and overpower their unexpected enemies. No sooner were the two good swords of Bacon and O'Reily flashing in the moonbeams, than corresponding motions of the savage war clubs gave evidence that they also were ready for battle. Many and hard were the blows which were given on both sides in the struggle, a mere protraction of which Bacon perceived was destruction. Accordingly bracing up his own nerves, and cheering O'Reily, he made a vigorous and successful lunge at his immediate antagonist, but not before the reinforcement of the enemy was on the ground to take his place. A contest of this kind, when the parties were any thing like equal in number, was generally not long doubtful—victory in most instances being upon the side of superior skill and weapons. But O'Reily, although a veteran soldier, had met his match in this instance, his antagonist being a tall and brawny warrior of most fearful proportions. Yet he laid about him stoutly, while Bacon, merely having time to catch his breath, renewed the unequal contest with two of the new assailants, the third at the same time joining his already too powerful chief against the Irishman. The conflict was now desperate and bloody; our adventurers fought well and skilfully, every blow was followed by a crimson stream, and they too in their turn were more than once beaten to their knees by the terrific sweep of the war clubs. At one time Bacon was entirely prostrated, but instantly recovering and rising to his knees he continued to defend himself until he had once more regained his feet.

This warfare had now lasted for some minutes, which seemed an age to the trembling maiden who stood an unwilling yet enchained spectator on the side of the hill above them. But victory appeared at length about to crown the desperate efforts of her friends, whose assailants were now reduced to exactly their own number, and one, the tall old chief opposed to Brian, covered with his own blood and just ready to fall, when a sudden and terrific yell immediately behind them announced a reinforcement; and Virginia sank upon the earth in terror and despair.

"Plunge into the stream and swim for your life," shouted Brian—"Oh! but I'll keep their hands busy till ye go clear, even wid a stack of the yellow devils afore me!"

Six horrid and painted human monsters, (so they seemed to our adventurers) now leaped into the midst of the conflict, relieving their own brethren and thundering their blows upon the heads of their already exhausted adversaries. In vain they made furious lunges, forgetting the cunning of fence in the perfect desperation of the hopeless conflict. At length they both fell under the weapons of their new enemies and two of the savages, flashing their knives from their sheaths, prepared to complete the sacrifice; indeed a despairing yell from O'Reily announced that the butchery had already commenced; when in an instant the head of the old Chief stooping over him was severed from the trunk, and in the next a second blow from the same gigantic arm prostrated the one about to tear the bloody trophy from the fallen Cavalier.

Virginia had by this time ventured another despairing look upon the fate of him who was the cherished companion of her childhood. In that moment, doubtless, all the warnings and injunctions of the Recluse were forgotten, or if remembered, instantly set aside as the over prudential suggestions of pride in rank, or wealth, or power, governing the feelings of her friends, or of him who undertook to give her counsel in their stead.

But there were still enemies left besides the two who had flourished the scalping knife over our prostrate adventurers. With these the Recluse (for he it was who had come so opportunely to the rescue) at once renewed the conflict. Placing his back against a tree, and throwing away his castor and scabbard, he joined in the strife with a zest like that of an epicure who bares his arm to the exercise of the carving knive—whirling his enormous weapon amidst the falling clubs with the precision, ease and coolness of a professor exhibiting his skill with the harmless foils. His first exertions were, of course, on the defensive, among so many assailants, but if his blows were rare they were sure and fatal. He was evidently but putting in practice a sort of exercise in which he must have both delighted and excelled in days long past.

At every blow or thrust a savage went down to rise no more, Bacon, too, now rallied his scattered senses and exhausted strength, and resumed his part in the conflict, with enough of both to render him a valuable auxiliary in the way of defence, which the Recluse perceiving, sprang into the midst of the enemy and speedily put to flight, or the sword, the exhausted and disheartened remnant. When Virginia saw this devoutly-prayed-for termination to the battle, she sank upon the ground as powerless and exhausted as if she too had heen actively engaged. The Recluse stooping over O'Reily and feeling his head and wrist, hastened to the boat, and seizing the wooden vessel with which the water was usually bailed out, returned and bathed his face and temples. Not so swift were his motions however as to prevent his stopping for a moment at the boat and gazing with astonishment at something which it contained ; but there was little time for wonder, and he hastened on his errand. When Brian's face was cleansed from blood it was found that the scalping knife of the old warrior had probably been struck from its intended destination so that the point had caught in one corner of his mouth and inflicted a wound of some magnitude across his face. While he was thus attended, Bacon hastened, with what speed he was able to exert, toward the spot where he had left his helpless companion. He found her just recovering from the listless stupor in which we left her. "Oh, Nathaniel!" was all that she was enabled to articulate as she fell into his arms, forgetting in the deep excitment of the moment every feeling save the strong and innocent affection which had so long existed between them.

Bacon placed her upon his horse, and taking the bridle in one hand, and holding her steady in her seat with the other, proceeded to the scene of the late mortal struggle. They found O'Reily sitting up, with his mouth already bandaged, and his late assistant and protector gone, having first, as Brian indistinctly muttered, pointed to the boat, as if there were something there which craved attention. Their own perceptions were now startled from the same quarter, by the sound of groans. Bacon ran to the spot, and found a female bound, and lying upon her face in the bottom of the boat. Having cut the cords and bathed her swollen face and temples, he speedily restored her to something like consciousness, and then bore her to the shore and laid her upon the ground. O'Reily now recognised her as Mrs. Jamieson, wife of Jamie Jamieson, principal fisherman to the town, whose hut, for convenient purposes in his avocation, was situated without the protection of the fort. This statement also accounted to Bacon for the presence of a quantity of fish netting in the boat, which doubtless excited the cupidity of the poor ignorant savages, who lay cold and lifeless at his feet.

New embarrassments seemed to stare our wanderers in the face at every step on this eventful night. Scarcely was O'Reily restored to his senses, and Mrs. Jamieson to such a state as to give hopes of recovery, when it occurred to our hero that something must be done with the dead bodies. But when he came to reflect upon the appearance which the battle ground itself would present, he determined to leave the rest to chance, and to say nothing himself or through his follower, and thus leave the gossips of the town to account for the slaughter of the Indians as they might. Mrs. Jamieson was now carefully replaced in the boat, and O'Reily assisted to his post at the *tiller*, while Bacon, having seated Virginia, occupied Brian's usual place at the oar, being the least injured of the two.

The former was for once in his life perfectly silent, perhaps owing to the awkward accident which had happened to his mouth, thereby rendering it difficult for him to enunciate with the true Hibernian pathos.

The females having been landed, Bacon desiring Virginia to sit by the still benumbed Mrs. Jamieson, returned for his horses, which were led by the side of the boat without any difficulty.

The whole party now proceeded to the fisherman's hut, Bacon supporting the feeble steps of its exhausted mistress. Here a new disaster awaited them. A few yards from the house towards the river, they discovered the body of the fisherman himself, cold, stiff, and lifeless. O'Reily was directed to remain with the woman of the house until she should completely recover her senses, but on no account to stay longer, or enter into any explanations.

Bacon and Virginia entered the gate of the fort unchallenged, and proceeded to the house of Mr. Fairfax, when the latter entered as quietly and as unperceived as she had sallied forth; while he officiated as ostler to his own steed, which service being finished to his satisfaction he sought his apartment; the morning being far advanced towards the dawn of day. His slumbers, it may be readily imagined, were not profound and undisturbed,—the restless nervousness of over exertion in mind and body, being very similar in its effects to that of too much repose.

CHAPTER V.

On the morning of the Anniversary of the Restoration, the sun was just emerging above the eastern horizon, the sky was unclouded and serene, the air balmy and elastic, and the volumes of misty drapery from the river were fast rolling away over the hills, as the Recluse stood upon one of the highest points of the river cliffs, with folded arms, surveying the scene around him.

Far back as the eye could reach to the west, all was interminable forest—the foreground exhibiting occasional specks of cleared land, where some planter, more adventurous than his fellows, had boldly trusted his fortunes to the mercy of the savage.

He looked upon the little city beneath, as the weary mariner on a long voyage may be supposed to look upon a green island in the midst of a desert of waters. His chest heaved as the swelling emotions of pent up years burst from his overloaded heart. Bacon, the manly and ingenuous youth, whom the reader will remember as having been appointed to visit him on this morning, had just sprung upon a mettled and pawing charger, which was now throwing the fire and pebbles from his heels in thick volleys, as his master with a fire and impetuosity scarcely inferior to his own, bent over his uncurbed neck as he descended into the plain. Several pieces of light artillery, together with volleys of musketry in quick succession, thundered over the smooth waters of the Powhatan, and reverberated in multiplied peals under the feet of the Recluse. There was something connected with this day, and its celebration, which seemed powerfully to have stirred up the still waters within him. Thick coming fancies connected with by-gone days were rolling over his soul in an uncontrolled torrent. But we must leave him for a time to his own reflections, amidst the solitary grandeur of the scene, while we pursue the road of the flying Cavalier towards the city.

The bells from the Church and State House were now also heard in the intervals of the cannonade, and as we approach nearer to the scene, a strange confusion of many sounds greet the ear. Drums and fifes, violins and banjoes, and even jews-harps, all lent their aid to swell the burst of joy and gratulation. Smiling and happy faces were grouped along the streets, while gay damsels, in their holyday finery, adorned the doors and windows of the busy citizens. A perfect Babel of commingled noises issued from the spacious area of a tobacco warehouse, which, after the usual fashion, consisted of an extensive roof, supported by colonnades to every front. Here was congregrated the rising generation—boisterous and happy in the midst of their games and sports. No schoolmaster was abroad on that day, to rush in upon the unwary urchins, and wreak upon them the vengeance of Samson upon the Philistines.

Our forefathers suffered their children to follow very much their own humours in the selection of those amusements suited to their age and condition. We see not but the result was as happy as that of the systems of our day, when every thing is regulated by system, even to the games and amusements of our children. The time is certainly not far distant when Geography will be taught by a game at cards ; Chemistry by set *conversations* upon the constituents of our edibles, and Natural Philosophy developed in nursery rhymes, that we may imbibe it with our lullabies.

On the morning in question, as merry a set of boisterous lads kicked up the dust in the old warehouse, as ever fought over a game of marbles, or laughed through one of leap-frog. And while the merry urchins, whom we have taken under our special protection, were thus enjoying a glorious holyday, their elders and superiors were moved by the same impulses. The mansion of the Governor itself was in visible commotion ; servants swelling with importance, aped the grandeur of their masters' looks, while they ran from room to room on their various duties. A provincial band of music was stationed under the windows, uniting their sweet sounds to the Babel-like uproar, in the well known tune of "Over the waters to Charley."

There was one little green spot upon the common inviting the contemplative mind to pleasing reveries. Here a few of the humbler maidens of the city were adorning the overhanging bushes with gay garlands of flowers, preparatory to the evening dance, which they contemplated celebrating in imitation of their superiors, who were to move in more stately measures at the mansion of the Governor.

The household of Gideon Fairfax was likewise earlier than usual on the alert, and he being one of the council of the Colony, came in also for a share of the honours noised forth under the windows of the most distinguished Cavaliers.

Breakfast had been some time waiting at the table, and the fondly indulged daughter had been repeatedly summoned, but still she came not. This excited the more surprise in the minds of her parents, as they supposed, that on this eventful morning, of all others in the year, she would be up with the lark. The truth was, that after retiring at such an unusual hour of the night, or rather morning—her slumbers were disturbed between sleeping and waking, by shadowy dreams of yelling savages, chivalrous youths, and mighty giants.

At length, however, she appeared, but instead of bounding into the room with gay and elastic steps, and more buoyant spirits, in happy anticipation of the promised enjoyments of the day, her movements were slow and heavy—her eyes red and swollen, and her whole appearance indicative of languor and dejection. Her fond parents were instantly at her side—each taking a hand as she walked into the room, and striving to learn from the fancied invalid the nature of her sufferings. She assured them that she had nothing to complain of but want of rest, and with this they were the more readily satisfied, as towards morning there had indeed been much firing of guns, and other demonstrations of loyalty. Her parents being thus satisfied, that her account of the matter was the true one, Virginia was suffered to assume her place at the head of the table—a place she had for some time occupied on account of the delicate state of her mother's health. Meanwhile the anxious parents assumed their own places, and endeavoured to beguile their daughter's languor by allusions to the merry sounds, and gay group without, not forgetting the assembly at the Governor's ; and it is more than probable that they would have succeeded, as few spirited and blooming beauties of sixteen can long listen unmoved to such details, had not Virginia, raising her half cheerful face at that moment to a large mirror which hung opposite, caught the reflection of a person in whose welfare she took a lively interest, standing in one corner of the room, and partly behind her chair, with a countenance and attitude which expressed the deepest misery. This was no other that Wyanokee, her own little Indian attendant, who officiated near the person of her mistress, in a medium capacity between friend and servant; the mistress only requiring the companion, and the maid spontaneously offering the services due both from affection and gratitude.

The figure of Wyanokee was diminutive, but like most of the aboriginal females, exquisitely proportioned, and graceful, after the fashion of nature's finest schooling. Her face was oval and between a brown and yellow colour, yet there was a vital tinge occasionally illuminating this predominant dark ground, which bespoke the refined female, in language intelligible to all, and far more eloquently than the tongue. Her hair was jet black, and folded upon her small round head after the fashion of the Europeans; and her brilliant teeth exhibited a striking contrast to the dark shades of her skin, and darker sparkling eyes. The delicately penciled brows, arched beautifully over a countenance strikingly feminine and lady-like; and the general expression was that calm sadness which has been remarked as characteristic of the domesticated aborigines from that day to the present. Her dress was essentially after the fashion of the whites of that day, just retaining sufficient of the Indian costume, however, to set off her slight but graceful figure to the best advantage. The exquisite proportions of her finely shaped foot and ankle were displayed in a closely fitting deer skin moccasin, studded around the eyelet holes, and wrought in curious, but not unpleasing figures, with party-coloured beads and porcupine quills,

Around her neck, and falling upon her gently swelling bosom, were many ingeniously wrought ornaments of wampum and silver—and around her wrists, bracelets of the same materials. Wyanokee was of the Chickahominy tribe, and had been taken prisoner after the murder of her parents by one of the neighbouring tribes, who at the time were at war with the Chickahominies. Nathaniel Bacon saw her in one of his hunting excursions, and struck with her native beauty, and pleading countenance, redeemed her from captivity at the expense of a string of blue beads. From thence he brought her to Jamestown, to remain until some opportunity should occur of restoring her to her tribe. Her parents having been slain, however, as we have already said, and much time necessarily having elapsed before such opportunity occurred, Virginia took advantage of it, and by mild and affectionate treatment, endeavoured to win her to herself. A mutual and peculiar attachment was the consequence, so that when the opportunity actually occurred, Wyanokee refused to return to the almost extinct tribe of her fathers. Two years had now elapsed since her introduction into the Fairfax family, during which time Virginia, an assiduous pupil herself, became in her turn instructress to her little protegée. Already had she learned many of the little feminine arts and accomplishments of civilized life, and made considerable proficiency in the English language—which, however, she never employed except in private to her instructress, or on some urgent occasion. Half the young Cavaliers in Jamestown would have been willing devotees at the shrine of Wyanokee's beauty, after the corrupt fashions of the parent court and country. But such celebrity was not suited to the taste or ambition of the Indian maiden. Whenever the little errands of her patroness led her to the shops of the city, instead of encouraging the forward and impudent gallantries of the young profligates, she would trip along like a frightened partridge—always turning a deaf ear to their flatteries, and keeping her eyes fixed upon the earth, in the most modest, natural and simple guise. Notwithstanding her habitual indifference to the flatteries of her many admirers, there was one youth whose very step upon the door sill her practised ear could detect. Not that her deliverer had ever taken advantage of her gratitude to him—her ignorance of civilized refinements, or her dependent situation, to poison her mind with the deceitful flatteries too common with his comrades of that day. The passion was perhaps the growth of time and reflection and the effect of gratitude, as the little Indian maiden became capable of instituting comparisons between his conduct towards herself and that of the young Cavaliers, whose assiduities have been already mentioned. Certain it is, that if it had been from some sudden impulse in their earlier intercourse, the customs of her race would have fully borne her out in declaring her passion to its object at once. At the time of which we write, however, this feeling was a profound secret within her own bosom, as she hoped and believed; and the more Virginia impressed upon her mind the necessity of reserve and modesty in her intercourse with the other sex, the more jealous she became in concealing the passion that possessed her heart. Nevertheless, it influenced all her after life, and gave a touching interest to the progress of her moral and intellectual development.

Some few of her Indian peculiarities were still retained by Wyanokee; her gesticulation was far more powerful and expressive than her small compass of language, and the ordinary indifference of her race to passing and exciting themes, was yet preserved by her. Her gentle mistress could indeed work upon her sensibilities through the medium of her affection and gratitude, like a skilful musician upon a finely toned instrument, but the master key was still wanting even to her. There was one peculiarity of her race not quite so agreeable or inoffensive as those already mentioned—namely, the silence and celerity of her movements; sometimes she would appear to Virginia in the middle of the night with the imagined abruptness of an unearthly spirit. Often would the fair maiden awake from her slumbers and find her stooping over her couch—with the saddest and most intense interest expressed in her countenance—and again she would glide through the silent apartments of the spacious mansion with a movement so shadowy and noiseless, that it seemed almost impossible to be effected by a substantial being.

When Virginia raised her eyes from the breakfast-table, and beheld Wyanokee's mute despair, as exhibited in the opposite mirror, her former nervous alarm and agitation instantly returned.

She was entirely at a loss to account for the unusual feeling exhibited by her attendant, except by connecting it in some way with her late nocturnal adventures. And it was a fearful supposition which flashed through her mind, that Wyanokee was acquainted with her last night's undertaking; yet at the same time ignorant of her motives. Hurrying mechanically through the meal, she rose, and taking the hand of the young Indian, was about to retire; but at that moment Nathaniel Bacon rode up to the door, his charger covered with dust and foam; leaping from his back and throwing the rein to an attendant, he entered the room at the very moment when the two maidens were about to make their exit. Under the peculiar circumstances of the case perhaps no one could have entered more mal-appropos. Mr. Fairfax himself and Bacon had parted, at the termination of their last interview, with excited and unpleasant feelings, both having lost command of temper. Virginia had last seen him under circumstances also which in themselves were calculated to excite no very pleasing reminiscences; but considering the precise attitude in which she stood at that moment with regard to Wyanokee, the interview promised to be still more embarrassing. Nor was the promise falsified—the salutations of the gentlemen were cold, formal, and embarrassing to both parties, while the two maidens stood on the eve of departure, each labouring under her own peculiar difficulties. Virginia felt as if all the adventures of the preceding night stood revealed to her parents, without any of the justificatory motives which had satisfied her own mind for embarking in them—while her attendant looked to her as if she too was labouring under a weight of surreptitious knowledge. Mrs. Fairfax was the only one of the party who preserved self-possession enough to welcome their young friend, after so long an absence, in intelligible language.

With the peculiar tact of the cultivated female mind she judiciously led the conversation to such subjects of universal interest at the time, as to induce her husband and the young Cavalier to forget their late unpleasant difference, and Virginia to resume her seat at the table, where she busied herself in helping the visiter to his breakfast. It was singular enough too, as Virginia no doubt thought, that one of these subjects should have direct reference to some personages who had so lately and so intently occupied her own thoughts—namely the Roundheads and Independents. Frank Beverly it seems had already blown abroad the meeting of these persons in secret conclave, as mentioned in the first chapter. The meal being concluded, Bacon again sprang upon his horse and hurried forward to the portico of the Berkley Arms, in which were now displayed no very equivocal evidences of loyalty, from the master of the house and his numerous guests, who thronged its area upon his approach. All the *elite* of the Cavalier youth were there in a perfect throng.

No sooner had Bacon alighted and made his way into the throng, than the tumultuous discussion of the youths was hushed into silence. This was not so much owing to any sternness in the dignity of the youth as to the peculiar nature of the discussion which was going on between Dudley and Beverly, and their several partizans, at the very moment of his entrance. The tumblers of julip were held in suspense, while heavy bets were offered, and about to be taken, upon the disputed question whether the very person who so suddenly appeared among them would be present at the celebration. No sooner had he set foot on the premises, however, than the fat landlord came waddling up, grasping the hand of our hero in one of his own, while in the other he presented him with a goblet of the national beverage.

"A pledge! a pledge!" now resounded from several quarters of the well filled Tap. It may well be supposed that the suspected one had no very great relish for julip after breakfast, but knowing the importance of such trifles on an occasion like the present, and under all the peculiar circumstances in which he was placed he took the cup, and elevating it, said—"Here's to the merry king Charles, who shall be king but Charley."

"Bravely done," shouted the host—and "huzzah for Bacon," shouted his own immediate partisans, many of whom belonged to a volunteer military company of which he was the commander, and whom to see was the very object of his visit to the Arms. Taking Dudley therefore by the arm, and calling to others of the corps, he invited them to a private interview in another apartment. As Bacon passed Frank Beverly a mutual but cold salutation was exchanged—dignified and polite on the part of the former, and cold, haughty and sneering on that of the latter—the ungracious feeling not at all lessened, it is probable, by the pointed exclusion of Beverly and his partisans from the private meeting just alluded to.

Although this was Bacon's first appearance in public, since his abrupt departure from the house of his friend and patron, it was not the first visit he had paid to the hotel, where he and his partisans now held their meeting. He had privately visited the landlord on the preceding evening, previous to the adventures related in the last chapter, for some purposes connected with the present meeting of his friends, but which he was by no means willing should be generally known. At that visit he was informed by the landlord of the mischievous plot laid by his rival to deprive him of the pleasure of Virginia's hand during the approaching festivities at the Mansion of the Governor, and his first intention was to counteract their machinations. But so intensely had his mind been engaged with the adventures of the preceding evening, that all minor interests escaped his recollection. It was the object of his visit on this morning, to remedy that oversight; but so cold and formal was his reception by Mr. Fairfax, and so embarrassed was that of his daughter, that he gave up the scheme for the present, leaving the house with any thing but pleasant emotions. Indeed, from the various combinations of parties and factions, he saw his own position becoming hourly more embarrassing and difficult, and still more so from the neutral position in which he was thrown—partly from the mystery connected with his origin, and partly from his connexion with the Recluse. But let the Independents on the one hand, and the Cavaliers on the other, plot and counterplot as they might, his course was clearly taken in his own mind. None of the doubts as to what cause he should espouse, which had been hinted at by some of the personages of our narrative, really existed in his mind. His course was plain, manly, upright, and straight forward. Nevertheless, as has been seen, he had not thus far entirely escaped suspicion. But trusting to the uprightness of his intentions, he took his measures on this eventful morning with a single eye to the public peace and the cause of truth, justice and humanity It was to promote these great ends, that he now assembled the members of the military company of which he was the commander. Upon what service they were to be engaged, will appear in the succeeding chapters.

CHAPTER VII.

While Bacon and his partisans were deliberating in one of the upper rooms of the Berkley Arms, and Beverly, Ludwell and their friends, still kept up their potations in the Tap below, all of a sudden the bells ceased to chime, and the cannons to roar, and the various other demonstrations of noisy mirth that pervaded the city, were hushed into silence. A corresponding stillness instantly prevailed throughout both the assembled parties, for a moment, in order to ascertain if possible the cause of this interruption to the public rejoicings. No one in either being able to explain the matter, both parties at the same moment rushed tumultuously into the street. They beheld men, women, and children, thronging in the direction of the public square, and naturally fell into the current, and were borne on its tide into the very centre of attraction. Here they found several ox-carts standing in the street, in the beds of which were stretched the dead bodies of eight Indians—fearfully mangled, and one with his head entirely severed from the body. Twenty voices at once were interrogating the gaping negroes who bestrode the cattle, but no other satisfaction could be gained from them than a mute reference to their master ;

a little busy important man, who resided on the main land, and was now holding forth with great energy and amplitude of expression, touching his various adventures of the morning, to a crowd of eager loungers gathered around him, as if to appropriate his wonderful disclosure entirely to themselves.

He stated that he had found the dead bodies upon the banks of the river, where there were still many evidences of a desperate conflict of both horse and foot. That the ground was covered with blood, and that one party must have been driven into the river, and drowned, as he had been enabled to trace them by their footmarks to the very edge of the water.

It will be readily imagined by the reader that Nathaniel Bacon was no unmoved spectator of this scene, or of the various conjectural explanations that were now given in his hearing, of a transaction in which he had been such a principal actor, and of which he could have given such an authentic history. He was rather rejoiced than otherwise, that the little planter of the main seemed so much disposed to indulge his imagination, as a discovery of his own part in the matter, and of Virginia's delicate position on the occasion, was thereby rendered less probable. But his self congratulations were too hasty; for scarcely had he revolved these things in his mind, before a sudden rush of the crowd towards some new object of surprise arrested his attention. This was no other than Brian O'Reily, bearing into the crowd upon his back the dead body of Jamie Jamieson, and followed by his wife, who to her bruises and misfortunes had applied the comfort of whiskey in great profusion. O'Reily, it seemed, had fully sympathised with the widowed lady, for his motions were any thing but accordant with the solemnity of the occasion. Bacon could scarce suppress a smile as he caught a glimpse of this group through the crowd. His first object, however, was to catch O'Reily's eye, and make him understand, if possible by a look, that he was to volunteer no evidence in the case. He had no sooner succeeded in gaining the notice of his attendant, than the latter applied his finger slyly to his lip, looking another way at the same time, and thus indicating that he understood the policy to be pursued, and that he was not so much intoxicated as he thought proper to seem. With this doubtful assurance Bacon was compelled to rest satisfied, walking about the square all the while in visible agitation.

The corpse of the fisherman being laid out in the market-place, the officer, whose duty it was, proceeded to summon an inquest to inquire into the manner and cause of his death. The first witness summoned before this tribunal, was, of course, the wife of the deceased. She testified that a party of savages had on the preceding night entered their house, and after having cruelly murdered her husband, beaten herself, and bound her limbs with cords, had carried away all their fishing nets. That having placed these in a canoe, they laid her in it also, and paddled across the river—where they were met by another party of savages, about fifty in number, as she supposed, and while they were busily engaged in dividing the spoil, a gigantic man, with a face flaming like fire, and a sword as long as a fishing pole, had suddenly fallen upon the murderers, and quickly put them to flight, or the sword. That having thus conquered the whole horde, he had placed her in the boat again, and brought her to her own house, where he left her, and where she remained alone until morning, when she was found by Mr. Brian O'Reily, who happened to be coming that way.

Improbable as some parts of this story were, it met with a ready credence from nearly the whole of the multitude; no tale, having any relation to the Recluse, being so marvellous that they would not readily believe it. But in no one of the assembled listeners did it excite greater surprise than in Bacon himself. It is true, that he readily recognised in the whole invention the joint influence of whiskey, and O'Reily's ingenuity, but even to these he had not supposed that he should be indebted for such downright falsehoods in his behalf. Mrs. Jamieson, too, seemed firmly to believe all that she had testified. Under these circumstances he did not feel himself called upon to set the matter right at the expense of Virginia's feelings, and the inevitable defeat of the measures in which he was that very morning deeply engaged.

How the Irishman was to manage his part of the narrative when called upon, as he certainly would be, and that so speedily that no time would be allowed to exchange a word with his master, Bacon could not divine. He knew right well that O'Reily was gifted with a strong tendency to the most outrageous and even ridiculous exaggeration, and that he would carry through whatever he should undertake to say, with wonderful shrewdness and imperturbable confidence; but how he was to make his story agree with that which he had put into the mouth of Mrs. Jamieson, and at the same time explain the wound upon his own face, and the contusion upon his head, without being guilty of some direct and palpable falsehood, was more than his master could imagine. At length Brian O'Reily was called to state what he knew touching the death of the fisherman. The first question propounded by the officer was, "Well, O'Reily, tell the jury how, and when you came to the house of the deceased."

"Oh! thin, and I'm bothered to know whether I got there by land or wather, and faix, I'm after b'leiven it was naither uv them."

"How then did you get there, if you went neither by land nor water?"

"An by the vestments, may be I wouldn't be far wrang, if I said it was the crathur that took me there, seein I can't deny it iny way, your haner."

"You saw no one strike or maltreat the deceased."

"It would be but ill manners in me to be conthradictin your haner."

"You are sure you did not strike him yourself."

"As sure as two tin-pinnies—Divil burn the man that Brian O'Reily ever ill used when he was down—much less when he was dead, your haner." (crossing himself.)

"How then came that cut upon the corner of your mouth?"

"Oh! murther, and is it these your haner's axing after?" and he ingeniously placed his finger upon a smaller wound made by his bottle on the previous night. "Yes, O'Reily, we wish you to state how you came by those wounds."

"Oh! but I'm bowld to show your haner, seein its you that axed me—sure here's the wapon that kilt me all out!" and as he spoke, he pulled out his broken necked bottle and handed it to his catechist.

"I see it has blood upon it, O'Reily, and this may explain the cut on your mouth, but how came that contusion on your temple?"

"Be dad but I run aginst a good big shelaleigh, an it broke me head so it did—sorra much head I had left at that same recknin, for the crather."

"You ran against a club, O'Reily? Was it growing in the ground or was it in the hands of an enemy?"

"It might be growin, your haner, or it might be in the hands of the great inimy himself, for all that Brian O'Reily knows—sure your haner isn't very particular in examinin the tixture of the timber that knocks you down. It might be a door-post—or may be the gate of the foort—as the thimber grows as thick here as paraties, and this gate was always too small for me when I had a dhrap of the whiskey."

"You ran against the gate-post, or the facings of Jamieson's door, then?"

"By the five crasses, an I've done that same many's the time—barrin always that it would be ill manners in me to conthradict your haner if I hadn't."

"You saw nothing then of the treacherous and thieving savages on the night of Jamieson's murder?"

"Oh then but I'm puzzled now intirely. By the holy father, I saw a power of sights on that same night. The whiskey was clane too strong for me. I saw all sorts of yeller nagres, and men widout shadows, and flamin counthenances, and the fire sparklin from the very eyes of me by the same token. Divil a word of a lie's in that iny way."

"But you saw no person strike or maltreat this man who lies dead here?"

"Divil the one, your haner! Brian O'Reily's the boy that wouldn't see foul-play to man nor baste. I never saw Jamie, till I saw him stretched all out as you see him there."

"You do not know then but that you may have encountered the murderers in your own drunken travels?"

"Faix and you may say that, your haner, widout a word of a lie in it; it bothers me intirely to tell what I did see. An, by the five crasses, if it wasn't for the wapon you've got in your hand—and poor Jamie that I brought here on my back—and this thump upon my head, I should say it was all a dhrame clane out."

"Well, you may go, O'Reily. I believe you know little of what happened to yourself or any one else last night."

"An that's thrue for you iny way; many thanks to your haner for your kindness and civility," said O'Reily, as he left the crowd, slily tipping a wink of triumph to his master.

Bacon certainly began to breathe more freely towards the conclusion, as having edged in with the crowd, he heard O'Reily's ingenious parries of the official's thrusts. But his trials were not yet over, for scarcely had he followed his attendant with his eye out of the crowd, before Mr. Fairfax stepped up to the officer and whispered something in his ear. In a few moments after a deputy was seen leading Wyanokee into the market-place—a look of the most profound dejection, still visible through her fright, at being brought into the presence of such a multitude.

She testified, that two of the Indians slain were her nearest kinsmen. That the one with his head severed from the body, was old King Fisher; and, upon examination, the blue feathers of his patronymic bird were found still sticking in the matted tuft of hair upon his crown. She farther stated that he was her father's only brother, and that another of the slain was his son—the only two remaining male relatives she had in the world. That all these savages were of the Chickahominy tribe; and that there were not more than two hundred warriors left of all that brave and powerful nation which had once thronged the banks of the Chickahominy river. And here the little Indian maiden seemed almost suffocated with overpowering emotions, as the memory of former days came gushing over her heart. No tear relieved her swelling emotions, but ever and anon she cast her eyes over the mangled bodies of her kinsmen, and once or twice turned with looks more rapid and of darker meaning towards Bacon. The general expression of her countenance, however, was one of profound and overwhelming sadness. Her soul seemed fully capable of realizing the melancholy destiny which awaited all the nations of the aborigines then inhabiting the country, from the sea board to the blue mountains,* and whose fiat was fast bearing her race from the loved places which had known them so long. It was doubtless in her mind a poor compensation for the destruction of her native tribe and their contemporaries, that she

* The Indians possessed no knowledge of any of the tribes beyond.

herself had been reclaimed from the happy ignorance of savage, to the more painful knowledge of civilized life.

She was asked if she knew of the visit of these unfortunate men on the preceding night. Her eye furtively ran over the eager faces gathered around, until it fell upon that of Bacon, when a momentary flash of some internal impulse illumined her countenance. It might be vengeance, or the hatred of unrequited passion—but let the cause be what it might, it glimmered with a demoniacal fire but for an instant, and then, like the expiring taper in the socket after its last flash, sunk for ever. The sadness of past and coming years seemed concentrated in the despair of one moment. She waived her hand and shook her head in silence, thus indicating that she could say no more—that human endurance had been stretched to its utmost verge. Walking deliberately out of the crowd until she came to the trunkless head of the last of the Chickahominy chiefs, she bent over the mutilated remains for a moment in unutterable sorrow, and then throwing her eyes to heaven, dark in despair, she stooped to pluck one of the blue feathers from the scalp, and then with sad and lingering steps, proceeded to her home.

All were impressed with involuntary respect for the bereaved maiden, and even the hardened officer suffered her to depart without having finished his examination. Sufficient, however, had been gleaned for the jury to bring in a verdict of murder by the hands of some of the Chickahominy tribe of savages. This tribe of Indians inhabited a small town called Orapacks, on the banks of the river which gave its name to the nation. They formed a part of the grand confederation which had first been united under Powhatan, and afterwards his successor, Opechancanough; the latter of whom so unfortunately fell, while a prisoner at Jamestown, by the hands of a dastardly soldier, who took his life in revenge for some petty wrong, real or imaginary. The depredation related in the foregoing pages, and the unfortunate result to so many of its perpetrators, was the first interruption to the general peace which Sir William Berkley had been enabled to secure for the colony, after various sanguinary massacres and conflicts, with the numerous tribes composing the empire of Virginia, as it was sometimes called, and reaching from the Peninsula to the present seat of Richmond.

It may be well, perhaps, to state that a process had been despatched, for form's sake, to summon the Recluse, but it was returned as similar messages had always been before—he was *non est inventus.*

The dead bodies were now removed,—that of Jamieson to the more consecrated ground around the church, and those of the Indians to a sort of Potter's-field or general burying ground, such as every city has possessed from the time of Judas Iscariot to the present day.

The necessary and justifiable sacrifice of some half

a dozen savages was, at that time, too common a circumstance in Jamestown, long to affect the gayeties of the day. Accordingly the afternoon found the daughters and wives of the hardy citizens gayly tripping it over the green common, to which we have already introduced the reader, inspired by the music of two sable musicians, who rattled and scraped defiance to all untoward interruptions whatsoever. The town was full of strangers from the neighbouring plantations, together with many members of the House of Burgesses from surrounding counties, who had arrived in preparation for the meeting of that body, summoned to be held on the third succeeding day. Many of these dignified personages had collected on the green, to witness the enjoyment of the humbler citizens and their wives and daughters.

A merry set of joyful lads and lasses were whirling through the giddy dance; when all at once a savage yell abruptly struck upon the ear, the music ceased, the youths stood still in the circle, while some of the maidens fled toward the public square, and others sought the protection of their fathers, husbands, or lovers. Consternation was visible in the boldest countenances. The transactions of the morning had unstrung the nerves of the females, and urged the sterner sex to thoughts of war, which had lain dormant since the general peace and the death of Opechancanough. But soon a jingle of little bells was heard, and the next moment the multitude burst into a loud laugh, and simultaneously cast their eyes up to a tall tree which over-hung the green, and upon which was seen a painted savage, descending with great agility ; he soon leaped into the middle of the area, where the dance had been in progress, and commenced shuffling away at a most indefatigable rate, the fiddlers striking at the same moment into the humour of this strange visiter, and he himself dexterously rattling a number of little bones which he held between his fingers—the bells all the while continuing to jingle, and producing the strangest effect upon the ear. His face was painted in the ordinary warrior guise, his head shaved close to the cranium, save a lock upon the crown, to which hung a tuft of scarlet feathers—his person was grotesquely ornamented with beads, bells and buttons in great profusion, interspersed with hundreds of red feathers, from which he took his name. He was called Red Feather Jack, and was remarkably fond of the music and all the ordinary diversions of the whites. In this respect he was the most remarkable Indian of his day—that race having been peculiar for the haughty and dignified contempt with which they looked upon the amusements of their civilized neighbours. He was known to be as desperate in battle as he was light hearted and merry at the sports of the white man, and had never been known guilty of any kind of treachery, and was a universal favourite at Jamestown among all the young people of both sexes. It may be readily imagined, therefore, that a shout of "Red Feather

Jack," which was instantly raised by the assembled throng, brought no slight accession to their numbers. The amusement thus afforded was kept up, intermingled with dances of their own, to which Jack beat time with his loudest bells, until the hour had arrived for the commencement of the more imposing and aristocratic ceremonies and amusements at the gubernatorial mansion.

Red Feather Jack was believed by many to be an admirer of Wyanokee's, though of a different tribe. He had once, on an occasion nearly similar to the one just related, offered to lead her to the dance, but the more refined maiden looked upon him with ineffable scorn and contempt, produced as much, doubtless, by his undignified and unnational habits, as by what she considered his inferior rank and understanding. After the cessation of the various sports upon the green—in the warehouse, and throughout the town, Jack was taken to the Berkley Arms, where his merry perfomances were kept up until a late hour of the night, to the great amusement of the loungers and the disappointed youths who had vainly aspired to a participation in the celebration of the Cavaliers.

There was one peculiar circumstance attending this day's celebration which became generally the subject of after remark. Not a sign of festivity or rejoicing was visible at the Cross Keys. Its master sat a solitary spectator in his own door, apparently regarding the passing levities with sovereign contempt. This of course did not escape without many comments from the more jovial landlord of "the Arms." It was likewise remarkable that none of the Independents were visible on this general holyday, and this was the more singular as many of the humbler followers of the late Lord Protector had been sold into temporary bondage, and of course might be supposed eager to enjoy one day's cessation from labour, even if they did not care to join the humbler citizens in their demonstrations of loyalty.

CHAPTER VIII.

As the sun went down upon the boisterous revellers in the ancient city, and closed the festivities of the day among the plebeians, the aristocracy of the vice-regal court began to roll along the streets in their carriages, and surround the door of the stout old knight who represented the person of his royal master in the colony. The members of the Council and of the house of Burgesses, with their wives and daughters, and all other citizens and sojourners of distinction were among the number. Now came the crash of carriages—swearing of footmen—cracking of whips, rattling of wheels—clattering of steps, and the pompous announcement of the man in office, as each party was marshalled into the long suite of apartments brilliantly lighted for the occasion. At the head of the largest room stood Sir William and Lady Berkley. The old knight was dressed in a blue velvet doublet, which being slashed below the belt or waistband, protruded out all round so as to show the yellow silk linings of the aforesaid garment, fringing and ornamenting the waist. His breeches were of pink satin, and were cut in what was called at that day* "the petticoats;" they were tied to

* See Holmes.

the large mouthed silk hose with gay ribands, and the lining of the breeches being longer than the garment itself, formed a sort of ornament for the overhanging hose; immediately over this row of knotted ribands ornamenting the knee, his breeches hung in ample folds. The sleeves of his doublet reached nearly to the elbow, and from the end of these the shirt was so fashioned as to bulge out in large flowing plaits to his ruffled wrists. His stockings were of white silk, and shoes ornamented with a profusion of ribands, knotted and bound into the shape of flowers. On one shoulder hung a short mantle, reaching to the haunches and falling in rich folds over one side of his person. Lady Berkley appeared for the first time without her farthingale, but still retained its cotemporary, the French hood. In place of the starched ruff, she wore the graceful and flowing collar, falling in folds and terminated in rich pointed lace round the upper half of the bust; she wore a stomacher indeed, but greatly modified from the long strait jacket fashion of the preceding reign.

A slight degree of pomp and formality characterized the profound inclination of the knight's magisterial person, as some guest of distinction was from time to time announced, while his lady performed her part of the ceremony in exact accordance with the stately habits of her lord, but softened by a native blandness of manner and sweetness of disposition. She was a lady in the most refined and polished acceptation of the term. They were both just sufficiently advanced in years to add the dignity of age to that resulting from their station, and command respect from those who moved within their sphere. The ladies began now to re-appear, after the momentary retouch of the toilet, and arrange themselves round the apartment apparently appropriated to the dance, from a band of musicians stationed some six feet above the floor in a temporary orchestra. The first touch upon the string of the leader's kit was magical—the chords of every young female heart in the room vibrated in unison. No letting down of one string and raising of another was required to bring them to concert pitch ; like the blooded charger in the field, in whose veins the first clang of the trumpet sends the vital stream glistening to the very eye-balls, their gayly decorated persons were at once glowing with animation ; their eyes sparkling and their bosoms heaving with impatience, joy, and anticipated triumph. But when the bow of an evident master was drawn over the strings of his rusty cremona in a long signal sweep, every heart palpitated in eagerness. The eyes of the gentlemen wandered over the multitude of youthful and lovely faces beaming with a delighted expression, and all were keenly alive to the coming pleasures of the dance. But there was a precedence in the arrangement of the first set which we must by no means neglect. Virginia Fairfax, by right of birth and consanguinity to the governor, invariably assumed her aunt's place at the head of the set.

The blooming Hebe issued forth from the impenetrable ranks of her compeers with the blushing grace and beauty of a nymph—her hand was slightly extended as though its owner were conscious that scores of the opposite ranks would have perilled life and fortune for its possession. She was clad in simple white; not a colour marring the chaste and perfect purity of her attire, save the transparent shadow of a crimson tint which rose and fell in vivid flashes over her complexion with the rapidity of thought. Near her stood a youth, his finely formed person set off to the best advantage by the gay and tasteful fashion of his time, and his dark hazel eye, brilliant with the momentary fire of excitement. Instinctively he moved forward to receive the outstretched and now trembling little hand, but scarcely had he gained it before a competitor appeared upon the field, of not less personal and far more aristocratic pretension. "With your leave, sir," said Frank Beverly, with a profound inclination of his finely dressed person, as he took the hand which Bacon, in the abstraction of the moment, was about to usurp. The latter retired in the most undisguised mortification; his rival moving to the head of the set with all the grace and ease of self-possession, rank, and consciousness of right in the present instan c.

Sir William himself bent his dignity to enjoy this scene, the most evident satisfaction beaming upon his countenance as he cast an intelligent glance toward his lady.

Our heroine had been too finely schooled in the etiquette and manners of the ball-room, to allow the most penetrating observer any means of ascertaining whether the incident just related was as pleasing to her as to her partner. Bacon's mortification was not long visible, for with a desperate sort of boldness, quite foreign to his general demeanour, he crossed the room and approached a young lady whose beauty shone conspicuous amid all the gay throng by which she was surrounded. Harriet Harrison was the daughter of one of the proudest and most wealthy families in the colony. They moved in the front ranks of those who radiated around the fashionable orbit of which the Governor and his family were the principal luminaries, and were esteemed by them as among their most honoured friends and supporters. Harriet was the intimate friend of Virginia Fairfax, and, after her mother, the most esteemed repository of her confidence. Though an idea of rivalry in any shape or form had never entered their young and guileless hearts, the youthful Cavaliers who floated upon the same fashionable tide, had frequently placed them in this attitude in their private discussions of the various personal and mental attractions of the maidens, each in her turn proving the reigning favourite, as their respective admirers happened to possess the supremacy over the minds of their companions. She was near the same age with Virginia, and undoubtedly possessed attractions of the most captivating quality, both in mind and person, yet they were finely contrasted with those of her friend. Harriet's complexion was brunette—her hair dark and shining as the raven's plumage—her eye black, keen and sparkling, her finely pencilled brows beautifully overshadowing the native archness of her countenance, and her mouth always expressive of amiable feelings, just sufficiently characterized perhaps by a dash of innocent humour and coquetry; or rather that coquetry which is the result of archness and humour as distinguished from premeditated design. Her figure was slight but finely proportioned. As Bacon approached this laughing little belle, his boldness visibly diminished beneath her sparkling eye, and his petition for her hand was uttered with the most courtly and deferential humility. The brunette cast a significant glance toward her friend at the head of the set, and then with promptitude accepted the offered partner, her intelligent and sparkling countenance turning towards Charles Dudley, who stood near, with a speaking archness, which conveyed as plainly as it could have been in words, her perfect understanding of the by-play which was going on at the expense of his friend. The set being completed, the music now struck up its enlivening notes, and the various contending passions and emotions of those engaged were soon lost for the time in the giddy whirl of excitement which succeeded. Every countenance was clad in joy and hilarity—Bacon himself seeming to forget, in the secret pleasure created by the occasional touch of Virginia's hand, that he himself was not the honoured partner. Nor was the exhilirating effect of the dance confined to those who partook in the exercise—the young enjoyed it present, the old by retrospection. The latter lived over again the gay and brilliant dreams of their own youth, and were what they beheld. The music perhaps touched upon some long forgotten associations of other days and other friends, when and with whom they had mingled in the merry dance under circumstances like the present. These hallowed and blessed associations were not unmixed with melancholy, but it was of the softest and most soothing kind; the tide of feeling flowed over the heart to the cadences of the music, rising and swelling like the waves of the subsiding storm, and irresistibly inviting to mental calm and repose. The elder matrons sat under its influence—their eyes half closed in a sort of pleasing abstraction—while a gentle and subdued smile of mixed emotions played upon their lips. They lived again in the persons of their gay and happy daughters, and with no more selfish wish than to see their offspring following quietly in their own footsteps.

The formality which had somewhat characterized the opening ceremonies was entirely banished —it could not live in the atmosphere of music and the dance. Sir William and his compeers in dignity seemed early to be sensible of this, for no sooner had the motion of "hands round" commenced, than he collected his forces, and retreated to the card room, where, from the excitement of the game and wine, they endeavoured to compensate themselves for their want of the more sentimental retrospects of their ladies.

Conversation, which till now had flagged under the withering influence of etiquette, burst forth in all the vivacity of unrestrained and unsophisticated nature. The eyes of Harriet Harrison sparkled like gems, as she and Virginia laughed and chatted together, when they occasionally met in the figures of the da ce. But with all Virginia's hilarity, an acute observer might have perceived a shade more than once passing over the sunshine of her countenance; whether owing to some vague presentiment of coming evil—to better defined apprehensions from those events which had so lately passed under her eyes—to the mysterious injunctions of the Recluse, or to some not altogether satisfactory arrangements of the dance, we shall leave the sagacity of the reader to determine. Certain it is, however, that she underwent no little badinage from her lively friend and confidant.

A certain emphatic declination in the notes of the leader, which all the initiated will understand, warned those in possession of the floor, that there is an order of rotation in happiness on these joyful occasions, a cadence, any thing but musical to those happily and mutually suited in partners, while to those not so fortunately coupled, it was a joyful relief. Each gentleman led his partner to her seat, which she had scarcely taken, perhaps, if one of the favoured few, before new applications for the honour of her hand were laid at her feet. Bacon had no sooner escorted Harriet to her place, than turning to her friend he again put in his claim in more formal parlance than his former instinctive aspirations, but again he was doomed to disappointment; Philip Ludwell on this occasion, with a smirking smile upon his countenance, claiming a prior engagement. Bacon scowled upon him with mingled scorn and rage, as he turned upon his heel and besought the honour of the first hand within his reach. But if he was disappointed, his friend Dudley seemed more fortunate, for at the same moment that the former led out his partner, he encountered the latter escorting the pretty Harriet—and certainly no one in the room claimed a larger portion of his sympathy. But he was struck with the change in the countenance of the lively brunette in the very short time which had elapsed between the two sets. During the first, there was a free, untramelled, mischievous expression in her countenance, which was now merged in one of partial embarrassment. The guileless and confiding air with which she had looked into the face of her former partner, was now exchanged for one of consciousness, as if the lively little belle expected retributive justice from her friends for her own previous badinage. The unpractised Dudley interpreted these appearances any thing but favourably to his own ardent hopes.

Bacon was more deeply studied in the workings of the "human face divine," especially when feeling no personal interest in their meaning, and he therefore amused himself in his ungrateful situation, by watching the changes of his friend's arch little mistress. He doubtless considered it a beautiful and interesting development of character, to see this lively little romp—so lately overflowing with vivacity and animal spirits—all at once transformed into the sensitive, sedate, and downcast maiden. He was certainly not less amused to perceive that these two interesting young personages were unconsciously playing at cross purposes. First the gentleman became cold and moody at the reserve exhibited by his mistress, which did undoubtedly exist, but from which his jealous anxiety made him draw a most erroneous conclusion; while she, on the other hand, resented this apparently ungrateful return for a partiality which her own consciousness induced her to believe was perceptible to its object; indeed this very fear of his knowledge was perhaps the moving impulse of her own wayward conduct. The resentment occasioned by his apparent coldness, and assumed indifference, produced a corresponding feeling in her bosom, and thus they mutually acted and reacted upon each other, departing farther and farther from a mutual understanding at every renewed attempt, until at the close of the set, Dudley retired, as he imagined, irreconcilably offended, folding his arms upon his breast, and looking the very picture of love in despair. While in this mood Bacon approached him, and tapped him on the shoulder, saying, "Hah, Charles, would'st drown thyself? Thou dost not set thy life at a pin's fee I'll warrant me. Why, what would'st thou have, man? Thou would'st not have her forward and pert enough to run unbidden into thy arms?"

"Run into my arms, forsooth! I think she was nearer running into thine own."

"Tut man, does thy knowledge of the sex extend no farther? Dost not know thou art quarrelling with the light of thine own eyes? Art thou not yet acquainted with the windings and apparent inconsistencies of the female heart? I say apparent, because when the *primum mobile* is once understood, all these little perversities of lovers' quarrels are beautifully consistent, and always traceable to the one great original cause. Once gain an insight of this leading motive, and you will admire where you now condemn—you will attribute to maidenly modesty and proper reserve, what you now censure as perverse and whimsical."

"I understand you not, Sir Professor."

"No, because you are interested in the matter. You cannot truly place the small end of the telescope to your eye, and see yourself at the other.

You cannot stand, for instance, as I stand, and see yourself as I see you. But study the subject a little before you give way to the identical petulant humours with which you would quarrel in your mistress."

"And how long is it, pray, Sir Sage, since you took the beam from your own eye. If mine deceived me not, I saw you but a little while since swelling with all the offended dignity of majesty itself—merely because some more fortunate swain had previously secured the hand of the Governor's fair niece."

"You are as far wrong in my affairs, Charles, as you were just now in your own. You seem peculiarly predisposed to-night, to see only the surface of things. Suppose that some half a dozen of those butterflies who are now congregating round Lady Berkley, were to form a plot by which you were to be deprived of the hand of that lady whom you most desired to lead to the dance? Nay, more, suppose that you considered it all important to your interests that you should possess the hand on this particular night, and that you should be thwarted by such a contrivance of *sub vice-royalty!* What would you do? Would you content yourself with spending your rage upon your own lips between your teeth?"

"No, by heavens, I would tweak the nose of a small sprig of royalty itself."

"What, under the circumstances and responsibilities that environ us to-night?"

"No! not to-night certainly; there is no hurry in the business—his nasal organ will be as tangible a week hence as now, I suppose; but who is it that has done this deed? I see you have many rivals."

"Frank Beverly, to be sure."

"I supposed as much."

"You see," continued Bacon, "that I have now removed the mote from my own eye, and that you did in my case exactly what you did in your own—you looked only at the surface. But really, Charles, between ourselves, I begin to entertain some fears that they will at last affect Virginia with their own aristocratic notions and pretensions, for the absence of which we have so often praised her. I have seen a strange unusual something stealing over her countenance whenever I have approached her of late, which I do not like. She evidently struggles with it herself, but it has obtained the mastery in every instance, so far. Think you they will succeed at last?"

"I know not, my friend! but step with me into the entry—a word in your ear." The parties stepped just behind the casings to the door of the room in which they had been dancing, so as to occupy a small entry-way between the two largest apartments of the mansion, and there Dudley continued in an under tone.—

"Do you think they will dare *the deed* to night?"

"As sure as there is truth in that strange old man—and he has never yet deceived me!"

"Tis well! and are all things prepared for their reception?"

"They are! As for myself, never did such occasion come more opportunely. I will raise a bloody monument to perpetuate the events of this night upon more than one memory in yonder gay assembly! And since the thought strikes me, Dudley, tis pity I disturbed the savage moroseness which was just stealing over you; however I shall retain a *quantum sufficit* for us both!"

At that moment they were about to return to the party which they had left, when Dudley elevating his finger, said, "Hist!"—and Bacon heard his own name pronounced, just on the other side of the partition against which they were leaning. The voice was Ludwell's. "Can you tell me Beverly," said he, "the reason why Bacon does not wear the love lock!"

"Yes, I can, nature stamped him for a Roundhead and Crop-ear at his birth. Have you not observed how obstinately his curling locks are matted to his head? I'll warrant me if the truth could be known, his father was as pestilent a Rumper as ever sung a psalm on horseback."

Bacon heard no more; he was seized with the most ungovernable rage, and the utmost endeavours and remonstrances of his friend could scarcely prevent him from bursting in upon the speakers. In his endeavours to effect this object he forced his person partly in front of the doorway, just sufficiently to perceive that Virginia sat near, for whom, he doubted not these observations were intended. Again he became nearly unmanageable, until Dudley said to him in a harsh tone. "Rash man, would you sacrifice the whole colony for the purpose of chastising a piece of unmannerly insolence upon the spur of the moment, when you can as well do it to-morrow? Nay, it is the more manly course of the two."

Bacon by a powerful effort seemed to master his feelings, and compressing his lips, and folding his arms so as entirely to deceive his companion, he marched deliberately into the room, as if he intended to cross to the opposite side. But when not more than three paces from the door, he wheeled suddenly round and addressed Beverly. "This is no place for a personal rencounter, Sir Slanderer, and I will no farther break through the rules of good breeding than to hurl defiance in your teeth, and even this much I would not do, only that the defiance may go abroad with the calumny;" and with these words he flung his glove in the face of him to whom they were addressed. Beverly was taken entirely by surprise; and for some moments did not seem to realize the extent of the insult, and the greater personal indignity which had been offered to him. He was not long, however, in comprehending the nature of the case, and deliberately stooping to pick up the glove he answered, "This, as you have better said than acted, is no place to quarrel, but I accept your gage, and dearly shall it be redeemed on your part."

During this short but pertinent dialogue, Virginia screamed and ran to the protection of her father and uncle, followed by the other ladies in that part of the room. A crowd instantly collected round each of the parties to hear their statements of the case. But Sir William, always prompt and energetic, ordered the orchestra to strike up and the dance to be resumed, which had ceased for the purpose of affording refreshment. "A mere boy's quarrel," said the old Knight with smiling visage, and the dance was resumed, as if nothing unusual had occurred.

General joy and hilarity were soon restored, for though the serenity and happiness of several important personages of our narrative might have been disturbed, there were still plenty of those left who were both light of heart and nimble of foot. The dance was again going round, wine circulating, wit sparkling, and merry faces and loud voices in all quarters, when a sudden explosion like the discharge of a broadside from a line of battle ship, seemed to shake the very foundations of the earth; windows rattled and fell—plastering came tumbling down—and ladies screamed and leaped from the casements, while others were borne off fainting to their friends. Bacon seized Virginia and Harriet, one under each arm, and bore them to a carriage, while Mr. Fairfax and Governor Berkley forced their ladies into the same vehicle, ordering the driver to speed for his life to the residence of the former. A bright red light in the midst of a dark column of smoke was now seen to ascend from behind the Governor's house. The powder magazine had been fired by the Cromwellians who were now in open revolt against the government. The schemes which they had been so long meditating, and which Bacon so truly anticipated, had now arrived at the crisis—the struggle was commenced which was to test whether a few scores of misguided but brave zealots were to triumph over the constituted authorities of the land, as they had before done in England.

CHAPTER IX.

The night was dark and lowering, and masses of heavy clouds enveloped the city, a bright red column of fire ever and anon shot fitfully up from the smouldering ruins of the magazine, tipping the clouds with a crimson tinge, and illuminating the city to the light of noonday, and again suddenly giving place to volumes of thick sulphureous smoke which involved the surrounding objects in tenfold darkness. Drums were heard beating to arms—trumpets sounding the charge—fifes piercing the air—bells ringing the alarm—muskets and petronels discharged in quick succession, swords clashing, women shrieking, and men were seen running hither and thither in all the tumult of popular commotion. Bacon had no sooner lifted his frightened protegées into the carriage, than rushing into the back court, he found Dudley at the head of their youthful corps already desperately engaged with the Roundheads. He immediately threw himself into the thickest of the fight. With all their desperate valour, however, the two young officers were quickly sensible that they had entirely miscalculated the number and appointments of their enemies. In vain they endeavoured to repulse the hardy veterans who forced their way to the doors and windows of the gubernatorial mansion. The assailants moved to their work in a solid phalanx, that veteran soldier Worley, conspicuous at their head, and literally hewing down all opposition. One line after another of the valiant and high born youths fell before the murderous weapons of the insurgents. In vain did Bacon and Dudley, and Beverly and Ludwell, all now united in a common cause, enact prodigies of valour; their impetuous lunges fell powerless upon the iron frames of their opponents. Crowds of citizens now rushed against the insurgents some armed with swords, others with scythe blades, others again with bludgeons, and the rest with such means of destruction as they could seize in the street as they hurried to the contest. The accession of strength to the cause of the government was as yet of little avail, Bacon and his followers being driven to the walls, while the insurgents were protected on each side by a high wooden fence or barricade. Tables, chairs and bedsteads were hurled upon the heads of the besiegers, and the lower windows were thronged with eager citizens, throwing their hastily seized weapons upon the heads of the foe in a vain effort to come within reach. The Cromwellians were now likewise receiving momentary reinforcements of those who leapt the high fences, and filled up the vacancies in the rear, as the front ranks fell in the desperate rencounter with the youths and citizens. To whom the victory would fall could not long prove doubtful, situated as they now were; this Sir William

Berkley and his kinsman Fairfax had no doubt perceived early in the engagement, for a shout from a multitude without the enclosure, in the midst of which might be heard the voice of Brian O'Reily, now announced the presence of the Governor. The welcome sound was speedily and cheerily answered by the sinking youths within, who took courage at the approach of succour, and fought with renewed spirit. The wooden barricade was now seen to heave and shake, with every motion and creak of which O'Reily shouted in chorus, until at length the whole yielded and fell with a loud crash. A rush of citizens quickly filled up the breach, and poured their blows into the flank of the Roundheads, who now changing their front charged upon their new assailants, at the head of whom were the Governor and Gideon Fairfax. The two old Cavaliers laid about them in a style worthy of their best and most chivalrous days, and the citizens as stoutly supported them although but poorly armed and equipped for such a rencounter. By this change of front the gallant little corps which had so long maintained its ground, was now in some measure relieved, and no longer subject to the murderous strokes of the iron-handed Cromwellians. By the order of Bacon they now poured their fire into the flank of the enemy, and by this double annoyance to their phalanx, would doubtless have speedily terminated the conflict, but the friends of the Insurgents without, taking example by the manœuvre of the governor and his party, now broke down the barricade on the other side, and rushed in their turn to the scene of conflict. As this new reinforcement were pushing through the court to jointheir friends, in storming the first breach, a loud explosion from Sir William's quarter was heard, followed by the groans and shrieks of a whole phalanx of the old and new assailants, in whose ranks a perfect lane was cut by this discharge of grape shot through the very centre of their column. A rush was now instantly made for the possession of the cannon, and as the citizens poured through the governor's house and the Roundheads through the new breach in the party-wall, a deadly scuffle ensued, which became more and more ferocious and sanguinary as each party received fresh accessions from their friends without. And though the Cavaliers and their supporters outnumbered their enemies, the latter had decidedly the advantage in equipment, strength and discipline; more especially in the hand-to-hand mode of warfare which now became necessary from the numbers crowded into so small a space. But there was another advantage which they possessed—they had but one commander, the veteran Worley, while the Cavaliers and citizens of the town were at one time commanded by Bacon, and at another by Sir William Berkley.

Bacon perceiving the effect of this circumstance, singled out and attacked the opposite leader in person, determined, if he lost his life in the unequal conflict, to make the attempt at least to place the two parties on a more equal footing. But

Worley quickly detected his aim, and being a not less expert swordsman than his antagonist, took advantage of an impetuous thrust, and quickly brought him to the grapple of close quarters. One excelled in strength, and the other in activity, but nothwithstanding the latter, superior powers of endurance would soon have ended the duel unfavourably for our hero, had not a blow from behind brought his powerful enemy to the ground. Before Bacon discovered O'Reily, he was well convinced that the bludgeon which had interfered so opportunely in his behalf, was wielded by no tyro at the weapon. However, he lost but few seconds, either upon his assailant or deliverer, but quickly directed his attention to matters of more absorbing importance in the direction of cannon. Meantime O'Reily seized the opportunity afforded by the engrossing nature of the conflict, in the quarter just mentioned, and stooping down he took one of Worley's feet under each arm, using his legs as shafts, and dragged him off to a horse stall hard by, where having deposited the insensible veteran upon the straw, he turned the key and consigned it to his pouch.

The battle now consisted almost entirely of numerous desperate individual conflicts, each citizen as he arrived singling out some hated Roundhead neighbour, and he in his turn as anxious to vent the party and personal hatred which had been so long festering within his bosom. Sir William Berkley perceiving that their veteran foes had a decided advantage in the position now occupied by the parties respectively, quickly devised a scheme, in concert with Mr. Fairfax, by which, while the Governor kept the enemy engaged over the cannon, the latter should take a score of sturdy citizens, and rushing in, regardless of consequences, drag this sole apparent cause of contention into the public square, and thus change the scene of action to a more open position, where the superior bodily strength of the insurgents could no longer avail them. The measure was executed with great spirit and promptitude, and succeeded beyond their most sanguine expectations; for no sooner had the citizens commenced dragging the piece at a brisk trot, than both parties tumultuously pressed round its wheels, and thus unconsciously were brought into a fair field of action. Bacon, as soon as he saw the design of the movement, wheeled his hardy youths through the Governor's house, and formed a line at the critical moment when the confused combatants arrived fighting over the gun: thus affording a rallying point for the friends of order and the government. The governmental troops immediately formed upon the line already partly established by Bacon and his corps, and thus the gun was at length brought to bear for a time upon the opposing ranks. The light which had hitherto fitfully gleamed upon the strife, was now sinking after long intervals, and emitting that unsteady and wavering flame which announces rapidly approaching extinction. A few rounds of musketry and one or two discharges from the small field-piece, and the arena of conflict was shrouded in impenetrable darkness, save from the momentary glare which preceded the explosions. The Cromwellians, locking their column more compactly together, rushed in a solid body upon the newly formed line of the citizens. So sudden and so impetuous was this movement, and so skilfully executed, that the brave but ill disciplined combatants, against whom it was directed, gave way before the solid phalanx of the enemy, leaving the long disputed fieldpiece surrounded by the Insurgents. They immediately turned its muzzle upon its late owners, and were about charging it with the usual silence and promptitude of their movements, when a bright light from a burning torch was seen forcing its way almost undisputed through their ranks. The Cromwellians stood aside for its passage with an irresolute sort of tardiness, produced by a doubt whether the bearer were a friend or an enemy. But they were not left long in suspense, for he had no sooner arrived at this point, now forming the line between the contending parties, than he sprang upon the carriage of the gun, holding his torch aloft, so as to shed a glaring light upon the assembled multitude of both parties, who stood now for a moment of truce, in wonder at the strange and gigantic figure before them.

"Hold!" said he in a loud authoritative voice, and waiving his hand with a commanding gesture over the ranks of the Roundheads who crowded round him. "Where is your commander, Worley?"

"He is slain," answered twenty voices.

"His blood be upon his own head. Where is he who commandeth in his stead?"

"Here am I," said a short black visaged thick-set man. "Here am I, Ananias Proudfit, whom the Lord hath commissioned this night to take away the wicked from the land, and to root out the Amalekite, and the Jebusite, and the Perizzite, and the Hittite, and the Girgashite and the Amorite. And are not this council and this wicked Governor justly comparable to the five Kings who took shelter in the cave of Makkeda, who were"—

"Peace, brawler, peace," thundered the gigantic umpire, "and cease to pervert the word of God to thy murderous and unholy purposes. Take warning by the fate of thy predecessor. Thou would'st not listen to a more safe and peaceable admonition, administered in humility and good faith. Now I tell thee that if thou art still deaf, this good sword shall cleave thy hardened skull," and he drew his formidable weapon and brandished it over the torch. "Hah! sayest thou so," said the enraged Proudfit, aiming a deadly blow at the gigantic figure towering above him, but which the stranger struck aside with the ease of a wary and practised swordsman, and in the next moment as he had promised, drove his ponderous weapon into the skull of his assailant. Then hurling his torch into the advancing throng of the Independents, he brandished the huge glittering blade in fearful circles around the besieged gun, and quickly cleared a space for its more dexterous and effectual employment.

The fight was now renewed in all quarters, but evidently to greater disadvantage on the part of the Insurgents, than they yet had to contend with. The loss of their commander a second time, even in the ordinary course of warfare, would doubtless have disheartened them, but the circumstances under which the last had fallen—the superstitious reverence in which they were accustomed to hold the Recluse—all contributed to damp their ardour, to say nothing of the bloody barricade he had already piled around his person. They were now, too, in a comparatively open field, where the greater numbers of their enemies could avail much, and where no opportunity was afforded for the fatal grapple which had so well served the rebels in the earlier stages of the conflict. They were assailed from all points of the square at the same moment, while the Recluse, in the very heart of their ranks, was literally hewing them down like weeds and cumberers of the ground. No quarter was asked or given—they had staked their all upon the success of their enterprise, and seemed determined, long after all hope of success in their first project must have failed, to leave a bloody monument to their foolhardy courage, if not to their wisdom and forethought. Nathaniel Bacon, exhausted by the loss of blood from wounds received in the desperate repulse of the insurgents during the early part of the engagement, and feeling his tremendous responsibility for his inadequate preparations, no longer so onerous or so urgent upon himself, fell upon the field, and was borne to the house of his early friend and patron.

With the powerful aid of the Recluse, and the accumulating reinforcements from the loyal citizens of the town, the remainder of the gallant but misguided zealots were soon either cut down, captured, or put to flight. The slain of the Cavalier party were laid out in the State House, while those of the opposite faction were deposited in the tobacco warehouse, so lately the scene of youthful revels.

The wounded were removed to the houses of their friends and relations throughout the city, and in a short time as profound silence reigned along its deserted streets as if no one had arisen to disturb its peace. Not an individual could be found who had seen the Recluse after the termination of the struggle. The slain were carefully examined, but no such huge proportions as his lay stretched in death, among the gory trophies of his prowess.

The veteran soldiers, so many of whom had fallen, while others were confined within the jail of the colony, were a remnant of Cromwell's soldiers who had been sent from the parent country, on account of their restless and dangerous propensities, some of them had been sold into temporary bondage, while others established themselves in business or planting on their own account. They had formed the desperate resolution of rising upon the governor and his guests while seated over their wine, supposing that, in the promiscuous massacre which they had intended to perpetrate, all the councillors, and leading men of the colony would be swept away, and themselves thereby enabled to revolutionize the government.

The Recluse had doubtless been vainly urged to join their desperate faction, and it would appear that they had either depended upon their threats of vengeance as a sufficient warrant for his fidelity, or trusted to his supposed predilection for their cause, and hatred against the authorities then at the head of colonial affairs. Nor does it appear that he did openly and boldly betray them. Bacon had by some means or other of his own, pryed so far into the secret of the incipient rebellion as to learn who were the prominent leaders—by the suggestion of the Recluse, obtained through the agency of Virginia, he had found access to the ear of one Berkenhead, an influential man among them, who, influenced by gold and liberal promises, betrayed so much of the conspirators' designs as enabled Bacon to adopt the preparations of which we have just seen the result. And though they were of themselves totally inadequate, yet they served the purpose of keeping the murderers at bay, until time was afforded for the intervention of the citizens, and thus had preserved the lives of the Governor and his Council, together with those of many members of the House of Burgesses. The Assembly, which convened three days afterward, unanimously voted three thousand weight of tobacco to the traitor Berkenhead, and passed sundry pious resolutions of thanks to the Almighty for their deliverance, besides setting the day apart as one of thanksgiving for ever after.

The ancient city presented a strange and desolate appearance on the succeeding morning, in the neighbourhood of the public square. Houses were deserted by their tenants, windows shattered, palings pulled down, the ground stained with blood; guns, petronels, swords, hats, and missiles of various descriptions lay scattered about in strange confusion.

At length the drowsy citizens were awakened to the importance of the day. A court of inquiry was assembled for the purpose of investigating the conspiracy which had so nearly proved fatal to the existing order of things on the previous night. The prisoners were brought from the jail to the Court House in irons, and all the witnesses supposed to know any thing of the matter, were in readiness. Nathaniel Bacon was the first called, but Mr. Fairfax came forward and stated that his wounds were so much more dangerous than had previously been supposed, that the surgeon strictly enjoined quiet and repose, and recommended if possible to postpone taking his deposition for the present. As the testimony was ample and satisfactory without his attendance, the examination of course proceeded. Berkenhead's deposition was essentially what we have already more succinctly stated in explanation of the insurrection, and most of the other witnesses testified only to what the reader has already seen or surmised. There was one witness, however, whose testimony was so novel and amusing, amidst the general scene of confusion and bloodshed, that we must by no means neglect it. Brian O'Reily was called in his turn to give evidence on behalf of the crown on a charge of treason against the prisoners at the bar.

"Well, O'Reily," said the examining officer, "please to tell the court what you know of the treasonable practices of any of the prisoners at the bar."

"Be the twelve Apostles and St. Patrick into the bargain, I caught one iv them in the very act."

"What act did you see, O'Reily, and which of these men was the perpetrator?"

"Faix it was just trason itself I caught him at; sure if I hadn't brought his head acquainted wid my shelaleigh, he'd iv murthered one of the king's officers iny way—young master Bacon."

"Well, tell us which of these men it was, and any thing you know concerning the getting up of this rebellion."

"The man's not there at all at all—he's at another bar, and has been this ten hours gone."

"He's at the bar of God, you mean?"

"I mane no sich thing, axing your honour's pardon for conthradictin you. Here's the key that's turned an 'im; besides, didn't I slape by the door all night wid nobody for company but a small dhrop iv whiskey, and didn't I spake to him this morning through the key hole, and didn't he coax and palaver wid me to let him out, and didn't he come over me wid his wife and nine childre, one at the breast, barrin that I knew it was a d—d lie at that same recknin, savin your presence, an didn't he fret about bein cooped up in sich a place all night wid nothin to ate an the same to dhrink, barrin the hay that was in the rack, an didn't I answer him from the contints iv the book, sayin that many a betther man than him had been born and brought up in a manger, (crossing himself) an didn't he call me all sorts iv hathen names; indeed an he did—the best iv them was cut-throat and horse-thaif, only they were in the Habrew language, an didn't I tell him he was a Judaite, an a wolf in sheep's clothin, an that he hated the very name iv Bacon. And may be he didn't call me a dam'd papist? An didn't I tell him he'd live to see his own funeral iny way? an didn't he answer me all about popes and bulls and papists? Oh! get away wid your blarney, says I, you're safe now as the Governor's old bull wid the short tail and the shambles on two of his legs, only I tould him he'd perhaps be likein the darbies on his hands instead of his trotters."

"And who was this, Brian, that you held this long discourse with through a key hole? You're giving us another of your drunken dreams I fear?"

"Divil a word iv a lie's in it, your haner, hav'nt

I just come from the stable door, and didn't I set ould growler, the bull dog to watch by him till I came back—sure he cant come over him wid his blarney about the wife and the nine childer—O be gorra I'm so tender hearted, it was a clane temptation to me."

"Who was it had the nine children?"

"Auld Nick fly away wid the nine he's got iv them; didn't I tell your haner it was all blarney to move the tinder feelings of Brian O'Reily?"

"Who was it then, you were talking to through the key hole?"

"An 'is it his name your haner's axing after all this time? couldn't you just say so at wanst, an not throw me out wid the story all thegither? It's the Divil's own aid-the-camp I'm thinkin. It's the man that makes swords all the time he's makin horse shoes, they call him Worley I'm thinkin."

"Worley! is it possible? have you seen him this morning?"

"Be the contints iv the book but I saw him not an hour gone, through the key hole; he was stanin up to hay like the Governor's horse, but his appetite seemed to uv left him intirely."

"Can you show the officers where he is?"

"I can do that same, I'm bould to say; didn't I tell your haner it's the key I had was turned an im?"

"And what is it the key of, O'Reily?"

"Faix it's the key to the Governor's stable."

(This answer produced a loud laugh from the spectators.) "Divel a word o lie's in it."

"Well, O'Reily, the officers are waiting on you; only prove to us that this is not another of your drunken reveries, and it shall turn out better for you than you now expect. Since it has been ascertained that this man Worley was not to be found among the slain, the Governor has issued his proclamation, offering two hundred pounds for his apprehension, dead or alive."

"Oh!" said O'Reily, as he was going out of the door, "but I'm afeard you'll find him rather in a state iv thribulation, I did some killen an im myself: Oh wasn't that a beauty iv a shelaleigh? Only to think of two hundred pounds; faix if I get it but I'll have it set in brass."

The officers in attendance, with Brian at their head, soon emerged from the Governor's stable amidst the shouts and cheers of the multitude. The unfortunate Roundhead commander was brought into court, suffering severely from thirst, and the effects of the contusion, produced by the violence of O'Reily's blow.

We will not detain the reader over revolting portions of the trial either now or hereafter; suffice it to say, therefore, in brief, that O'Reily received the interest of two hundred pounds ever afterwards, for his capture of the Rebel Chief. Four of the ringleaders at the second, and final trial were condemned and speedily executed, and the others recommended to mercy. Thus was terminated this sanguinary conflict, the last convulsive throe of the Independent faction in the British dominions of North America.

As our tale is no farther directly connected with this ill-advised and hopeless insurrection, we proceed in the next chapter with the direct thread of our narrative, the principal personages of which were so directly concerned in the bloody affair just related, that we could not pass it over with any kind of regard to historical accuracy.

CHAPTER X.

During the whole of the day succeeding the insurrection, our hero lay in the most precarious and dangerous state; and the violent inflammatory action produced by several large sabre wounds so much unsettled his reason, that the surgeon was compelled still farther to deplete his already exhausted frame. Towards night his mind recovered its powers, but his strength was still gone, and he lay upon his couch in all the helplessness of infantile impotency; and toward evening, exhausted by the previous night of turmoil and strife, succeeded by a day of feverish restlessness, he at length fell asleep.

There was one never-wearying eye that watched the fitful slumbers of the invalid. Conscious, perhaps, that Bacon could never be more to her than a friend and protector, Wyanokee delighted in rendering him those quiet, but constant and indispensable services which his situation required. Not a change of his ever-varying countenance, as the workings of a diseased and excited imagination, were from time to time portrayed upon his pale and already attenuated features, escaped her, while her own beautiful and expressive countenance, vividly displayed, in rapid and corresponding changes, her sympathy with the sleeping sufferer. If any one approached the door, her keen glance immediately arrested the intruder, her finger upon her lip, and a frown upon her brow, in her powerful and national pantomimic token of silence. If the eye of the sleeper opened for an instant in bewildered amazement at the difference between the real scene before him, and the one from which in sleeping fancy he had just escaped; her wild and imaginative susceptibilities were instantly on the alert.

The mind of the aboriginal, even when partially cultivated, is overcome with superstitious reverence and awe, in the presence of one under the excitement of a diseased imagination. Such had been the state of feeling with Wyanokee during the whole of Bacon's mental hallucinations throughout the day, and now as she watched at his bedside, during his uneasy slumbers, her keen perceptions were tremulously alive to each successive demonstration. There was one member of the family, however, who entered and departed from the room unchallenged—Virginia! At this moment she entered—her own tender sympathies wrought upon by all the late harassing events; although differing in their developments and cause in some respects, they were in no wise inferior in degree to those of her protegée. She moved with noiseless step and suppressed respiration until she stood over the couch of the wounded youth. Long and feelingly she gazed upon the sharp and pallid features; there was naught of passion in that gaze —it was pure and heavenly in its origin, as in its motive. Her moistened eye, with a movement almost peculiar to the sick room, or the funeral chamber, turned slowly upon her attendant. No melting and sympathizing tear softened the brilliant and penetrating eye which met her gaze; there was excitement, deep excitement, but not the mellowed emotion of regulated sympathy; in Wyanokee, the imagination controlled the heart —in Virginia, the heart subdued and softened the imagination.

There was something touchingly beautiful in the moral development of these two young and innocent hearts. There was a mutual instinctive understanding of each, with regard to the position of the other, in relation to the wounded youth before them; yet it had never been admitted even to their own consciousness, because they had never analyzed their own feelings, and circumstances as yet had never openly betrayed them to each other. As they mutually exchanged glances, something like an electric thrill passed chilly through their veins, but it was only for an instant; the reasoning faculties of the mind examined it not—they were not in a situation to examine it—imagination controlled the whole mental organization of the one, and the tenderest and purest emotions of the heart that of the other. Virginia came to relieve the faithful and indefatigable Indian maiden, and as the only practicable means, sent her under some pretext to her mother. She now occupied a seat near the foot of the couch, in full view of the sleeper's countenance, faintly illuminated by the subdued rays of a shaded lamp. She had watched the varying and magnetic vibration of muscle and nerve for nearly an hour, when the eyes of the sleeping youth slowly and wildly opened upon her in a bewildered stare, and at length he spoke.—

"The senses are not the only vehicles for communicating passing events to the mind," said he, his voice already hollow and sepulchral from the previous excitement of the brain. Virginia understood him not, but supposed that his mind was again wandering, but it was not so; his mental perceptions were preternaturally clear, as they sometimes are after painful cerebral excitements.

She made him no answer, hoping that he would again close his eyes to repose. But he continued, "How else can we gain knowledge of things which have transpired when all the senses are shut up in profound slumber? Just now I slept deeply, but not soothingly, and I thought I was on the brink of destruction, from which none but you could save me; and that Wyanokee persisted in attempting the rescue, and the more she struggled the more irremediable became my difficulties. At length you appeared upon the scene, leaning upon your mother's arm, and she carried away Wyanokee while you redeemed me from destruction. This is indeed no farther true than that you have taken the place of your attendant, and that your mild sympathizing countenance is far more genial to my present weakened state, than her wild and startling glances. But does it not seem as if my mental perceptions had caught a glimpse of passing events without the intervention of the animal senses?"

Virginia put her finger upon her lip and shook her head, to remind her charge that strict silence was enjoined. For this there were other motives acting upon her perturbed feelings besides the injunction of the surgeon, had they been wanting.

The invalid closed his eyes, and in a short time seemed to sleep more calmly and soundly than he had yet done. It being the portion of the night through which Virginia had insisted upon watching, she moved quietly to a couch by the window looking upon the river and the blue hills beyond, and threw herself upon it and gazed out at the enchanting scene. Her own flower garden lay beneath the window, stretching away towards the river, and ornamented midway with a tasteful little summer-house designed by herself, and decorated by the hands of the ingenious youth who now lay so helpless before her. The air was balmy and serene, and redolent of the richest perfumes of fruits and flowers just bursting into maturity with the advancing summer. Millions of stars twinkled in the high cerulean arch of heaven, and were reflected back from the broad expanse of waters beneath, with an enchanting brilliancy. The murmuring waters of the Powhatan rippled alogn the sandy shore with a melancholy monotony, indescribably soothing to her harassed and troubled mind. The various noises of the busy world around were one by one sinking into silence. Occasionally the profound stillness which succeeded, disturbed by the distant bark of a watch-dog, or the more rural cackling of geese, faded away in the distance so imperceptibly as to leave the mind at a loss to know whether they were real sounds, or those associations with the scene which the imagination often conjures up to bewilder us on such occasions. Her eyes were half closed for a moment under these soothing and seducing influences, and the next, quickly opened to catch the fiery track of some darting meteor as it winged its way through the starry heavens, or to follow the humbler lights borne through the air by myriads of fire flies which brilliantly floated upon the transparent atmosphere. A wild and startling note from some beast of prey, as it roamed through the trackless and unsubdued forests beyond the river, occasionally struck upon her ear, and ever and anon she turned her eyes toward her sleeping charge, and all the painful and harassing feelings of the last few days returned. It was like awaking from a delicious dream, to the stern reality of some pressing and constantly obtrusive misfortune. Her previous life had been tranquil and unruffled; until now her spirits buoyant and elastic. Suddenly the scene had changed, and all the unmarked and unrecorded pleasures of her youthful years were lost in the cares and troubles of the present. She imagined herself the most irremediably wretched being in existence. So new was unhappiness to her, that the slight cloud which now hung between her and the happiness she had enjoyed seemed fearfully dark and lowering.

But again the soothing influences of the scene without imperceptibly stole upon her senses, and she fell into a slumber. Her imagination, now uncontrolled by the sterner qualities of mind, mingled the images retained from the stirring events of the last few days in the most fantastic forms. She saw her mother enter the garden with a slow and solemn step, clad in the habiliments of the grave.

Her form was aerial and graceful, and her features supernaturally beautiful and glorious. Presently this figure was met by another of colossal proportions, approaching the summer house from the opposite end of the garden ; his step was grand and majestic, and his countenance stern and warlike. He was clad in complete armour, and his mailed heel as it struck the gravel, sent the blood cold to her heart, and at once convinced her of the reality of the scene. As the figures met they paused and seemed to hold communion for a time, and then pursued their way together ; but when they returned to view, the relations of the parties were changed, the colossal figure was using the most violent gesticulation, to which his companion seemed to bow her head in meekness and submission, but not in conviction. At this the other suddenly sprang forward, seized his victim, and was about to leap the garden walls when an attempt to scream dispelled the illusion. Virginia opened her eyes and glanced around the room to assure herself of the reality of the scene before her. The wounded youth still slept soundly, and the lamp still threw its flickering shadows on the wall. By a slower and more cautious movement of the eyes she next examined the garden without; all was still and quiet as the grave, and gazing long and abstractedly upon the little arbour she again gave way to the exhaustion of her physical powers, and again the same figures rose upon her fancy. Now all doubt of their reality was discarded from the very circumstance of the former's having proved a delusion. She knew the other was a dream, but this she felt was truth, and she even went so far as to reason in her mind upon the strange coincidence of the dream, and the present real scene. The gigantic figure was now clad in the gray garb of the Recluse, his limbs manacled with chains, while her mother knelt apart in the attitude of deep and unutterable wo. A crowd was gathered round as if to witness a public execution; soldiers and citizens, knights and nobles mingled in the confused throng. The criminal was kneeling upon his coffin, the cap was drawn over his face, and the fatal word was given! She awoke with the sound of firearms still ringing in her ears, and the piercing shrieks of the female figure thrilling through her veins.

It may be readily imagined that her startled perceptions were by no means tranquillized on perceiving, as she opened her eyes, the shadows of moving figures upon the wall before her. In order to see from whom these reflections came she must turn her head and look in the direction of the opposite wall, but for her life she dared not move! Terror chained her to the couch. At length the shadows moved towards the door! By a desperate effort she turned her head in that direction, and to her amazement beheld her mother dressed in white, exactly as she had seen her in her dream, slowly and steadily leaving the apartment. She clasped her hand to her forehead and endeavoured to recall her bewildered senses. The confused images of her slumbering and waking perceptions were so inextricably mingled together that for a time she was utterly at a loss to know whether the whole was real or a dream. Certainly the actors were the same, and the impressions continuous. She had not long lain in this bewilderment when she heard the door leading into the garden, just beneath her window, softly opened, and her mother in a few moments walked down the avenue in the very direction she had before seen her take.

Her eyes were intently riveted upon the movements of her parent, until they were hid from her view by the intervening trees and shrubbery.

But she removed them not—they were still fixed upon the spot where she had last seen her, until her white robes emerged here and there from the foliage, when her eyes instinctively followed her, straining her already weakened organs to catch the slightest change of position, and seemingly desirous to penetrate the sombre shadows of the night, whenever the figure upon which she gazed was lost to view. At length the door again softly opened beneath her window; and she saw the figure no more. But a very few moments elapsed, however, before another appeared upon the scene, of far more gigantic proportions and questionable business at that place and hour. It was the same figure which she had before seen associated with the one which had just departed; and now that she really saw them in flesh and blood, she was more than ever at a loss to know which and how many of her visions of the night were real and which illusory.

The one now before her eyes was clad in his usual, half puritanical, half military tunic, and as usual he was fully armed, but the weapons hung quietly by his side; his arms were folded upon his breast, and his whole carriage and demeanour was subdued, sad, and melancholy. He stood leaning against the vine-clad column of the arbour, with his eyes intently fixed upon the spot where the preoccupant of the scene had disappeared. His chest heaved with emotion, which ever and anon found vent in laboured respirations of unspeakable misery.

At this moment a fierce watch-dog sprung at the intruder with savage ferocity, and to one less accustomed to danger in all its shapes, would doubtless have proved a formidable foe; but in an instant a heavy blow from his iron sheathed sabre laid the animal struggling at his feet. He stood leaning upon his weapon for an instant, and then moved slowly away until he came near the river, when he laid his hand upon the palisade running along the foot of the garden, and leapt upon the beach like a youth of twenty. In a short time Virginia saw his boat upon the water, his gigantic form rising and bending to his work with desperate and reckless efforts, the frail bark gliding over the smooth waters, "like a thing of life," until it faded away in the distance to a mere speck.

Her eye followed the receding object as it became more and more indistinct, until a mere undefined point was left upon the retina, her own voluntary powers sinking more deeply in repose from the intentness with which she pursued the single object.

How long she slept she knew not, but when she awoke the horizontal rays of the rising sun were beaming through the parted curtains, and the misty drapery from the river was rolling over the hills, and pouring through the intervening valleys in thousands of fantastic forms, weaving, here a rich festoon round the summit of one blue hill, and there spreading out a curtain of mellow tints before another.

The cool and invigorating morning breeze from the river, joined to the effects of her last refreshing and uninterrupted sleep, completely dispelled the shadowy illusions of the night, and she arose comparatively cheerful and happy. She was frightened when she cast her eyes upon the couch of the sufferer and found him awake, to think how much and how long she had neglected him. There was one indefatigable and untiring nurse watching by the bedside, however! She had stolen in unperceived during the night, and now sat upon an humble seat at the foot of the couch; her eye as brilliant as if it was not subject to the ordinary fatigues of humanity. The invalid too had slept soundly, and awakened this morning refreshed and invigorated, and with all his inflammatory symptoms much abated.

With all these cheering influences around her, Virginia's countenance would have been soon clad in her wonted smiles, had it not been for an unbidden scene which every now and then was conjured up before her imagination, in which those near and dear to her were principal actors. But these, painful and inexplicable as they seemed to her, were far from being well defined in her own mind. For her life, she could not separate the real evidences of her drowsy senses from the vivid images of her imagination. She was firmly impressed, however, with the belief, that some parts of them were true and real transactions! She firmly believed that she had seen her mother and the Recluse during the night—not together certainly, but near the same spot and in quick succession; and she as firmly believed that she had seen the latter disable the watch-dog, mount over the palisade, and hurry away in his boat. So much was indeed true; her mother had actually visited the wounded youth during the night, and she had actually walked in the garden, and the Recluse was actually there, but no meeting took place, except in the imagination of the worn-out maiden.

She entered the breakfast room with these various impressions, real and imaginary, curiously mingled and confused, and bearing upon her own countenance an expression of embarrassment not less surprising to her mother, who was the first person she encountered. Twenty times she was on the point of asking her mother whether she had walked in the garden during the night, but as often a strange embarrassment came over her, resulting partly from what she thought she had seen, and partly from words dropped by the Recluse in her hearing—the whole confused, unarranged and undigested—the latter perhaps being entirely unrecognised by her consciousness, but still operating imperceptibly upon her conduct. She was not a little astonished, therefore, when her mother came directly to the point occupying her own thoughts at the moment, saying, as she approached her, and affectionately smoothed down the clustering ringlets upon her brow. "You slept upon your post last night, my dear daughter? Nay—no excuses—there needs none. You wanted rest, little less than he whom you watched."

"I did not sleep so soundly as you imagine, my dear mother; I saw you, methought, either sleeping or waking, and to speak truly, I scarcely know which state I was in;" and as she spoke she cast a searching glance at her mother, but her countenance was calm and unruffled as she replied, "You must have been sleeping, my dear Virginia, I stooped over you and kissed your cheek as you slept."

"And did you not walk in the garden?"

"Yes I did! is it possible you saw me and spoke not?"

"I did see you, dear mother, but I was afraid to speak."

"Afraid to speak! Oh! you were afraid of waking Nathaniel?"

"No! no! I was frightened at the appearance of your companion in the garden."

"My companion in the garden! my poor child, you must indeed have dreamed; I had no companion in the garden."

Mr. Fairfax coming in at this moment, Virginia hastily took her chair at the head of the table, and busily commenced her duties at the table, her thoughts all the while occupied upon any thing else.

"What a strange being is that Recluse," said Mr. Fairfax, with apparent *non chalance*, "have you ever seen him, my dear?" addressing his wife.

Virginia dropped the plate she was in the act of handing to her father and was seized with, to her parents, the most unaccountable embarrassment. She endeavoured to make some excuse in order, as she supposed, to hide her mother's inevitable confusion. But the latter calmly replied, "No, my dear, I have never seen him. I have always had some curiosity to behold him, but now that he has proved himself such a public benefactor, I shall not be satisfied till the wish is gratified. Nathaniel had before excited us much by his account of him, but now I suppose the whole city will be eager to pay him their respects."

Virginia stared at her mother during this speech in the most undisguised astonishment, until she saw the calm serenity of her countenance—the expression of truth and sincerity, which had never deceived her, so strongly portrayed there, when she was again lost in bewilderment, which lasted throughout the meal. Her parents, however, were too much engaged with their own subject of discourse to observe her unusual abstraction, and the meal therefore and the dialogue came to a close without any farther development pertaining to our narrative.

CHAPTER XI.

"The eager pack from couples freed,
Dash through the bush, the briar, the brake,
While answering hound, and horn, and steed,
The mountain echoes startling wake."

The Wild Huntsman.

A FEW days after the events recorded in the last chapter, the denizens of the ancient city were roused betimes by the sounds of the hunter's horn, the echoing chorus of the eager hounds, and the neighing of the fiery steeds, as they were led forth to the gallant pastime of the chase. The river and overhanging hills were enveloped in an impenetrable veil of mist, and the dew settled in a snowy cloud, upon the hair and castors of the Cavaliers as they issued from their doors, rubbing their eyes and preparing to mount the mettled coursers which pawed the earth and blew thick volumes of smoke from their expanded nostrils. These preparations for the enlivening sports of the field were not confined to a small number of the civic youth, or to the keener sportsmen among their elders—all the gentry of the town and colony, with few exceptions, were assembled on the occasion.

Sir William Berkley wih his numerous guests,

Gideon Fairfax, with his fellows of the Council, the members of the House of Burgesses, now principally occupying the hotel of the "Berkley Arms," Frank Beverly, Philip Ludwell, Charles Dudley, with the Harrisons, the Powells, &c. all now came curvetting into the public square, dressed in their gay hunting jerkens and neat foraging caps, some with bugles swinging from their shoulders, and others with firearms suspended at their backs.

A stately gray-headed old negro, known by the cognomen of Congo, was in command of some half score of more youthful footmen of his own colour, in the livery of the Governor, each of whom held the leashes of a pair of hounds.

These, from time to time as old Congo wound a skilful blast upon his bugle, opened a deafening chorus, which echoed through the surrounding forests, and awakened from their slumbers the drowsy citizens of the town. Many a damsel peeped from her lattice to catch a glimpse of the gay Cavaliers as they wheeled into the place of rendezvous in parties of tens and twenties, all noisy and boisterous; some with the anticipation of the promised sports, and others from the more artificial stimulus of a morning julip. The sound of Congo's bugle had reverberated through the silent streets in signal blasts to the grooms of the gentry at a much earlier hour of the morning, so that many of the high-born damsels inhabiting the purlieus of this little court, were also on the alert. Among these our heroine, awakened by the echoing chorus of the "hunter's horn," was already dressed and smiling from her window, like one of her own sweet flowers, upon the gay young Cavaliers, as they passed in review before her.

In an adjoining window was another inhabitant of the same mansion, roused by the same cheering notes, but he smiled not upon the joyous throng as they gathered around the spot occupied by Congo and his canine favourites, nor yet upon those of the gay youths who rode up and touched their beavers respectfully to the smiling maiden as they singly or in pairs cantered away over the bridge in pursuit of their day's sport. It was Bacon! his head bandaged and his countenance pale and wan from his late illness and loss of blood.

Nevertheless he was dressed, and as eager for the sport as any youth among them, but exhausted nature negatived his feeble efforts and longing aspirations, and he had seated himself at the window in sullen disappointment. This latter feeling was in nowise subdued by the sight of Frank Beverly, already recovered from his slight wounds, dressed in a scarlet jerken and hunting cap, a bugle over his shoulder, and mounted upon a noble animal apparently as eager to display his fine proportions as his master. The thundering clatter of the chargers' heels as this numerous cavalcade now passed in long succession over the bridge before the gazing citizens, thus untimely awakened from their slumbers, at length began to die away in silence, broken at intervals by the measured tramp of an occasional party of the more staid, older and less eager Cavaliers, pursuing the main body at a pace more suited to their age; or by the gallop of some slumbering sluggard hastening to overtake his more punctual comrades of the chase. Now and then a note from the bugle of some overjoyous youth, as he entered the forest, brought a frown upon the brow of old Congo, whose look was turned in silent appeal against these irregular proceedings, to his master, who rode apart in earnest conversation with Mr. Fairfax. While our sportsmen are thus joyously moving on their way to the appointed spot, we will pursue the thread of the dialogue between the two dignitaries just alluded to, as it had reference to the leading personages of our story.

"Nay, treat not my apprehensions lightly, Fairfax; is not that youth who leans so disconsolately out of your window this morning, a proper knight to catch the errant fancies of a girl of sixteen?" said Sir William.

"He is indeed a right well-favoured boy," replied Mr. Fairfax, "and one calculated to win his way to a colder heart than that of a maiden near his own age. Was he not the means of your own preservation, Sir William, from the knives of yonder murderous fanatics cooped up in the jail of the city?"

"Ay!" said his companion, drily, "I grant

him to be all that you say he is; but does not that enforce more powerfully what I have been saying? Ought you not under such circumstances, to acquaint him with the necessity of his finding another house than your's for his home, where your daughter is constantly before his eyes, and what is more important, where he is constantly before her's, not only with the attractions of his own well-favoured person, but in the interesting character of her father's and her uncle's preserver?"

"If the poor youth had ever presumed upon his position in my family, to make advances to my daughter, then indeed there might be some propriety in the course you recommend, Sir William. But I have observed him closely since our last conversation on this subject, and I am satisfied that there is nothing more than fraternal affection between them."

"It is very difficult, Fairfax, for the parties themselves to draw an exact line, where the one kind of affection ends, and the other begins; the gradation from mere brotherly regard to love is so very imperceptible, that the very persons in whom it takes place are often unconscious of it, until accident or warning from others forces it upon their apprehension."

"But where is the necessity of examining into these fine distinctions now, Sir William? Where is the point of the matter."

"To that it was my purpose to come presently,

but you are always so impetuous and sanguine, if you will permit me to say so, that I have found it difficult to discuss this matter in your presence, with all the coolness and deliberation which ought to attend the negotiation of an alliance between the kinsman of his majesty's representative in the Colony, and the daughter of his nearest relative—the heiress probably of both their fortunes."

"But has not the match between Virginia and Frank been a settled matter for years?"

"Ay, truly, Fairfax, and I am rejoiced that you remember it; but was it not also agreed, for wise purposes, that the parties themselves should know nothing of the contract until Frank became of age?"

"True, and what then?"

"That time has been passed some months."

"Indeed!"

"Ay, and what is more important to the happiness of the young pair, Frank himself has moved in the business without any prompting from me. This, you know, was what we desired, and the very end for which the matter was kept from their knowledge."

"He has then proposed himself to Virginia, and she has doubtless accepted him! All right, all right, Sir William. I always told you it would turn out just in this way. Every thing turns out for the best. You see the advantage of leaving the young people to themselves."

"Yes, yes, it has all turned out very happily in your sanguine imagination; but you run away with the matter without hearing me out."

"Did you not say it was all settled? I certainly understood you so!"

"No, I said nothing like it. I said that my young kinsman had moved in the business without my prompting; and I intended to say, if you had permitted me, that he had authorized me, this day, to make a formal tender of his hand and fortune to your daughter, through you; which I now do."

"Well, why did you not say so at first, Sir William, and there could have been no trouble about the matter. Instead of that, you read me a long lecture about the danger of harbouring handsome young fellows in my house generally, concluding in particular with a recapitulation of the various debts of gratitude due from me and my family, and yourself, to poor Bacon. But as far as I am concerned, I give my hearty consent to the proposed union, and you may so assure Frank from me, and tell him that he has nothing more to do, but to appear as every way worthy in the eyes of Virginia as he does in mine."

"There, you see, you are coming in your own immethodical and precipitate way, to the very point with which I set out. I was merely hazarding a few observations upon the various prepossessing qualities of your protegée, and expressing some fears of the intercourse subsisting between him and your daughter, with a view to put you on your guard at once. This was not done with a view to read you a lecture, as you are pleased to say, but from the best grounded apprehensions that things were not proceeding well for our scheme."

"Is there any ground for the fears you mention?"

"There is, Fairfax! Lady Berkley has often of late mentioned her apprehensions to me, that there is a growing and mutual attachment between your ward and your daughter. Frank has observed the same thing, and indeed the very proposals I have just had the honour of making to you, have probably resulted from a desire on his part to bring the matter to an eclaircissement at once."

"I will speak to Virginia and her mother on the subject, and my word for it, my daughter will show you that she knows what is due to her birth and standing in society. But as to turning Nathaniel out of my house! I could as soon turn Virginia herself out. Poor boy, he has a farm of his own, it is true, but my house has always been a home to him, and it always shall be, as long as he continues worthy, and I continue the head of it."

"Ay, that farm! There was another ill-advised piece of generosity; not content with bringing up a foundling like your own son, you must purchase him a farm and stock it."

"Indeed, Governor, you give me credit for much more generosity than I have exercised. *I* purchased him no farm, or if I did, it was merely as his agent and guardian. He furnished the means himself."

"That was very strange! Very strange indeed, that a youth without occupation, and without any visible fortune, should purchase and stock one of the most valuable plantations in the colony."

As they arrived at this point in their discourse, they had ascended to the top of one of the highest hills within many miles of the city. Here they found the sportsmen who had preceded them, closely grouped together, and all talking at once, while Old Cong, (as he was familiarly called by the youths,) was engaged in slipping the leashes. One pair after another of the fleet animals snuffed the air for a moment, and then bounded down the slope of the hill, carrying their noses close to the earth, and eagerly questing backward and forward through the shrubbery; sometimes retracing their steps to the very point from which they started.

At length one of the foremost of the pack opened a shrill note as he ran, indicative to the uninitiated, only of eagerness and impatience in the pursuit of the game, but Old Congo's experienced eye instantly brightened up, as with head erect, he uttered a sharp shrill whoop, and mounting his fleet courser, he shot down the hill with the fleetness of the wind, making the woods echo with his merry *hip halloo*, as he cheered them on. By this time the pack were following the leader in the devious trail on which he was now warm; the whole chorus sometimes opening in joyous and eager concert as they came upon the scent, just from the impress of sly Reynard's feet, and then again relapsing into silence. These intervals in the cheerful cry announced the doubt which as yet existed, whether the trail upon which they had struck was any thing more than the devious windings made by the game on emerging from his den, for the purpose, as the negroes stoutly affirmed, of throwing his pursuers out. It seemed indeed as if such had been the intention of the cunning animal, for a plan of the intricate mazes which the pack were threading, if laid down upon paper, would very much resemble a complicated problem in Euclid, or the track of a ship upon a voyage of discovery in unknown seas. Meanwhile Old Congo was in the thickest of them; now cursing one refractory member, and again cheering a favourite. The Cavaliers stood in groups—one foot in the stirrup and a hand on the pummel of the saddle, or smoothing down the curling mane of their impatient chargers. At length the problem was solved, and the hounds were seen coursing in a circle round the brow of the hill, a continuous yelp from the leader, and an answering chorus from the pack, announcing to the waiting gentry, that the game was up. They instantly mounted, and were presently flying over the uneven ground at a speed and with a reckless, yet skilful horsemanship, which bade defiance to all the perils of the chase. Here one lost his cap by the limb of a tree; there another measured his length upon the ground by the stumble of his charger; the main party speeding apace, regardless of all, save the fox and his pursuers.

The chase, like misfortune, is a wonderful leveller of distinctions. Foremost in the field were the proud Sir William and the keener Fairfax; one upon either side of Congo, whooping and yelling in unison, and all distinctions forgotten for the moment, but the speed and bottom of their coursers; the countenances of the three alike expressive of concentrated eagerness in the sport. To a spectator on the summit of the hill, the scene was not wanting in picturesque and striking features. The sun was just peeping over the blue hills, and lifting the vapours from the valleys beneath, in all the variegated and beauteous tints of the rainbow, as they arose in majestic masses and encircled the summits of the cliffs. The cool and invigorating breeze of a young summer morn, as it was wafted through the romantic dales and glens, came loaded with the richest sweets of forest and of flower. And when the music of the hounds was softened in the distance to a faint harmonious swell upon the air, the feathered tribes, luxuriant in beauty, warbled forth their richest strains of nature's melody as they hopped from twig to twig, flashing their brilliant colours in dazzling contrast to the pendant dew-drops glittering in the sunbeams. On the other hand the rays fell in broad sheets of light upon the tranquil waters of the noble Powhatan, as seen through the deep green foliage of the woodland vista. The city too was dimly visible in the distance, its towering columns of smoke shooting high up towards heaven through the clear calm air, and expanding into fleecy waves as they were lost or scattered in the higher regions of the atmosphere. These morning glories of a southern sunrise were, however, lost upon our sportsmen, who now came sweeping round the base of the hill from the opposite side, the horses covered with foam, and riders making the welkin ring again with their shouts of gladness and excitement. The dignity of station and of birth, affairs of state, and all other considerations foreign to the business of the time, were utterly forgotten and abandoned, while their late proud possessors vied with the youngest and the humblest in seizing the pleasures of the chase. The horses seemed in the distance as if their bodies were moving through the air, a foot and a half nearer the ground than they were wont, their legs nearly invisible; while their riders bent over their necks as if impatient even of this headlong speed.

Hitherto the hounds as usual, when in pursuit of the fox, had moved in the figure of a rude circle, never departing to any great distance from the point whence they had started, but moving round and round the hill; and there was every appearance that the chase would be thus continued until the game was either fairly run down, or had gained the shelter of his hole.

In the present instance, however, an unexpected reprieve was granted to the hard pressed animal. The dogs, as they came round the brow of the hill for the third or fourth time, struck off abruptly from their regular circuit; the foremost chargers were reined up, and in a short time the whole cavalcade was brought to a stand at the point where the dogs had quitted the track.

The cause of this interruption to the sport was readily understood by the experienced Cavaliers. A buck had crossed between the dogs and the fox, and the former, contrary to their usual discipline and stanchness, broke off to follow the newest scent. Many were the imprecations hurled at the head of Old Congo and his deputies for this misconduct of their charge, the consequence, as was affirmed, of their having been set upon the trail of a buck on the previous Sabbath. It was now, however, too late to remedy the evil, as Congo's bugle itself was not sufficient to recall the eager pack.

Firearms were immediately unslung from the shoulders of such as bore them, and Mr. Fairfax, as the keenest sportsman, leading the way, nearly half of the youths were quickly seen following him up the opposite hill. Sir William Berkley and such of the company as had already been worn out, retraced their steps to the picturesque point from which they had set out, and which has already been described.

Here some of the footmen, retained for the

purpose, speedily constructed a rude table under an umbrageous tree, upon which was laid out a tempting display of cold viands, wines and strong waters. Horses were now tied to the surrounding trees, and their riders threw themselves upon the sward to repose their wearied limbs, and regale their longing eyes upon the good things which only awaited the return of their comrades. This delay seemed likely, however, to prove rather tedious to the longing appetites of the former, who had not as yet broken their fast.

Full two hours had elapsed, and yet no token came of hounds or huntsmen. The patience even of the formal and ceremonious Sir William began to flag, and he forthwith ordered the bugles to sound a recall from the highest spot in the neighbourhood. In vain the reverberating blasts reechoed from hill to hill, and from river to cliff; in vain they paused to listen for the music of the hounds or an answering signal from the keener sportsmen. After repeated trials the patience of the Governor gave way, and having set apart a share of the provision for their comrades, they fell upon the tempting display with knife and dagger. Cups of horn, and silver flagons were speedily produced, and in a short time their absent compeers were almost forgotten in the general destruction of cold capons, tongue and ham.

Towards the conclusion of the repast, the absent sportsmen began to drop in singly and at intervals. The bridles of their foaming horses were thrown to the grooms, and they fell upon the wine and fowls like famished soldiers, after a long day's march. Then came a panting hound, crouching beneath the legs of a horse, with his tongue hanging from his mouth; then another, and another, until they had all obeyed the summons of the bugle.

None of the huntsmen who had returned as yet, had been in at the death; but it was supposed that Mr. Fairfax, the only one now missing, had been more fortunate, as the hounds that came in last were covered with blood. He was momentarily expected, but they listened in vain for the sound of his horn. Old Congo was despatched over the hills to summon him with his bugle, but he likewise returned without any tidings of the absent Cavalier, and without having heard any answering notes to those of his own horn. Hours were spent in waiting for him, at first occupied by the younger Cavaliers in various games and athletic sports, but as the day waned apace, and still no news of him arrived, uneasiness began to engross the minds of his associates.

By the orders of the Governor, the whole Cavalcade spread themselves, and scoured the forests for miles in the direction he had been seen to take, but no answer was returned to their shouts and bugles, and no token of his presence and safety was discovered. Occasionally two parties were brought together by a supposed answer from his bugle, but it was found to be only the reply of one scouring party to another.

After a long and fruitless search, they resolved to hasten to the city, in hopes that he had reached his home by some other route, and in case this supposition should prove fallacious it was resolved that the whole male population should be called out to the search. The distance was accomplished with a speed and recklessness quite equal to that with which they had performed it in the morning, but with feelings very different. A general and gloomy silence pervaded their ranks. Gideon Fairfax was one of the most universally popular Cavaliers in the Colony; he was generous, hospitable, and sincere, with his equals, and humane and affable to his inferiors. His own slaves idolized him, and would have readily perilled life and limb in defence either of his person or his reputation.

When the cavalcade arrived at the bridge, their painful suspense and anxiety were little relieved by perceiving an immense crowd assembled round the house of Mr. Fairfax. That some accident must have befallen him they had too good reason now to apprehend, else what could have drawn the multitude together? The arrival of a successful huntsman, was an affair of too frequent occurrence at Jamestown to excite the present visible commotion. The returning and anxious Cavaliers were soon met by the eager throng, who pressed around them in crowds, each party demanding of the other news respecting their absent fellow-citizen.

The assemblage of the crowd around the house was soon explained by the appearance of his favourite charger, upon which he had set out in the morning, so full of health, vigour and animation. He was held in the midst of the assemblage, his head-gear broken, the saddle bloody, and his sides dripping with mud and water, as if he had just crossed through the river. In this condition he had presented himself at the stable door where he was usually kept, without his rider, and this was all they knew in the city concerning the fate of the missing horseman. This was enough to excite the most distracting fears in the minds of his own family, and the worst apprehensions in those of his immediate friends and more humble admirers.

Horses and men were speedily volunteered for the purpose of scouring the whole forest in the direction of the chase. Many of the Cavaliers barely dismounted from one horse to mount another; and in a very few minutes, hundreds of citizens, some on horseback and others on foot, had assembled. While they were thus speedily collecting their forces, a scream from some washerwomen on the bank of the river, quickly drew the crowd in that direction. Men, women and children rushed to the spot with feelings of anxiety and alarm, wrought to the highest pitch. They were not left long in doubt, for a boat was just nearing the shore, in which were two men rowing, while another supported upon his lap the head of the still living but wounded Cavalier.

CHAPTER XII.

Mr. FAIRFAX was borne to his own dwelling upon a litter, amidst the universal regrets and lamentations of the people. The condition of his own immediate family may be more easily imagined than described. The most heart-rending shrieks pierced the air when it was announced to the female part of it that the amiable and generous head of their house had been basely shot,—by whom he knew not, nor could he form a conjecture. The deed was perpetrated a few moments after he had himself shot the buck. He immediately fell from his horse and was for a time perfectly unconscious of his condition. When he revived he found his horse gone and himself so weakened from loss of blood that he was unable to stand. His only resource was his trumpet, upon which he made repeated efforts to summon his companions, but even the sound of his horn was so feeble that it could not have been heard more than a few rods from the spot. While he was in this helpless condition he chanced to discover three men fishing at the base of the river bank, whom he attempted to summon to his aid, but the sound of the water prevented them from hearing him. With great difficulty and suffering he was at length enabled to crawl down the hill to such a distance that he might be heard, and was thence borne to the city in their boat, as the reader has already been informed.

The surgeon, after examining his wound, pronounced it to be of the most alarming character, and assured Bacon, apart from the family, that he had little hopes for the life of his patron, who after the exhaustion of his painful journey and the succeeding intense pain caused by the probing of his wounds had fallen into a deep sleep.

Sometime during the morning which has been described in the preceding chapter, and while the hunting party were yet enjoying themselves undisturbed by any untoward accident, Bacon had invited Virginia to accompany him in his first stroll through the garden since his illness. She complied with more alacrity than had been usual with her of late, hoping that the refreshing sweets of a summer morning and the cheering sight of birds and flowers, would dispel the gloomy misanthropy which had settled upon his countenance, since his disappointment at not being able to join the chase.

After a silent promenade through the shady walks, they seated themselves in the little summer house already mentioned, and Bacon thus broke the embarrassing silence.

"Virginia, the current of events seems to be hurrying us on to a painful crisis! It is impossible for me to shut my eyes to such of them at least, as relate more particularly to myself. My position in the society in which I now move, is daily becoming more painful to me. I am constantly subjected to the impertinence of those who imagine that they have, or perhaps really have, some reason to complain of the protection and countenance afforded to me by your noble father."

"Trust then, Nathaniel, to his and our continued confidence and esteem, and less to the morbid sensibility which disturbs you, and all will soon be well again."

"Not so, Virginia. If we were in a little community by ourselves, I could indeed give my whole mind and soul to such enjoyments as the society of your family has already afforded to me, forgetting all the world besides, and never listening for a moment to ambitious hopes and aspiring thoughts. But in this proud and aristocratic circle, I must soon be either more or less than I am at present."

"Why must you be more or less than you are, Nathaniel?" said Virginia, with unaffected and bewitching *naiveté*.

"Is it possible, Virginia, that you do not see the reason why? Have you witnessed the fierce struggles contending at my heart and never formed a surmise as to the real cause?"

"Except the morbid sensitiveness to which I have already alluded, and its very insufficient cause, I declare that I know of none."

"Is it possible. Good Heavens! and must I at

last break through the restraints which I had imposed upon myself? Must I trample upon the generous hospitality of the father to lay my heart open before his daughter?" Her countenance underwent an instantaneous change, and while he continued, her eyes fell beneath his ardent gaze, and her head sank upon her bosom in confusion.

"I will indeed trust to the flattering delusion which hope whispers in my ear, that perhaps your father himself knows enough of me and of my origin to absolve me from these restraints. It must be so, Virginia—else he had never trusted a heart, young and susceptible like mine, to the constant influence of beauty like yours," and he took her unresisting hand, "joined with such perfect innocence and such childlike simplicity as never till this moment to be conscious of its power. Oh, Virginia, I would fain believe that he foresaw and approved of the result which he could not but anticipate. What he approves will his daughter's voice confirm?—No answer! Will you not vouchsafe one little word to keep my sinking hopes alive!—You are offended; your countenance speaks the language which your tongue is unaccustomed to utter!"

"What should I say?" answered Virginia; "would you have me promise a return of love whose indulgence is dependent on contingency? Is it kind, is it proper to urge me upon this subject under existing circumstances?"

"By heavens, Virginia, there shall be no contingency of my making! I have crossed the Rubicon, and you shall have the knowledge as you have had possession of my whole soul from the days of our infancy. 'Tis yours, Virginia, wholly yours; soul, mind and heart, all yours. Mould them as you will, reject me if you must, they are still yours. I swear never to profane the shrine of this first and only love by offering them up on any other. They are offered now, because my destiny so wills it. We are the creatures of circumstances. I have vainly struggled against the overwhelming tide which has borne me to this point. I am goaded onward by insult—beset with menaces, and torn by the storms of such a passion as never man before encountered. Can you, dear Virginia, vouchsafe to me some measure of relief from these distracting emotions? Say that you would have been mine under other circumstances! Say that you will never wed that proud and imperious Beverly! Say any thing, Virginia, which shall calm the tumults of my bosom, and feed my hopes for the future." While he thus spoke, the blushing maiden was evidently labouring under emotions little less powerful than his own. Her previous air of offended feminine dignity was fast melting into sympathy, with the impassioned feelings of the excited youth. She felt for his peculiar griefs and cares, and shared his warmer sentiments. The youth perceived the softening mood, and continued.

"Speak, I pray you, Virginia, I am in your hands. Speak me into existence, or banish me from your presence!"

"I do not know, Nathaniel," said Virginia, after many attempts to give utterance to her thoughts, "whether it is proper at all times to speak the truth, but I will not deceive you now. There does indeed seem to be a peculiar concurrence of circumstances around us, and more perhaps than you are yourself aware of. I did not intend to deceive you, or lead you astray; when I told you a few moments since that I knew nothing of any other struggle than that arising from your own excited feelings, I spoke the truth, but perhaps not the entire truth;" and as she spoke, a lovely blush suffused her neck and downcast face; "I knew of other struggles indeed, but not your's, Nathaniel."

"Were they your's, Virginia, and of the same nature? say they were, and heaven bless for ever the tongue that utters it."

"That you have to ask, does more honour to my discretion, than I have ascribed to it myself of late. I have had painful fears that I should have little to tell on an occasion like the present, should it ever come, with my father's approbation. And if I have now overstepped the bounds of that proviso, it was in the hope of calming your troubled spirits, and preventing a catastrophe upon which I have looked with dreadful anticipation, since the night of the insurrection."

"And will you indeed be mine?"

"I will, Nathaniel, whenever you gain my father's approbation; but without it, never."

At this moment the garden gate was heard to creak upon its hinges, (most unmusically to Bacon's ears,) and Harriet Harrison came tripping over beds and flowers, all out of breath, her cheeks glowing with the heightened colour of exercise, and her eyes sparkling with mischief just ready to explode.

"Oh, Virginia! Virginia! such news!" was her first exclamation; "But shall I tell it before Mr. Bacon?"

"Yes, if it is of the usual kind."

"Well, upon your own head be the consequences. I have accidentally overheard such a secret! You must know that your Aunt Berkley has been at our house this morning, and I overheard her tell my mother that there was to be a great wedding immediately, and that I was to be one of the brides-maids. What! no tell-tale guilty blush? Well, who do you think is to be the bride-groom, and who the bride?"

"Indeed, Harriet, I cannot even guess."

"The blissful man, then, is Beverly—but can you name his bride?"

"I should not go far hence for an answer, if you had not announced your nomination for a secondary office."

"O fie, fie, Virginia, I did not think you could play the hypocrite so well. I will tell you who it is then, but you must not breathe it even to the winds, nor you, Mr. Bacon. It is a sly arch little damsel, about your age and figure, by name Virginia Fairfax!" And with these words, she burst into a loud laugh, pointing to her companion with her finger, and then tripped away again towards the gate without waiting to see the effect of her communication; but stopping with the gate in her hand, she cried—"But remember, Virginia, Charles Dudley is not to stand up with me; we don't speak now." And then she flew away, her hat hanging by the riband round her neck, and her raven ringlets flying loose around her temples. Virginia sat as one without life or motion, her face deadly pale, and her eye preternaturally clear and glassy, but without a tear. Her respiration was hurried and oppressed, and her countenance expressive of high and noble resolves in the midst of the keenest mental suffering. She knew whence her aunt obtained her information, and in its communication to others in the confidence of the Governor, before she had been consulted, she saw the tyrannical determination of that arbitrary old man to consummate this hated union without the least regard to her wishes or her feelings.

As these convictions flashed upon her mind, they called up firm and resolute determinations, even in her gentle bosom! she was stung into resistance by the tyrannical and high handed measures of her uncle, and resolved to resist upon the threshold. Bacon's physical frame was not so steady, or his nerves in his present mood so well strung by high resolves of independent action. He too saw by whom the blow was aimed, and upon whose head it would principally fall, and he trembled for the consequences to his gentle companion. He did not know the strength of her independent mind, and the endurance and fortitude with which she would carry her purposes into execution. He knew her to be gentle and kind and superlatively lovely, but as yet she had endured no trials,—her courage and fortitude had been put to no test. The very amiable qualities which had won his affections, served only to increase his doubts as to her capacity to resist and endure what he too plainly saw awaited her. He had yet to learn that these are almost always found united in the female bosom with a signal power of steady and calm resistance to oppression. To this resolution had Virginia arrived, when his more turbulent and masculine emotions burst from his tongue as he seized her hand, "Swear to me, Virginia, before high Heaven, that you will never marry this proud heir of wealth, and worldly honours."

"Upon one condition."

"Name it! if it is possible, it is done."

"That you from this moment give up all idea of a meeting with Frank Beverly, which I know has only thus long been delayed by your wounds and illness." He dropped her hand and writhed upon his seat in agony—the cold perspiration bursting from his pale forehead, as he covered it with his hands. But presently standing up he exclaimed, "Great God! and can you ask this of me, Virginia? Is my honour of so little value to you, that you can ask me to betray it? You heard the insult! You saw the dagger aimed in the dark! Ay, and saw it strike upon a bare and wounded nerve! Shall I not resist? Is an assassin to thrust the point of his steel into the very apple of my eye, and meet with no resistance? Instinct itself would strike back the cowardly blow. Another might forego the measure of his revenge for an ordinary insult, but placed as I am, an elevated mark for impertinence and malignity to shoot at, with nothing but my single arm to defend me; no line of noble and heroic ancestors to support my pretensions, and my rank in the community; no living relations to give the lie to his calumnies! Standing alone amidst a host of powerful enemies, shall I be stricken down by a cowardly maligner, and never turn to strike one blow for my good name, my mother's honour, my father's memory, and my own standing in society? No, no, Virginia; you cannot, you will not, require me to promise this. One evidence I must and will give to the calumniator, that I come of no churl's blood."

"But, Nathaniel, did you not resent and thus return his injury upon the spot?"

"Ay, truly, I did hurl defiance in the craven's teeth, but that only throws the demand for satisfaction upon his shoulders, so that when it is made,

I may at once atone for his, and take ample reparation for my own deep wrongs."

"Promise me, then, that you will but act with Frank henceforth on the defensive? Remember he is my kinsman."

"I do promise; and now promise me in your turn never to marry this kinsman, unless I give my consent, or you should be absolved from your obligation by my death, or some other irremediable barrier."

"I promise, Nathaniel."

Scarcely had the words issued from her lips, when the clanking of stirrups and clattering of a horse's hoofs at full speed, were heard outside the garden wall.

Into what a state of consternation and dismay the family was thrown by the appearance of the bloody and panting charger at his stable door without his master, the reader may already have imagined.

CHAPTER XIII.

It was the hour of midnight; the softened rays of a shaded lamp threw a flickering and uncertain light upon the paraphernalia of the sick chamber, as our hero sat a solitary watcher at the side of the wounded Cavalier. The long and apparently profound sleep into which the invalid had fallen, completely deceived the females of the family, so that they were more easily persuaded by Nathaniel to leave the charge, during the first half of the night, to his sole care. He had for a long time sat a sad and silent beholder of the unconscious sleeper, watching with breathless eagerness every change of muscle, as some sharp and inward pain vibrated in horrible contortions upon the countenance of the wounded Cavalier. In one of these he started suddenly up in the bed, his eyes glaring wildly upon his unrecognised attendant in utter amazement. First looking into his face and then to the bandages around his own person, he fell back on his couch—a grim and frightful smile of remembrance and recognition playing for a moment upon his features, as he placed his cold hand within that of Bacon, which had been softly laid upon his breast to soothe his startled perceptions.

"Nathaniel," said he, his voice already hollow and thrilling, "My hour is come! It is useless to disguise it. I feel and know it to be so, whatever the surgeon may pretend. You need not place your finger upon your lip; I owe to you a duty which I must perform while yet I may. You have often importuned me, and sometimes impatiently, which I did not enough, perhaps, consider to be natural to your situation, but you must forgive me—you have often importuned me upon the subject of your origin. If I had possessed any full or satisfactory knowledge on the subject, you may be sure I would not long have detained it from you. Indeed, I was little less anxious than yourself to place you upon an equal footing in every respect with your associates." Here a smile of inward satisfaction beamed upon his auditor's countenance, unobserved, however, by the speaker, as he continued: "There were some reasons too, connected with the history of my own family, which prevented me from divulging what little I did know of your's. If I have erred, for this too you must forgive me. The wrong shall now be repaired. You have now been a member of my household for fifteen or sixteen years.

"One cold and rainy day our sympathies were excited, by seeing an athletic young Irishman in the street, near our door, carrying upon his back a well dressed boy, apparently six or seven years of age. The child was crying most piteously with cold and hunger. We called in the Irishman, and after furnishing him and his little charge with food, inquired whose child it was, and whither he was taking it. He answered, in his own expressive language, that he did not know to whom the child belonged, nor whither he was taking it. That it had beeen a fellow passenger with him across the ocean, until they were shipwrecked at the mouth of the river, outside of the Capes. That a woman who had two boys near the same age, either of her own, or under her protection, he did not know which, had most earnestly prayed him to take one of them upon his back, as he was preparing to swim to the beach. He did so, and succeeded in landing with his charge in perfect safety. What became of the woman and the other child he never knew, as shortly after the waves broke over the vessel, and she went to pieces. Many of the passengers and crew, however, had been saved and were scattered about through the neighbouring plantations, driven to seek employment by the urgency of their immediate wants. Whether the woman and the child were among the number he could not learn, as those who were saved had necessarily landed at distant points upon the shore. He brought the child to Jamestown in hopes that it would be recognised, and if not, that some humane person would take charge of it. His hopes had thus far proved fruitless, as to the first expectation, but we undertook cheerfully the latter task, and likewise gave employment to the kind-hearted Hibernian. I caused it to be made as generally known through the Colony, as our limited means of communication would permit, that such a child was in our possession, particularly describing his person and clothes, but all in vain. I also caused search to be made for the woman with the other child, through the southern plantations, but no tidings of them were ever heard, and we naturally concluded that they had gone down with the vessel.

"Some months after the little stranger had been thus domiciliated among us, I one day received an anonymous letter, which stated that the writer knew who were the parents of the child, but for important reasons of a political nature, he could not then divulge their names or history. He stated so many circumstances connected with the shipwreck, and described so exactly the child, that we were compelled to believe him. This letter was followed by others at various intervals, from that time to the present, often enclosing drafts for large sums to be drawn for in England, for the benefit of the child. I need scarcely tell you that the child was yourself—and your preserver, Brian O'Reily. The name by which you are called is the nearest that we could come to that by which, both yourself and Brian stated, you were known on board the vessel. The money enclosed for your benefit, has been suffered to accumulate until the late purchase of the plantation at the falls, of which you are now in possession. Around your neck, at the time of your arrival, was a small trinket, enclosing the hair of two individuals, curiously interwoven, and on its outside were some initials corresponding with your own name, and the date of a marriage. This, together with the letters I have mentioned, you will find in the left hand drawer of the secretary which stands in the corner of my library. After opening the outside door, you will perceive the key hanging beside the drawer. These letters were never shown, nor the contents mentioned to my wife, for a reason which I am now about to explain to you, if my strength will permit, and which will also unfold to you the cause of my reluctance to communicate with you on this subject.

"When I first saw Emily in England, she was a young and beautiful widow. Early in life a mutual attachment was formed between her and the son of a neighbouring gentleman, in rather more humble circumstances than the father of my Emily. In consequence of this disparity in the fortunes and standing of the two families, their attachment was kept a profound secret between themselves, until the youth having joined the army of the Commonwealth, they eloped. This was their last and only resort, because her father was as determined a Loyalist as his was indefatigable in the cause of the Independents and Roundheads. For two whole years she followed the perilous fortunes of her husband, now become a distinguished officer, during which time she gave birth to a son. For a season she resided with her infant at a retired farm-house, in a distant part of the country from the scene of strife; but her husband becoming impatient of her absence, directed her to procure a nurse for her boy and again partake of his hazardous fortunes. Her child was accordingly left in the charge of the nurse, and she set out to join her husband. On the eve of meeting him, as she supposed, she was met by the news of a desperate engagement, in which the party opposed to her husband had been victorious, and very shortly afterward, she was herself, with her attendants, overtaken in the highway, and captured by a party commanded by one of her own brothers. He immediately sent her under a strong escort to her father's house, not however before she had time to learn from some of the prisoners taken in the engagement, the heart-rending news of the death of her husband. She gained these sad tidings from one of his comrades, who saw him receive the wound and fall at his side.

"She found her father so exasperated against her that she dared not even mention to him or her brothers the existence of her child, lest they should take some desperate means to separate them for ever. For a time, therefore, she contented herself with such clandestine communications with her nurse as the perilous nature of the times permitted. At length the sum of her afflictions was consummated by the death of her infant, the account of which was brought to her by the nurse in person.

"When I first saw her, these many and severe misfortunes had been somewhat softened down in the lapse of years. She was still a melancholy being, however, but I belonging to her father's party, and being of a gay and volatile turn of mind, and much pleased with her beauty and amiable temperament, offered to bring her out to America as my wife, whither the success of the Protector's arms was then driving so many of the Nobles and Cavaliers of England, and where I already had a sister married to the then late, and now present Governor of Virginia. After candidly stating all the foregoing circumstances, she agreed to accept my hand. And we were accordingly married and sailed for the Capes of Virginia. You will perceive, upon a perusal of the anonymous letters, that the writer displays a most intimate knowledge of all the foregoing particulars of our family history. The design, as you will doubtless perceive, was to operate upon our superstitious feelings, by this mysterious display of knowledge, in matters so carefully guarded from the world. This was not at all necessary, because we had already adopted, and treated you as one of our own family. Nevertheless he partially succeeded with me. I confess to you that it has always appeared to me one of the strangest circumstances that ever came under my knowledge, that any living person should be acquainted with the facts contained in those letters. I have made the most strenuous and unceasing efforts to discover their author, by means of the European drafts, but all to no purpose. You will now readily comprehend the reason, why I did not communicate with Emily on this subject. It would only have been opening old wounds afresh, and would probably have excited her more sensitive feelings to a painful state of anxiety and suspense. The same reasons which influenced my conduct in this respect, will doubtless operate upon your own judgment when I am gone. In the same drawer is a will, by which you will perceive, when it is properly authenticated, that I have left to you, in conjunction with others, the most sacred of all human trusts. You will find yourself associated in the management of my affairs, with persons whom I knew at the time to be uncongenial with you in your general feelings, but upon this one subject you will all be influenced by one desire. Governor Berkley and Mr. Harrison will never thwart you in the active management, which I have left principally in trust to you.

"I have now rapidly sketched what you will better understand from the papers themselves, and I have finished none too soon, as I am admonished by the return of these cutting pains."

After another agonizing paroxysm, he fell again

into one of those death-like slumbers, which often fill up the intervals of suffering after a mortal wound.

When Bacon perceived that he slept profoundly, he at once gave way to the restless anxiety to see the papers, by which he was consumed. Eagerly, but softly, he sought the library, opened the doors of the high old fashioned black walnut secretary, with its Lion's claws for feet, and his grisly beard and shining teeth, conspicuous from every brass ornament with which it was adorned.*

He returned to his post and opened the package of papers with a trembling anxiety, and intense interest, similar to what one might be supposed to feel who was about to unseal the book of fate.

He had no sooner cast his eye upon the hand-writing, than the package fell from his grasp in the most evident disappointment. Until this moment he had indulged a vague undefined hope that from a single glance at the characters, he should at once possess a clue to unravel the whole mystery. His mind had instantly settled upon one peculiar and remarkable individual in the Colony, as the only one likely to possess such knowledge, and from the interest which that person had always manifested in his fate, he had almost persuaded himself that he would prove to be the writer. With

* Some idea of the rude state of the mechanic arts of the period may be formed by those who have seen the antiquated chair, in which the speaker of the Virginia house of delegates sits to this day. There are many specimens too of ancient furniture still preserved in the older Counties of Virginia.

his handwriting and the peculiarly dignified and stately character of his language, he had long been familiar. The first few lines over which his eye glanced rapidly and eagerly, convinced him of his error ; neither the characters nor the language were his. Nevertheless they possessed sufficient interest, after the momentary disappointment had passed away, to induce him to grasp the magain and once more commence their perusal. In this occupation he was soon so completely absorbed as to be unconscious of the time which elapsed, the situation and circumstances in which he was placed as regarded himself, as well as the wounded Cavalier, who lay in the same apartment. In unfolding one of the papers he came upon the gold trinket mentioned by his benefactor. Here again was a new subject of intense interest. "This," said he to himself, "was worn by my mother and was placed around my neck at our last parting." Here was a fragment of her tresses precisely similar in character and colour to his own, interwoven with the darker shades of those of his father. Here too was the date of their marriage and the initials of their names agreeing sufficiently well with his own supposed age. These were all subjects of earnest contemplation to the excited imagination of a youth rendered morbidly sensitive on the subject of his birth and parentage, by many painful occurrences with his aristocratic young associates, and still more by recent developments with the idol of his affections. The trinket was laid down and the manuscript resumed, of whose contents as much as is important to our narrative has already been communicated to the reader. The characters in which it was written, were successively compared in his mind to those of every person in the Colony who handled the pen. In that day it was not hard to remember who they were from their great number, chirography having been an art with which the Cavaliers were less familiar than with the use of the small and broad sword. Not a scribe in the country wrote in characters similar to the one he held in his hand, so far as he could recollect. He thought they resembled those of Governor Berkley more than of any other, yet that sturdy old knight had invariably frowned so much on his attempts to assume the place and standing in society to which his education and intelligence entitled him, that he could not believe him concerned in benefiting him, even as an agent.

The Recluse was the only individual upon whom his mind ould rest as the probable author, notwithstanding the variance of the writing. Yet against this conclusion there were many powerful arguments. The first that suggested itself to his mind was the money. Could he command such large sums? And if he could, was it possible with his known habits and peculiarities, not to mention his occasional abberration, to arrange complicated pecuniary affairs in Europe? Then again, if he was the writer, why were these communications continued after he had himself arrived at years of discretion?

Every reason seemed to favour the idea that he himself would have been chosen as the depository of these communications, had the Recluse been the man, especially when he reflected that he was at that very time possessed of more of his confidence than any other person in the Colony. The papers were perused and re-perused, and the locket turned over and over listlessly in his fingers, while a shade of deep sadness and disappointment settled upon his countenance.

From this unpleasing revery he was suddenly aroused by the groans of the wounded sufferer, who now awoke in the greatest agony. When Bacon came to his bed-side a melancholy change was visible in his countenance. He was making his last struggle with the grim monster. He was however enabled to express a desire that his family should be called, but when they arrived, he could not give utterance to his ideas. He took first the hand of his wife, and next that of his daughter, and successively resigned them into those of his young executor. This, under the existing circumstances of the moment, attracted no particular attention, but was the subject of many an after-thought and remark. A few convulsive struggles followed, and then the generous and noble spirit of the Cavalier deserted its prison house.

We will not attempt to describe the heart-rending scene which ensued. Suffice it to say, that after a decent and respectful delay, (far more than is allowed in our day,) the much loved and much lamented Mr. Fairfax was borne to the grave, amidst the lamentations and regrets of the whole assembled gentry of the Colony. The long line of mournful pageantry moved in slow and melancholy steps to the sound of a solemn dirge through the streets of the ancient city, and after the usual sad, but appropriate rites of the established church, the corpse was deposited in the burying ground, which to this day preserves the crumbling ruins of many monuments of the ancient Cavaliers.

CHAPTER XIV.

It was some weeks after the funeral of Gideon Fairfax, that Bacon, attracted by the genial warmth of a summer day, sauntered out for the first time, in company with his friend Dudley, to seek the usual *rendezvous* of the young Cavaliers. Scarcely were they seated in the Tap of the "Arms," before Philip Ludwell hastily entered, touched his castor formally to Bacon and Dudley, and handed to the former a note, fastened with a silken cord, and sealed with the arms of the House of Berkley. Bacon cut the cord and read the note, without changing countenance, and then handed it to Dudley, who had no sooner perused its contents, than they both arose, retired to a private room, and called for pen, ink and paper. The latter soon returned with an answer, sealed in like manner, and handed it to Ludwell, who again formally bowing retired. The first ran thus:

Jamestown, June —, 16—.

To Nathaniel Bacon, Esq.

Sir—I seize the first moment of your appearance in public, restored to health, to demand the satisfaction due for the grievous insult put upon me, on the night of the Anniversary Celebration, in presence of the assembled gentry of the Colony. All proper arrangements will be made by my friend Ludwell, who will also await your answer. I have the honour to be your most obedient servant,

FRANCIS BEVERLY.

Bacon's answer was no less courteous and explicit.

Berkley Arms, June —, 16—.
To Francis Beverly, Esq.

SIR—Your note by the hands of Mr. Ludwell was this moment received. Your challenge is accepted. To-morrow morning at sunrise I will meet you. The length of my weapon will be furnished by my friend Dudley, who will convey this to Mr. Ludwell, as well as make all other arrangements on my behalf. I have the honour to be, yours, &c.

NATHANIEL BACON.

The following morning at sunrise, two parties of Cavaliers landed from their boats at a secluded inlet, on the southern extremity of Hog Island, immediately opposite the city, but screened from view by the depth of the overshadowing forest. A surgeon with his assistant soon followed.

The two parties exchanged formal but courtly salutations, and immediately proceeded to the business of their meeting. A level grass-plot, firm under the pressure of the foot, and sufficiently cleared for the purpose, had long been set apart as the battle ground on similar occasions, and was now easily found.

When all the parties were arrived at this spot, the seconds proceeded to measure the swords in presence of their principals. This of course was a mere formality required by the usages of the times, as the length of the weapons was already known and settled between themselves.

The two young Cavaliers about to engage in deadly strife, were perhaps as nearly matched in skill and courage as any that could be found in the Colony. Both were in the daily practice of the foils, as a matter of education no less than of amusement. Both were impetuous by nature, and rash in their actions, and both came upon the field longing for vengeance in requital of wrongs which each supposed he had received at the hands of the other.

Beverly was in the enjoyment of ruddy health, and buoyant animal impulses, but his antagonist was pale, thin, and evidently labouring under depression of spirits, as well as feebleness of body. To a hasty and superficial observer, this state of the parties would have seemed decidedly unfavourable to the latter; but it is very questionable whether the high health and robust strength of Beverly were not more than counterbalanced by the subdued but steady composure evinced by his antagonist, the result of long confinement and depletion.

With a slight inclination of the head in formal salutation, each advanced a foot and crossed his blade with that of his antagonist. The eyes of each were instantly riveted upon his enemy, with the steady and deadly ferocity of two wild beasts of prey. The pause continued a few moments, as if each were striving to measure the hatred of the other; a few rapid and skilful thrusts and parries were exchanged, and then another interval of suspense and inactivity ensued. The next effort was longer and more fiercely contested, and the intentions of each in this uncomplicated warfare were more readily distinguished. Beverly was at each successive trial becoming more and more ferocious, while his antagonist was as evidently acting on the defensive, if not attempting to disarm him. This now apparent intention of the latter, might be the necessary result of his present comparative debility, of policy--aiming to take advantage of his opponent's impetuosity, or of his promise to Virginia. But from whatever cause it sprung, Dudley thought it a most hazardous experiment to depend upon disarming so skilful a swordsman, and was accordingly under the most lively apprehensions for the fate of his friend. These were not however of long continuance, for at the next onset, Beverly, forgetting himself for a moment, as he impetuously flashed his weapon in deadly and rapid thrusts, cried, "Ha, Sir Bastard, have at your coward's heart." In the next instant Bacon's sword pierced his body—his eyes glared wildly for an instant, his sword fell from his powerless hand, and as Bacon withdrew the weapon, Beverly uttered a groan and fell prostrate upon the earth.

Bacon stood listlessly wiping his sword-blade upon his handkerchief, his eyes abstractedly fixed upon the fallen youth, like one without thought or reason, or rather so deeply buried in thought as to be almost unconscious of the scene before him. His thoughts were upon his promise to Virginia, to act only upon the defensive. This he had interpreted far more literally than the fair girl herself had designed, and it was his intention so to act throughout the struggle, had not his patience and forbearance been overcome by the taunting exclamation of his adversary, just preceding the last fatal onset.

All the circumstances passed rapidly through his mind, until his meditations settled into the most poignant regret; not a little aggravated when Beverly opened his eyes, and held up his hand to Bacon, feebly exclaiming, "Bacon, forgive me; I wronged you both first and last. I see it now when it is too late, but it is never too late to ask forgiveness for an injury." Bacon grasped his hand, and flung himself prostrate at his side in an instant. "Before God, Beverly, it was not my intention, when I came to the field, to do this deed; my whole effort at first was to disarm you. Forgiveness lies with you, not with me. I have done you an irreparable injury, yours was but the result of thoughtless impetuosity, for which I as freely forgive you, as it was hastily and heedlessly offered. May God forgive us both."

The surgeon and his assistant now interfered in the prosecution of their professional duties. While these were in progress, all parties were silent in breathless attention; not a change of the doctor's countenance escaped them. At length he arose, and deliberately wiping and replacing his instruments in their case, walked thoughtfully some paces from the wounded youth.

Bacon dared not follow to ask the fate of his patient, but Dudley, with breathless eagerness pursued his footsteps, and demanded to know in few words his fate. "Life or death, Doctor?" he hastily exclaimed, as if he expected an answer in like short and expressive terms.

"Ours is not one of the exact sciences as to prognostication," said Dr. Roland. "The wound extends from the anterior part of the thorax."

"Dont tell me about the thorax, doctor, tell me whether there is life or death?"

"The pleura and the right lobe of the lungs have been wounded, consequently there will be great inflammation succeeding, both from the pleuretic and pulmonary excitement. These are the unchangeable laws of the animal economy, and will not yield were the son of Charles himself lying before us."

"O damn the animal economy. Can't you say in one word, life or death?"

"No, I cannot, Master Dudley. All I can say at present is, that it is my hope and belief, if properly managed, that he will not die from the hemorrhage, and that his chance of life depends upon his weathering out the inflammation mentioned."

"There is a reasonable hope then! Thank you, doctor, thank you; may God send that his life be spared." Uttering this fervent ejaculation he joined his companions, who now held a consultation as to the most judicious plan of removing the wounded youth. One proposed that he should remain at a cottage upon the island; but the surgeon decided that he might be removed in a boat to the city as easily as he could be carried to the cottage. He was accordingly extended upon a rude litter, and deposited in the most convenient boat, upon such a bed as they could hastily construct of cloaks and bushes.

They had scarcely emerged from the shrubbery overhanging the margin of the river, when a rustling noise was heard, similar to that made by the flight of a large flock of birds, and in the next instant a shower of Indian arrows fell harmless in the water, succeeded by an astounding yell of twenty or more savages, indistinctly seen through the dense fog rising from the stream. Their light bark canoes, of variegated colours, could scarcely be distinguished as they rode upon the waves like huge aquatic birds. The savage warriors were standing perfectly erect, notwithstanding the motion of the waves and the vigorous exertions of those squaws who officiated at the oar and helm. Bows were already strung in their hands, and they were again in the act of leveling them upon the party, when Bacon, seizing a duck gun from the bottom of the boat, fired into the midst of the foremost canoe. Three huge painted warriors leaped into the water and yelled and struggled for an instant before they sunk to rise no more. Another discharge of arrows, and another shot from Bacon's weapon, with like success, considerably damped the ardour of the pursuit. Bacon and his party had in the mean time urged the boat containing Beverly and the surgeon far ahead and out of reach of their missiles, while they protected their retreat. Having suffered the enemy to come within striking distance, he was now enabled to see that they were Chickahominies, and readily comprehended their motives. He was himself the object of their pursuit. They had watched his movements for the purpose of avenging the death of their chief and his followers. So prompt and efficient, however, was the defence of the party sought, that after a few harmless flights of arrows, and a few returns from the firearms of the white party, they hastily retreated, and in a short time their canoes were only seen like distant specks on the circumscribed horizon, as they scudded away before the rising volumes of vapour for fear the dawning day should betray them and their hostile attitude to the notice of the citizens.

As Bacon and Dudley stepped upon the shore in front of the palisade, the other party having landed and disappeared before their arrival, they stood to gaze over the water for an instant to ascertain whether any of the savages yet lingered upon the scene. The fog was rapidly rising from the water, so that their line of vision was uninterrupted for some distance over the bay between the islands.

They could just perceive their late enemies doubling the southern point of the island upon which they stood, and were about to retire, supposing all further apprehension from that quarter at an end, when they discovered the dim outlines of some one upon the southern end of the island, making signals with a white handkerchief. They immediately and silently moved along the shore, under cover of the palisade, until they came within such a distance of the object which had attracted their attention, that they could discern who it was themselves, at the same time remaining undiscovered. It was Wyanokee! Her appearance at this early hour and solitary place, and her equivocal employment, produced the greatest astonishment and mortification in the mind of Bacon. Until this moment he would have pledged his life for her truth and fidelity. Ever since the encounter with the Indians, he had been wondering in his own mind, how they had pursued him so exactly to the secret place of their rendezvous. Now he recollected that Wyanokee had passed through the gallery of the State House on the preceding evening, where Dudley and himself were practising. She might have overheard some of their conversation. Her presence at such a place had excited a momentary surprise at the time, but it all passed over, under the usual idea that Wyanokee was every where. She often glided about like a spirit, yet no one knew whither she was going, or the purpose of her movements. "Can it be possible," said Bacon to himself, "that Wyanokee has been treacherous?"

All these corroborating circumstances, together with her present attitude, answered in the affirmative. Notwithstanding the strong conviction of this unwelcome fact which now settled on his mind, he could not believe her deliberately bent on his destruction. He had seen her exhibit many noble traits of character in trying situations. Besides, she was somewhat under his protection, and we are always inclined to love those whom we have served. She was also Virginia's pupil, and the latter was proud of her as such, and he himself had felt a sort of complacency at the progress of the maiden under her tuition. His imagination had often dwelt upon her imaginary perfections, as so many reflected beauties from Virginia's guileless heart and cultivated mind. No, he could not believe her thus meanly treacherous. Some native impulse must have been roused, some secret spring of her long hidden and dormant nature, must have been touched. Her savage ideas of patriotism had fired her to revenge the death of her nation's chief.

Notwithstanding these palliating suggestions which rose in his mind on the doubtful attitude in which he had detected her, his reflections were by no means pleasing, as he locked his arm in

Dudley's, and retired from the shore. Every thing seemed to him to conspire against his happiness. First, there was the old and ever present cause of solicitude in relation to his own origin, the doubtful nature of which had been the remote cause of the unhappy rencounter of the morning. Then there was the new attitude in which he was placed towards Virginia, by the death of her father, together with the tantalizing, partial revelations of the anonymous letters and gold locket, which that event had thrown into his possession, with the thousand surmises, half formed hopes, and resolutions resulting from them. Upon the whole, however, he could not but feel, in the midst of these various depressing circumstances, that his chance for success in an application for the hand of Virginia was greater with the widowed lady of the murdered Fairfax than it would have been were he alive. He knew the high position in which he stood in that lady's favour. He knew her contempt for worldly show, pomp and circumstance—he had always known it, but now he knew something of the cause in the revelations of her own history. He knew that she had boldly indulged the first predilections of her own young heart at the expense of her father's and her brother's favour; and his hopes were strong, that when he should present himself before her in something of a like attitude, as an applicant for the hand of her fair daughter, her own recollections would rise up before her in his favour. That there would be difficulties to surmount, and prejudices to subdue, he knew full well. That Sir William Berkley would exert his power to the utmost, to prevent such a consummation he also knew; but the consent of Mrs. Fairfax once gained, he resolved to brave the opposition if he could not subdue the prejudices of the Governor.

The unhappy business of the morning would in all probability hasten the contending elements to a crisis. The Governor would soon know of the meeting and its result; he would in all probability inquire into the cause of the quarrel, and his shrewd insight into the motives of human action would very soon discover that there were hidden impulses operating, which caused the insult to be given, and kindred ones in the opposite party which rendered the offence so much the more heinous and unpardonable. In short, he would discover that there was a lady at the bottom of the whole affair; and that this lady was his own fair niece; and that the two gentlemen who had just contended in deadly strife, were rivals for the possession of her favour. Such being the process of reasoning in the Governor's mind, Bacon knew him too well to suppose that he would delay the matter long before he endeavoured to bring it to a conclusion. Indeed he believed (and the reader knows how truly) that his excellency already saw the advantages of the connexion as vividly as his nephew apprehended the sterling qualities of the lady. Such being the case, the result of the morning's meeting, if it did not prove fatal to his rival's life, would in all probability precipitate the matter at once to an issue. The Governor would no sooner ascertain that Beverly was out of danger than he would take the business in his own hands, and how he would manage it, and what means he would take to accomplish his ends, Bacon's personal experience in other matters fully taught him. He resolved therefore to be beforehand with him, to present his own claims first, to attempt to conciliate the lady of his late patron, before her ear had been poisoned by the violent abuse which he knew would be heaped upon him, as well as by contempt for his origin. But could he imbrue his hand in the blood of his rival and then present it for acceptance? Could he precipitate his claims before the family in their present melancholy state?

These were the subjects of his reflection, as the two youths entered the gates of the city,—and here another difficulty arose; if he should immediately present himself before the family, the news of the meeting having preceded him, even without broaching the subject before alluded to, would not the feelings excited in the mind of Virginia and her mother be unfavourable to his claims? Then again, should he leave rumour with her hundred tongues to explain to the maiden the reasons which had induced him to accept the challenge from her kinsman, would not his cause be still more prejudiced? Finally, therefore, after taking all these things into consideration, he came to the conclusion that it was best to wait some favourable news from his wounded rival before presenting himself, or in case of the worst result, to absent himself from the city altogether for a time.

Accordingly the youths bent their footsteps to Dudley's lodgings, there to await intelligence concerning Beverly. It is hardly necessary to remind the reader that duelling in that day, so far from being considered criminal, was the sole test to which all differences between gentlemen were submitted. The influence of the custom has been handed down, variously modified by the circumstances of the times, from one generation to another, until it has reached our own.

CHAPTER XV.

For more than a week Frank Beverly lay in the most precarious state, and more than once during that period his friends were summoned to his bed-side, expecting every moment to be his last. Bacon, torn and racked with suspense, moved about the house of his late patron like one distracted. He had already made his peace with Virginia, by explaining to her the unequivocal and unconditional demand for satisfaction made upon him by Beverly, as well as the unjustifiable taunt upon the field, by which he had been driven from his defensive attitude. But even her society failed in its usual attractions, while Beverly remained in danger. Doctor Roland, with all his technical formality, was as indefatigable in his attentions as he was oracular and mysterious in his announcements from hour to hour, and day to day, concerning the state of his patient. These, reported to his master from the lips of Brien O'Reïly, would form no unamusing subject for the reader, were not our attention called to the more important personages and graver incidents of our narrative.

As Bacon had surmised, Sir William Berkley was not long in understanding the real cause of the quarrel; he had himself heard partial reports of the affront and its cause on the night of its occurrence. As Bacon had also expected, he seemed to await the fate of his young kinsman, before he took any farther steps towards promoting the alliance between him and Virginia. This however did not prevent him from giving way to the most ungovernable rage at Frank's condescension in meeting an adventurer, "the son of no one knew whom."

At length the invalid was unequivocally pronounced to be out of danger, by Dr. Roland himself. The Governor had no sooner received the information, than he despatched a footman with his most respectful compliments to Mrs. Fairfax, and requested the pleasure of an hour's conversation with her, on the most important business; in answer to which, a message was returned to the Governor, that she would be pleased to see him, at any moment which might suit his convenience. That time soon arrived, and the formal old gentleman, after many apologies for the untimely intrusion upon the privacy of her sorrows, and condolence for their cause, thus introduced the subject to which he solicited her attention.

"It was perhaps not known to you, Madam, that your late lamented husband and myself had long since formed a prospective arrangement, by which we hoped to dispose of our fortunes in such a manner as to add honour and dignity to our families, at the same time that we should preserve them united, and confer happiness upon our nearest relatives and presumptive heirs. His will, as I understand, has not yet been authenticated, but doubtless when it is so you will find that he has provided for the fulfilment of this design."

"I do not fully comprehend your Excellency."

"I mean, madam, that we contemplated uniting in marriage, your fair daughter and my young kinsman, Beverly; by this means I will be enabled to entail my fortune on their male descendants, which will meet all my desires concerning my niece, at the same time that it will be doing no injustice to my young relative."

"The plan seems ingeniously contrived, Sir William, to prevent future heart-burnings concerning the disposal of your estate; but were the young people to know nothing of the arrangement?"

"The knowledge of it was kept from them, at the suggestion of your late lamented husband, in order that they might imbibe no prejudices against the scheme as they grew up, but rather be thrown into each other's way, as the time for its consummation approached, and thus perhaps discover its propriety themselves. This has in part proved true, for on the very day of the unfortunate accident which deprived your house of its inestimable head, I had the honour to lay Frank's proposals before him."

"Sir William—I do not know my daughter's sentiments on the subject,—the fulfilment of the scheme will depend entirely on her feelings."

"With due deference, madam, would it not be more politic to treat the matter as already, and long since settled, between her father and myself, and sacredly sealed by his death?"

"I must be plain and candid with your Excellency—I have no desire to use policy in the affair; if my daughter gives her free and hearty consent, you have mine; but if the match is repugnant to her feelings we will drop the subject, with many thanks to your Excellency for your kind purposes, and to Mr. Beverly for the intended honour."

Virginia was now called in; but while the servant performed that duty, Sir William replied, "I am exceedingly mortified, madam, that you seem to place the fulfilment of this long-treasured scheme upon a contingency so light."

"Do you then consider a young lady's being permitted to have a voice in choosing her partner for life, a light contingency, Sir William?"

"I think, madam, that her parents are more capable of making a selection which will confer honour upon them and her, than she can possibly be. Our best families would soon arrive at a very plebeian level, were every female descendant to be permitted to indulge her love-sick fancies, instead of consulting the interest and honour of her house. But it may be that this discussion is useless in the present instance. Here, madam, comes your daughter, who will decide."

Virginia entered, pale and trembling with alarm and vague presentiments of evil; her hands were crossed upon her breast, and her eyes downcast. After making a reverential courtesy to the Governor, she instinctively stood before him, awaiting his commands as one upon trial. However harsh the Governor's opinions to the mother, policy dictated a very different course toward the daughter; he accordingly led her to a seat beside himself, and with the most bland and courteous manner, thus addressed her,

"I come, my niece, as an ambassador from poor Frank, with full powers to ask of your mother this fair hand in marriage; and I must take the same opportunity to declare the happiness it would give Lady Berkley and myself, to receive you into our mansion as the wife of our kinsman, and the daughter of our affections."

The mildness and the unusual condescension of her formal uncle completely threw Virginia from the stately and unequivocal answer which she had meditated when first summoned; for it will be recollected that she had already had an intimation of his intentions. She could do no less than feel grateful for his own undoubted affection, and she felt it extremely difficult properly to express this feeling, connected as it must be with the overthrow of his dearest hopes. After the most painful embarrassment, she was enabled to answer: "To you, my dear uncle, I have always felt grateful for the more than paternal affection which you have shown to me, and I must feel not less so for the motives which prompted you to undertake the present mission; but with all my affection for yourself and desire to please you, and all my gratitude to Mr. Beverly for the honour which he intended me, I must beg leave to decline his offer."

"Wherefore must you decline it, Virginia?" asked Sir William, with the most evident chagrin and surprise.

"Simply because I cannot reciprocate the affection which I am informed Mr. Beverly entertains for me."

"You have never made the trial, niece; you have not taken five minutes to consider the importance of the proposition which I have had the honour to lay before you. Reconsider your hasty answer; take time to form a mature opinion of the many advantages which the connexion holds out. See Frank himself when he recovers, and my word for it, he will make as many love-sick speeches as would woo a lady from Charles' court."

"It is not necessary, my dear uncle; I have long meditated upon the subject, having by accident heard of the proposed union before you were pleased to communicate it in person."

"What is your objection to Frank? It is certainly no satisfactory answer, to say you cannot reciprocate his affection, when you have never yet given him an opportunity to plead his cause in person. He is unquestionably as well favoured a youth in regard to personal attributes, as any in the Colony, and I flatter myself as well born and of as bright expectations?"

"I have no objections to urge, Sir William; Mr. Beverly is undoubtedly all that you say he is, but he never can be more to me than he is at present; for this determination I have many reasons satisfactory to my own sense of propriety, but which it is neither necessary nor proper for me to urge. One I will however give you, with the hope of for ever setting the question at rest. My affections are already engaged!"

Had a thunderbolt hurled the old Cavalier from his seat, he could not have been more astounded. Mrs. Fairfax was scarcely less so. Sir William glanced from her countenance to that of her daughter, as if he expected the former to overwhelm her daughter with reproaches, his own anger all the while displaying itself in the contortions of his inflamed and glowing countenance. But seeing her astonishment subsiding into complacency instead of anger, his own broke forth—

"What! bestow your affections unasked? and upon whom pray!"

"I have not bestowed them unasked, Sir."

"Has any gentleman asked and obtained permission of you, to address your daughter?" he inquired, turning to Mrs. Fairfax.

"None, Sir."

"Who then is the favoured swain? Who has dared to interfere in this matter unauthorized by the consent of your only surviving parent or myself?"

"For him I have neither the right nor the will to speak. At the proper time he will doubtless do it for himself," said Virginia, as she arose with offended dignity to leave the room.

"Hear me yet a moment," cried Sir William, with the most ill disguised efforts to appear calm. "If the person, who has thus intruded into your family, is of proper birth, connexions, and expectations, and his suit should meet with your mother's approbation, I of course have no right to interfere. But remember, should you attempt to form an alliance with an individual who would disgrace my family, to which you are nearly connected, I will, if there be none other to perform the office, with mine own hands tear him from the very foot of the altar, and mete to him such a reward as his temerity demands."

At this moment the door opened, and Nathaniel Bacon entered, with an expression of unalloyed delight upon his countenance. He had just heard the joyful tidings from the medical attendant of his rival. He met Virginia face to face, just within the sweep of the door, and perceiving no other object at the moment, attempted gayly to seize her hand, but no corresponding movement being perceptible, he paused to examine her countenance, at the same time glancing at the offended visiter, whose scowling eyes were fixed upon him. Virginia's countenance was like a mirror to reflect her feelings, and had there been no intelligible expression upon the face of the Governor, Bacon would readily have comprehended the attitude of the various parties. These observations, however, were the work of an instant, for Sir William no sooner perceived his presence, than he sprung to his feet, his brow growing darker every moment. He had entirely misinterpreted Bacon's appearance at that critical juncture. His suspicions had all along pointed to him, and he now imagined that his presence was the result of preconcerted design. "To what motive, Sir," he cried, "am I indebted for this intrusion? Have you come to congratulate me upon the recovery of my young kinsman, of whom your murderous hand had well nigh deprived me?"

Bacon wheeled partly upon his heel, as if endeavouring to force himself out of the room, without answering the choleric old Cavalier, but seeing Virginia turn her head and cast an indignant glance at the offender, his own hard schooled feelings broke forth also. "To no particular motive, Sir, are you indebted for this visit: it was the result of the purest accident. I knew not that your Excellency was in the house, and came into this room in the ordinary free and unchallenged mode of intercourse, to which the inmates of this most hospitable and generous family are accustomed."

"Ay, Sir Stripling, and unless I am grossly deceived, your intercourse has not gone unchallenged for nothing."

"To what is your Excellency pleased to allude."

"Have you not studiously endeavoured to undermine the most important family arrangements of those who cherished and protected your infancy? Have you not stung the bosom that warmed you into existence? Have you not been callous to the claims of gratitude, due alike to the living and the dead? Have you not attempted to beguile the only daughter of your patron into a disgraceful alliance?"

Bacon resisted the mild and persuasive endeavours of Mrs. Fairfax to lead him from the room, whence Virginia had already departed, while he replied, drawing himself up to an erect and perfectly composed and dignified attitude,

"If your Excellency chooses so far to forget, what is alike due to your station—to yourself, to the present company, and to me, as to permit yourself to ask such questions, you cannot expect me so far to forget myself as to answer them!" and with this reply he left the room.

The Governor, after indulging in the most vehement bursts of passion, and threats of vengeance against Bacon, should he dare to connect himself with his family, and in vain endeavours to extort a promise from Mrs. Fairfax, never to give her consent, left the house in the most towering and ungovernable rage.

He had scarcely crossed the threshold, before Bacon returned to the same room, leading Virginia by the hand, having held a very interesting conversation with her in another apartment. Mrs. Fairfax was sitting apparently absorbed in the most painful reflections. As the youthful pair entered, a slight clearing away of the clouds which had gathered upon her countenance might be perceived. They walked deliberately up to where she sat, and seated themselves one on each side of her: when Bacon thus spoke—

"It was not my intention, dear madam, thus to intrude upon your sorrows, but I may be pardoned for presenting myself as a petitioner at your feet, when another, high in station and dignity, has thought proper to forget those claims. Had he confined himself to the legitimate object of his mission, I had perhaps still forborne, but when he has stepped out of his way rudely to thrust me before you as the disorganizer of your family arrangements, and as the serpent who has stolen into your house in order to poison your brightest hopes and fondest anticipations, I have thought it became me at once to state to you how far I have offended.

"It is true, dear madam, that I have not been insensible to the many charms of your daughter's person and disposition. You have witnessed, I would fain hope, not unobservantly, the dear delights of our first childish intercourse, when our minds and hearts were drawn together by an affection and a congeniality of taste and sentiment which we supposed, if we thought of it at all, was purely fraternal; and then when our minds began to expand, and our affections to assume and to display their real character, and finally when we came thoroughly to understand each other and ourselves, you were not a heedless spectator of these progressive changes and developments; and having seen, I cannot believe that you would have permitted this mutual affection to grow to its present maturity and strength, intending to deny its sanction at the last, when the cure might so easily have been made by nipping the tender flower in the bud. Speak, I pray you madam! Our fate hangs upon your words!"

"I will not pretend to you, my children, that I have not observed the mutual affection which has grown up between you from its earliest dawn. Nor will I disguise from you that it gave me pleasure mingled with much pain. Many long and dreary nights have I lain upon my pillow, anticipating what I then supposed would be the fierce struggles of this moment. I calculated with the usual short sightedness of mortals, that he who will ne'er partake in our councils more, would have been here to decide upon your wishes.

"I supposed that his own family pride would first have been to conquer, then I thought of the fierce resistance which the greater pride of his kinsman, Sir William, would offer—the interview of this morning shows how truly. After all these painful misgivings, however, and the maturest judgment that I could bestow upon the subject, I came to the resolution to suffer what seemed the predestined current of events to run its course. Providence has by a most painful process removed the only obstacle you had to fear, my children, and he, had he been alive, would doubtless have finally given his consent rather than attempt to tear up forcibly by its roots a passion like yours, the growth of years and intimate knowledge of each other. I therefore give you my consent, my children, that you be united in marriage, and the sooner the better, as the first storm upon its announcement once over, all these contending passions which drive you into broils and strife will cease."

As she concluded speaking, Virginia, down whose cheeks the tears had been rapidly coursing each other, sunk upon her knees, in which position she was instantly joined by her now acknowledged and betrothed lover. Mrs. Fairfax placed her hands upon their heads, tears bedimming her own eyes, and blessed them, and then kissed her daughter as she was about to leave the room. When she was gone, Bacon resumed the subject of their discourse. "O say, dear Madam, how soon will you consent to the completion of our happiness? I address myself to you in the first instance, in order that I may use your name in my appeal to your daughter for an early day."

"As soon as you can persuade Virginia to consent. I would seriously and earnestly recommend two things with regard to your nuptials, the rest I leave to yourselves, namely, that they take place as privately as possible, for fear of Sir William's violence; and secondly, as soon as possible, in order that you may anticipate the complete recovery of young Mr. Beverly."

"Oh, madam, may Heaven bless your wisdom and benevolence. I am now doubly armed, and will seek your daughter, and I hope soon return with a favourable answer."

Accordingly he flew out of the room, and in a few moments she heard him loudly calling her daughter's name through all the portals of the house, and rapping at every door, but no Virginia was to be found. At length, however, he sallied forth into the garden, when he found her in her summer-house, apparently in profound study of some favourite Author's new publication, perhaps Milton's "Paradise Regained." His arguments fell apparently upon a deaf ear. She continued to read, regardless of his passionate gesticulations and burning words. Her cheeks glowed vividly enough, but she gave no other evidence that she was conscious of his presence. At length he seized her hand, and forcibly but gently led her before her mother, like a culprit, as she doubtless felt herself, for her eyes were downcast, and a crimson blush suffused her neck and temples. Mrs. Fairfax attempted in vain to assume a grave and judicial expression. She succeeded, however, in convincing the young pair that the safety and the peace of many of their family circle depended upon their speedy nuptials. It was doubtless for these reasons alone, that they soon agreed amicably upon an early day, until which time we will leave the imagination of the reader to follow the young pair through flowery beds of roses and tulips, and the more flowery anticipations of "Love's young dream."

CHAPTER XVI.

The appointed day at length arrived—it was ushered in by no cheering omens from without or within the mansion of Mrs. Fairfax. No warbling songsters from the feathered tribes perched upon the window of our heroine, or hopped from flower to flower through the graden beneath, to woo her from her slumbers; and the heavens themselves gave lowering and sultry evidence of an approaching storm. In the east it was misty and unsettled; while a long curtain of dark frowning clouds, heavily charged with electric fire, hung in portentous masses along the whole line of the western horizon. The atmosphere was hot and oppressive, the whole aspect of the weather such as invariably casts a damp upon the spirits.

Virginia required no sweet serenade to call her from her slumbers. She was already awake, as indeed she had been through most of the night. A feverish dread of undefined approaching evil, had dimly floated through her excited brain during her waking hours, and yet more shadowy horrors disturbed her partial and unrefreshing sleep. Her morning habiliments were donned earlier than usual, without the assistance of her Indian attendant; yet she marvelled at her unwonted absence. She usually slept in an adjoining apartment, and hither Virginia bent her steps to chide the tardy maiden for her strange neglect on so important an occasion. No little surprise was visible in her countenance, when she found not only the apartment untenanted, but that the bed upon which Wyanokee usually slept, was undisturbed, or that if used at all, it had been slightly disarranged, only as if with a deceptive purpose. She repeated her name throughout the house and garden, but no answer was returned. Her voice soon aroused her mother, who was no less surprised at the circumstances related by her daughter. Together they went to the apartment, and again examined the bed, which had evidently not been slept in. And now other appearances struck them, which had not before attracted their attention. The dress she had worn on the previous day, hung in a closet answering the purposes of a wardrobe, together with the whole of her apparel, the gift of Virginia or her mother. Not an article could be recollected of these, which was not there. They seemed, moreover, to have been studiously arranged so as to attract attention in this particular. On the other hand, every garment of Indian fabric which she had preserved through her captivity, was gone. The moccasins she had worn on the previous day—the Indian beads, wampum, and other ornaments of native origin, were nowhere to be seen.

All the gifts of Bacon and Mr. Fairfax, some of which were of gold and silver, were conspicuously arranged upon a shelf in the same apartment. Many of these she had hitherto constantly worn in her ears, and upon her wrists and ankles.

As they were pursuing their researches Virginia discovered the window of the room in which her attendant had always slept, shut down upon the end of an Indian arrow. She raised the sash and drew in the missile, in the end of which, inserted in a split and bound with a strip of the fibre of a sinew, was the identical blue feather Wyanokee had plucked from the gory locks of the slain King Fisher, the last of the Chickahominy chiefs. The arrow was pointed in the direction of the nation's hunting ground. The language of these symbols Virginia understood but too well; she had too long made Wyanokee a subject of study, as well as of instruction, not to understand that the feather indicated her flight to the dwellings of her tribe. She also thought she saw many collateral indications in the time chosen for her elopement—the arrangements of her English garments, and more especially of the gifts she had received from Bacon. She doubted not in her own mind that the resolution of Wyanokee was in some way connected with the approaching ceremony, but she did not communicate her suspicions to her mother, because they were as yet not clearly defined in her own thoughts. They received momentary corroboration however, as many circumstances recurred to her mind, which were trivial in themselves, but important in connexion with the present discovery, and which have been from time to time hinted at in the progress of our narrative.

The impression left upon the mind of our Heroine by these incidents produced any thing but the joyous, elastic and happy mood, her young dreams had always anticipated for her wedding day. There were many other subjects of apprehension to mar the pleasures of the time. Governor Berkley had left her mother's house overflowing with wrath, and threatening speedy vengeance against her betrothed.

Few persons ever became indebted to Sir William Berkley in a matter of personal hatred or ill will, who did not sooner or later find him a hard and exacting creditor. With all her love for her uncle she knew his harsh and unyielding nature, and dreaded his power.

The natural apprehensions of a modest, gentle, and tenderly educated maiden on her wedding day, are at all times sufficiently powerful of themselves; but joined to the unfavourable omens and sources of anxiety by which Virginia was surrounded, they were overpowering. Her breakfast remained before her untouched, notwithstanding her mother's endeavours to cheer her drooping spirits.

A short and animated conversation with her lover, as the day began to wane, partially recalled her wonted cheerfulness, but when he was gone she relapsed into her former mood. The aspect of the heavens seemed to her to grow momentarily more portentous. Already the thunder was heard rolling in the west, and black masses of threatening clouds were gradually closing in from every point of the horizon. The wrath of Heaven itself seemed to our heroine gathering over the city. This nervous excitement of mind will not be wondered at when it is remembered that a short time only had intervened since dark and mysterious injunctions had been urged against the marriage, of which the appointed time was now so near at hand; and to this must be added the state of alarm and agitation in which she had since been kept by insurrections, outrages, personal strifes and deadly feuds between her friends; and above all, by the violent and sudden death of her father. In the short space of a few weeks her once tranquil and happy existence had been changed into one of painful trials and vicissitudes. The night was rapidly closing in. There hung the bridal garments, and there stood the tire woman waiting her commands. At this juncture a carriage drove up to the door, steps were let down, the knocker sounded, and in the next moment the gay brides-maid bounded into the room, arrayed for the occasion. Her countenance was radiant with smiles as she entered, but perceiving her friend's sombre mood she walked round her sundry times and then raised her hands and eyes in pretended astonishment, as she exclaimed, "Do I mistake! Was it indeed to your wedding that I was invited? For shame, Virginia!

shake off these sickly fancies. Come, rouse yourself, and I will be your tire woman. Our family will soon be here, the carriage has gone back for them. Will that not move you? Then your lawful lord and"—

Here Virginia rose and placed her hand upon the lips of the lively girl, yet with a look which seemed at the same time to intimate no unwillingness to be cajoled or rallied from her present serious humour.

The wedding was to be kept a profound secret from all but the invited guests, and those who were to officiate at the ceremony. The former consisted only of Mr. Harrison's family, and the latter of the clergyman of the Established Church, who officiated at Jamestown—Charles Dudley who was to give away the bride, and Harriet as bridesmaid.

The appointed hour of nine at length arrived. Assembled in the parlour below, the various parties awaited the appearance of the bride. Carriages were already at the door; the chapel lighted, and the priest habited in the robes of his sacred office.

Bacon, after sundry movements towards the door at which she was expected to enter, could subdue his impatience no longer, and at once mounted the staircase. He met the two maidens on their way down; Virginia apparently having imbibed some of her friend's spirit and vivacity, which she so much needed. She placed her hand timidly but confidingly in that of Bacon as they entered the room. Both she, and her attendant, were robed in virgin white—and certainly never were dresses more appropriate;—they were both young, innocent, beautiful, and intensely interesting, in the position which they now occupied.

Bacon and Dudley were dressed exactly alike, and rather in the costume of the preceding, than of the present reign; the latter not yet having made its way to Jamestown. They wore doublets of scarlet velvet, with large loose sleeves slashed up the front; the collar covered by a falling band of the richest point lace, with a vandyke edging. Their breeches were of white silk, and fringed at the bottom, where they united with their silk stockings, amidst a profusion of ribands and ornaments of lace. Their shoes were ornamented over the buckle straps, with white bridal roses wrought in silk. Hanging gallantly upon one shoulder, they wore the short and graceful blue cloak of the period: not in such a manner, however, as to conceal in any degree the gay appearance of the costume which it completed, but so as to be thrown aside and resumed at a moment's notice. This latter article being light and graceful, and worn more for ornament than use, was always thrown aside for the military buff coat on warlike occasions.

The party, preceded by the priest, entered the waiting vehicles. Just as they were seated according to the order of previous arrangement, vivid flash of lightning shot athwart the horizon, succeeded by a crash of thunder loud and fearful, as if the eternal hills themselves had again been shattered into chaos. The females drew themselves into the corners of the carriage, covering their eyes, and the gentlemen were silent, while the God of the Universe, spoke through his thunders.

The drive to the church was as short as it was silent. The priest entered his desk and laid open the sacred volume, while the various parties arranged according to order in a semicircle round the altar, waited upon his words.

The chapel was dimly lighted, except immediately around the parties, in accordance with the strict privacy of the celebration. Mrs. Fairfax was as calm and benignant as was consistent with her usual settled melancholy. Virginia was pale as a marble statue, her head just sufficiently inclined forward to suspend her bridal veil in graceful and flowing folds before her exquisitely formed figure. Harriet's vivacity was subdued to respectful and mute attention. The sound of the clergyman's voice could just be heard at intervals between the awful peals of thunder, while the lurid flashes contrasting with the feeble rays of the lamps, rendered the surrounding gloom more impressive. The words which fell from the lips of the sacred functionary were something like the following:

"Dearly beloved, we are gathered together here

in the sight of God, and in the face of this company, to join together this Man and this Woman in holy matrimony; which is an honourable estate instituted of God in the time of man's innocency, signifying unto us the mystical union that is betwixt Christ and his church; which holy estate Christ adorned and beautified with his presence and first miracle that he wrought in Cana of Galilee; and is commended of Saint Paul to be honourable among all men; and therefore is not by any to be enterprised or taken in hand unadvisedly—lightly, or wantonly—to satisfy men's carnal lusts and appetites, like brute beasts that have no understanding; but reverently, discreetly, advisedly, soberly, and in fear of God, duly considering the causes for which matrimony was ordained.

"First, it was ordained for the procreation of children to be brought up in the fear and nurture of the Lord, and to the praise of his holy name.

"Secondly, it was ordained for a remedy against sin, and to avoid fornication, that such persons as have not the gift of continency might marry and keep themselves undefiled members of Christ's body.

"Thirdly, it was ordained for the mutual society, help, and comfort that the one ought to have of the other—both in prosperity and adversity.

"Into which holy estate, these two persons present come now to be joined. Therefore if any man can show any just cause, why they may not lawfully be joined together, let him now speak, or else hereafter for ever hold his peace."

A solemn silence prevailed through the dimly lighted aisles, as the usual pause was allowed for the answer. At this juncture, and while the small party around the altar held their breath in mute astonishment and wonder, the door was rudely thrust open, and a gigantic figure strode down the hollow sounding aisle. His heavy footfalls rung upon Virginia's sensitive organs like the funeral knell of departed peace. He walked directly towards the altar, until he stood immediately behind the youthful pair about to plight their faith, his tall figure towering far above their heads.* Over his face he held a black mask, as he thus spoke, in answer to the general challenge of the priest.

"Well mayest thou say that now or never is the time to speak the just cause which interposes to prevent the consummation of this union. That cause know I! But its revelation, now rendered imperative, will be like unto tearing up with irreverent hands the mysterious secrets of the charnel house beneath our feet. Oh God, why could not this duty have been spared to me!"

His huge frame shuddered with convulsive emotion as he paused and seemed to view from beneath his mask his astounded and breathless audi-

* The reader will perceive when the proper timecomes for disclosing from what authentic annals this character is taken—that we have but described his person as the grave words of History portrayed him.

tors. The clergyman seized the opportunity to repeat with solemnity the challenge. "If any man can show any just cause why this youthful pair may not lawfully be joined together, let him now speak, or else hereafter for ever hold his peace!"

"They cannot lawfully be joined together because they are the children of the same mother!"

The silence of death prevailed throughout the chapel. Respiration and reflection itself seemed suspended upon the awful announcement of the Recluse, while he fell back upon one of the seats of the aisle and covered his face with his hands in unutterable anguish.

Mrs. Fairfax had been visibly agitated from the first moment of this startling interruption, by some more dreadful emotion than the surprise and vague alarm of those about her, but now desperation itself nerved her sinking powers, as she stepped a pace forward and uttered in a distinct voice. "It is false! proceed with the ceremony." Harrison and Dudley instinctively felt for their arms, the former exclaiming, "He is mad—staring mad! be it our business to prevent this irreverent interruption!"

But the Recluse immediately sprung upon his feet, throwing his mask upon the floor as he stood full in front of Mrs. Fairfax, and exclaimed, pointing with his index finger to his time-worn countenance; "Look thou upon these long forgotten lineaments, and then upon these (laying his hand upon Bacon's head) and testify before Heaven and earth whether I have not spoken truth! a fearful truth!"

The person appealed to stood for some moments like a statue, her eyes protruding from their sockets, as if a tenant of the grave indeed stood before her—her hand at length slowly rose from her side and wandered through the vacant air as if she would have submitted the spectre to the test of feeling—imperfectly measuring the distance however between her own person and the object sought, it fell again powerless by her side. Her lips moved as if she were in the act of holding a conversation with the being who had addressed her, but no sound issued from them. The pupils of her eyes were painfully distended, and their whole expression wild and bewildered. At length her chest began to heave convulsively, when she made a wild and desperate effort to rush upon the object of her gaze, but fell prostrate on the floor before she had attained half the distance between them. As she fell she cried in the most piteous accents, "Charles! Charles!" and then swooned away.

Charles Dudley, who had till now assisted Bacon in supporting his fainting bride, resigned his charge to Mr. Harrison and ran to Mrs. Fairfax, supposing himself to be the person thus piteously apostrophized. He took the fallen lady in his arms and raised her partly from the floor, but no symptoms of returning animation were visible. While he thus supported her head upon one knee, kneeling upon the other, assisted by the clergyman and friends, and Bacon and Mr. Harrison supporting Virginia, who was in little better condition, a tumultuous crowd rushed in at the door, headed by Sir William Berkley himself, exclaiming to his minions, "Tear him from the altar! tear the upstart from the altar."

But as he ran with his drawn sword towards the pulpit, something in the attitude and expression of the various parties at once arrested his hand and voice.

There is a power of expression in deep and irremediable sorrow which cannot be looked upon without emotion. Boisterous and outrageous as Sir William Berkley had entered the chapel, his fierce nature was instantly subdued by the appearance of his sister-in-law and her daughter. The crowd which followed were instinctively awed into silence by the same powerful and speaking appeals.

When the announcement of the lawful cause which prevented the consummation of the union first fell upon Bacon's ear, his head sank upon his breast, and although he mechanically clasped Virginia round the waist, as he felt her clinging to him, and sinking at his side; he stood stupified with horror, holding up his lifeless burden, entirely enable to think or act. His habitual and superstitious reverence for every thing uttered by the Recluse, induced him to receive the first impression of his words unchallenged even in his own mind.

By the time that Sir William Berkley and his

party arrived, the Recluse had disappeared; every one was so much absorbed by the instant and pressing calls for assistance and sympathy from the suffering females, that the time of his departure was entirely unnoticed.

The Governor had no sooner recovered from his first shock and surprise, than he made his way to one of the young Harrisons to learn the cause of the present appearance of the parties, so different from what he had been taught to expect. Although he did not believe that there was one word of truth in the cause assigned for the interruption of the ceremony, he was well enough satisfied that the parties themselves, and Mrs. Fairfax should believe it. No matter to him what horrors they suffered, he considered it all but a just punishment for their attempted mesalliance. As for Bacon, and his horror-stricken feelings, Sir William did not deign to bestow a thought or word upon them, after the first hasty exclamation with which he had entered the door. By his orders, the female sufferers were placed in a carriage, and removed to his own house. Bacon resigned his charge with a listless apathy, bordering on stupefaction, and to a superficial observer, such would doubtless have been the impression; but his was the deadly deceitful calm which precedes the coming storm. The most horrible of all human sufferings is that where no tear is or can be shed—where no enemy presents himself for vengeance—no hope for the future, all having been perilled and lost upon a single throw. Bacon felt himself thus situated—the cherished hopes of a lifetime were blasted in an instant, not only for the present, but under such circumstances as to cut off all hope for the future. The object of his passion could not henceforth be enshrined in a holy secret worship of the soul, such as is sometimes kept up through a long life of celibacy for the lost one.

No mortified pride arose to his relief! he could not hate—he dared not love the object around which his whole heart and soul were entwined. The very light of his eyes—the sun of his existence—his delights of the present—hopes of the future—all, all were blotted from existence in a moment. The very retrospects of the past were poisoned. Could he bear to dwell upon the enrapturing delights of their young loves, when the object and participator was now discovered to be his own sister? To whichever aspect of the case he turned, he as speedily revolted in horror. It was while these things were tearing and racking his soul, that he appeared to feel externally less than might have been expected. His mind and feelings were precipitately rolled back upon their own resources, and the suddenly dammed up waters of bitterness sought vent at every avenue. Virginia was no sooner taken from him, however, than his perceptions seemed roused at once to the full horror and hopelessness of his fate. Without his castor, and still decked in his gay bridal attire, he burst from the crowd, prostrating the Governor's minions to the right and left, as he felled a passage to the door. His eye had lost its abstracted expression; it was deadly fierce and terrifically wild as he rushed forth into the kindred storm without—no one knew whither.

END OF VOLUME FIRST.

THE

CAVALIERS OF VIRGINIA,

OR THE

RECLUSE OF JAMESTOWN.

AN HISTORICAL ROMANCE OF THE OLD DOMINION.

BY THE AUTHOR OF

"THE KENTUCKIAN IN NEW-YORK."

IN TWO VOLUMES.

VOL. II.

NEW-YORK:
PUBLISHED BY HARPER & BROTHERS,
NO. 82 CLIFF-STREET,
AND SOLD BY THE PRINCIPAL BOOKSELLERS THROUGHOUT
THE UNITED STATES.

1835.

THE

CAVALIERS OF VIRGINIA.

CHAPTER I.

The lightning streamed athwart the heavens in quick and vivid flashes. One peal of thunder after another echoed from cliff to cliff, while a driving storm of rain, wind and hail, made the face of nature black and dismal. There was something frightfully congenial in this uproar of the contending elements with the storm raging in Bacon's heart, as he rushed from the scene of the catastrophe we have just witnessed. The darkness which succeeded the lurid and sulphureous flashes was not more complete and unfathomable than the black despair of his own soul. These vivid contrasts of light and gloom were the only stimulants of which he was susceptible, and they were welcomed as the light of his path! By their guidance he wildly rushed to his stable, saddled, led forth, and mounted his noble charger, his own head still uncovered. For once the gallant animal felt himself uncontrolled master of his movements, fleet as the wind his nimble heels measured the narrow limits of the island. A sudden glare of intense light served for an instant to reveal both to horse and rider that they stood upon the brink of the river, and a single indication of the rider's will was followed by a plunge into the troubled waves. Nobly and majestically he rose and sank with the swelling surges. His master sat erect in the saddle and felt his benumbed faculties revived, as he communed with the storm. The raging elements appeared to sympathize with the tumult of his own bosom. He laughed in horrid unison with the gambols of the lightning, and yelled with savage delight as the muttering thunder rolled over his head.

There is a sublime stimulus in despair. Bacon felt its power; he was conscious that one of the first laws of our organization, (self-preservation,) was suddenly dead within him.

The ballast of the frail vessel was thrown overboard, and the sails were spread to the gathering storm with reckless desperation. Compass and rudder were alike abandoned and despised—they were for the use of those who had hopes and fears. For himself he spread his sails and steered his course with the very spirit of the storm itself. Nature in her wildest moods has no terrors for those who have nothing to lose or win; no terrors for them who laugh and play with the very elements of her destruction; they are wildly, madly independent. It is the sublimity of the maniac! Nevertheless there is a fascination in his reckless steps as he threads the narrow and fearful windings of the precipice, or carelessly buffets the waves of the raging waters. There are other sensations of a high and lofty character in this disjointed state of the faculties. The very ease and rapidity with which ordinary dangers are surmounted, serves to keep up the delusion, and were it not for the irresponsible condition of the mind, there would doubtless be impiety in its developments. Such were Bacon's sensations as he wildly stemmed the torrent. He imagined that he was absolved from the ordinary responsibilities and hazards of humanity! and to his excited fancy, it seemed as though petty fears and grovelling cautions were all that lay between humanity and the superior creations of the universe! that power also came with this absolution from the hopes, fears and penalties of man's low estate. In imagination "he rode upon the storm and managed the whirlwind." The monsters of the deep were his playmates, the ill-omened birds of the night his fellows. The wolves howled in dreadful concord with the morbid efforts of his preternaturally distorted faculties, as the noble and panting animal first struck the shore with his forefeet.

Emerging from the water, he stroked down the dripping mane with a wild and melancholy affection. The very consciousness of such a feeling yet remaining in his soul, which he dared indulge, produced for the moment a dangerous and kindred train of emotions. These as before led him upon forbidden ground, and again the wild tumult of his soul revived. Striking his heels into the animal's flanks, and bending upon his neck, he urged him over the ground at a pace in unison with the impetuosity of his own feelings.

The fire and gravel flew from his heels, as he bounded through the trackless forests of the unsubdued wilderness. The frightened birds of night, and beasts of prey, started in affright, wild at the appearance upon the scene of one darker and wilder than themselves. The very reptiles of the earth shrunk to their hiding places, as the wild horseman and his steed invaded their prescriptive dominions.

Mrs. Fairfax and her daughter, according to the commands of Sir William Berkley, were conveyed to his mansion. To them all places were now alike. The mother after a long and death-like trance, revived to a breathing and physical existence; but her mind was overrun with horrors. Reason was dethroned, and her lips gave utterance to the wildest fantasies. Events with which, and persons with whom, none of those about her were conversant, were alluded to in all the incoherency and unbridled impetuosity of the maniac. The depletion and anodynes of the physician were administered in vain. The ravages upon the seat of nervous power had rendered the ordinary remedies to the more distant chords of communication utterly powerless. From a mild, bland, feeble and sickly state of melancholy, she was suddenly transformed into a frenzied lunatic. Her muscular power seemed to have received multiplied accessions of strength. Yet there was "a method in her madness"—the same names and scenes frequently recurred in her raving paroxysms. That of Charles was reiterated through the wild intonations of delusion; sometimes madly and revengefully, but more frequently in sorrow.

There was occasionally a moving and touching pathos in these latter demonstrations—tearless it is true, but thrilling and electrifying in the subdued whisper in which they were sometimes uttered. A flood of pent up emotions was poured forth with a thrilling eloquence which had their origin in the foundations of the soul. Scenes of days long past, were revived with a graphic and affecting power, which imagination cannot give if their mysterious source and receptacle be not previously and abundantly stored with the richest treasures of the female heart and mind.

Because the by-standers do not happen to be in possession of all the previous history of the sufferer, so as to put together these melancholy and broken relics, they are generally supposed to be the creations of a distempered fancy.

So it was with Mrs. Fairfax; her detached reminiscences fell upon the dull and uninstructed ears of her attendants as the wildest hallucinations of the brain, yet there was more connexion in these flights than they imagined. They supposed that she thought herself conversing in her most subdued and touching moments with young Dudley, merely because his name was frequently pronounced, and that he happened to be present at the disastrous ceremony, which resulted so dreadfully to all parties.

Among all these, Virginia's was the hardest lot—so delicately and exquisitely organized, so gentle—so susceptible—so full of enthusiasm—so rich in innocence and hope, and all so suddenly prostrated. Bacon was nerved with the wild yet exalted heroism of manhood in despair. Her mother was wrapt in a blessed oblivion of the present, but she was sensitively and exquisitely alive to the past, present and future. One fainting paroxysm succeeded to another in frightful rapidity, for hours after she was removed to her uncle's house.

The painful intervals were filled up with a concentration of wretched reflections, which none but a finely organized and cultivated female mind could conceive or endure. No proper conception of these can be conveyed in language, unless the reader will suffer his imagination to grasp her whole condition at once.—Beginning at the first inception of the unsuspected passion for the noble youth who is the hero of our tale—in her earliest infancy; and afterwards following her as it matured and strengthened by the reflections of riper years.—Every faculty, both perceptive and intellectual, had combined to impress his image in the most indelible colours upon her heart. He had himself ripened these very faculties into maturity by the most assiduous culture, and won her esteem by the most touching, delicate, and respectful attentions.

All these things in detail were painfully revolved in her mind. Every landscape, every book, every subject, reminded her most forcibly of him whom it was now criminal to think of. Her's was the sorrow that no sympathy could soften, no friendship alleviate. The sight of her intimate and confidential friend drove her mad, for her presence instantly revived the horrid recollections of the chapel. Long after the clouds had cleared away, the thunder still roared in her ears. The sudden slamming of a door sounded to her nervous irritability, like the report of a cannon. Her own shadow conjured up horrible images. The most violent and the most acute paroxysms of the human organization, however, have a tendency to wear themselves out, when left uninterruptedly to their own action. Such was necessarily, in some measure, the case with Virginia; her mother's more alarming condition calling so much more loudly for attention, and Wyanokee having fled, and Harriet's presence proving so evidently hurtful, she was consequently left with a single sable domestic. Essentially she was in profound solitude; and after the first paroxysms which we have described, her mind naturally and irresistibly fell into a train of retrospective thought. Startling and horrifying they certainly were at first, but still the mind clung to them. Many of the circumstances of the late disastrous meeting were to her as yet unexplained. To these she clung as to the last remnants of hope; they were the straws at which she grasped with the desperation of the drowning wretch. She had at first received her mother's tacit acknowledgment of the mysterious stranger's statement, or rather the effect produced by that statement as irresistible confirmation of its truth. But now she doubted the propriety of her hasty conviction. She marvelled at the effect produced upon her mother—yet there were other means of accounting for it. Would she not have exhibited a like sensibility, had a like statement been made, however false, under such circumstances?—did she not deny it, positively deny it at the moment? Such was the train of reasoning by which her mind began to reassure itself; and it must be recollected that she had never heard more of her mother's history, than that she was a childless widow when her father married her. Sufficient was left however of first impressions to render her situation one of intense suffering and suspense. She dared not ask for Bacon, yet a restless and gnawing anxiety possessed her, to know whether he acknowledged the truth of the dreadful tale without a murmur, and without investigation. But her physical organization could not keep pace with the ever elastic mind; her gentle frame gave sensible evidence that the late violent shocks had made sad inroads upon her system. One chill was succeeded by another, until they were in their turn followed by a burning fever. In this condition she fell again into the hands of the physician, and all mental distress was soon lost in the paramount demands of the suffering body.

Toward the hour of midnight, the storm subsided. Fragments of the black curtain which had hung over the face of the heavens, shot up from the eastern horizon in stupendous blue masses, every now and then illuminated to their summits with the reflection of the raging elements beyond. The violence of the conflict in Bacon's breast had also subsided. He rode along the banks of the Chickahominy, his charger dripping with wet and panting with the exhaustion of fatigue. The bridle hung loose upon his neck, and his rider bent over his mane like a worn-out soldier. His own locks had unbent their stubborn curls to the driving storm, and hung about his neck in drooping masses. His silken hose were spattered with mud, and his gay bridal dress hung about his person in lank and dripping folds. His horse had for some time followed the bent of his own humour, and was now leading his master in the neighbourhood of human habitations. The boughs of the tall gloomy pines were fantastically illuminated with broad masses of light, which ever and anon burst from the smouldering remnants of a huge pine log fire. Its immediate precincts were surrounded by some fifty or more round matted huts, converging toward the summit like a gothic steeple. Around the fire, and under a rude shelter, lay some hundred warriors, wrapped in profound slumber while one of their tribe stood sentinel over the camp.

When Bacon had approached within a short distance of this picturesque group, the sentinel sprung upon his feet, and uttered a shrill war-whoop. The horse stood still, erected his neck and pricked up his ears, while his master folded his arms upon his breast and calmly surveyed the scene. Those warriors who slept under the sheds near the fire, assumed the erect attitude with a simultaneous movement, joining in the wild chorus of the sentinel's yell as they arose.

Hundreds of men, women, and children poured from the surrounding huts,—most of the grown males, with their faces painted in blue and red stripes, their heads shaved close to the cranium, except a tuft of hair upon the crown, and all armed in readiness for battle. Bacon assumed the command of his horse and rode into the very centre of this wild congregation,—the fore hoofs resting upon the spent embers of the fire.

He was greeted with another yell, after which the savages stood back and viewed his strange and untimely appearance with wonder not unmixed with awe. His bridle again fell from his hand, and his arms were crossed upon his breast. His countenance was wild and haggard, and a flash of maniacal enthusiasm shot athwart his pale features. His dress under present circumstances was fantastical in the extreme.

A grim old warrior with savage aspect after staring some time intensely at the intruder, was suddenly struck with something in his appearance, and stepping out a few paces from the mass of his companions began to address them in his own language, now and then pointing to the horseman, and using the most violent gesticulations. At another time the youth would have been not a little alarmed at certain significant signs which the speaker used when pointing to himself. These consisted in twirling his war club round and round, as if he was engaged in the most deadly conflict. Then he placed his hand to the side of his head and bent it near the earth as if about to prostrate himself, and finally pointing to Bacon. When he had done this, several of the crowd closed in toward his horse, and seemed intensely to examine the lineaments of his countenance. Having satisfied themselves, they set up a simultaneous yell of savage delight. He was quickly drawn from the saddle, his hands tied behind him, and then placed in the centre of the assembled throng.

Their savage orgies now commenced ; a procession of all the grown males moved in a circle of some fifty feet in diameter round his person. Several of the number beat upon rude drums, formed of large calabashes with raw hides stretched tight and dried over the mouths; while others dexterously rattled dried bones and shuffled with their feet to their own music. Others chanted forth a monotonous death song; the whole forming the rudest, wildest, and most savage spectacle imaginable.

Bacon himself stood an unmoved spectator of all these barbarous ceremonies. He felt a desperate and reckless indifference to what might befall him. Human endurance had been stretched to its utmost verge, and he felt within him a longing desire to end the vain struggle in the sleep of death. To one like him, who had in the last few hours endured the mental tortures of a hundred deaths, their savage cruelties had no terrors. A faint hope indeed may have crossed his mind, that some warrior more impetuous than his comrades, might sink his tomahawk deep into his brain in summary vengeance for the death of their chief. But they better understood the delights of vengeance. After performing their rude war-dance for some time, they commenced the more immediate preparations for the final tragedy. His hands were loosed, his person stripped and tied to a stake, while some dozen youths of both sexes busied themselves in splitting the rich pine knots into minute pins. These being completed, a circular pile of finely cleft pieces of the same material was built around his body, just near enough for the fire to convey its tortures by slow degrees without too suddenly ending their victim. A deafening whoop from old and young announced the commencement of the ceremony. Each distinguished warrior present had the privilege of inserting a given number of splinters into his flesh. The grim old savage who had first identified Bacon as the slayer of their chief, stepped forward and commenced the operation. He thrust in the tearing torments with a ferocious delight, not a little enhanced by the physical convulsive movements of his victim at every new insertion. Worn out nature however could not endure the uninterrupted completion of the process, and the victim swooned away.

His body hung by the thongs which had bound his waist and hands to the stake, his head drooping forward as if the spirit had already taken its flight. He was immediately let down and the tenderest care observed to resuscitate him, in order that they might not be cheated of their full revenge. His head and throat were bathed in cold water and his parched lips moistened through the medium of a gourd. At length he revived, and strange as it may appear, to a keener consciousness of his situation than he had felt since he left the church. All the wild horrors of his fate stared him in the face. The savages screamed with delight at his returning animation. Copious drafts of water were administered as he called for them. The most intense pain was already experienced from the festering wounds around each of the wooden daggers driven into his flesh. Again he prayed that some of them might instantaneously reach his heart, but his prayer was not destined to be granted. He was again fastened to the stake, and the second in dignity and authority proceeded to perform his share of the brutal exhibition. At this moment a piercing scream rent the air, and all tongues were mute, all hands suspended.

The sound proceeded from the extreme right of the encampment. Here a larger hut than the rest stood in solitary dignity apart from the others, like an officer's *marqueé* in a military encampment. In a few moments the rude door was thrust aside and an Indian female of exquisite proportions rushed to the scene of butchery, and threw herself between the half immolated victim and his bloodthirsty tormentors. Upon her head she wore a rude crown, composed of a wampum belt tightly encircling her brows, and surmounted by a circlet of the plumes of the kingfisher, facing outwards at the top. Around her waist was belted a short frock of dressed deer-skin, which fell in folds about her knees, and was ornamented around the fringed border with beads and wampum. Over her left shoulder and bust she gracefully wore a variegated skin dressed with the hair facing externally; from this her right arm extended, bare to the shoulder, save a single clasp at the wrist; and she carried in her hand a long javelin mounted at the end with a white crystal. The remaining parts of her figure exhibited their beautiful proportions neatly fitted with a pair of buck-skin leggins, extended and fringed on the seam with porcupine quills, copper and glass ornaments. Similar decorations were visible on her exquisitely proportioned feet and ankles. Thrusting her javelin in the ground with energy, and proudly raising her head, she cast a withering glance of scorn and indignation upon the perpetrators of the cruelty. Her address, translated into English, was to the following purport: "Is it for this," and she pointed to Bacon's bleeding wounds, "that I have been invested with the authority of my sires? Was it to witness the perpetration of these cruelties that I have been almost dragged from the house of my pale faced friends? Scarcely has the fire burned out which was kindled to celebrate my arrival among you, before it is rekindled to sacrifice in its flames him who redeemed me from captivity. Is this the return which Chickahominies make for past favours? If so, I pray you to tear from my person these emblems of my authority among you."

She was immediately answered by the old warrior who had commenced the tortures; "Did not the *long knife slay the chief of our nation?"

He was answered by a yell of savage delight from all the warriors present. Wyanokee (for it was she, as the reader has no doubt already surmised) continued, "Ay, he did slay King Fisher and his son—but were they not unjustly attempting to take away the property of the pale faces? and did they not commit the deed against their solemn promise and treaty, and after they had

* This term originated in Virginia.

smoked the pipe of peace ? For shame, warriors and men—would ye turn squaws, and murder a brave and noble youth because he had fought for his own people and for the preservation of his own life ?"

Her harangue was not received with the submission and respect which she expected—many murmured at her defence, and claimed the death of the captive as a prescriptive right and an act of retributive justice. She advanced to cut the cords which bound the prisoner, but twenty more powerful arms instantly arrested her movement. Tomahawks were raised in frightful array, while deep and loud murmurs of discontent, and demands for vengeance rent the air. She placed herself before the captive, and elevating her person to its utmost height, and extending her hands before him as a protection, she cried, "Strike your tomahawks here, into the daughter of your chief, of him who led you on to battles and to victory, but harm not the defenceless stranger." The principal warriors held a consultation as to the fate of the prisoner. It was of but short duration, there being few dissenting voices to the proposition of the old savage, already mentioned as principal spokesman of the party. They soon returned and announced to their new queen that the council of the nation had decreed the prisoner's death. "Never, never !" exclaimed the impassioned maiden, "unless you first cleave off these hands with which I will protect him from your fury. Ha!" she cried, as a sudden thought seemed to strike her; "there is one plan of redemption by your own laws. I will be his wife!" A deep blush suffused her cheeks as she forced the reluctant announcement from her lips. An expression of sadness and disappointment soon spread itself over the countenances of the revengeful warriors, for they knew that she had spoken the truth. Another council was immediately held; at which it was determined that their youthful queen, might according to the usages of the nation, take the captive for her husband, in the place of her kinsman who was slain. When this was proclaimed, Wyanokee slowly and doubtingly turned her eyes upon Bacon to see whether the proposition met a willing response in his breast. A single glance sufficed to convince her that it did not. Instantly, however, recovering her self-possession, she cut the cords and led him to her hut, where after having been reinvested with the sad remnants of his bridal finery, we must leave him for the night.

CHAPTER II.

"THE several causes of discontent in the colony of Virginia long nourished in secret, or manifesting themselves in partial riots and insurrections, were now rapidly maturing, and only the slightest incident was wanting to precipitate them into open rebellion.

"Since the death of Opechancanough, the Indians, deprived of the benefits of federative concert, had made but few attempts to disturb the tranquillity of the colony. Several of the tribes had retired westward, and those which remained, reduced in their numbers and still more in strength by the want of a common leader, lingered on the frontiers, exchanging their superfluous productions at stated marts with their former enemies. A long peace, added to a deportment almost invariably pacific, had in a great measure relaxed the vigilance of the colonists, and the Indians were admitted to a free intercourse with the people of all the counties. It was scarcely to be expected that during an intercourse so irregular and extensive no grounds of uneasiness should arise. Several thefts had been committed upon the tobacco, corn, and other property of the colonists."

These depredations were becoming daily more numerous and alarming, and repeated petitions had been sent in from all parts of the colony calling upon Sir William Berkley in the most urgent terms to afford them protection. The Governor remained singularly deaf to these reasonable demands, and took no steps to afford that protection to the citizens for which government was in a great measure established. Some excuse was offered by his friends and supporters by pleading his great age and long services. Sir H. Chicerly, who had some time before arrived in the colony, clothed with the authority of Lieutenant Governor, and who had till now remained an inactive participator of the gubernatorial honours, began to collect the militia of the state; but Sir William was no sooner informed of these proceedings, so well calculated to allay the rising popular ferment, than he at once construed it into an attempt to supersede his authority, and forthwith disbanded the troops already collected, and countermanded the orders for raising more, which had been sent by his subordinate through the several counties. These high-handed measures of an obstinate and superannuated man, inflamed the public mind. Meetings were called without any previous concert in almost every county in the province, and the most indignant remonstrances were sent in to the Governor. These, however, only served to stimulate his obstinacy, while the continued depredations of the Indians wrought up the general feeling of dissatisfaction into a blaze of discontent. While these things were in progress, a circumstance happened, which, while it brought the contest to an immediate issue, had at the same time an important bearing upon all the principal personages of our narrative. On the night succeeding the melancholy catastrophe at the chapel, related in the last chapter, the tribes of Indians which had formerly been leagued together in the Powhatan confederacy, simultaneously rose at dead of night and perpetrated the most horrid butcheries upon men, women, and children, in every part of the colony. The council had scarcely convened on the next morning before couriers from every direction arrived with the dreadful tidings. Among others, there came one who announced to the Governor that his own country seat had been consumed by the fires of the savage incendiaries, and that Mrs. Fairfax, who had been removed thither for change of scene by the advice of her physician, was either buried in its ruins or carried away captive by the Indians. Public indignation was roused to its highest pitch, but it was confidently expected, now that his excellency himself was a sufferer both in property and feelings, that he would recede from his obstinate refusal to afford relief. But strange to say, in defiance of enemies, and regardless of the remonstrances of his friends, he still persisted. The result ensued which might have been expected; meetings of the people, which had before been called called from the impulse of the moment, and without concert, were now regularly organized, and immediate steps taken to produce uniformity of action throughout the different counties.

While these elements of civil discord are fermenting, we will pursue the adventures of our hero, whom we left just rescued from the hands of the relentless savages. The new queen of the Chickahominies, after having conducted Bacon to her own rude palace, retired for a short period in order to allow him just time to prepare himself for her reception. An Indian doctor was immediately summoned and directed to extract the splinters and dress the wounds. The departure of this wild and fantastical practitioner of the healing art was the signal for her own entrance. Slowly and doubtfully she approached her visiter, who was reclining almost exhausted upon a mat. Upon her entrance he attempted to rise and profess his gratitude, but overcome with pain, sorrow, and weakness, he fell back upon his rude couch, a grim smile and wild expression crossing his features. She gracefully and benignantly motioned him to desist, and at once waived all ceremony by seating herself on a mat beside him. Both remained in a profound and painful silence for some moments. Bacon's mind could dwell upon nothing but the horrid images of the preceding hours of the night. Regardless of her presence and her ignorance of those circumstances which dwelt so painfully upon his memory, he remained in a wild abstraction, now and then casting a glance of startled recognition and surprise at his royal hostess.

She examined him far more intently and with not less surprise, after the subsidence of her first embarrassment. Her sparkling eyes ran over his strange dress and condition, with the rapidity of thought, but evidently with no satisfactory result. She was completely at a loss to understand the cause of his visit, and the singular time and appearance in which he had chosen to make it. It is not improbable that female vanity, or the whisperings of a more tender passion, connected it in some way with her own recent flight. These scarcely recognised impressions produced however an evident embarrassment in her manner of proceeding. She longed to ask if Virginia was his bride, yet dreaded to do so both on her own account and his. She had lived long enough in civilized society to understand the signification of his bridal dress, but she was utterly at a loss to divine why he should appear in such a garb covered with mud, as if he had ridden in haste, in the midst of a warlike nation, and on the very night appointed for the celebration of his nuptials, unless indeed she might solve the mystery in the agreeable way before suggested. Catching one of the originally white bridal flowers of his attire between her slender fingers, she said with a searching glance; "Faded so soon?" He covered his face with his hands, and threw himself prostrate upon the mat, writhing like one in the throes of expiring agony.

His benevolent hostess immediately called a little Indian attendant, in order to despatch him for the doctor; but her guest shook his head and motioned with his uplifted hand for her to desis. She reseated herself, more at a loss than ever to account for his present appearance and conduct. She had supposed that he was suffering from the pain of his wounds, but she now saw that of these he was entirely regardless. She became aware that a more deeply seated pain afflicted him. Again he turned his face toward the roof of the hut, his hands crossed upon his breast, and his bosom racked with unutterable misery.

"Is the pretty Virginia dead?"

The blackness of hell and horror was in his face as he turned a scowl upon his interrogator, and replied, "Is this a new method of savage torture? If so, call in the first set, they are kind and benignant compared to you." But seeming suddenly to recollect that she was ignorant of the pain she inflicted, he took her hand kindly and respectfully, and continued, "Yes, Wyanokee, she is indeed dead to me. If you regard the peace of my soul, or the preservation of my senses, never whisper her name to the winds where it will be wafted to my ears. Never breathe what she has taught you. Be an Indian princess, but for God's sake look, speak, or act not in such a way as to remind me of passed days. Tear open these wounds, inflict fresh tortures—yea, torture others if you will, so I but horrify my mind with any other picture than her's. O God, did ever sister rise before man's imagination in such a damning form of loveliness? With most men, that little word would suffice to dispel the horrid illusion! but with me, cursed as I have been from my birth, and as I still am deeper cursed, the further I pursue this wretched shadow called happiness, I would wed her to-morrow, yea were the curse of the unpardonable sin denounced upon me from the altar instead of the benediction. For her I would go forth to the world, branded with a deeper damnation than ever encircled the brows of the first great murderer. I would be the scorn, the jest, the by-word of present generations, and a never dying beacon to warn those who come after me."

As he proceeded, Wyanokee fixed her dark penetrating eyes upon his face, until her own countenance settled into the expression of reverential awe, with which the Indian invariably listens to the ravings of the maniac. At every period she moved herself backward on the mat, until at the conclusion, she had arrived at a respectful distance, and crossed her hands in superstitious dread. A single glance conveyed her impressions to his mind, and he resumed, "No, no, my gentle preserver, reason is not dethroned, she still presides here, (striking his forehead,) a stern spectator of the unholy strife which is kept up between her sister faculties." Leaning toward her upon his elbow, he continued in a thrilling whisper, "You have heard me read from the sacred volume of the tortures prepared for the damned! of a future existence, in which the torments of ten thousand deaths shall be inflicted, and yet the immortal sufferer find no death! His soul will be prepared for the endurance! I have already a foretaste of that horrible eternity! And yet you see I preserve the power to know and to endure! Is it not a dread mystery in this frail compound of ours— and portentous of evil to come, that this faculty of supporting misery so long outlives the good? The wise men of our race teach us that every pain endured is a preparation of the opposite faculty to enjoy pleasure! that our torpid fluids would stagnate without these contrasted stimulants; 'tis all a delusion, a miserable invention of the enemy. Man can suffer in this life a compound of horrors, for which its pleasures and allurements have no equivalent; yea, and he suffers them after all chance for happiness has vanished for ever. The pleasures of the world are like the morning glories of a sea of ice. The sun rises and sparkles in glittering rainbows for an hour, and then sinks behind the dark blue horizon, and leaves the late enraptured beholder, to feel the chill of death creeping along his veins, until his heart is as cold and dead as the icebergs around 'an atom of pleasure, and a universe of pain.'"

His hearer sat in the most profound bewilderment; much of his discourse was to her unintelligible, and notwithstanding his protestations to the contrary, she still retained her first impressions as to the state of his mind. She knew something of the various relations existing between the most important personages of our story, and in her own mind, had already begun to account for his present state. She supposed him to have been rudely torn from his bride. Her object therefore in the following words, was to learn something more of these particulars, and at the same time to soothe the excited feelings of her guest.

"The great Father of the white man at Jamestown will restore your bride. Does not your good book say, 'whom the' Great Spirit 'has joined together let no man put asunder?'"

"Ay!" replied Bacon, "but what does it say when they are first joined together by the ties of blood? Besides, he never did join us together in the holy covenant. He stamped it with his curse? He denounced his veto against it at the very foot of the altar. The same voice which thundered upon mount Sinai spoke there. His servant stood up before him and asked, 'If any man can show just cause why they may not lawfully be joined together let him now speak, or else hereafter forever hold his peace.' And lo, both heaven and earth interposed at the same moment. The thunders of heaven rent the air, and that most fearful man appeared as if by miracle." Again lowering his voice to a whisper, he continued, "As I rode upon the storm last night, and communed with the spirits of the air, some one whispered in my ear, that the heavens were rent asunder and he came upon a thunderbolt. And then again as I walked upon the waves, and the black curtains gathered around, a bright light darted into my brain and I saw the old Roundheads who were executed the other day, sitting upon a glorious cloud, mocking at my misery! yea, they mouthed at me. Ha, ha, ha!" The sound of his own unnatural laughter startled him like an electric shock—and instantly he seemed to recollect himself.

He covered his face with his hands, and rested them upon his knees in silence. Some one entered and spoke to the queen in a low voice, and she immediately informed her guest that his horse was dead. "Dead!" said he, as he sprang upon his feet. "His last—best—most highly prized gift dead! All on the same night—am I indeed cursed—in going out and in coming in? Are even the poor brutes that cling to me with affection, thus cut down? but I would see him ere he is cold."

A torch-bearer soon appeared at the summons of his mistress, and the royal hostess and her guest proceeded to the spot. There lay the noble animal, his once proud neck straightened in the gaunt deformity of death. His master threw himself upon his body and wept like an infant. The tears, the first he had shed, humanized and soothed his harrowed feelings. Slowly he arose, and gazing upon the lifeless beast, exclaimed with a piteous voice, "Alas poor Bardolph, thy lot is happier than thy master's!"

The day was now dawning, and the morning air came fresh and invigorating to the senses, redolent of the wild perfumes blown upon the moor and forest, from the influence of a humid night. These reviving influences however fell dead upon the benumbed faculties of our hero. In accordance with the urgent solicitations of his hostess, he agreed to swallow an Indian soporific, and try to lose his sorrows and his memory in that nearest semblance of death. He did not fail, as he re-entered the wigwam, to observe that the whole village (called Orapacs) was busily preparing for some imposing ceremony, and that great accessions had been made to the numbers of the previous night.

Long and soundly he slept; when he awoke the sun was coursing high in the heavens. The air was balmy and serene, and his own monomaniacal hallucinations were dissipated, partly worn out by their own violence and partly dispelled by many hours of uninterrupted repose. Dreadful is that affliction which sleep will not alleviate. It is true that one suffering under a weight of misery which no hope lightens, no reasoning assuages, wakes to a present sense of his condition with a startling and miserable consciousness, yet upon the whole, the violence of grief has been soothed and moderated. So it was with our hero, and he walked forth a new and revived creature.

But as he stepped from the wigwam, a spectacle greeted his eye more akin to the fantasies of the previous night than to stern reality. The village was situated on a plain near the banks of the river. The forest remained much as it first grew, save that the undergrowth had been burned away and the ground afterwards overgrown with a luxuriant coat of grass. This summary method of trimming the primitive forest gives it much the resemblance of a noble park, cleared of its shrubs, undergrowth, and limbs, by the careful hands of the woodman. The scene, as Bacon looked along the woodland vista, had a wild novelty, and its aspect would doubtless have been sedative in its effect had it not been for the spectacle already alluded to, which we shall now endeavour to describe. An immense concourse of Indians was collected just without the external range of wigwams. They were seated in groups, in each of which he recognised the distinguishing marks of separate tribes, the representatives of each distinct nation of the peninsula having a distinct and separate place. At the head of this warlike assemblage, on a rude throne sat the youthful Queen of the Chickahominies. Immediately around the foot of this elevation were seated the few grim warriors yet remaining of that once powerful nation, and on her right hand the Powhatans. A fantastically dressed prophet of the latter tribe, with a curiously coloured heron's feather run through the cartilage of his nose stood in the centre of the assembled nations, and harangued the deputies with the most violent gesticulations, every now and then pointing in the direction first of Jamestown, and then of Middle Plantations, (now Williamsburg,) and in succession after these, to the other most thickly peopled settlements of the whites. His rude eloquence seemed to have a powerful effect upon his warlike audience, from the repeated yells of savage cheering by which each appeal was followed. He concluded his harangue by brandishing a bloody tomahawk over his head, and then striking it with great dexterity into a pole erected in the centre of the area. Numerous warriors and prophets from other tribes followed with similar effect and like purpose, to all of whom the stern savages listened with an eager yet respectful attention. When they had concluded, the youthful queen of the Chickahominies descended one step from her throne, and addressed the assembled nations; but her discourse was received in a far different spirit from that which had attended the eloquence of her predecessors. She was evidently maintaining the opposite side of the question which occupied the grave assembly, and it was apparent that the feelings of her auditors were hostile to her wishes and opinions. No evidences of delight greeted her benevolent counsels, and she resumed her seat almost overpowered by the loud and general murmurs of discontent which arose at the conclusion of her "talk." She felt herself a solitary advocate of the plainest dictates of justice and humanity—she felt the difficulty and embarrassment of addressing enlightened arguments to savage ears and uncultivated understandings, and a painful sense of her own responsibility, and of regret for having assumed her present station, pressed heavily upon heart.

Bacon saw only the eloquent language of their

signs and gestures; but some knowledge of the outrages already perpetrated easily enabled him to interpret their intentions. He knew that bloodshed and murder were the objects of their meeting, and he resolved to seize the earliest opportunity to escape, in order to take part in the defence of his country. His mind turned eagerly to this wholesome excitement, as the best outlet which was now left for the warring impulses within his breast.

CHAPTER III.

The retirement of Wyanokee from her temporary presidency in the grand council of the confederated nations, was the signal for beginning the general carouse, by which such meetings were usually terminated. Two huge bucks, with their throats cut, had been some time suspended from a pole laid across a pair of stout forked saplings, driven into the ground at the distance of a few feet from each other; these were now brought into the centre of the area, and quickly deprived of their skins. The neighbourhood of civilized man had already introduced that bane of savage morals, whiskey; and plentiful supplies of this, together with pipes and tobacco, were now served to the representatives. A general scene of rude and savage debauch immediately followed. Meat was broiled or roasted upon the coals—whiskey was handed round in calabashes, while the more gay and volatile members of the assemblage found an outlet for their animated feelings in the violent and energetic movements of the Indian dance. The sounds which issued from the forest were a mingled din of tinkling metals—rattling bones, and the monotonous humming of the singers, occasionally enlivened by a sharp shrill whoop from some young savage, as his animal spirits became excited by the exercise. The squaws performed the part of menials, and bore wood, water, and corn, to supply the feast for their lords and masters.

The new queen of the nation, upon whose ground these carousals were held, retired to her own wigwam, as much disgusted with the moral blindness and depravity of the deputies, as with the commencing revels. Besides her disgust of what was left behind, there was an attraction for her in her own sylvan palace, which, till a few hours back, it had sadly wanted in her eyes; not that she approached it with any hope that her passion would now or ever meet with a return from its object—but still there was a melancholy pleasure in holding communion with one so far superior to the rude, untutored beings she had just left. She felt also a longing desire, not only to learn more of the mysterious transactions of which she had gathered some vague indications from Bacon's discourse, but to take advantage of present circumstances in returning some of the many favours heaped upon herself by her white friends. There was a nobler motive for this than mere gratitude; she wished to show to Bacon and Virginia, that she could sacrifice her own happiness to promote theirs. She felt now satisfied that both of them had discovered the existence of her passion, long before she was aware of the impropriety of its exhibition according to civilized usages, and she was anxious to evince to them how nobly an Indian maiden could cover this false step with honour. Full of these ennobling, and as it proved, delusive ideas, she entered the wigwam with a mien and step which would not have disgraced a far more regal palace.

Bacon was found upon a mat, reclining in melancholy mood against the side of the apartment, intently eyeing the movements of the savages upon the green. She followed his eye for a moment in shame and confusion for the spectacle exhibited by the men of her own race.

"Do you mark the difference," said Bacon, "between the dances in yonder forest and those at Jamestown? Why do not the women join in the merry-making? We consider them worthy to partake of all our happiness."

"Ay, 'tis true, there is no Virginia there!"

His brow settled into a look of stern displeasure and offence, as he replied, "Would you renew the scenes of the last night?"

"No, Wyanokee desires not to give pain, but to remove it—as she came here now to show. You heard me claim you last night as a husband."—A crimson tint struggled with the darker hue of her cheek, as she forced herself to proceed.—"But it was only to save you from the cruel hands of my countrymen. You may, therefore, give up all uneasiness on that subject—I know well that the Great Spirit has decreed it otherwise than I desired, and I submit without a murmur. It is useless for me to conceal that I had learned too quickly to feel the difference between a youth of your race, and one of yon rude beings; but it was more owing to my ignorance of your customs than any want of proper maidenly reserve. That is now passed, you are a married man, and as such I can converse with you in confidence."

"Yes," said Bacon, a bitter smile playing over his countenance, "I am married to stern adversity! 'Tis a solemn contract, and binds me to a bride from whom I may not easily be divorced. Death may cut the knot, but no other minister of justice can. I must say too, that the ceremonies of last night were fitting and proper. I wooed my bride through earth, air, and water; in thunder, lightning, and in rain. Nor was she coy or prudish. She came to my arms with a right willing grace, and clings to me through evil and through good report. I am hers, wholly hers for ever. It is meet that I should learn to love her at once. Ay, and I do hug her to my heart. Is she not my own? do we not learn to love our own deformities? then why not learn to love our own sorrows? Doubtless we shall be very happy—a few little matrimonial bickerings at first, perhaps, but these will soon be merged in growing congeniality. Man cannot long live with any companion, without bestowing upon it his affection; the snake, the spider, the toad, the scorpion, all have been loved and cherished: shall I not then love my bride? Is there not a hallowed memory around her birth?

was she not nurtured and trained by these very hands? Is there not wild romance too, in her adventures and our loves? Is she not faithful and true? yea, and young too! not coy perhaps, but constant and devoted."

Although this language was prompted by very different states, both of heart and head, from that of the preceding night, yet its literal construction by the Indian maiden betrayed her into very little more understanding of its import. She better comprehended the language of his countenance. That, she saw, indicated the bitterness of death, but the cause was still a mystery. She therefore continued her kind endeavours with something more of doubt and embarrassment. "My intention was to offer you and Virginia a home as soon as these warlike men are pacified and gone—that you might come here and live with me until her grand uncle will receive her and you. Oh, it will make Wyanokee very happy."

She would, no doubt, have continued in this strain for some time, but his impatience could be contained no longer. "Is it possible that you do not yet understand the depth and hopelessness of my misery? Know it then in all its horrors. I was half married last night to my own half sister! Did fate, fortune or hell ever more ingeniously contrive to blight the happiness of mortal man at one fell blow? View it for a moment. There was the game beautifully contrived—the stake was apparently trifling, but the prize glittered with India's richest rubies—the very thoughts of them conjured up scenes of fairy land. The richest fantasies of romance sparkled before the eye of the player. The wildest dream of earthly happiness allured him to each renewed attempt. First a little was staked—then another portion—then another to insure the two former, and so on until houses and lands and goods and chattels—yea and life itself, or all that made it valuable, were hazarded upon the throw. Lo, he wins! Joy unutterable fills his breast—he is about to place the jewels next his heart, but behold they turn into scorpions. Rich and beautiful in all their former ruby colour—but there is a fearful talismanic power in their beauty. There is a deadly poison in the sight! They charm to kill. Lay them not near the heart or else the great magician, the king of evil—the prince of darkness himself, has bought you body and soul! That was my case. I won the glorious stake, I had it here (striking his breast), yea, and have it now, and the devil is tempting me to lay it next my heart. I have wrestled with him all the night, but again he is at work. See that you do not help him!"

Again she was lost in reverential awe. As his paroxysm by slow degrees returned, she exhibited in the mirror of her own countenance the passion, the wild enthusiasm, reflected from his, until the final charge to herself, when she was overcome with wonder and fear. His own preternaturally quick perceptions caught the effect produced, and he again folded his arms and leaned back in grim and sullen silence, but with the keen eye of the serpent watching the changing countenance of his auditor. She was sunk in abstraction for some moments, and then, as if rather thinking aloud than communing with another, she said, "Is it possible?"

"Yea, as true as that the serpent infused his poison into the ear of the mother of mankind. As true as that man was the first creature that died on the face of the earth by the hands of his fellow. As true as death and hell! As true as that there is a hereafter. Happiness is negative! Misery positive. There is always a subtle doubt lingering upon our most substantial scenes of happiness; but with misery it is slow, certain and enduring; the proof conclusive and damning. It is more real than our existence, and exists when it is no more. Our nerves are strung to vibrate to the touches of harmony and happiness only when played upon by inspirations from above, but they vibrate in discord to the earth, the air, the winds, the waves, the thunder—the lightning. They are rudely handled by men, beasts, reptiles, devils, by famine, disease and death. Am I not a wretched monument of its truth? Are not these miserable and faded trappings, the funeral emblems of my moral decease? Am I not a living tomb of my own soul? A memento of him that was, with an inscription on my forehead, 'Here walks the body of Nathaniel Bacon, whose soul was burned out on the ever memorable night of his own wedding, by an incendiary in the mortal habiliments of his own Father, with a torch lit up in pandemonium itself? His body still walks the earth as a beacon and a warning to those who would commit incest!'"

The door was darkened for a moment, and in the next the Recluse stood before him. His giant limbs lost none of their extent or proportions as viewed through the dim light which fell in scanty and checkered masses from the insterstices of the sylvan walls. He stood in the light of the only door,—his features wan and cadaverous, and his countenance wretchedly haggard. "Why lingerest thou here in the lap of the tawny maiden, when thy countrymen will so soon need the assistance of thy arm? This night the torch of savage warfare and cruelty will in all probability be lighted up in the houses of thy friends and kindred. Is it becoming, is it manly in thee to seek these effeminate pastimes, in order to drown the images of thy own idle fancy? If thou hast unconsciously erred, and thereby cruelly afflicted thy nearest kindred, is this the way to repair the evil? Set thou them the example! Be a man—the son of a soldier. Thy father before thee has suffered tortures of the mind, and privations of the body, to which thine are but the feeble finger-aches of childhood as compared to the agonies of a painful and protracted death. Rouse thyself from thy unmanly stupor, and hie thee hence to the protection of those who should look up to thee. Be not anxious for me, maiden; I see thy furtive glances at the besotted men of thy race, and thence to me. I have long watched their movements. They see me not; they will attempt no injury—and if they should their blows would fall upon one reckless of danger—who has nought to gain or lose,—who has long had his lights trimmed, and lamp burning, ready for the welcome summons."

When he first entered the wigwam, Bacon sprang upon his feet, and gazed upon the unwelcome apparition as if he doubted his humanity; but as his hollow and sepulchral voice fell upon his ear in the well known, deep excited intonations of the chapel, he moved backward, his hands clasped, until his shoulders rested against the wall. There, shuddering with emotion, he gazed earnestly and in silence upon his visiter, whose words fell upon an indiscriminating ear. The Recluse perceived something of his condition as he continued, "Hearest thou not?—seest thou not? Rouse thee from this unmanly weakness. I saw thy dead horse upon the moor. I will leave thee mine at the head of the Chickahominy Swamp. When night closes upon yonder brutal scene, mount and ride as if for thy life, even then thou mayst be too late! Remember! This night be thou in Jamestown!"

Having thus spoken, he stooped through the door, and vanished among the trees behind the wigwam, as he had come. Bacon still gazed upon the place where he had been, as if he still occupied the spot, his eyelids never closing upon the distended iris, until he fell upon the floor in a swoon. Such restoratives as an Indian wigwam afforded, were speedily administered, and very soon the desired effect was produced. While he lay thus worn down by the sufferings produced by the tortures of the previous night, and the cruel excitement of his feelings, Wyanokee discovered, as she was bathing his temples, the small gold locket, which he had worn suspended from his neck, since the death of Mr. Fairfax. Apparently it contained nothing but the plaited hair and the inscription already mentioned. She caught it with childlike eagerness, and turned it from side to side, with admiring glances, when her finger touched a spring and it flew open; the interior exhibited to view the features of a young and lovely female.

At this juncture Bacon revived. His countenance was pale and haggard from the exhaustion of mental and bodily sufferings. His perceptions seemed clearer, but his heart was burdened and oppressed—he longed for speedy death to terminate the wretched strife. The prospect was dark and lowering in whatever direction he cast his thoughts; no light of hope broke in upon his soul—all before him seemed a dreary joyless waste. In this mood he accidentally felt the open trinket within the facings of his doublet, and inserting his hand he drew it forth. His head was elevated instantly, his eyes distended and his whole countenance exhibited the utmost astonishment. His first emotion was any thing but pleasant—as if he had drawn from his bosom one of his own figurative scorpions, but this was speedily succeeded by one of a different nature. The first sensation of pleasure which he had felt since he left Jamestown beamed upon his mind; it was mingled with the most unbounded surprise; but quick as thought the light of hope broke in upon his dark and cheerless prospects. Again and again the picture was closely scrutinized, but with the same conviction, never before had he beheld that face. It was resplendent with smiles and beauty. The dark hazel eyes seemed to beam upon him with affectionate regard. The auburn tresses almost fluttering in the breeze, so warm and mellow were the lights and shadows. But what rivetted his attention was the want of resemblance in the picture to the lady whom he had been so recently and so painfully taught to believe his mother. The latter had light flaxen ringlets and blue eyes, and the *tout ensemble* of the features were totally dissimilar. He imagined he saw a far greater resemblance between the picture and himself, and hence the ray of hope. But in the place of despair came feverish suspense—he now longed again to meet the Recluse, whose presence had so lately filled him with horror. His mind sought in vain within its own resources for means to bring the question to an immediate issue. Was he the first-born son of Mrs. Fairfax or not? Perhaps Brian O' Reily could tell something of the picture, or had seen the original. No sooner had this faint glimmering prospect of unravelling the mystery dawned upon his mind, than he was seized with the most feverish desire to set out for Jamestown.

The savages still kept up the carouse, but it would be hazardous in the extreme, as he was assured by his hostess, to attempt to leave Orapacs until the conclusion of the feast, which perhaps would last till night. At that time they were all to proceed to the Powhatan domain. He was compelled therefore to content himself with reading the lineaments of the interesting countenance just opened to his view.

Upon what a frail foundation will a despairing man build up his fallen castles in the air. Such was the occupation of our hero until the light of the sun had vanished over the western hills. He lay upon his mat in the twilight gloom, indulging in vague uncertain reveries. He had examined the picture so long, so intently, and under such a morbid excitement of the imagination, that he supposed himself capable of recollecting the features. He had called up dim and misty shadows of memory (or those of the imagination nearly resembling them) from a period wrapped in obscurity and darkness. He endeavoured to go back step by step to his years of childhood, until his excited mind became completely bewildered among the fading recollections of long passed days. As the rippling waters of the purling stream mingled with the monotonous whistling of the evening breeze, his versatile imagination fell into a kindred train. The music of the nursery, by which his childish struggles had been lulled to repose, floated over his memory in the tenderest and purest melancholy. Who that has music in his soul has not, at a like season and hour, refreshed his heart with these early impressions? Nor are they entirely confined to an inviting melancholy mood and the hour of twilight. In the full vigour of physical and mental power, and when the spirits are bounding and elastic—in the midst of dramatic representations or the wildest creations of Italian musical genius, these stores of memory's richest treasures will suddenly flood the soul, touched perhaps by the vibration of some kindred chord. Bacon's harassed mind was refreshed by the tender and softened mood into which he had fallen. Besides, he was now stimulated by the glimmering dawn of hope. When therefore darkness had completely covered the face of the land, he arose to go upon his mission, a different being. Although his own emotions on parting were faint compared to those of Wyanokee, they were yet sorrowful and tender. He lamented the lot of the Indian maiden, and respected the virtues and accomplishments which elevated her so far above those by whom she was surrounded. He bade her adieu with the most heartfelt gratitude for her services, and aspirations for her welfare.

When he stepped from the wigwam he was astonished to see the huge fires, upon which they had cooked the feast, still burning with undiminished brilliancy, and still more startled to observe twenty or more savages lying drunk around them, and half as many sober ones holding vigils over their slumbers. He immediately changed his intended direction, and skirted round the forest in which they lay, so as to arrive at the place pointed out by the Recluse by a circuitous rout.

When he came opposite to the fires, and half way upon his circuit, he was not a little alarmed to hear the astounding warwhoop yelled by one of the sentinels. Casting his eyes in that direction he saw that all the guard were on the *qui vive*, and some of the slumberers slowly shaking off their stupidity. He supposed that one of the sentinels had heard his footsteps, and thus alarmed the rest. Taking advantage of the trees, and the distance he had already gained, he was enabled to elude their vigilant senses. But when he came to the spot pointed out by the Recluse, a greater difficulty presented itself. The horse was already gone, but not taken by the one who brought him there, as he saw evidently from the impressions of his feet in the earth, where he had stood most of the afternoon. He soon came to the conclusion that the Indians had found and carried him off. This was the more probable as they adjourned their council about the time he must have been taken. His call to Jamestown was too urgent to be postponed, and however feeble in body he determined to exert his utmost strength to arrive there during the night.

CHAPTER IV.

Our hero reached Jamestown late on the very morning when the couriers arrived in such rapid succession, with the startling intelligence of the Indian massacres. All night he had wandered over the peninsula, vainly endeavouring to discover his way; light after light shot up amidst the surrounding gloom, and more than once he had been misled by these, almost into the very clutches of the swarming savages. His heart sank within him as he saw plantation after plantation, in their complete possession; the illumination of their incendiary trophies lighting up the whole surrounding country. It seemed indeed to his startled senses as if the Indians had simultaneously risen upon and butchered the whole white population of the colony. With the exception of a small remnant, they had already once perpetrated the like horrible deed, and he again saw in his imagination the dreadful scenes of that well remembered night. Feeble old men, women and children indiscriminately butchered—perhaps Virginia, whom he once again dared to think of, among the number. True, Wyanokee had assured him otherwise, but might not the grand council have determined upon the deed at the more appropriate time of their nightly meeting?

As the dawning day unfolded to his view the relative bearings of the country, these gloomy anticipations were partly realized. Every avenue to the city, both by land and water, was crowded with people of all sexes, colours and conditions, flying to the protection of the Fort. Wagons, carts, negroes, and white bondsmen, were laden with furniture, provisions, and valuables. Ever and anon a foaming charger flew swiftly by, bearing some Cavalier to the city, doubly armed for retributive vengeance. By these he was greeted and cheered upon his way, as well as informed of the depredations committed in the neighbourhood whence they had come. From one of these also he procured a horse, and joined a cavalcade of his associates and friends, proceeding to the same centre of attraction. To them also he unfolded so much of his recent adventures as related to the general interests of the colony. Long, loud, and vindicative were their denunciations, as well of the treacherous savages as the stubborn old man at the head of affairs in the colony.

Although evident traces of his late bodily sufferings were perceptible in Bacon's countenance, no vestige of his mental hallucinations on one particular theme was perceived; his mind was intently occupied upon the all absorbing topic of common safety. As they proceeded together to the city, it was proposed to him to assume the command of a volunteer regiment, which they undertook to raise as soon as they arrived in Jamestown. His military talents and daring bravery were already well known by most of his associates, but he doubted whether he was the most proper person in the colony to assume so responsible a command. As to his own personal feelings, never did fortune throw the chance of honourable warfare more opportunely in the way of a desperate man. True, it would have come still more seasonably twenty-four hours sooner, but then he would only have been better qualified for some desperate deed of personal daring, not for a command upon which hung the immediate fate of all the colonists, and the ultimate supremacy of the whites in Virginia. He promised, however, to accede to their proposal, provided, after the regiment was raised, in which he must be considered a volunteer, the majority cheerfully tendered him their suffrages. He stated the hostility of the Governor to him personally, without enlightening them as to its most recent cause; but they were now as resolute upon disregarding the feelings and wishes of Sir William, as he had already shown himself in disregarding their own. In short, they resolved at once to assume that authority to protect their lives and property, which they now felt, if they had never before known, was an inalienable right. Here was sown the first germ of the American revolution. Men have read the able arguments—the thrilling declamations, the logical defence of natural and primitive rights, which the men of '76 put forth to the world, with wonder at the seeming intuitive wisdom that burst so suddenly upon the world at the very exigency which called it into action. But in our humble opinion, the inception of these noble sentiments was of much earlier date—their development not so miraculous as we would like to flatter ourselves. Exactly one hundred years before the American revolution, there was a Virginian revolution based upon precisely similar principles. The struggle commenced between the representatives of the people and the representatives of the king. The former had petitioned for redress, "time after time,"—remonstrance after remonstrance had been sent in to Sir William Berkley, but he was deaf to all their reasonable petitions. The Cavaliers and citizens of the colony now arrived at the infant capital, resolved to take upon themselves as much power as was necessary for the defence of life, freedom, and property. While the gathering multitude flocked to the State House and public square in immense numbers, Bacon alighted at the Berkley Arms, in order to change his dress, and before he joined them, perform one act of duty which it would have been difficult for him to say whether it was anticipated with most pain or pleasure. It was a visit to Mrs. Fairfax and her daughter. He walked immediately from the hotel to the quarters usually occupied by the servants of the Fairfax family, in hopes of finding O'Reily —to despatch for his effects, which he supposed he could not obtain in person, without suddenly and unpreparedly exposing himself to the notice of the family. But the house was silent as the tomb! No gently curling smoke issued from the chimney; no cheering light broke in at the windows; all was dark, noiseless, and desolate. The domestic animals still lingered around their accustomed haunts, apparently as sad in spirit as he who stood with his arms folded gazing upon the deserted mansion. The streets were indeed crowded with the eager and tumultuous throng, but after the first unsuccessful essay at the door of the servant's hall, he had passed round into the garden of the establishment, and stood as we have described him, a melancholy spectator of the painful scene. There hung Virginia's bird cage against the casings of the window, perhaps placed by her own hands on the morning of the unfortunate catastrophe, but the little songster was lying dead upon the floor. The blooming flowers around her windows hung in the rich maturity of summer, but seemed to mock the desolation around with their gay liveries. The dogs indeed lazily wagged their tails at his presence, and fawned upon him, but they too, slunk away in succession, as if conscious of the rupture which had taken place in his relations with the family.

What a flood of tender recollections rushed upon his memory as he stood thus solitary in the flower garden of her who was the sole object of his youthful and romantic dreams, and gazed upon the well known objects,—each one the memento of some childish sport or pleasure. There too stood the shaded seats and bowers of more mature adventures, redolent of the richest fruits and flowers, and teeming with the hallowed recollection of love's young dream. Nor were tears wanting to the memory of that early friend and patron who had given him shelter in his helpless days, from the cold neglect and inhospitality of the world, and thus, perhaps, saved him the degradation of a support at the public expense. These softened and subdued emotions humanized the savage mood which sprung up from similar reminiscences on a previous occasion. The current of his feelings had been changed by a single ray of hope. The fountain was not now wholly poisoned, and the sweet water turned to gall and bitterness. The scene therefore, painful and melancholy as it was, produced beneficial results. But he marvelled that the house should be so totally deserted. He supposed that the lady and her daughter might be sojourning for a time with the Governor, but what had become of their numerous domestics? They too could not be quartered at the gubernatorial mansion. And above all, what had become of his own Hibernian follower? Certainly, he was not thus provided for. He knew his privileged servant's warm partialities and hatreds too well to believe that he had accepted any hospitality from his master's bitterest enemy. At that moment a servant of the Berkley Arms was passing, and having called him into the garden, Bacon raised a window leading to his own apartments, procured such of his garments as he most needed, and despatched them to the hotel. When he had encased himself in these, somewhat to his own satisfaction (and most young Cavaliers in those days wore their garments after a rakish fashion) he sallied out to perform the duty which he felt to be most incumbent on him. He knocked at the door of Sir William Berkley's mansion, with very different feelings from any he had before experienced on a similar occasion. The relations so lately discovered to exist between himself and those for whom his visit was intended, as well as his feelings toward those who had the right of controlling in some measure the persons admitted to visit at the mansion, awakened anxious thoughts not a little heightened by the anticipation of meeting Beverly, with whom an unexpected interview promised few agreeable emotions. The family seemed determined too that he should have the benefit of all these reflections, from the length of time they kept him standing in the street. At length the porter opened the door with many profound inclinations of the head, still standing however full within the entrance, and continuing his over wrought politeness. "Is Mrs. Fairfax within?" was the inquiry.

"She is dead! may it please your honour!"

"Dead!" uttered Bacon with a hoarse and trembling voice. "When and how?"

"His Excellency has just received the news—

she was murdered last night at his country seat by the Indians."

"Was Miss —— was his niece there also?" he asked with a bewildered doubt whether he had better inquire any further.

"No, Sir, she lies ill of a fever up stairs. Dr. Roland scarcely ever leaves her room, except to tell Master Frank the state of his patient."

"I will enter for a moment and speak a few words with the good doctor."

"Pardon me, your honour, it gives me great pain to refuse any gentleman admittance, but my orders are positive from Sir William himself to admit no one to the sick room, and above all not to admit your honour within these doors. I have over and over again turned away Miss Harriet, who seems as if she would weep her eyes out, poor lady, at my young mistress' illness and the Governor's cruelty, as she calls it."

"I see you have a more tender heart than your master; here is gold for you, not to bribe you against your duty or inclinations; but you will fully earn it by informing Dr. Roland that Mr. Bacon wishes to speak with him for five minutes at the Arms, upon business of the last importance."

"I will tell him, sir; but I do not think he will go, because he has himself given the strictest injunctions that your name shall not be whispered in the room, or even in the house. No longer than this morning, sir, she heard them announce the death of her mother down stairs. Her hearing is indeed extraordinary, sir, considering her so poorly. Since that she has been much worse."

Bacon did not choose to expose himself to the chance of insult any longer by meeting some of the male members of the family, he therefore took his departure from the inhospitable mansion, and skirted round the unfrequented streets, in order to avoid the immense multitude collected in the square and more frequented passages. He could hear the shouts and cheering which echoed against the houses as he proceeded, but little did he imagine that they welcomed his own nomination to the responsible station of commander to the colonial forces. His intention was to proceed to the Arms, and there await the arrival of the doctor; but he no sooner entered the porch than he was seized by the hand in the well known and sympathizing grasp of Dudley.

While the friends were yet uttering their words of greeting, and before they had propounded one of the many questions which they desired to ask, Bacon was seized under each arm with a rude, but not disrespectful familiarity—saluted by the title of General, and borne off toward the state house in spite alike of remonstrances and entreaties.

It was with great difficulty they could gain the square, so dense was the barricade of ox carts loaded with furniture, and wagons thronged with negro children; while families in carriages and on horseback, and thousands of the multitude promiscuously huddled together, increased the difficulty of making way. Since he had heard the startling news of the death of Mrs. Fairfax, his mind was more than ever bent upon joining the proposed expedition; and had it not been for the interruption to the anticipated meeting with the Doctor, no one could have appeared upon the rostrum with greater alacrity.

The contumaceous conduct of the Governor toward the respectful remonstrances and petitions of the citizens, and more especially his unwarranted and disrespectful treatment of himself, recurred to his mind in good time. He mounted the rude platform hastily erected in front of the state house, burning with indignation, and glowing with patriotism.* "He thanked the people for the unexpected and unmerited honour they had just conferred upon him. He accepted the office tendered to him with alacrity, and none the less so that yonder stubborn old man will not endorse it with his authority, and sanction our proceeding under the ordinary forms of law. What has produced this simultaneous explosion in the colony? What are the circumstances which can thus array all the wealth, intelligence and respectability of the people against the constituted authorities. Let your crippled commerce, your taxed, overburdened and deeply wronged citizens answer? The first has been embarrassed by acts of parliament, which originated here, the most severe, arbitrary and unconstitutional, while your citizens

* This is an abstract of the speech really delivered by Bacon.

both gentle and hardy, have been enormously and indiscriminately taxed in order to redeem your soil from the immense and illegal grants to unworthy and sometimes non-resident favourites.

"There was a time when both Cavalier and yeoman dared to be free; when your assembly, boldly just to their constituents, scrupled not to contend with majesty itself in defence of our national and chartered rights. But melancholy is the contrast which Virginia at this time presents. The right of suffrage which was coeval with the existence of the colony, which had lived through the arbitrary reign of James, and with a short interruption through that of the first Charles, which was again revived during the commonwealth, and was considered too sacred to be touched even by the impure hands of the Protector, is now sacrilegiously stolen from you during a season of profound peace and security.

"The mercenary soldiers, sent from the mother country at an immense expense to each of you, fellow-citizens, where are they? Revelling upon the fat of the land at distant and unthreatened posts, while our fathers, and mothers, and brothers, and sisters, are butchered in cold blood by the ruthless savage. Where is now the noble and generous Fairfax, the favourite of the rich and the poor? Where his estimable and benevolent lady? Murdered under the silent mouths of the rusty cannon which surmount yonder palisade. Look at his sad and melancholy mansion, once the scene of generous hospitality to you all—behold its deserted halls and darkened windows. But this is only the nearest evidence before our eyes—within the last twenty-four hours hundreds of worthy citizens have shared the same fate.

"Shall these things be longer borne, fellow-citizens?"

"No! no! no!" burst from the multitude—"down with the Governor, and extermination to the Indians."

He continued. "Already I see a noble band of mounted youths, the sons of your pride and your hopes—flanked by a proud little army of hardier citizens; from these I would ask a pledge, that they never lay down their arms, till their grievances are redressed."—

"We swear—we swear," responded from all, and then, three cheers for General Bacon, made the welkin ring. At this juncture the trumpet, drum, and fife, were heard immediately behind the crowd, and a party of the royal guard, some fifty in number, halted upon the outskirts of the assemblage, while their officer undertook to read a proclamation from the Governor, ordering the mob, as he was pleased to style the meeting, to disperse under penalty of their lives and property. The *army of the people*, already getting under arms, immediately commenced an evolution by which the temporary commander of the mounted force would have been thrown directly fronting the guard, and between them and the multitude. Bacon saw the intended movement, and instantly countermanded the orders, "Let the people," said he, "deal with this handful of soldiers; we will not weaken our force, and waste our energies by engaging in intestine broils, when our strength is so much called for by the enemies of our race upon the frontiers." The suggestion was immediately adopted; before the hireling band could bring their weapons to the charge, the multitude had closed in upon them, and disarmed them to a man. This accomplished, they were taken to the beach, in spite of the remonstrances of many of the more staid and sober of the Cavaliers and citizens, and there soundly ducked. Very unmilitary indeed was their appearance, as they were marshalled into battle array, all drooping and wet, and thus marched to the music of an ignominious tune to the front of the Governor's house.

The frantic passion of Sir William Berkley can be more easily imagined than described. He saw that he was left almost alone—that those citizens most remarkable for their loyalty had deserted him. However wilful and perverse, he saw the necessity of making temporary concessions, although at the same time more than ever bent upon summary vengeance against the most conspicuous leaders of the opposing party whenever chance or fortune should again place the real power of the colony in his hands. At present he felt that he was powerless—the very means which he had taken to thwart and provoke the people now became the source of the bitterest regret to himself, namely—sending the mercenary soldiers of the crown to distant posts on fictitious emergencies. He resolved therefore to disguise his real feelings until the departure of the popular army, when he could recall his own regular troops, and thus take signal vengeance upon such of the agitators as should be left behind, and thence march immediately to the subjugation of the force commanded by Bacon. Scarcely had the presence of the dripping guard, as seen through his window, suggested these ideas, before an opportunity offered of putting in practice his temporary forbearance.

A committee was announced, at the head of which was Mr. Harrison, his former friend and supporter—they were the bearers of a conciliatory letter from General Bacon. In this letter the young commander in chief, in accordance with the suggestions of the older Cavaliers, respectfully announced his election to the command of the volunteer army, and concluded by requesting the Governor to heal all existing breaches by sanctioning his own appointment, as well as that of the appended list of young Cavaliers, to the various stations annexed to their names; and that no delay might occur in the pursuit of the enemy, an immediate answer was requested. The stout old Cavalier was ready to burst with ill suppressed rage as he marked the cool and respectful tone of this epistle, coming from one he most cordially detested and despised, both on public and private grounds.

The committee waited until he had penned his answer, which was cold and formal, but polite. In it he declined signing the commissions in the absence of the council, but promised to convene it early on the ensuing day, when he stated that he would despatch a courier after the army, if the council thought proper to approve of the popular proceedings. He promised also to dismantle the distant forts, and immediately to call in the foreign troops for the defence of the capital.

With this answer, the committee, he to whom it was addressed, and the populace were well satisfied. It really promised more than they had expected of the obstinate old Governor. Little did they dream of the lurking treachery in the old man's heart, much less did they truly interpret the equivocal language contained in the note itself, concerning the foreign soldiers, and the defence of the capital. Little did they imagine that they themselves were the foes against whom he proposed to employ the mercenaries.

The army now took up its line of march across the bridge, amidst the cheers and blessings of the multitude; men, women, and children following them to the boundaries of the island.

Part of the force was sent up the river in sloops, in order to co-operate with the main army in their design of driving the tribes scattered along the water courses of the peninsula, to a common point of defence, and thus forcing them, if possible, into an open, general, and decisive engagement. The youthful commander in chief was intimately acquainted with all the localities between the seat of government, and the falls of the river, (where Richmond now stands,) and he very ingeniously arranged his forces by land and water, so that he might at the same time drive the treacherous enemy before him through the peninsula, and avoiding a premature battle, concentrate the enemy at the point already indicated. It was with this general view, that one part of his force was now sent up the river, while the other pursued the route between the Chickahominy and the Pamunky rivers. These general views were discussed, and the plan decided upon at a council of war, held on the main land, immediately after the troops had passed the bridge. Bacon having imparted to Charles Dudley, his Aid-de-Camp, such orders as the emergency required, turned his horse's head again toward the bridge, and retraced his steps to Jamestown.

CHAPTER V.

THE martial sounds of drums and trumpets had scarcely died away over the distant hills, when Sir William Berkley despatched couriers to the various military outposts of the colony, peremptorily ordering the commanders to march forthwith to Jamestown with the forces under their command. To these couriers also were given secret instructions for the private ears of such of his loyal friends among the Cavaliers living on their routes, as he knew would adhere to him under any circumstances, urgently soliciting their immediate presence at the capital. After these were despatched, he summoned a secret conclave of such friends, equally worthy of his trust, as were yet to be found in the city.

Thus were they engaged, as General Bacon, habited in the rich military fashion of the day, rode along the north western skirt of the city, his own gay attire, and the splendid trappings of his horse wretchedly mocking the desolation within. He drew up at the back court of the Berkley Arms, dismounted, and passed immediately into a private room. Having despatched a servant for the landlord, he employed the time before he made his appearance, in meditations upon the singular and protracted absence of Brian O'Reily, the new responsibilities which he had just assumed, and the present condition and future destinies of the fair invalid at the gubernatorial mansion.

When the landlord entered he quickly demanded if Doctor Roland had inquired for him during the forenoon, and was answered that he had not. A servant was despatched with a note to the Doctor repeating his request for an interview of five minutes at the Arms. After he had waited some time in the most intense impatience, the servant returned with a verbal message stating that the doctor would wait on Gen. Bacon immediately.

"From whom did you obtain this answer?"

"From the porter at the door, sir."

"Very well, you may retire!"

As he sat impatiently listening for the heavy footsteps of the doctor, he heard a light fairy foot tripping up the stairs toward his room, and in the next instant a gentle tap at the door. His heart almost leaped to his mouth as he indistinctly bade the applicant to come in. "Can it be possible," said he to himself, "that Virginia has escaped from her jailers? Was the story of her illness but an invention of the Governor's?"

Before he had answered these questions to his own satisfaction, the door was suddenly thrust backward and Harriet Harrison stood before him.

She was pale, agitated, and gasping for breath, as she threw herself unasked into a seat. Bacon was from his previous emotions scarcely more composed, and his heart beat tumultuously against his doublet, as he endeavoured vainly to offer the courtesies due to her sex and standing.

"Oh, Mr. Bacon!" (gasped the agitated girl) "fly for your life."

"On what account, my dear young lady?"

"I'll tell you as quick as I can. I had just obtained admission to-day to Virginia's room for the first time, when, after having spent the time, and more, allotted to me by the doctor, as I was coming down the stairs I had to pass the door of Sir William's library, and I accidentally overheard him giving orders to an officer to collect some soldiers from the barracks and make you a prisoner in this house. How he knew you were here I know not; but I was no sooner out of the door than I flew to the back court below, demanded of the servant holding your horse to point out your room, and rushed in in this strange manner to put you on your guard. Now, fly for your life—you have not a moment to lose!"

"One word of Virginia, your fair friend, and I am gone. Will she survive? Is her reason unsettled? Does she believe the strange story of the Recluse?"

"In a word then, she is better—of sound mind, and in her heart does not believe one word of that story, though sober reason is strangely perplexed."

"One word more, and I have done. Does she inquire for me?"

"The very first word she said to me was, 'Does Nathaniel believe it?' Now go, while yet you may. Should any new emergency arise in your absence I will despatch a courier after you."

"Yet one message to Virginia. Tell her that I have accidentally discovered in the trinket preserved by her father, and worn by me in the days of my infancy, the likeness of her whom I have every reason to believe my mother. Tell her not to hope too sanguinely, but to give that circumstance its weight, and trust to the developments of time; and now I commit you both, my dearest friends, to the protection of an overruling Providence; farewell."

With these parting words he rushed down stairs, mounted his fleet charger, and swiftly left the court just as the Governor's emissaries entered the front porch of the house to arrest him.

Harriet drew her veil closely over her face, and almost as fleetly sought her father's dwelling.

Our hero in a very few minutes placed the river which separates the island from the main land between him and his pursuers. The sun was yet above the western horizon, and the clouds which spread in fleecy and stationary masses, were tinted with the softest hues of the violet and the rose, filling the mind with pleasing images of repose, cheerfulness, and hope. These soothing and delightful influences of the summer evening were in a great measure lost however upon our hero as he pursued his solitary way through the unbroken forest in the immediate footsteps of the army.

Besides the inevitable suspense attending the developments of his own origin and destiny—there were immediate anticipations before him of no pleasing character. He had just assumed the responsibilities of an office, which at the very outset was attended with the most painful embarrassments. His keen military eye ran over the ground occupied by the enemies of his country, and perceived at once that to make his enterprise completely and permanently successful, the savages must be driven entirely from the peninsula.

The very first on the list of these nations was the Chickahominy, at the head of which was the youthful queen, who had so lately perilled her life and her authority for his own salvation from the tortures of her countrymen. His decisive and energetic mind perceived the stern necessity which existed of driving these melancholy relics of once powerful nations far distant from the haunts of the white man. The question was not now presented to his mind, whether a foreign nation should land upon the shores of these aboriginal possessors. That question had long since been decided. It was now a matter of life or death with the European settlers and their descendants—a question of existence or no existence—permanent peace or continual murders. The whites had tried all the conciliatory measures of which they supposed themselves possessed. Peace after peace had succeeded to the frequent fires and bloodshed of the savages. The calumet had been smoked time after time, and hostage after hostage had been exchanged, yet there was no peace and security for the white man. The right of the aboriginals to the soil was indeed plain and indisputable; yet now that the Europeans were in possession, whether by purchase or conquest, the absolute necessity of offensive warfare against them was equally plain and unquestioned in his mind. These views had been hastily communicated to the council of officers held on the banks of the river, at the commencement of the march, and unanimously concurred in by them. Notwithstanding this unanimity of opinion among his associates in command, the very first duty which presented itself in accordance with these views, harrowed his feelings in the most painful manner. His imagination carried him forward to the succeeding morning, when his followers would in all probability be carrying fire and sword into the heart of the settlement ruled by his preserver. As the refined and feeling surgeon weeps in secret over the necessity of a painful and dangerous operation upon a delicate female friend, yet subdues his feelings and steels his nerves for the approaching trial, so our youthful commander silenced the rising weakness in his heart, and urged his steed still deeper into the forest. He determined to temper and soften stern necessity with humanity.

A few hours' ride brought him up with the

baggage and artillery of the army. The sun had already gone down, but a brilliant starlight, and a balmy and serene air revived his drooping spirits, as he swiftly passed these lumbering appendages.

Scarcely had he placed himself at the head of the marching column, and perceived that the flower and chivalry of his command—the mounted Cavaliers, were still in advance of him, before the sharp quick report of their firearms was heard at some three quarters of a mile distance in advance. These were quickly succeeded by the savage war-whoop, and in a few moments a bright red column of fire and smoke shot up towards the heavens immediately in front. His spurs were dashed into his charger's flanks, and he flew through the fitfully illuminated forest toward a gently swelling hill from beyond which the light seemed to proceed.

When he had gained this eminence, a sight greeted his eyes which awakened all the tenderest sympathies of his nature. Orapacs, the sole remaining village of the Chickahominies—the scene of his late tortures—as well as his preservation, was wrapped in flames. Ever and anon a terrified or wounded savage came darting through the forest heedless alike of him and of the martial sounds in his rear. He reined up his courser on the summit and sadly viewed the scene.

His commands were no longer necessary for the existing emergency. The deed, for which he had been so laboriously and studiously preparing his mind was done. The royal wigwam, the very scene of his shelter, and of Wyanokee's hospitality, was already enveloped by the devouring element. A few struggling and desperate warriors still kept up the unequal contest, but in a few moments, even the despairing yells of these were hushed in the cold and everlasting silence of death. Painfully and intently he gazed upon the crumbling walls of the once peaceful home of his Indian friend. He could perceive no appearance of the unfortunate queen. His imagination immediately conjured up the image of the heroic maiden, her form bleeding and mutilated as it lay among the last defenders of the land of her fathers. By a singular sophistry of the mind, he consoled himself by the reflection, that the orders had not proceeded from his lips—that his hand had no part in the matter, although he had himself laid down the plan of the campaign, of which the scene before him was the first result. True, he had mentioned no exact time for the accomplishment of this measure, and the ardour of his young companions in arms had outstripped his own intentions; nevertheless, the design was his, however much he might soothe his own feelings by the want of personal participation.

By the time that the infantry and heavy artillery had arrived upon the spot occupied by their General, the village of Orapacs was a heap of smouldering ruins. The scene was again covered with darkness, save when it was illuminated at intervals by a fitful gleam, as some quivering ruin fell tardily among the smouldering embers of the walls which had already fallen. He assumed the command of his troops, and marched them into the plain between the place they then occupied, and the site of the melancholy scene we have described. By his orders also, the trumpets were ordered to command the return of the impetuous Cavaliers. Dudley and his compatriots soon came bounding over the plain, exhilarated with the first flush of success, and not a little surprised at the cold and respectful salutations which greeted them from their commander. Most of them, however, were acquainted with his late sufferings and feeble bodily health, and to this cause they were willing to attribute his present want of euthusiasm.

Bacon had no sooner issued the necessary orders for the night than, taking Dudley by the arm, he walked forth into the forest beyond the sentinels already posted.

"Tell me, Dudley," (said he in a hurried and agitated voice,) "was she slain?"

"Was who slain?"

"The queen of these dominions!"

"No, I believe not. I think she was borne from the scene early in the conflict, by some of her tribe."

"Thank God!" he fervently ejaculated, and then addressing himself to his aid, he continued, "Return, Dudley, to the camp—superintend the execution of the orders I have issued for our security, in person, but follow me not, and suffer no one, either officer or soldier, to approach the ruins. I will return in the course of a couple of hours."

Having thus spoken, he suddenly disappeared through the forest, and his companion returned to the camp.

With slow and melancholy steps our hero approached the late busy and animated scene. The beasts of prey were sending up their savage, but plaintive notes in horrible unison with his own feelings. The cool evening breeze fanned the dying embers, and occasionally loaded the atmosphere with brilliant showers of sparks and flakes of fire. As these rolled over his person and fell dead upon his garments, he folded his arms, and contemplated the ruins of the wigwam in which he had found protection.

"There," said he, "was perhaps the birthplace of a hundred monarchs of these forests. Until civilized man intruded upon these dominions, they were in their own, and nature's way, joyous, rosperous, and happy. They have resided amidst the shades of these venerable trees, perhaps since time began! The very waters of the stream bubbling joyously over yonder pebbles, have borrowed their name. Where are they all now? The last male youth of their kingly line was slain by these hands, and the last habitations of his race fired and plundered by soldiers owing obedience to my commands. The plough and the harrow will soon break down alike their hearth-stones and the scene of their council fires. Yea, and the very monuments of their dead must be levelled to meet the ever craving demands of civilized existence. But pshaw! is this the preparation to steel a soldier's heart, and fire it with military ardour and enthusiasm? Let me rather ponder upon my own sufferings on this spot. Let me remember the groans of dying old men, women, and children, which rent the air twelve hours since. And above all, let me bear in mind the despairing shrieks of her, who was more than a mother to me, of her who clothed and fed and protected me in infancy. Where is she now?"

"She is alive and well!" answered a feeble and plaintive voice from the wild flowers and shrubbery which grew upon an earthen monument erected to the savage dead.

"Who is it that speaks?"

"One that had better have slept with those who sleep beneath!"

"Wyanokee?"

"Ay, who is left but Wyanokee and these mouldering bones beneath, of all the proud race that once trod these plains unchallenged, and free as the water that bubbles at your feet."

He approached the rude monument as she spoke. It consisted of a grass-grown mount some thirty feet in length, by ten in height and breadth, and was surmounted by thick clustering briers and wild flowers. The youthful queen was sitting upon the margin of the tumulus, her head resting upon her hand, and it in its turn supported on her knee. As the officer approached, she stood erect upon the mount. Her person was clad and ornamented much as when he had last seen her, except that above one shoulder protruded a richly carved unstrung bow, and from the other, a quiver of feather-tipped arrows crossing the bow near her waist. The soldier replied,

"It is almost useless for me to profess now, how wholly, how profoundly, I sympathize with you in witnessing this scene of desolation. Naught but the dictates of inevitable necessity could have induced the army under my command to perpetrate this melancholy devastation. But I trust that the soothing influences of time, your own good sense, and the ministrations of your kind white friends, will reconcile you to these stern decrees of fate."

"Kind indeed is the white man's sympathy—very kind. He applies the torch to the wigwam of his red friend, shoots at his women and children as they run from the destruction within, and then he weeps over the ruins which his own hands have made."

"It is even so, Wyanokee. I do not expect you to understand or appreciate my feelings upon the instant; but when you are once again peacefully settled at Jamestown with your sorrowing young friend, and will cast your eyes over this vast and fertile country, and see to what little ends its resources are wasted, and on the other hand, what countless multitudes are driven hither by the crowded state of other parts of the world, you will begin to see the necessity which is driving your red brethren to the far west. You can then form some conception of the now unseen power behind, which is urging them forward. You will see the great comprehension and sublime spectacle of God's political economy! you will see it in its beauty and its justice. You feel the partial and limited effects of these swelling waves of the great creation now upon yourself and your nation. I grant they are hard to be borne, but once place yourself above these personal considerations, and compare the demands of a world with the handful of warriors lying dead around those ruins, and you will bow to the justice of the decree which has gone forth against your people!"

"Does your Great Spirit then only care for the good of his white children? You taught me to believe that he too created the red men, and placed them upon these hunting grounds, that he cared as much for them as he did for their white brethren—but now it seems he is angry with the poor red man, because he lives and hunts as he was taught, by the Great Spirit himself. These hunting grounds are now wanted for his other children, and those to whom he first gave them, must not only yield them up, but they must be driven by the fire and the thunder, and the long knives of those who have been professing themselves our brethren."

"Your view of the case is a very natural and plausible one, yet it seems to me you have overlooked that point in it, upon which the whole matter turns. Let us for one moment grant the necessity of making room on your hunting grounds for your white brethren, who are crowded out of the older countries. There seemed at first no need to disturb the red men, there was room enough here for all, we were content to live upon this kind and neighbourly footing. Had your brethren been equally content, the great purposes of the Creator would have been answered without any destruction of his red or white children. Have the red men so demeaned themselves toward the whites that we could all dwell here together? Let the massacre of last night speak! You point to yonder smouldering ruins and bloody corpses. I point to the bleeding bodies of my countrymen and friends, and their demolished dwellings as the cause—the direct cause of the desolation you behold."

"The white man talks very fast—and very well—he talks for the Great Spirit and himself too; but who talks for the poor red man, but Wyanokee. All you say is very good for the white men upon our hunting grounds, and the white men driven from over the great waters, and for the white men left behind. It leaves room to hunt and plant corn *there* for the white men, and finds room *here* to hunt and plant corn, but you do not give the poor red man any hunting ground. You say we must go to the far west, but how long will it be the far west? How many of your white friends are coming over the big waters? How far is this place, where the red man will not be driven from his new hunting ground? If we cannot live and smoke the calumet of peace together, we must have separate hunting grounds. Where are our hunting grounds? Ah, I see your eye reaches where the clouds and the blue mountains come together—to the end of the world, we must go, like those beneath us to the hunting grounds of the Great Spirit."

"Not so, Wyanokee, we would willingly spare the effusion of blood, and when our arms have taught the men who assembled here two days ago, our firm determination always to avenge the murder of our friends and the plunder of their property, it is our intention to propose a fair and permanent peace. We will endeavour to convince them of the necessity of abandoning for ever the country between these two great rivers, and moving their hunting grounds where the interests of the two races cannot come in conflict."

"O yes, you will run the long knives through their bodies, and then smoke the calumet! You will drive us from our homes, and then you will persuade us to give them up to the white man."

"You are not now in a proper mood to reason upon this subject calmly, my gentle friend, nor do I wonder at it; but the time will come when your views of this matter will be similar to my own."

"No, Wyanokee cannot see through the white

man's eyes; she has not yet learned to forget her kindred and her country. She came here to-night to sit upon the graves of the great hunters and warriors who slept here with their calumets and tomahawks beside them, long before the long knives came among us. She will carry away from this place to night, this little flower planted by her own hands over the graves of her fathers and brothers. She would leave it here to spread its flowers over their ancient war paths and their graves, but even these silent and peaceful bones, and these harmless flowers must share the fate of them who buried the one and planted the other. Wyanokee will never see this place more—never again be near the bones of her fathers, until she meets them all at the hunting ground of the Great Spirit. Farewell, home and country and friends, and fare thee well, ungrateful man; when next the Indian maiden steps between thee and the tomahawk of her countrymen repay not her kindness with the torch to her wigwam and the long knife to her heart."

With these bitter words of parting, she descended from the mound with dignity, and disappeared through the forest, notwithstanding the urgent entreaties of Bacon, that she would return. She gave no other evidence of heeding him than turning back the palm of her hand toward him, and leaning her head in the opposite direction, as if she were exorcising an evil spirit. He made no other attempt to stay her progress; once indeed the thought occurred to him to hail the sentinel and arrest her for her own sake, but the idea was as speedily abandoned. He determined to leave her destiny wholly in the hands of him who first decreed it. For a moment he ascended the mount and cast his eye over the wide-spread and melancholy desolation, and then rapidly retraced his steps to the camp. When there, his first orders were to have the slain warriors of the expatriated tribes, buried in the tomb of their forefathers, while his own personal attention was bestowed upon the condition of the prisoners taken during the demolition of the village.

They sat round the tents appropriated to their use, in stern and sullen dignity. Wounded or whole, no sound escaped their lips; and their food and drink remained untouched before them. They noticed the entrance of the commander in chief no more than if he had been an insignificant creeping reptile of the earth; no signs of recognition lighted up their features, though most or all of them must have been present at the scene of his own tortures. While Bacon stood no unmoved spectator of the calm unshaken fortitude with which they bore their misfortunes, an incident occurred that served to exhibit the stern qualities of their pride in still bolder relief. One of the old warriors had been taken while attempting to escape with one of his children, after having fought until there was not a vestige of hope remaining for the preservation of his people and their homes. He was brought into the camp, together with his child. While the prisoners were all sitting round in sullen dignity, and the general of the invading army stood surveying them as we have mentioned, this little child came entreatingly to its father's knees, and begged for the food which stood untouched before his face. He made no verbal reply—a momentary weakness softened his countenance as he gazed into the face of the tender petitioner, but in the next, he raised his tomahawk and sank it deep into the brain of his child before any one could arrest his arm. The innocent and unconscious victim fell without a groan or struggle, and the stern old warrior reinserted the handle of his weapon in his belt, crossed his arms upon his breast, and resumed his former attitude of immobility. Bacon gazed at him in astonishment and horror for an instant, and then wheeled suddenly round to retire from an exhibition of humanity, so rude, ferocious, and appalling. But as he was about to emerge from the portal of the tent, Wyanokee was rudely thrust into the door, and they stood face to face.

His first impulse was to draw his sword, and rush upon the two soldiers who had guarded the prisoner, but a moment's reflection served to remind him that they had but obeyed his own general orders. He returned the half drawn weapon therefore, and stood an embarrassed spectator of the captive maiden's searching glances, as her eyes wandered around the room, first resting upon her unfortunate companions in captivity, next upon the corpse of the slain infant, and lastly upon the commander himself. He had seen her previously when her subdued manners and lady-like deportment, inclined him in communing with her to forget her Indian origin, but he saw her now with all her native impulses roused to their highest tension. Her eye flashed fire as it rested upon him after completing her survey, and she thus addressed him, stepping a few paces backward, while her person was drawn up to its utmost height, and her bosom heaved with struggling emotions.

"Are you the same person who sometime since undertook to inspire noble sentiments into the mind of the purest being that ever honoured a white skin? Are you the same youth who aspired to her hand and renounced it on the marriage night, because of kindred blood? Are you the youth whose fair and deceitful form, and apparently noble nature, once made Wyanokee look with contempt upon this heroic race of warriors? If the form, the person be the same, the Great Spirit of evil has poisoned the fountains of your heart, and turned your goodness and your honour to cruelty and cunning. How far has the great light gone down behind the sea, since you stood upon the ruins of all that Wyanokee loved, and professed sorrow for their destruction, and sympathy in her misfortunes? When you stood before her, and dared not lay your own hands upon her person!—you could leave her untouched upon the grave of her great warriors—you dared not seek to injure her, lest their spirits should return from the happy hunting ground and kill you on the spot. But you could deceitfully order these poor long knives to stand in her path and prevent her from taking the last look, and heaving the last sigh that should ever be looked and uttered in these forests."

"I gave no orders for your arrest, Wyanokee; I have not spoken to the sentinels since I saw you!"

"But you could stand and mourn with Wyanokee over the ashes of her fathers' wigwam, when you had just come from ordering these to carry her into captivity. They told me themselves that they acted by your orders. Oh how cruel, how deceitful is the white man! He gladdens the poor Indian's eyes with his glittering toys, till he cheats him of all the corn laid up for his squaws during the winter. He smokes the calumet with the chiefs, while his own followers are burning down the houses of their nation. You, sir, redeemed Wyanokee from captivity, to carry her into a more galling bondage. You taught her the knowledge of the white man, only that she might multiply her sorrows, when this long foreseen night should come. Was it for this that she redeemed you from the red hot tortures of these chiefs? Did you come upon their hunting ground to learn how to torture in preparation for this occasion, and trusting to Wyanokee's soft and foolish heart for your safe return? Lead them and her to the stake! we will show the white warrior how to endure the tortures of our enemies without fainting like women."

"You will not listen to me, Wyanokee, else I could have told you long ago, that I had given no orders to the sentinels. We do not desire your captivity? you are free to go now whithersoever you choose, provided you keep beyond the range of our sentinels. What our race has done against yours, has only been done to protect their own lives and property, and to make that protection secure and permanent. You know that we never torture prisoners; when the war is ended and peace obtained, these warriors shall go free and unharmed. I see that they have refused to touch their food, under the belief that they are to suffer, but I will leave you to undeceive them, after which you are free to go or to remain. If the latter be your choice, a tent shall be provided for your sole accommodation."

Having thus spoken, he hastily left the tent and sought the marquée occupied by the higher grade of officers and the more aristocratic of the Cavaliers. Gay sounds of song and minstrelsy greeted his ears as he approached the spot—Bacchanalian scraps promiscuously chimed in chorus with more sentimental ditties, and all occasionally drowned in boisterous shouts of laughter. These evidences of the mood in which he should find his associates deterred him from entering, under his present feelings, and he therefore passed on to his own solitary quarters. In a few moments he was extended upon such a bed as a camp affords, with no external source of interruption to his repose, save the distant cries of the wild beasts, and the more monotonous tread of the sentinel, as he paced his narrow limits in the performance of his duty.

The sun rose the next morning over the ruins of Orapacs and the scene of the late strife in unclouded splendour. The enlivening notes of drums and trumpets had long since roused the soldiers from their slumbers, and having despatched their morning meal, they were speedily forming into marching order. The commander of this imposing little army mounted his charger, and galloped along the forming battalions; his eye bright and serene, his spirits, in comparison with the previous night, bounding and elastic. Having detailed to his council of officers his intention of next attacking the king of Pamunky, the orders for the march were given, and the lines wheeled into columns, headed by the gay and brilliant *cortége* of youthful Cavaliers.

The prisoners were marched into the centre of the column, and as they assumed their station, the general ran his anxious eye eagerly over their persons, to ascertain whether his former pupil had availed herself of the accommodations provided by his orders. But no such graceful form greeted his sight, and he learned from the Captain of the guard that she had departed soon after he had himself left the prisoners—entirely alone. A momentary sadness shaded his brow, as he reflected upon the desolate condition of the Indian maiden, but it was soon lost in the absorbing duties of his station.

Toward evening, of the ensuing day, as the army pursued their route between the Chickahominy and Pamunky Rivers, the vanguard discovered several of the Pamunky tribe, skulking among the trees of the forest immediately in advance of them. The general, apprehending an ambuscade, immediately ordered the Cavaliers to fall back upon the main body of the army, while a practised band of rangers were ordered to examine the cover of the wood. Scarcely had these orders been transmitted to their various destinations, before a bright beacon fire shot its spiral column of smoke and flame high above the surrounding trees. What this new device portended the commander could not divine, nor could the council, which was immediately summoned, give to it a satisfactory interpretation. The Rangers returned without discovering any signs of an ambuscade, though they had penetrated to the huge fire which lighted up the forest. Not an Indian was to be seen there or beyond. Bacon and his staff rode forward to the scene in person —but the aid of a glass enabled him to discover nothing more.

The army was again put in motion, and every precaution used which some experience in Indian warfare had taught the general was so necessary. For miles they proceeded with the most watchful caution, until the absence of the undergrowth in the forest taught them that it had been fired, and thereby disclosed the probability of their being in the near neighbourhood of the town of the Pamunkies. The verdant glades were lighted up at intervals by broad masses of red light from the setting sun, as they fell between the natural interstices of the trees. The appearance of the woodland vista before them was romantic and picturesque in the extreme. The forest had the aspect of a country which had been settled for ages. The venerable trees, surmounted with green and brown moss, were now occasionally richly bronzed with the rays of the sun as they fell horizontally upon their hoary trunks, and the whole more resembled an ancient and venerable park, which some wealthy gentleman had inherited from careful and provident ancestors, than a wild woodland, fresh from the hands of nature, in which the woodman's axe had never been heard, and upon which no other care or culture had been bestowed than the occasional torch of the savage.

They were not left long to revel in these wild beauties—a more appalling scene awaited them.

The sun was fast declining behind the river hills of the Chickahominy and darkness encircling the sombre groves in which they rode, when suddenly a hundred fires cast a lurid glare across their path, and the army instinctively halted on beholding the town of the Pamunkies wrapped in flames. Again they were put in motion, and cautiously approached the spot. Bacon fearing that some treachery lurked beneath these unexpected measures of the Indians, could scarcely restrain the impetuosity of his mounted force, spurred on by curiosity to see in what new device of savage warfare they would terminate.

They arrived upon the skirts of the town, however, and within the influence of the heat, without hindrance or adventure; and what no less surprised them, not a living creature was perceptible, around or near the conflagration.

The first idea that suggested itself to the mind of Bacon was, that the savages had, in despair, thrown themselves into the burning ruins of their own dwellings. He now understood the meaning of the beacon light on their route; "it was the signal for commencing the tragedy," he muttered to himself as he reined up his steed and ordering his troops to halt, brought them into line along the outskirts of the burning village, which, like the one they had themselves fired, was constructed upon the banks of the Pamunky river. While the troops thus stood upon their arms, some of the officers rode through the blazing wigwams, very much against the will of their rearing and plunging chargers. It was completely deserted; but while they were consulting upon the measures to be taken, a tumultuous and astounding yell burst suddenly upon their startled ears. The intense light of the burning village rendered the twilight gloom around as dark as midnight by the contrast, and not a savage could anywhere be seen. The mounted troop made a wide sweep round the alignment, but with no better success. Another astounding shout of savage voices ascended to the clouds. Many of the frail and tottering wigwams tumbled in at the same moment—throwing the light in a lower line of vision over the water, so that they were enabled to discover a large body of mounted Pamunkies drawn up like themselves on the opposite bank of the river. Their grim and painted visages, close shaven crowns, scalp locks, and gaudy feathers, appeared through the medium of the red and flickering light reflected from the water, in horrible distinctness. A legion of devils from the infernal regions, clothed in all the horrors of German poetry, never startled the senses and aroused the imagination more than did this spectacle its amazed beholders. With another yell and a flourish of their tomahawks above their heads, the Indians simultaneously wheeled their horses and flew over the plain towards the source of the river. In a few moments all was silent as death, save the crackling of the burning wigwams. The squaws and children seemed to have been long since removed. Again the colonial army—or to speak more properly, the army of the people, encamped before the ruins of an ancient and venerable settlement.

Here were no painful reminiscences for the sensitive but energetic commander. The savages were flying before his as yet scarcely tried army, in the very direction in which it was his purpose to drive them. He knew them too well to believe that the whole peninsula would be thus tamely abandoned, and he issued his orders, before lying down to rest, for redoubled vigilance through the night, and an early march in the morning toward the falls of the Powhatan, where he had every reason to believe that the tribes of the former confederacy were again drawing to a head.

CHAPTER VI.

Our hero was not deceived in his supposition, that the savage tribes inhabiting the Peninsula would make a desperate effort to retain possession of a country so admirably adapted to their mode of life. Two noble rivers, one on either hand, abounding with a variety of fish, and a fertile soil, yielding its treasures with little culture, were considerations in the eyes of these ignorant but not misjudging sons of the forest, not to be surrendered without a struggle.

As the army of the colonists pursued its march toward the point already indicated as the rendezvous of the again confederated tribes, it was constantly harassed with alarms—signal fires and flying bodies of mounted warriors, first cutting off their communication with the river—now assailing the vanguard, and then hovering upon the rear. Three weeks and more were thus consumed in partial and unsatisfactory engagements; the skirmishers first approaching one river, upon the representation of some treacherous savage, and then hurrying back in the opposite direction to meet some illusive demonstration made by the cunning enemy. The youthful commander soon perceived that this mode of warfare was the one exactly suited to the nature and condition of his foes, and the least adapted to the impetuous courage of his own troops. He saw too, that the savages had the double design of wearying out their invaders in the manner we have described, and of collecting and concentrating their forces, at some point where their own mode of warfare could be rendered available, without exposing themselves to the destructive discharges of artillery which they still held in superstitious terror. A very little reflection satisfied him that there would be no immediate danger in pursuing the direct route between the Powhatan and Chickahominy rivers, toward the falls of the former, where he had already some intimation that the enemy were collecting in great force. He was well satisfied that the tribes already dislodged had removed all their winter provisions, and their wigwams being destroyed, there could be little hazard to the city in disregarding their daily demonstrations in his front, flank, and rear. Accordingly his troops were concentrated in a solid column, and marched directly toward the falls, entirely disregarding the petty annoyances which had already detained them so ingloriously in the Peninsula.

While they were marching toward the scene of the great and final struggle for supremacy between their own race and the Aborigines, in this narrow neck of land, which had so long been the scene of contention, we will retrace our steps for a short space, in order to bring up the proceedings at Jamestown to the point at which we have just arrived.

In doing so, however, it is not our intention to fatigue the reader with a minute account of the long and tedious days, and still more wretched nights, spent by our heroine after the shock given to her delicate constitution by the painful and unexpected adventure in the chapel, and by the subsequently reported death of her mother under peculiarly awful and afflicting circumstances. The reader has doubtless more truly imagined her condition during the first paroxysms of the fever, than we could describe it. Down to the time when her favourite and confidant was permitted to enter her room, the daily occurrences of her yet endangered life were sad and monotonous enough, but the paramount cravings of diseased nature once assuaged, her mental excitement once more rose in the ascendant. Not that her reason ever became deranged, except from violent febrile action during the height of the attack; however feeble her physical organization, her mental powers were clear and unclouded, and her spirits, though of necessity somewhat broken, were firm and elastic. The truth is, that she did not believe the assertion of the Recluse by which the nuptial ceremony was so dreadfully interrupted. She had indeed a feeling of superstitious reverence for whatever came from his lips, but she had also seen the wild fire of his eye when under deep excitement, and she did not therefore give implicit confidence to any declaration he should make.

This questioning of his oracular authority was an after-consideration it is true, and was itself prompted by other feelings, having their foundation in the affections of the heart. She could not believe that her lover was her own brother ; her feelings toward him were peculiar—powerful, and different from the love of mere kindred. Besides, there were little almost undefinable circumstances in the intercourse of their halcyon days, which she did not believe, could in the nature of man, have taken place between brother and sister. She most truly thought that her lover and herself were expressly created for each other ; that their union had been decreed in heaven. That in the first dawnings of their mutual understanding of each other, there had been electrical, spiritual and ever sublime transmissions of mutual intelligence and exquisite pleasure, which could not exist between children of the same parents. These were some of the reasonings which first led her to doubt the infallibility of the Recluse, or rather this was something like the process by which she arrived at firm and undoubting conviction. She viewed the case in this light from the very first moment of unclouded perception, but at first it was a wild tumultuous and suffocating mixture of vague perceptions, and scarcely permitted hopes. As she gradually analyzed her feelings, and examined the reasons for her convictions, the truth dawned more and more clearly upon her view. She was one day sitting, propped up on her couch, during the three weeks in which Bacon was engaged in his Indian campaign, the doctor sitting by her side with his finger upon her pulse. Both were silent and abstracted. The pale beautiful countenance of the invalid was fixed in deep and earnest thought. Her eyes wandered through an open window, and sought a resting place upon some sunny spot of green and refreshing nature. Her lips moved just perceptibly, as if she were conversing with some one in an under tone. At length she slightly raised her head, her eyes sparkled with the brilliancy of stars, waxing brighter and brighter, and her head rising higher and higher from her pillow, until she screamed in wild delight, "The light of heaven and love's inspiration itself declare it false."

The doctor rose with a grave and anxious look, and placing one hand upon her shoulders, and with the other removing the pillows that supported her, laid her gently down, saying,

"I fear there is more excitement about your head to-day, my dear young lady; if it continues you must lose blood again."

"Oh, dear doctor, there is indeed excitement about my head and my heart too, but it is not the excitement of fever; or if it is, it is a dear delightful fever, which I trust in God will never leave me, for it came just now wafted on my brain as if by the music of the spheres."

"Your room must be darkened again, and the cold applications to your head repeated."

"You think I am losing my senses again, dear doctor, but I assure you I am just regaining them, as I will show you from this time forward. I have now done with physic. I have a medicine here," (and she laid her hand upon her heart, while a bewitching smile played around her mouth, that staggered the good doctor,) "which is worth more to me than all the costly drugs of India, or the islands of the sea."

And the event justified her words. Her mind was no sooner settled in deep conviction, and her heart comparatively at ease, than she began rapidly to recover. It was some days before the scene just related, when Harriet Harrison was admitted to her presence, and when, as the reader has already learned from that maiden herself, Virginia propounded to her the questions touching her lover's belief in their reported relationship, which were repeated by Miss Harrison to Bacon.

So long as that interview continued between the two intimates, untramelled by the presence of a third person, it was one of deep interest; but unfortunately the heir of the house had too much reason to suspect that Harriet's feelings were engaged in another's interest, long to indulge them with an unbroken interview. Virginia barely had time to ask those questions, and whisper to her friend the tidings of her own dawning hopes, before the doctor entered, attended to the door as Harriet perceived through the partial opening, by Frank Beverly himself; she therefore took her leave, promising a speedy return.

As she retired from the chamber of the invalid, she accidentally overheard the Governor's orders for Bacon's arrest, the result of which has already been relàted. Her next visit to the house was on the day of the scene between the doctor and his patient, which we have just attempted to describe. She was ushered into the room of state, usually occupied by the Governor for the reception of his most distinguished guests. No formality was neglected in duly receiving her at the door, and conducting her to this presence chamber of his Excellency, by the official who acted as master of ceremonies.

"I have no business of state to communicate to the Governor, Sir Porter; I came to see his niece!"

The porter bowed profoundly as he replied, "But his Excellency has some business with you, madam, as he informed me, when he directed me to usher you into this apartment." Another profound inclination followed, with an accompaniment of rubbing hands and shuffling his feet backward; while the arch, but somewhat alarmed and astonished maiden, was left to con her speech to the Governor at her leisure. After a most tedious interval of half an hour, the formal representative of majesty made his appearance, with such a profusion of bows that his merry master himself would have smiled to witness them. Of course Harriet bit her lips in order to restrain their mirthful inclinations. While the old knight drew a chair, and after sundry hems, and stroking his chin, thus gravely addressed her: "I am informed, Madam, that you are desirous of an interview with me; will you be so good as to enlighten me as to the cause of the unexpected honour?"

"Some one must have deceived you with a most egregious story, Sir William. I desired no such thing. I came here to see my friend, Virginia Fairfax."

"I am exceedingly pained to inform you, Miss Harriet, that from certain late circumstances, which it is needless to particularize, and in which you were somewhat a participator, I, as Virginia's natural guardian, have thought proper to end the intercourse between you at once. My niece is destined soon to become the wife of my young kinsman, Beverly, and it is most prudent to keep her from the sight of such persons and things as might remind her of that most strange and disgraceful transaction of which I will not speak more openly. I am very sorry to give you pain, but there was no other course left for me to pursue than to be plain and candid with you."

"And does this marriage take place with Virginia's consent?"

"She has not been consulted as yet; her health, in the first place, did not admit of it, and in the second, the evidence which she so lately gave o being utterly incapable of choosing a husband calculated to secure her own happiness, or reflect honour upon her family and connexions, has caused that duty to devolve on me."

"But, Sir William, suppose she should refuse to accept the husband of your choice? You certainly will not enforce your determination."

"Her lamented father and myself entered long since into a covenant by which these young people were to be united. On the very morning of his death, we talked the matter over; he freely and fully consented to the completion of the engagement, and forthwith it shall be carried into execution, if sufficient authority remains to me in these turbulent and rebellious times to enforce it."

"But you will give her time to assuage her grief, and make up her mind to the lot which awaits her. You surely will not precipitate her into the celebration of these nuptials?"

"You talk, young lady, as if it were some horrible and revolting monster to whom I intended uniting her, instead of the presumptive heir and nearest kinsman of Sir William Berkley, well favoured and highly accomplished, as you must acknowledge that he is. She has had time enough to recover her equanimity, and as soon as her health is equally restored; the ceremony shall be performed; and whether or not, it is my purpose to complete it before the return of that arch-rebel Bacon to the city. Please God, however, I intend he shall return in irons to undergo the penalty demanded by the outraged laws of his country."

"And you will not permit me to see my friend for five minutes—only five minutes?"

"No! lady, you are now advised of my intentions touching the disposal of my niece, and you may readily comprehend the reasons of your exclusion from her presence, without my entering into further and more painful explanations."

With this answer, Harriet was compelled to be content, and therefore making a reverence, more than usually formal, to his Excellency, she withdrew. It was not in her nature, however, to resign her friend to the fate which threatened her, without an effort to relieve her. From the gubernatorial mansion she immediately hastened in pursuit of O'Reily, in order to despatch him with a communication for his master. But Brian was nowhere to be found; her own researches and those of the servant whom she despatched in pursuit of him were of no effect; she was therefore compelled to entrust her message to one of her father's negroes, who was well mounted, and despatched upon his errand, within less than two hours from the time of her interview with his Excellency.

During the absence of the army in the Peninsula, Sir William Berkley had not been idle, as has already been intimated. The commands borne by his couriers to those Cavaliers throughout the colony, who were yet well affected to his government, began now to bring them in from all directions, and the regular soldiers stationed at the forts, which were so offensive to the citizens, were marching rapidly upon the capital from every quarter. Some had already arrived, and the city was once more thronged with eager faces. Sounds of martial music were again heard through the streets, and the more quiet citizens again disturbed with the stern preparations for war.

The present military and Cavalier assemblages in the capital were, however, of a very different political character, and brought together with very different motives from those which had preceded them. They were not less in numbers, spirit and appointments; but their object was not to cope with the savage—it was to measure arms in deadly strife with their own countrymen and fellow-citizens. The army now assembling, was intended by the Governor to suppress what he called the rebellion, and his purpose was, as soon as his forces should all arrive, to march at once to the Falls of the Powhatan, and while the popular army were engaged in front with the savage enemies of their country, to fall upon their rear, and either cut them in pieces, or compel them to surrender as rebels found bearing arms against his majesty's authority in the colony.

Seldom have political parties of any country presented so strange an aspect as did those of Virginia at this period. First, the people of the city had been divided between the Cavaliers and Roundheads. The latter were no sooner brought into complete subjection, than a new amalgamation took place, by which their distinctive character was lost. Then, growing out of the puerile obstinacy of Sir William Berkley, in refusing to repel the incursions of the Indians merely because he had at first maintained that there was no danger to be apprehended from their hostility, the popular or conservative party sprang into existence. Against these were now arrayed the loyalist faction, and most of those descended from noble ancestors or bearing titles, headed by the Governor himself.

In a very few days this latter party had assembled their whole military force in the city, and the most active preparations were made to march against Bacon and his followers who were carrying fire and sword into the very heart of the country occupied by the real enemies of the colony.

The temporary duties of the government were resigned into the hands of Sir H. Chicherley, while Sir William Berkley, Sir Herbert Jeffries, Francis Beverly, Philip Ludwell, and their compeers, assumed the most important stations of command in the army of the loyalists. Much the larger portion of the regular troops were composed of foreign mercenaries, sent over from England to perform those very duties which Bacon and his followers were now to be punished for assuming. The very soldiers who ought to have protected the whites against the incursions of the Indians were to be turned against the patriot band which had volunteered to perform a service no longer to be deferred with safety to the colony. It is true that the commissions of Bacon and his officers were not legally signed by the constituted authorities; but an emergency had arisen which threw the citizens back at once upon their original rights and powers. The government having failed to afford them protection for their lives and property, they had assumed that office for themselves. This was the condition of the colony at the juncture of which we write.

While Sir William and his coadjutors were thus busily collecting and disciplining their forces, the citizens of the capital were not uninterested spectators of this unwonted succession of military preparations. Most of those remaining in the city had friends and relations in the ranks of the popular army, and though they dared not openly express their disapprobation of the Governor's proceedings, their discontent was deep and settled, and only awaited the departure of the present overpowering force, again to burst into open resistance against the government.

While these preparations for civil strife were going on in the streets of the city, a discussion of not less interesting import to some of the leading characters of our story, was carried on within the walls of the Governor's mansion. The stout old Cavalier had fixed upon the day preceding the departure of his army, for the solemnization of the marriage between his niece and his kinsman Beverly. He had himself held several interviews with the former, but had failed to make the least impression on her mind, either by his reasoning or his more artful appeals to her filial duty and affections.

In vain had he detailed her father's plans and expectations. In vain had he appealed to her love and respect for his memory. In vain had he descended from his dignity to reproach her with the late disastrous occurrence at the chapel. In vain had he coarsely charged her with desiring an alliance, contrary alike to the laws of God and man. She was deaf to his arguments and his threats. But the time approached with fearful rapidity, which he had appointed for the ceremony. The intended bridegroom held an important command in the expedition now preparing, and it was Sir William's intention that he should be married and set out on the succeeding morning. Notwithstanding our heroine's apparent firmness, therefore, in presence of her stern relative, every note of preparation which was wafted into her chamber sent the blood oppressively to her heart. Her naturally mild and gentle nature shrunk from the contemplation of the violence which her fears and her knowledge of her kinsman induced her to believe would be used to overcome her resolution.

His pretended dread of the disgrace which he charged her with desiring to bring upon his family she knew was exactly the apology he wanted for the arbitrary measures necessary to the completion of the plan.

She was alone in the world. No one now stood ready to give her rescue from the relentless hands which placed restraint upon her inclinations. Her nearest kindred had, as she believed, fallen by the savage tomahawk, and her only remaining relative was about to force her into a marriage which she detested. Notwithstanding all these depressing circumstances, her elastic mind and sanguine temperament had hitherto risen above the accumulating weight of her misfortunes. She had still preserved the vague yet constant hope, so natural to youth, that some fortunate occurrence, some unexpected accident would yet take place to mar the well laid plans of the Governor. But as the time approached, and the preparations moved steadily forward without any evidence of coming succour, or the fortunate event which was to release her from her dreadful situation, her heart began to misgive her—she was compelled in some measure to assume an humbler posture towards the stern old man in whose hands her destiny seemed placed. Her ingenuity had turned the subject in all its various aspects—every chance of escape was provided against. Even the presence of her friend Harriet, upon which she had founded most of her hopes, was rigidly and perseveringly denied to her. As a last and desperate resort, she humbly supplicated her uncle for an uninterrupted interview with him to whom he purposed to marry her; and Sir William seeing nothing in this request calculated to defeat his plans, but on the contrary hoping that it proceeded from a wavering resolution, granted the request.

She sat upon a large leathern-backed chair, her head leaning upon the window sill, and her flaxen ringlets clustering around her pale and attenuated, but still beautiful features. Her *robe de chamber* was white and simple in its fashion, and her hands were listlessly and languidly twined into its folds, seeming, every now and then, as if her delicate fingers would pierce the yielding texture. A solitary tear seemed as if it had already departed from its pure fountain, as tremblingly it hung upon the long dewy eyelash, the mere closing of which dissipated it into a thin misty veil of sadness to her liquid melancholy blue eye, as it was turned in fearful expectation towards the door.

At length Beverly entered. She had until this moment strenuously resisted all endeavours to promote an interview, and once, on a former similar occasion, had covered her face and pertinaciously resisted all attempts on his part to lead her into conversation. He now entered with the knowledge that the invitation came from herself; he felt his supposed power; and a lofty smile played upon his proud but handsome features. As he approached, she sank upon her knees, and clasped her hands in supplication. The tears had now burst the restraints of thought and internal oppression, and rapidly coursed each other down her cheeks as she spoke, "You see before you, sir, a solitary female and an orphan, bereaved suddenly and cruelly of her natural protectors—deserted or oppressed by those who should have supplied their place. Before the distracting grief for these afflictions has had time to lose its first intensity, she has been cruelly beset and importuned to become a party to a marriage, of which she had never before thought. You, sir, are the other party! I entreat, I implore you on my knees, at least to postpone this intended ceremony. If it is performed to-night, as my uncle has appointed, the wrath of Heaven will be poured out upon such a desecration of its holy institutions. You, sir, will wed a corpse or a raving maniac! Interpose then, I pray you. Petition Sir William, as from yourself alone, for its postponement, at least until your return from the intended campaign, and I will pray for your happiness until the end of my existence. I will then indeed believe that you desire mine."

He made several attempts to raise her from her supplicating posture, during her appeal, but she maintained her attitude. Having paused to catch her exhausted breath, he seized the opportunity to say, "Are you sure, madam, that there is no lurking weakness, no sinister design, in this demand for farther time?"

"Of what design, what weakness do you suspect me?" she exclaimed, raising her head boldly, and losing almost instantly the subdued tone of entreaty.

"Of base and criminal affections for one who should be blotted from the tablets of your memory for his villany, if not for his kindred blood!"

She was on her feet in an instant; her ringlets wildly tossed back by a quick motion of the head, and a corresponding effort with both hands, which she held still clasped in her hair, as she stared at him an instant before she replied,

"Are you a man? A gentleman? A Cavalier? That you come here to insult and trample upon one already deserted of all mankind? Her whom you pretend to desire for a companion through joy and wo! How base, how cowardly, to insult a helpless female, and that female your kinswoman—one whom you pretend to love. Out upon you, sir, for a dastard! Were he now here whom you so basely slander, you would not dare employ such language!"

"Softly, softly, my dear lady. You are only betraying your own feelings, and counteracting the relenting mood into which your well acted appeal was near betraying me."

"Oh, then, forget what I have said, and be indeed the high minded, generous Beverly, I once believed you! We were children together, caressed by the same friends and owning a common origin. Can you then witness unmoved my forlorn condition, without one feeling of compassion?"

Beverly was not wholly without tender feelings, although they were so concentrated upon himself, that it required the touch of a master hand to reach his heart. Selfish men, however, are sometimes easily worked upon by allusions or appeals to their family pride. Their connexions are a constituent part of the idol of their worship —self; and it is not the least remarkable feature in their characters, that such men are almost always affectionate husbands and devoted parents. These are but a part of self; their kindred by a farther remove are generally valued in proportion to their ability to confer honour upon the common stock.

"He that feels not love," says Goethe, "must learn to flatter." Doubtless the great German poet was contemplating the difficulties of the supremely selfish man in love, when he penned this aphorism. But Beverly was not so profoundly skilled in the human heart; he ardently desired to possess the hand of his fair kinswoman, as well on account of her many personal attractions, as of the rich inheritance of which she was the heiress; but he had not learned his own harsh defects of character, and of course could not substitute the arts of flattery for the softer eloquence of love. He felt and enjoyed his power, as compensating in some degree for the want of admiration of himself in his intended bride, and such were the feelings operating upon him when he entered her chamber; but her last appeal seemed to move his selfish nature, as he paused to contemplate the eloquent suppliant before he replied.

"Suppose that I obtain from Sir William his consent for the postponement of the ceremony, will you then give me your hand of your own free will?"

She paused before replying. The case was desperate; no succour seemed now within the bounds of probability. The shades of evening were fast gathering around the gloomy precincts of her secluded apartment. She knew her uncle's determination of character. One only chance of escape appeared remaining open to her, and she desperately resolved to seize it. Such was the train of reasoning by which she rapidly arrived at this conclusion, and replied,

"Our inclinations are not always within our own control, but if you obtain this reprieve, I promise to give you my hand upon the return of the present expedition, provided that nothing occurs in the mean time to free me from the necessity. For I will be plain and honest with you, and avow mydetermination to escape this marriage if I can."

"I understand you, fair cousin; you expect deliverance at the hands of your degraded and new found kinsman; but trust me, he will need succour himself before that time arrives. I expect to march him through these streets in irons on my wedding-day. Frown not—gather no storms of indignation upon your brow—it shall be even so. But time wears apace; so pledge yourself before Heaven, that if I obtain Sir William's consent to this delay, you will be mine upon the return of the army."

"Before Heaven I promise you, under the condition I have named."

"It is then a bargain, and I will seek the Governor to fulfil my part of it; should he consent, see that you remember your plighted faith. As for your condition, I take no thought of that;" and with this remark he left the room.

It was with the greatest difficulty that she could suppress her rising indignation, upon his again alluding to her new found kinsman; but she did so far suppress it as to force herself through the required promise. The door had no sooner closed upon his retreating footsteps, than she clasped her hands, and exclaimed fervently, raising her eyes toward heaven, "Thank God! I am now freed from the immediate apprehension of this most hated union. Oh, if he does but come within the allotted time! and come as my flattering hopes persuade me that he will—a conqueror! hailed a the deliverer of his country—the champion of her oppressed and outraged people, and the preserver of the most wretched of her maidens! what blessings will be his! Be he brother or kinsman or lover, he shall live for ever in this grateful heart. Brother indeed! He is a brother in kindness, devotion, and disregard of self; but a brother in kindred blood, my heart assures me he is not."

The door was again opened after the lapse of a short time, and Beverly entered to say, "I have seen Sir William, and presented my request; he refused at first, but when I told him that you had promised to be mine at the expiration of the required time, he yielded his consent. I purposely concealed from him that there was any condition in the case, first, because I take no heed to it myself, and secondly, because it might have precluded his concurrence, and would most certainly be a motive with him for placing you under still more rigid restraint. You see, sweet coz, that I study your happiness far more than you give me credit for. Why will you not freely then make me its guardian for life?"

"How very different is the selfish man," thought Virginia, "who thus blazons his own little acts of merest charity, for refined and delicate attentions, from him who possesses innate benevolence and gentleness of heart? He would have studiously concealed a hundred greater kindnesses than this." But under present circumstances, even such unfavourable comparisons did not prevent her from replying,

"For every act of kindness towards me, Mr. Beverly, I am sure I try to feel very grateful, and since I have been within these walls, my feelings have been so little exercised in that way that it is really refreshing to feel under their influence, even in the smallest degree. The very servants treat me as a lost and abandoned creature. Those of my own sex that once professed love and respect for me, fly from the apartment when I speak to them, as if there were contamination in my very voice. I know that some horrible tale has been told them about me: would you but take the trouble to correct the false impression, before you depart, my solitary lot might be greatly softened, and I would then have double cause for gratitude."

"With the domestic arrangements of the house I dare not interfere—Sir William has directed all those things himself."

"And is it by his orders too that my aunt comes not to see me, nor sends a kind word of inquiry as to my health these long sad days, or a book to while away the longer and more gloomy nights?"

"It is. She has wept as many foolish tears almost as yourself, since your confinement to this room."

"Thank God! You have taken a load from off my heart. There is then one soul within the house, of my own sex and blood too, who sympathises with me during these stern severities."

"Your trials will soon be over, my pretty coz, and then we will remove to a house of our own, and you shall lord it over some of these blackies, in revenge for their want of respect, to your heart's content." Attempting to chuck her under the chin, as he spoke, she was compelled to turn her head suddenly toward the window, for the double purpose of placing herself beyond the reach of his

10*

hand, and of concealing the rising flush of anger and contempt that glowed upon her countenance. She saw that he treated her as a child—that he imagined such conversation suited to the level of her capacity, and longed to humble his proud self-sufficiency, but dared not under present circumstances. For the first time in her life, she found herself compelled to disguise her natural feelings, and suppress the bitter words which rose upon her tongue. She therefore, by way of changing the conversation, and knowing not what else to say, inquired, "How soon does your army expect to return?"

"Soon, my dear coz, very soon. In ten days at farthest, I hope to lay some of the trophies of victory at your feet, and twine you a bridal turban from the standard of the rebel chief." Again she was forced to turn her head away. And the harmony of their meeting, constrained and unnatural as it was, would probably very soon have been ruptured by the almost bursting indignation which agitated her bosom, had not the martial summons to the evening parade called her tormentor from her presence.

By dawn of day, on the morning after the interview just related, the army under the command of Sir William Berkley took up its line of march toward the falls of the Powhatan.

Virginia was a sad and silent spectator of the imposing pageant. She stood at her window facing one of the cross streets, through which their march was directed, and examined the devices of banner after banner, as they moved along in martial pomp, to the soul-inspiring music of the drums and trumpets. No sympathizing emotions or half embodied supplications to the Ruler of Nations for the safety of their persons or the success of their arms burst from her lips. She saw the proud and self-satisfied Beverly curvetting by on his equally proud steed; she even saw him gayly wave his towering plumes in recognition of her presence without an answering nod or a single indication of approval. Her heart and hopes followed the standard of the youthful Captain who commanded the force which these were summoned to scatter and destroy. Long after the last ensign had passed from her sight, and the music was heard only in faint and distant echoes as it swelled and died away upon the air, she stood in the same spot, her eyes apparently still occupied with passing objects. It was not so—she was endeavouring to look into futurity. She pictured in her imagination the army of the Cavaliers, under Bacon, struggling in the murderous ambuscade of the concentrated savage tribes in front, and mercilessly cut down by their own countrymen in the rear. She saw the stern and uncompromising Sir William and his veteran compeers, brandishing their sabres over the heads of the younger Cavaliers, and Beverly and Bacon engaged in the deadly contest of personal rivalry and political hatred. Notwithstanding the disadvantages of the latter's position, youthful hopes and a sanguine temperament, awarded the victory to the cause which she believed the just one. She had already, as by miracle, escaped a fate which she considered far more to be deplored than death, and resolved to trust her own cause, and that in which it was involved, to him who rules the destinies of battles. She remembered, with feelings of adoration, that he had said that the race was not always to the swift nor the battle to the strong.

CHAPTER VII.

The army under the command of General Bacon had succeeded in concentrating the confederated tribes of the Peninsula, which had so long annoyed its flank and rear, at the falls of the Powhatan. Here they had erected a rude fortification, composed of fallen trees, having an entrenchment surrounding it, with the excavated earth thrown up as an embankment. This was situated upon an eminence commanding the more even ground on each side of a small stream, which ran nearly at right angles with, and fell into the river below the falls. The army of the Colonists arrived within sight of the Indian fires, just after the sun had sunk behind the horizon. General Bacon's plantation* was situated but a short distance from the very spot on which the savages had erected their fort, and consequently he was well acquainted with the ground. After halting a short time to examine the position of the enemy, he marched his troops to the open plain beneath their strong hold, in perfect silence. Here they bivouacked for the night, with the intention of storming the intrenchments at the first dawning of the morrow. Every thing was noiselessly put

* Historical.

in readiness for this final struggle for supremacy between the whites and the Aborigines. The latter had collected in overwhelming numbers, and seemed determined to make a desperate effort to regain their lost footing in the land of their fathers, while the former, having daily improved in discipline, were in high health, buoyant with the youthful hope and courage, and impatient for the dawn, that they might strike a blow at once, to answer the high expectations of their friends at home, and terminate the war. Little did they imagine that an army of those very countrymen was treading in their footsteps, under the command of Sir William Berkley, with the avowed purpose of meting to them that chastisement which they were so impatient to bestow upon the enemy before them.

Their commander was not long left in ignorance upon this point, however, for scarcely had the columns made their arrangements for the night along each side of the small stream, before a courier from the capital was brought into his quarters, by one of the sentinels stationed upon the outskirts of the encampment. He was the bearer of a proclamation, signed by Sir William Berkley as Governor of his Majesty's Colony in Virginia, in which Bacon and his followers were denounced as traitors and rebels, and commanded forthwith to lay down their arms and return to their allegiance, under pain of death, and confiscation of their property. The surprise and indignation occasioned by this singular document had not subsided, when another messenger was dragged into the presence of the commander in chief. It was a negro, trembling from head to foot with visible terror at the very uncivil treatment which he had received, and more, perhaps, at the warlike preparations around, and the glaring effects of the Indian fires on the hill. All attempts to gain an intelligible account of his mission proved for a length of time, utterly unavailing, until Bacon, recognising something of old acquaintance in his features, dismissed his attendants. He then quickly disclosed, in his mongrel dialect, that he had been ordered to deliver a letter into the general's own hands, and when no person was present. A greasy and rumpled document was then drawn from his pouch, which, notwithstanding its hard treatment, and discoloured exterior, Bacon instantly recognised as the writing of Harriet Harrison. The date was rather more remote than seemed necessary for its regular transmission to its present destination, which the sable messenger explained by stating that he had been some days dodging in the footsteps of the army, but that as often as he approached it he had been frightened back again by the flying hordes of savages, hanging upon their skirts. If Bacon felt disposed to indulge in merriment at the ludicrous detail of poor Pompey, the contents of the note, which he now began to decipher by the light of a lamp, speedily restored his gravity. Harriet briefly related to him the nature of the conversation she had held with Sir William Berkley at his own house, and the treatment which Virginia suffered at his hands; she concluded by stating the preparations then making in Jamestown by the Governor and his party, to pursue and capture, or cut them to pieces. This information was truly startling to the youthful general; that concerning Virginia was most moving; but the imminent peril of those gallant spirits entrusted to his command required his immediate attention. He despatched a chosen mounted band on the instant, to scout along the late route of his army, far enough to ascertain whether that under the command of Sir William was within such a distance, as to enable him to interrupt the contemplated attack upon the savages at the dawning of the coming day.

Bacon's character was eminently prompt and decisive. He determined, should such be the case, to commence the attack upon the instant he should receive such information.

Having provided for the safety and accommodation of Pompey, and ordered the courier of the Governor into close but respectful keeping, he sallied out along the outposts, to examine the scene of future operations. The stars twinkled brilliantly in the heavens around the horizon, but the glaring light of the savage fires upon the hill threw the mellowed rays of the heavenly orbs into dim contrast immediately round the two camps. As he walked along the margin of the little stream, upon the borders of which his own troops were stationed, toward the river, the night-scene presented to his view was reviving and exciting to his imagination. The ascending columns of fire upon the hill reflected the trees and other objects upon its brow in gigantic shadows over the plain beneath. The bright red light fell upon the broad sheet of water below the falls, in long horizontal rays, stretching far away over its shining surface toward the opposite shore. The island in the middle of the stream, a little higher up than the point at which he stood, was clothed in verdant impenetrable shrubbery—the darkness gathered around its shores more palpable from the contrast of the neighbouring fires. The roar of the falls fell monotonously upon his ear, ever and anon interrupted by the sharp shrill whoop of some overjoyous savage, engaged in orgies within the fort surmounting the hill. As he pensively stood upon the banks of the Powhatan, and surveyed the illuminated scene immediately around, and the darker shadows of the hills stretching away in the distance and skirting the margin of the river, the shining waves beneath his feet, and the dusky outlines of the rocks and islands beyond, it little entered his imagination that upon that romantic spot, in future time, there should spring up a noble city—the capital of an empire state—that the natural lawns upon which he stood, would be exchanged for docks and quays—that the hills on his right hand (which to a scholar might, even then, have recalled the Acropolis) should support classic colonnades, and spires pointing to the clouds; and that the diminutive stream upon the banks of which his troops were bivouacked, should receive, from the sanguinary battle in which he was about to engage, a name to outlive the very monuments of his generation.* Without these deeply interesting associations, however, the scene in its natural and unreclaimed features was eminently captivating and romantic. No site in the country abounded more with bold and enchanting objects. On the one hand were the picturesque hills,† commanding a prospect seldom equalled, never surpassed, of landscape varied with woodland, dell and meadow, through which the shining waters of the Powhatan were now visible, glowing like a sheet of fire, and now lost in the shadows of the towering forests, as it held its devious course beyond the reach of the reflected fires in the back ground.

Our hero might have stood gazing upon this enchanting scene until the sound of the reveillé in the morning had roused him from his revery, had not his quick eye caught a glimpse of moving lights within the Indian encampment. With hurried steps he retraced his way through the line of sentinels, and issued immediate orders for his subordinates in command to assemble in military council. He was satisfied in his own mind, as he walked up the stream, that some unusual occurrence

* The little rivulet skirting the south eastern end of Richmond is called "Bloody Run" to this day.

† On one of these the present capital of Virginia stands.

had taken place within the palisade of the Indians —perhaps the presence of his own stationary columns, as they stood in their dark frowning outlines, had been discovered by the ever cunning and watchful enemy. He had more than once stood in wonder at the apparent absence of their usual stratagems and devices. He supposed, however, that, trusting to their immense superiority of numbers, and the protection of their breastworks, they had resolved to risk an engagement, in which courage and strength alone should be the implements of victory.

The council of war had scarcely assembled, before they were astounded with the report of musketry in answer to the usual accompaniments of a savage sortie, in the most remote direction of the camp. General Bacon issued his orders promptly and decisively. The columns whose rear had been surprised by a sortie from the enemy, were, by a prompt movement, instantly wheeled into line, changing their front so as to face the assailants, while the mounted Cavaliers, under the command of young Harrison, fiercely attacked them in flank. The desperate band of warriors were speedily driven within their breastworks. It was doubtless only their intention to harass the outskirts of the army, and then, by retreating, draw their pursuers within reach of the ambuscade stationed behind the breastwork. They were pursued by the mounted troops, who had no sooner driven them within the palisade, than they in their turn suddenly wheeled and retreated upon the main body.

These sallies were kept up through the first watches of the night, with so much perseverance on the part of the enemy, and so much annoyance to the ardent and impatient troops of the patriot army, that General Bacon determined to give way to their martial ardour, and at once storm the strong hold of the enemy.

The plan of battle in this straight-forward mode of warfare was simple in the extreme. Seldom had the Aborigines given their white enemies a chance of testing the relative valour of the two races; and protected as they were even now by a formidable breastwork, General Bacon did not hesitate as to the propriety of trusting to the discipline and skill of his soldiers, and the immense superiority of their arms, against the greater numbers and defensive preparations of the enemy.

The fires within the palisade were apparently flickering upon their dying embers, and an unsteady flash, gleaming at intervals, was the only light shed over the contemplated battle-ground. A profound quiet reigned within the camp of the enemy, indicative to the mind of Bacon of some new treachery or savage scheme. Having warned his officers against these, he despatched mounted scouting parties to hover round both camps, and took every other human precaution against surprise ; orders were now issued preparatory to a general attack upon the enemy's entrenchments.

By a prompt evolution, his battalions of foot were wheeled into a solid column of attack on the northern side of the stream, while the mounted Cavaliers were stationed as a reserve on the right. The former were marched in compact order, directly up the face of the hill, not a trumpet or a drum disturbing the silence of the funeral-like procession. The various colours of their plumes, as they waved in the night breeze, and the occasional glitter of burnished arms, as a flash of light fell athwart the solid phalanx from the flickering fires above, presented one of the most striking scenes imaginable.

General Bacon assumed the immediate command of his columns in person. He sat upon his impatient charger on the right wing, and examined the ominous appearance of the enemy's camp with intense interest. Not a warrior's head was to be seen above the breastwork as they approached. All was silent, gloomy, and portentous; not a sound was heard, save the measured tramp of his own troops, as they moved through the bushes.

Once indeed he thought he heard the wild shrill scream of a female, very different in its intonations from the harsh voice of the savage squaw. But so many unearthly sights and sounds had haunted both his sleeping and waking hours of late, that he drove the impression from his mind, to rest with hundreds of others of like import.

When the front lines had arrived within some forty yards of the dark and frowning breastwork, a sudden and momentary check was given to their farther progress. A rushing sound, as of the flight of many birds, and the clatter of Indian arrows against their arms and persons, simultaneously struck upon their senses, followed by the fall of many soldiers, and the short involuntary exclamations of pain, which, from the impulse of the moment, escaped the unfortunate individuals.

Trumpets and drums instantaneously broke the stillness of the march. Their martial notes reverberated over the surrounding solitudes in enlivening peals. The ill-omened birds of night flapped their wings, and swooped through the unsteady lights of the scene in utter dismay at this untimely invasion of their prescriptive dominions. These were quickly followed by a discharge of musketry, poured into the formidable palisade. It was scarcely discharged, however, before Bacon discovered the utter uselessness of such a waste of ammunition. He saw that the breastwork was so constructed, that, while it admitted of the discharge of missiles from within, it afforded a secure protection to its occupants against the musketry of their assailants. In the mean time his soldiers were exposed to the murderous discharges of poisoned arrows.

In this emergency no time was to be lost; placing himself, therefore, at the head of his troops, he ordered the walls to be torn down. These, as before related, were composed of large trees piled one upon another, with their green boughs still protruding in many places over the shallow intrenchment, and the earth excavated from the latter thrown up on the outside agaist a rude wicker-work of fine bushes, filling up the interstices of the trees. Trumpets sounded the charge, and the columns moved at a quick pace to the onset. Still not a savage head was seen until they had arrived at the very borders of the intrenchment. Here some two hundred of the stoutest and ablest bodied of his soldiers were marched up to the projecting limbs of the largest tree, forming the basis of the breastwork. Bacon saw at a glance that if he could manage to seize hold of these projecting arms and turn the tree across the fosse, it would at once open the way for his mounted troops, and perhaps carry with it some forty or fifty feet of the palisade, and thereby bring the opposing armies face to face. They had already seized the projecting limbs, and were shaking the frail protection of the savages to its very foundations, when simultaneously a thousand lights gleamed over forest, hill, and dale— A thousand voices united their shrill clamours in one deafening yell of savage ferocity. The troops engaged in tearing down the breastwork instinctively loosed their hold, and flew to their arms, as they threw their eyes upward to the spot whence these blinding lights and deafening noises came. It was but the work of an instant, for little more time were they permitted to examine,—they were called upon to act, and that vigorously, for their own preservation. In a single instant, and apparently at a given signal, the whole of the rude terrace surmounting the fortification literally swarmed with painted warriors, each bearing in his left hand a pine torch, and in the other, a tomahawk, a war-club, or a battle-axe.* They sprang from their commanding position into the midst of their assailants, and scattered themselves in every direction through that part of the army already advanced to the breastwork.

Human ingenuity could not have devised a mode of warfare better calculated to suit their numbers, position, time, courage, and limited means of resistance. It at once rendered the mounted troops useless—prevented the colonists from using their fire-arms, because those immediately engaged were at too close quarters, while those at a greater distance were as likely to kill friends as enemies. The savages dealt their murderous blows with wonderous rapidity and precision, and though the hardy planters in the front ranks turned upon them with the butt ends of their muskets, the savages had evidently the advantage. The blazing fagots were often thrust into the very faces of their opponents, and while

* These were made of stones ground into the shape of our axe, with a groove round the centre for a handle made of withe.

writhing under the confusion and agony of the fire and smoke, they were stricken down like helpless beasts.

Bacon saw the imminent peril of his troops, and though he was at first astounded by the rapidity and daring courage with which the plan was executed, he did not despair, nor yet sit listlessly upon his horse to see his friends and countrymen slaughtered. He saw at a glance too that only the front columns were engaged—that a part of these must now necessarily fall, but he determined at the same time, that their deaths should be dearly avenged, and his remaining troops brought off victorious. He immediately placed himself between the forces already engaged and those rushing to the rescue. The latter he wheeled into line immediately in front of his mounted reserve, thereby changing their front to the flank of the contending parties, while their own right wing rested upon the top of the hill, and the left on the little stream already mentioned. Having completed this evolution to his satisfaction, the mounted Cavaliers were brought round to the position just occupied by the foot, so that they immediately faced the struggling combatants, and the latter were ordered to give way. The retreat was sounded from the brazen mouths of the trumpets over their heads, and Bacon in person and his mounted aids, rode furiously and recklessly among them, crying for them to fall back toward the line stationed on the right.

These various movements were but the work of a few moments. Meantime the painted and ghastly warriors, rendered still more horrible by the flaring lights which they bore in their hands, and by the reeking instruments of death which they swung over their head with such unerring precision, were pouring over the walls upon the devoted band in countless hordes. So intently were they engaged, that the evolutions of their enemies had entirely escaped their attention; and indeed the Colonists themselves, who were fighting hand to hand with the savages, had not observed the movement, until the voices of their commanders urged them to fall back upon the newly formed line. As Bacon had calculated, no sooner were the engaged troops made to understand the orders, and induced to recede, than a partial separation was effected, which was fatal to the Aboriginals. The retreating Colonists were almost immediately under the protection of the line already braced in solid column, and standing to the charge* ready for the expected pursuers. A company of the mounted Cavaliers was broken up into squads, and these were actively engaged in hewing down the pursuers, or cutting off their retreat to the protection of the fort. In a short time a complete line of separation was formed between the two armies, save where, here and there, two athletic men of the op-

* The bayonet was just then coming into use, but was inserted into a round piece of wood, which was thrust into the muzzle of the musket.

posite races, both having lost their arms in the contest, struggled in the death gripe. Here an iron handed mechanist of the city clenched a warrior's throat—the eyes of the victim protruding frightfully from his head in the glaring light, and his tongue hanging from his mouth like that of a rabid animal, until he fell as a lump of clay among the hundreds of both parties who had gone before. There a grim warrior struggled with another, making desperate efforts to reach his knife, which the soldier as constantly struggled to prevent. Yonder among the heaps of slain, lay two of the differing races, fallen to the earth in a mutual but deadly clasp, each holding the other by the throat, until the struggle became one of mere endurance, and, strange to say, the white man generally conquered.

While, however, these desperate personal struggles were occurring, the tide of battle was fast turning against the most numerous party. It was with the greatest difficulty that Bacon could restrain the ardour and impetuosity of the troops stationed in line for the protection of the devoted corps which had led the van, the straggling members of which were momentarily retreating behind the solid bulwark of their countrymen's pikes and bayonets. But no sooner was this duty of humanity performed, and a complete line of demarcation distinctly drawn, than all restraints were removed. A volley of musketry was poured among the scattering savages along the face of the hill, in order to convince them that hereafter they would be kept at a respectful distance. A simultaneous movement of horse and foot now swept the brow of the hill; the horse charged immediately in front of the palisade, while the infantry drove in the extended line of savages at the point of the bayonet. The most inextricable confusion ensued in the ranks of the red warriors. While the cavalry cut them down on one hand, and the bayonets of the infantry transfixed them on the other, hundreds were tumbling over hundreds as they tumultuously leaped over the palisade. Some hung by the projecting bushes—others fell upon the terrace, and were cast down and trodden under foot by their companions; while multitudes were cut to pieces in making the attempt. In a short time the open field was left in complete possession of the whites—the brow of the hill was literally covered with the wounded and the slain, both of white and red. Yet the battle was not ended; hundreds upon hundreds had escaped within the fort. The savage force amounted at the commencement to something like three thousand warriors of various tribes, and that of the Colonists to about one thousand.* Bacon earnestly desired to spare the effusion of human blood, and hazardous as the Indians were as neighbours, either professing friendship or enmity, he resolved to send them a flag of truce and propose a permanent peace upon condition of their

* Burke says 600.

abandoning the Peninsula for ever. He knew that they understood the sacred rights and privileges of that peaceful banner, for it had already been recognised among some of their own tribes. Accordingly a young and promising officer was thrust up to the top of the palisade. He waved his flag and laid his hand upon his heart in token of friendship, and grounded his sword in order to convince them that he came upon a peaceful errand, but instead of sending out their interpreter or prophet, he was treacherously murdered by a tomahawk—thrown some twenty yards by the hand of a warrior, and buried in his brain. All hopes of peace were now abandoned, and Bacon determined to complete the victory which he had commenced, and won thus far at the expense of so many valued lives.

Orders were again issued for tearing down the palisade, while a chosen band of prompt and expert marksmen were stationed at the distance of some thirty yards, to shoot down the savages as they should show their heads above the breastwork Instead of the infantry being stationed to protect the miners as before, the cavalry formed a column flanking the marksmen, so that they could at a moment's warning, rush in between the descending hordes and the corps engaged in pulling down the barricade.

Again the trees composing the palisade were seized by the projecting limbs, and a sudden wrench brought the earth piled against its outer side tumbling into the ditch beneath, and shook the whole fabric to its foundation. Again an ominous and inexplicable silence prevailed within the enclosure, which was the more remarkable, as there was left no known method of escape, and by their own treachery to the officer who had borne the flag of truce, they were reduced to the alternative of dying in their ditches or desperately cutting their way through the solid phalanx which enclosed them on every side. Hitherto the marksmen stationed in front for the purpose of clearing the terrace of the savages, as they should mount the breastwork from the inside, had little to do. At length a group of savages displayed their painted faces above the barrier, apparently endeavouring to drag some unwieldy burden to the top of the works. They were instantly shot down, but their places were as speedily supplied by others. A faint but piercing shriek rent the air, which promptly arrested the attention of Bacon, Dudley, and young Harrison, who sat upon their horses superintending the operations of the miners, and holding an occasional discourse among themselves. The voice came evidently from a female, and reminded Bacon that he had once before during the night heard a like sound from the same direction. He waved his sword to the marksmen stationed on his left, to withhold their fire, while his own attention and that of his two associates were intently rivetted to the occupation of the group ascending the wall from the other side. At this moment the large tree which the troops in front had been some time shaking loose, came crashing over upon its limbs, and bringing with it those which had been piled above, thus exposing to view the interior of the fort, but not yet affording an uninterrupted passage for the besiegers. The battalions of foot, however, were tumultuously rushing toward the breach, reckless of the interposing branches and trunks of the prostrate trees, when Bacon, in a voice of thunder commanded them to halt! The very moment the fort gave way a sight was revealed to his eyes, and those of his two comrades, which made the hair rise on end upon their heads, and the blood in their veins run cold with horror. The Indians, who had so long struggled to ascend the fort some twenty or thirty yards from the breach, had at length succeeded, bearing one of the objects which so powerfully arrested the attention of the officers on horseback. Two grim warriors supported between them the body of a woman of the European race, while a third stood behind her, on the top of the palisade with uplifted tomahawk. With one hand he held the weapon suspended over the head of the drooping victim, while with the other, he pointed to the neighbouring breach in the breastwork, with a look and gesture that seemed to say, "advance, and her fate is sealed!" Although the light from the smouldering fires was dim and unsteady, enough was caught of the outlines of this figure to thrill to the very heart-strings of the three spectators; she was upheld on either side by the mere strength of her guards—her feet seemed to have sunk from under her—but her head was erect and turning with wonderful rapidity from side to side, as she gazed with wild and glaring eyes upon the scene around her. Her fair silken tresses fell unrestrained upon her shoulders or were blown about in fluttering streams, as the unsteady light fell now in broad masses, and then in dim and shadowy rays. Her dress was white, and fell in ample folds around all that was left of a once symmetrical figure. Her features were ashy pale and attenuated to the last degree of human wretchedness, her eye shot forth the wild flashes of a frenzied mind. She was entirely unconscious of her danger, and though she seemed to examine the wild scene around, it was not with fear and trembling. A sickly smile played upon her death-like features, as if she rather took pleasure than suffered pain in these unusual sights, or saw embodied before her in palpable form somewhat of the fleeting phantasmagoria which had so long eluded her senses, yet she was speechless—and so were the late combatants.

A profound and solemn silence prevailed throughout the ranks of both parties. The fate of battle, or the life of an individual, was suspended upon the results of the moment. It was soon interrupted, wildly, fearfully interrupted! The threatened victim burst into a convulsion of frantic laughter, the wild unguided tones of a voice once rich and musical, were borne along the still night air, and resounded through the dark forest like some unearthly mockery of human merriment. As if a thunderbolt from heaven had instantaneously stricken her dumb she ceased. The sounds of her own voice startled and astonished her; perhaps some dim rememberance of its former tones, as it rose and fell upon the air, floated darkly through her mind. The grim old warriors who supported her, were impressed with awe and fear, and the very executioner was almost overcome with his native superstitious reverence. The events we have just described occupied but a few moments of time,—far less than we have taken to describe them. At this juncture, and while the three stern Indians maintained their posts, Wyanokee sprang upon the terrace, struck the tomahawk from the hands of the ready executioner—pushed him backward over the palisade, and threw herself recklessly upon the unfortunate lady, encircling her with her arms. At the same instant her two astounded countrymen fell lifeless from the terrace, pierced to the heart by the unerring balls of the sharp shooters.

The Colonial army now broke tumultuously into the fort. Here another threatened victim had been held as a suspended pledge over their fires, for the safety of this their last strong hold, but so intense had been the interest excited in behalf of the unfortunate Mrs. Fairfax, that little attention was bestowed upon him. It was none other than

Brian O'Reily. When the breach was made in the fort, he was discovered in the centre of the area, tied fast to a stake driven into the ground. A quantity of resinous pine wood was built high up around his body, and half a dozen torch-bearers stood ready to apply the flame. The report of the muskets had no sooner announced the death of their comrades on the wall, than this pile was fired in a a hundred places. Already the victim began to writhe as the intolerable heat scorched his flesh, and the smoke rushed into his eyes and throat. As the soldiers entered through the breach with Dudley, who had dismounted, at their head, he rushed toward the suffering victim, and, assisted by his followers, hurled the burning brands upon the heads of those who kindled them.

Meanwhile Bacon had also dismounted. He saw that the contest would now be short, and giving his orders to Dudley, he leaped upon the palisade where Wyanokee was vainly endeavouring to support and restrain his former patroness, who had repeatedly and fruitlessly endeavoured to stand erect, and as often had fallen back into the arms of the Indian maiden. As Bacon approached, his whole soul agitated with deep and thrilling emotions, she was sitting upon the wall, forcing herself farther and farther back, like a frighted infant, into the arms of her protectress. Her eyes stared wildly upon the approaching youth, and the lids fell not over the painfully distended orbs. She did not recognise him, even when he approached within a few paces and kindly and soothingly addressed her. At one moment she seemed about to make some reply, but the half formed words died upon her lips—they moved as though she held the desired discourse, but no sound was audible. The wild noise and confusion of the onset, breaking upon her ears, she started up and cried "Hah! see you not that the king's troops put those of the commonwealth to the sword? Behold his giant form weltering in gore! 'Tis gone! It was not he! No, no; I saw not the bloody hand. It was merely one of these puppet warriors dressed out to frighten babes. He lives! did he not tell me so, with his own lips? Do the dead tell the living lies? That were a trick of the devil indeed." Again she burst into a horrible and appalling laugh, fell back into the arms of Wyanokee, and her mortal pains and sorrows were for ever ended.

The long-disputed contest was now drawing to a close; the Indians fought desperately, as long as there was a hope left of repulsing the troops which rushed in at the breach, burning with ardour and roused to indignation by their wanton cruelties; but the superior arms and skill of the Colonists rendered the contest in a short time utterly desperate on the part of the besieged. When farther resistance was put out of their power, by the besiegers closing in upon them on every side, and thus confining their exertions within a narrow space in the centre of the fort, the stern warriors threw away their tomahawks and war-clubs, and fell prostrate on their faces. It was a moving sight to behold these hardy veterans of a hundred battles, gradually encompassed by a more skilful and powerful enemy, until they were forced to surrender this last foothold upon the land of their fathers. Their prostrate attitude was by no means intended to express an abject petition for mercy; it was the custom established by their people, and its impulse was utter desperation. They neither desired nor expected quarter, but threw themselves upon the earth, to signify their willingness to meet the tortures of their enemies. When placed under the vigilance of the troops appointed to guard them until dawn, they sat like statues, not a muscle or feature expressing emotion of any kind.

Bacon stood over the body of his late kind and unfortunate patroness, as still and motionless as his own prisoners, contemplating the sad change which a few short days had made upon her mild and benignant features, until reminded by Dudley that he had other duties to perform. The latter approached and informed him that the garrison had surrendered. He heeded him not. He repeated his information, and touched the general upon the shoulder. Bacon started wildly for an instant, but seeing who spoke, a meaningless smile flitted across his features while he answered, "True, true, Dudley, I will attend you in a moment;" and was about to relapse into his former mood, but rousing himself, he issued orders for pitching his own marquée, and then directed that the dead body of Mrs. Fairfax should be borne thither and deposited under its shelter with all due respect. Till now, Wyanokee had sat near the cold and lifeless form. Not a tear was shed nor any other indication given that she had lost a friend, esteemed by her one of the first of the earth. There was, perhaps, just a perceptible expression of wildness and mystery in her steady and abstracted gaze on vacancy, as if in thought she was following the departed spirit to the verdant forests and blossoming meadows of the happy hunting-ground beyond the sky. It is true that she had been somewhat instructed in the doctrines of our religion, but he has made little progress in the study of mankind who does not know that the peculiar opinions—the forms of worship, whether of superstition or religion, which have been infused into the mind in the tender years of infancy, will ever after give a tinge to the views of the recipient. But Wyanokee had by no means renounced the doctrines of her father's worship, and however much her mind may have been worked upon while under the influence of the whites, and of the imposing form and ceremonies of the Established Church, since her abjuration of their friendship, she had imperceptibly lapsed into most of her aboriginal notions.

When the body of Mrs. Fairfax was laid out under the marquée of the commander in chief, and a line of sentinels was established around its limits,

Wyanokee was the sole living tenant of the apartment. She sat by the corpse, in precisely the same state which we have before described.

In a very short time from that in which Dudley announced the termination of the conflict to his commanding officer, profound quietness reigned over the fort and brow of the hill, so lately the scene of bloodshed and strife, save where it was disturbed by the movements of those engaged in burying the dead, and rescuing the wounded who lay suffering under the weight of their dead comrades.

Never had such a battle been fought in Virginia, either as regarded the number of Indians engaged, the consequences depending on the result, or the sanguinary nature of the conflict itself. It was the last struggle for supremacy between the whites and the Indians in the Peninsula.

CHAPTER VIII.

General Bacon apprehending that the rising sun might disclose to view the approaching columns of the army under Sir William Berkley, had ordered the dismantled fort to be refitted in such a manner as to afford some protection to his exhausted troops. The trees were again brought round to their former position, and the limbs by which themselves had gained entrance lopped off. The sun, however, rose above the horizon without betraying any sign, either of the expected army, or of the mounted scouts whom he had sent out just before the battle. This latter circumstance gave him not a little uneasiness, as he could account for their protracted absence in no other way than by supposing that they had fallen into Sir William's hands.

Most of the troops were yet indulging in repose, after the extraordinary fatigues of the night, and were cheerfully indulged by their officers, in the hope that they would rise with renewed ardour and courage for the expected attack.

At about ten o'clock in the morning, the troops having been roused from their slumbers, and partaken of a hasty breakfast, the sentinel pacing to and fro upon the top of the walls, announced the approach of the expected foe. Bacon and his staff quickly mounted the breastwork to examine the number and appointments of his confident enemy; but to his great joy and relief, the approaching troops proved to be his own missing scouts. He mounted his charger and galloped over the intervening ground in order to learn the cause of their strange absence; so impatient was he, not only on that score, but likewise to learn tidings from his pursuers. He very soon met the advancing horsemen, who, upon perceiving their general, halted in the road. The information communicated by the commander of the party was not less surprising to Bacon than was the account of the battle to the officer, who had been absent from its dangers and its glories. The latter stated, that after having ridden about twenty miles on the previous night, they suddenly came upon the encampment of Sir William's army, but having discovered their fires in sufficient time, had avoided their pickets. They scouted round his camp for a considerable length of time, endeavouring to learn something of his intended movements—the number of his soldiers, and their disposition toward themselves, but found no means of gaining information. At length they narrowly escaped being discovered and intercepted by a foraging party, and having discovered that the troopers composing it, had come last from the house of a planter, living not far from the encampment, they resolved to present themselves before him, candidly explain their business, and throw themselves upon his patriotism for any information which he might possess. They did so, and were fortunate enough to find that the planter was not only able, but willing to give them important information, and was anxious for the success of Bacon's expedition—his own son being engaged in it. The amount of his information in few words, was, that Sir William Berkley had that very evening received an express from Jamestown, urgently summoning him back to the capital, with all his forces. That two influential citizens residing in the counties south of Jamestown, by name Walklate and Ingraham,* having heard of his expedition to cut off the return of General Bacon and his army, had immediately raised a force of horse and foot scarcely inferior to his own, and were marching upon the capital. Nor was this all the unfavourable news communicated by the express: it farther stated that the House of Burgesses, then in session, (contrary to the promise of Sir William to dissolve it,) were engaged upon some resolutions, very injurious to the reputation and farther influence of the Governor, and that they had already approved of the proceedings of General Bacon, and resolved to require the Governor to sign his commission as commander in chief of the colonial forces, besides having transmitted to the

* Historical.

ministry at home, testimonials of his patriotism, talents, and bravery.

The foraging party from the army of Sir William, had farther informed the planter, that it was the intention of his excellency to break up his camp by dawn of day, and return by forced marches, to the protection of the capital.

At this juncture, the Colony of Virginia presented the singular spectacle of three distinct and independent armies, assembled at one time. One at the falls, commanded by Bacon—another in the Peninsula, commanded by Sir William Berkley, and the third in the south, commanded by Generals Ingraham and Walklate. The first and last were nothing more than disciplined assemblages of volunteers from among the people, while that under the command of the Governor in person, was composed in part of veteran regular troops, and partly of loyal subjects, called together by the urgent appeals of him who had so long been the honoured organ of his majesty's authority in the colony.

When General Bacon returned to the camp, and had assembled his associates in command, and communicated to them the foregoing particulars, he also announced to them his intention of leaving the temporary command of the army with his next in rank, and repairing in person immediately to the capital.

His views having met the approbation of the council of officers, the sloop which had brought up the marine part of the expedition was promptly put in readiness, and forty chosen men embarked for his escort.*

His unfortunate valet and devoted adherent, Brian O'Reily, although much enfeebled by long confinement and want of wholesome food, was, at his own earnest request, added to the number. So urgent had been the various claims upon the time of General Bacon, that he had not yet heard Brian's account of his sufferings and privations.

Before embarking he issued the strictest orders for the safety, comfort, and protection of the numerous prisoners, and of Wyanokee in particular. He directed that she should be conveyed in the same wagon, then preparing for the purpose of transporting the remains of Mrs. Fairfax to Jamestown.

Before taking leave of his comrades in arms, he entered the marqueé containing the honoured remains. The sentinel was walking his solitary rounds of monotonous duty, with solemn aspect. Strange that the ceremonies attending the laying out and decently guarding this lifeless body should more powerfully impress this sturdy soldier than all the heaps of slain piled into one common grave during the night.

Bacon entered the marquée alone. There sat the last daughter of the kings of Chickahominy, in precisely the attitude in which he had seen her five hours before. She was the sole mourner at

* Historical.

the feet of her whom in life she had most honoured. He was powerfully affected by the sight of many little personal ornaments, not worn on the previous night, but which had been collected by Wyanokee and placed conspicuously upon the corpse. He was struck, too, with the delicate consideration of the Indian maiden in these native observances in honour of the dead. Conspicuous among the things valued by her friend while living, was a small silver clasped pocket bible; it was spread open upon the neat folds of her white garments, surrounded with a profusion of wild flowers, such as he had often known her to transplant into her own garden.

But time pressed, and urgent circumstances called him to the capital; he therefore lifted the covering (a white handkerchief) from her face, and gazed for the last time upon those features impressed upon his heart and memory from infancy. Almost involuntarily he drew from his doublet the diminutive locket, reassured his heart by a momentary comparison of the features—and then forced himself away and proceeded to the bank of the river, where the sloop already spread her sails to the ready breeze.

The prisoners taken at the battle of the Falls, or of the Bloody Run as it was more frequently called, were placed in the centre of the army, with the exception of Wyanokee, and the fort burnt to the ground, after which the Colonial troops took up their line of march for the capital. Toward this central point three separate armies were now advancing, while the House of Burgesses were passing a series of resolutions in which all three were deeply interested. A more important juncture in the affairs of the Colony had never occurred, and the approach of the various hostile parties toward the capital excited the deepest anxiety in all the reflecting inhabitants of the city.

The courier announcing the successful issue of Bacon's campaign against the tribes of the Peninsula, which had so long disturbed the peace and tranquillity of the planters, was received with general manifestations of joy and expressions of gratitude to the youthful commander of the expedition.

By a resolution of the assembly, the State House was ordered to be illuminated, and the inhabitants generally were requested to follow the example. These, with other voluntary demonstrations of rejoicing on the part of the citizens, were about to be carried into execution, when the vanguard of Sir William Berkley's army, commanded by the sturdy old knight in person, arrived at the gates of the bridge. When he was informed of the cause of this unusual measure, and of the resolutions which had been passed by the House of Burgesses, both in regard to himself and his young rival in the popular favour, he burst into a most ungovernable fit of rage—threw his sword into the river, and swore he would embark for England the next morning. He was no sooner dissuaded from the rash step, than he resolved upon an expedient equally inconsiderate. It was nothing less than to march his army into the streets of the city, and thence, with a chosen band of followers, disperse the assembly at the point of the bayonet. It was with the greatest difficulty, and after long efforts, that his more discreet friends were enabled to dissuade him from this step likewise, nor even then until they had compromised the affair, by agreeing that he should issue a proclamation with the same view, and forthwith issue writs for a new election. Accordingly, having marched his troops into the heart of the city, and encamped them immediately round the State House and public grounds, he carried his threats into execution.

The dissolution of the assembly was immediately proclaimed, and writs were issued for the election of their successors. To such a length had Sir William Berkley carried his high-handed measures, from time to time, since his reaccession to the vice-regal chair, that he imagined the people would submit to any dictation emanating from so high a functionary as himself—that it was only necessary to make his will and pleasure known to the good citizens of Jamestown, at once to put an end to all the demonstrations of joy by which his arrival was so unwelcomely greeted. He was led into this error, partly by his own overweening pride, and partly by the respect which so many years of unclouded prosperity in the same station had naturally engendered in the people. And doubtless they would have endured much, and did submit to many oppressions, rather than resist the authority of one who had so long held the reins of government. But the true secret of the change in the character of that government, was in the erroneous views conceived by the captious old knight, during the government of the commonwealth. He had fallen with his first Royal master and risen with the second—and thus had come into power the second time, with all the extravagant notions of prerogative entertained by his transatlantic prototype, without having derived any wholesome lessons of experience from the fate of his first unfortunate master.

The people heard the proclamation dissolving the assembly, with murmurs indeed at the spirit and motive in which it originated, but without feelings of opposition to the measure, because it was one which they had themselves demanded before his departure. They therefore moodily acquiesced, and even submitted to be bearded by the foreign mercenaries in their streets and public walks, but when the Governor, emboldened by this apparent tameness undertook to issue another document, proclaiming Bacon, Dudley, Harrison, Walklate, Ingraham, and their followers, rebels, the people could submit no longer. The muttered thunders of popular discontent burst out into all the fury of a storm. His officers were forcibly prevented from reading his proclamations in the streets, and public places—a general meeting of the citizens voluntarily assembled at the State House, surrounded as it was by his soldiers, and there passed resolutions, condemning his recent conduct, in the most unmeasured terms. They also appointed a large committee to wait on him forthwith, and not only demand the suppression of the last proclamation, but that he should sign the commissions, already prepared by the assembly for the very persons so denounced. After making these demands of the infatuated old man, they farther informed him that two expresses were already mounted—one to be despatched to the army under Bacon, and the other to that headed by Ingraham and Walklate, both of which were probably within a short distance of the city. That besides these preparations for any extreme measures to which he might think proper to resort, the citizens generally were arming themselves, and even that many members of the late House of Burgesses, which he had just dissolved, were taking up arms, and held themselves in readiness to assist in disarming and expelling the mercenaries under his command. Sir William demanded two hours for deliberation and consultation with his friends. These were soon assembled, and the committee withdrew to await the expiration of the allotted time.

Again the Governor was destined to be mortified. The officers assembled, most of whom had been with him in his recent expedition, stated that the popular spirit of revolt and insubordination, had spread among the soldiery to such an extent that no dependence could be placed upon them in case of a rupture with the citizens. In this emergency he was compelled to listen to the admonitions of the friends, who advised that he should endeavour to turn the popular current in his favour, by signing the commissions, and withdrawing the offensive proclamations. To this he was forced to accede, and accordingly when the committee of the citizens returned he signed the commissions. Scarcely had he dismissed them, however, before he began devising measures to counteract the very purpose of his act. He ordered a representation to be immediately drawn up for ministers, in which the now commissioned officers in question were represented as traitors—directed the most resolute and trust-worthy of his adherents to embark for Accomac, whither he resolved to transfer the seat of Government until the citizens of the capital should be taught that respect for his majesty's representative in which they had shown themselves so deficient within the last few hours; and commanded all the armed ships not engaged in transporting his own troops across the bay,* (and there were many of them in the river,) to cruise up the stream, in order to intercept the sloop conveying General Bacon and his suite to the city, with strict orders to bring him dead or alive to Accomac. Having issued these various orders, and seen them

* See Burke.

put in a regular train of execution, he embarked the same night on board an armed brigantine, with his own family and suite, not forgetting his imprisoned and deeply injured niece.

Meanwhile General Bacon was calmly reclining upon the deck of his little sloop; it was the second night from his embarkation—the moon was shining brightly in the heavens, and the stars sparkled brilliantly through a hazy but not damp atmosphere, and not a breath of air filled the white sails as they flapped idly against the mast. The vessel was drifting slowly toward her place of destination it is true, but not with a velocity in accordance with the ardent desires of the passengers. Every soul on board had retired to rest except himself, Brian O'Reily, and that part of the crew to which belonged the duty of the watch. It was the same night the reader will remember, on which Sir William Berkley arrived at, and afterward so suddenly departed, from the capital.

Brian O'Reily was for the first time explaining to his master the manner in which he came into the hands of the Indians. Bacon had readily surmised the whole process, but knowing that O'Reily must be indulged with the relation at one time or another, and being unable to sleep in his present excited state of mind, he had given the impulse to Brian's garrulity, not inadvertently, however, by the simple question,

"So Brian, you were in pursuit of me when the Powhatans made you a prisoner?"

"Ay, by St. Stephen the martyr, and the

twelve Apostles, barrin one iv them that was a thraitor, I was near bein a martyr myself, only the bloody nagres had a notion to fatten me, and that's the rason they kept me tied on me back all the while, jist as I used to fix the misthress's blind calf, the saints bless her soul."

"Fatten you, Brian, for what?"

"To ate me, to be sure!"

"Pshaw, O'Reily, they are not cannibals."

"Oh the divil burn my eyes, but I saw thim roastin babies by the fire, and ating them like pathriges, widout so much as salt to season them!"

"You just now told me you were tied in a dark hole, and fed on parched corn, all the time you were a prisoner."

"Divil a word iv a lie's in that, any way, your honour, and sure enough I did'nt jist see thim kooking the young ones, but didn't I smell thim roastin? Sure and Brian O'Reily wouldn't be after being decaived in the smell of a pig for a sucking baby. Didn't the divil tempt me wid that same smell any way? may be he didn't? Wasn't I starvin myself upon short allowance iv their murtherin popped corn, and didn't the bloody nagers roast a baby jist whin me unconscionable bowels came up into my throat every day, begging for muttin and turnips? and didn't they want to fatten me like the misthress's blind calf—me bowels I mane? and didn't I put thim aff wid a half score o' parched corns? Oh! if they had only been stilled into whiskey, may be it wouldn't iv cured the smotherin I had about the heart."

"I suppose, Brian, you were never sober for such a length of time together in your life before."

"Oh! be our Lady you may say that—there was jist nothing to ate, and the same to dhrink, barrin the parched corn, and the babies, and may be, an oldher sinner for Sundays, by way of a feast."

"You travelled on foot, I suppose, from place to place, until they concentrated at the falls!"

"Divil a foot iv mine touched the ghround, since they pulled me off my horse at yon town of theirs over the river. I rode on a horse ivery foot iv the way, your haner, and had one iv the nagers to attind me; may be he did'nt ride behint me on the same baste, and put his arms around me like a butcher taking a fat wether to the shambles."

"You were in right good case too, when you fell into the hands of this singular butcher, that deals in human flesh, according to your account?"

"Ay was I, but I lost it asier than I got it—by the five crasses, but the sweat run down to me shoes every time I looked round at the painted divil sittin on the same baste wid me—his nose ornamented wid a lead ring like a wild steer. Sure I thought the ghreat inimy was flyin away wid me, before I was dacently buried."

"What did he say to you, Brian?"

"Say to me, your haner! By the holy father, but he addressed none iv his discourse to me. Maybe he was talkin to the divil that was in him as big as a sheep—didn't he grunt it all away down in his pipes like a pig in a passion? Or may be he was talkin to the horse, for he grunted too, and one iv thim jist discoursed as well as the t'other, to my mind."

"Could you not tell upon what subject he spoke, from his gestures or signs.—Did he not point to Jamestown frequently?"

"Not he—he pointed to the colour iv me hair, more belikes, and when they gat to yon place where your haner put so many iv thim to slape, they all gathered round me to see it. They had their own crowns painted the same colour, and they wonthered at the beauty iv mine, and faith, that was the most rasonable thing I saw among thim, barrin that they brought me the paint-pot, and wanted me to figure off one iv their beautiful gourds like Brian O'Reily's. I towld thim it was a thing out iv all rason, and pulled out some iv the hair to show thim, and divil burn the bloody thaives, but they cut it all aff jist for keepsakes among thim."

"They left you a top-knot, I see, however."

Before O'Reily could make a reply, the sailor on the watch cried out that there was a large ship bearing down upon them. Bacon sprung upon his feet, ordered Brian to alarm the soldiers, and walked hastily forward. At the first glance, he saw a crowd of warlike heads, and caught the reflection of the light upon their arms. A second look at the strange movements of the vessel, and the hostile preparations of those on board served to convince him that he was himself the object of their pursuit. Taking two of the first soldiers who made their appearance on deck, he silently entered the boat swinging from the tafferel of the sloop, motioned the two soldiers to follow him, and then ordered the boat to be let down with all silence and despatch. O'Reily seeing these preparations as he came on deck from the performance of his orders, sprung into the boat as one end struck the water; it was too late, and the circumstances too urgent for his master to order him back—the frail bark was pushed off, therefore, with muffled oars, and as much within the shadow of the approaching vessels as their destined course would permit. Scarcely were they without the protection of these, before they discovered the yawl of the ship full of armed men, rapidly gliding into the water, and in the next moment, they heard musket balls whistling over their heads, accompanied by the momentary gleam and then the quick report of firearms. Seizing an oar himself, and ordering Brian to follow his example, they pulled with all their strength for the shore; this once gained, he hoped that the protection of the forest and the increasing haziness of the atmosphere settling upon the high banks of the river, would effectually protect his retreat. But in spite of their utmost efforts, the superior power with which the yawl was propelled through the water was rapidly shortening the distance between them. Brian threw off his jerkin, and strenuously exhorted his master to trust himself to the mercy of the waves, though he knew not the nature of the threatened danger. On this point, Bacon himself could only conjecture, that it was some device of his old enemy to get him secretly into his power, and hence his anxiety to reach Jamestown at the present juncture. He knew nothing of the change which had taken place at the capital in his favour, but he knew his own power over the populace, and he preferred being made prisoner in public, to trusting himself to the tender mercies of Sir William Berkley. In spite of all his exertions, and the hopes of reward held out to the soldiers in case of success, their boat was cut off from the shore by the pursuers interposing between it and themselves. He saw that resistance would be madness, as the boat now wheeling exactly in front of them contained five times their number, and would doubtless, in case of a struggle, be promptly sustained by assistance from the ship, which was now nearer to them than their own vessel. His only course, therefore, was to submit with as much philosophy as he could muster. He was deeply mortified and chagrined however, for his presence seemed to him to be most urgently called for at the capital. These views were founded upon the information he had received, now two days old. Could he have known what had taken place at Jamestown only a few hours before, and only a few miles distant from his present position; could he have known that Sir William Berkley was at that very moment an adventurer upon the same waters, but a few miles below, and driven thence by the firmness of the patriotic citizens who belonged to his own party, he would doubtless have made a desperate resistance. Perhaps it was more fortunate for all parties that he was thus ignorant of existing circumstances at the capital, for had he fallen at this juncture, (which was most probable) the fate of the Republican party in the infant state might have been very different.

He and his party soon found themselves on board of the hostile ship, which was commanded by Capt. Gardiner, an Englishman—a devoted loyalist and adherent of Sir William Berkley. He was politely received by that officer, but informed that he must consider himself a prisoner until he could exculpate himself before the Governor in person, at Accomac. Until this moment Bacon had been partially reconciled to his mishap, trusting to his known popularity among the people of the city, which he knew would not be diminished by the eclat of his Indian victories; but now that he was informed of the present residence of the Governor, and the destination of the ship, his hopes were totally prostrated. He began to suspect that something was wrong with Sir William at Jamestown, from his present singular location, and was not a little uneasy at the secret and unusual measures he had taken to get him into his power. He knew the turbulent and impetuous temperament of the old knight, and how little he was given to consult right and humanity in too many of his summary measures of what he chose to call justice, to think that he would hesitate one moment to summon a court-martial of his own partizans—try, condemn, and execute him and his three unfortunate followers, if not the more numerous body, now also prisoners, in the sloop. As he stood upon deck in the midst of his guard, weighing these various aspects of his position, the ship was silently gliding within view of the lights from the city. He observed that the captain steered his course as far from the island as the channel of the river would permit, which confirmed his previous suspicions as to the state of popular feeling in the capital, and increased his uneasiness as to the secret designs of the Governor upon himself. From Captain Gardiner he could gain no satisfactory information—he merely replied to Bacon's demand for his authority, that Governor Berkley had commanded him to bring him (Bacon) to Accomac, and to deliver him dead or alive into his hands.

When it was too late, Bacon saw the rashness of the councils which had induced him to abandon his army, and trust himself among the numerous ships floating in the river, the commanders of which were known adherents of his enemies.

The reflections of our hero, as he paced the quarter deck toward morning, were bitter in the extreme. He saw all the bright hopes of his reviving spirits vanish like a dream, as the vessel now just emerging from the waters of the Powhatan, and propelled by a fresh morning breeze from the land, was plunging with every swell of the buoyant waves into the waters of the Chesapeake, and receding farther and farther at every plunge from the objects of his highest and dearest aspirations.

That portion of the magnificent bay into which they were now entering immediately ahead, was expanded and lost to the eye on the limitless waves of the ocean. On the starboard tack, like a black cloud joining the sea and the sky together, lay Cape Henry, and on the larboard, still more faintly pencilled against the horizon, lay Cape Charles. Between the two, the white bordered waves of the Atlantic rolled their swelling volumes into the Chesapeake.

The faint yellow tinge of dawn could just be discerned, like a moving shadow, now upon the waves and then upon the hazy clouds, dipping into their bosom, while hundreds of aquatic birds, interposed like a black cloud at intervals to intercept the view in the distance, or more suddenly flapped their wings from under the very prow of the vessel as they swooped along the surface of the stream and dipped the points of their wings like a flash of light into the sparkling waters.

A steady breeze was blowing from off the land, and the white sails of the ship swelled proudly and the tapering spars bent under its influence, as she ploughed up the waves foaming and falling in divided masses before her prow. On any other occasion than the present, Bacon would have enjoyed the prospect on this grandest of all inland seas, but now his mind was oppressed with gloomy doubts and forebodings. Every plunge of the vessel was bearing him more within the grasp of his relentless foe. But the mishap of his own personal adventure, every way unfortunate as it was both for himself and the cause in which he had engaged, was not that which weighed most oppressively upon his mind. Ever since the discovery of the miniature contained in the locket, he had been gradually giving way to his reviving hopes, and building upon that slender assurance bright and glorious superstructures of imagination. He had endured and lived, and fought and conquered with that hope, as the polar star to his otherwise dark and dreary course. Now again his destinies were almost wrecked by a storm from a quarter in which he had scarcely cast his eyes. How could he imagine that Sir William Berkley would be driven from the capital, by the stern and independent resistance of the unarmed citizens? How could he know that being thus driven from it he would yet retain a sufficient naval force to capture him and his escort upon the very eve of his triumphal entry into the city? These were the reflections which made him look with a feeling of dark misanthropy upon the glorious beauties of the Chesapeake. His ambition, his pride, and his conscience were satisfied; but his love for a bride, already once led to the very steps of the altar, was again thwarted upon the eve of what he had supposed and hoped would prove the final and happy fulfilment of his most ardent hopes. His feelings toward the devoted and interesting maiden, who had perilled and suffered so much on his account, were enthusiastic in the highest degree. She stood toward him not only in the relation of his betrothed, but his wedded bride; and the more endearing and captivating she became to him as he contemplated her in these relations, the more he cursed in his heart the hard-hearted and perverse old man who had been the cause of all his troubles.

Every chance of escape was intensely examined; not a word was suffered to fall unheeded from Captain Gardiner and his subordinates. He noted carefully the distribution of the prisoners in the vessel in which he was himself confined, as well as of those in the sloop following in their wake. He took careful observations of the most prominent objects on their route—the state of the tide in the river which they had just left. He examined the boats—how they were secured—the equipments and appearance of the crew on board, and resolved if he must fall in the midst of his reviving hopes, to die as became the conqueror of Bloody Run and the lover of Virginia Fairfax.

CHAPTER IX.

Amid all his misfortunes and gloomy anticipations, Bacon discovered one bright spot in his horizon. He had inquired of Captain Gardiner whether Mr. Beverly had accompanied the Governor to Accomac, and was answered in the affirmative. This was the source of rejoicing, because he believed that Virginia was yet in Jamestown. Harriet Harrison's letter had been perused over and over again, during the first part of the voyage, and was one cause of that restless anxiety to escape which we have attempted to describe.

He chafed the more as his imagination pictured his rival leading, or rather forcing Virginia to the altar, while he was thus ignobly detained. But now having satisfied himself that Beverly was not left behind, his mind was comparatively at ease on that score. Nevertheless his desire to escape was not diminished; the state of parties might change in the capital—Beverly might return and perpetrate his design while he was yet in confinement. That Sir William Berkley intended more than to keep him in temporary duress, he could not now in his cooler moments believe—his repinings were caused by the interruption to his own cherished schemes and ardent desires. He had hoped before this time, to be in Jamestown—a conqueror—the accepted lover of Virginia Fairfax, and to satisfy the Recluse himself, that he was deceived as to his birth and parentage. That there was some mysterious knowledge of Mrs. Fairfax's history possessed by that strange man, he doubted not; but he doubted as little that it had led to error with regard to himself.

The dark shadows of night had already closed over the broad expanse of waters on whose bosom our hero was thus far borne without chance of escape. He could discern numerous lights flitting along the circumscribed horizon, which he supposed to be upon the shores of Accomac, from the dark curtain which skirted along as far as the eye could reach, between the sky and the water. He was not left long in doubt upon this point, for the sailors were busily engaged furling the broad sheets of canvass and heaving over the anchor. In a few moments a bright flash illuminated the darkness around, followed by the booming sound of a piece of ordnance let off from the ship. This was answered by another from the shore, and Bacon perceived the lights which had before attracted his attention, moving, as he supposed, toward the boat landing, there being no facilities for running the ship close in upon the land. These he could perceive now rising and falling with the swelling and receding waves, and very soon faintly distinguished voices in confused murmurs as they were borne along the water, and lost amidst the roar of the waves lashing against the sides of the vessel, and the confused noise and merriment of the ship's crew.

Captain Gardiner took up his trumpet and hailed the approaching boat, after which a dead silence ensued on board, all hands listening intently for the expected answer. Hoarse and confused sounds came sweeping on the wind, as if the person answering spoke through his hand instead of a trumpet, but no distinct words could be made out. Again the captain hailed, "boat ahoy," and again with the like result. The wind was unfavourable for the transmission of sound, and he gave up the attempt. He had scarcely left the deck, however, before the boat came riding by on the buoyant waves, both parties having been deceived as to the distance, by their inability to intercommunicate. The Captain ran eagerly upon deck, and inquired of those in the boat, whether the Governor had arrived? The answer was in the affirmative. Bacon now understood the anxiety of Captain Gardiner to communicate with the shore. He learned too, from the dialogue going on, that the Governor and himself were probably crossing the bay at the same time.

When it was announced to the boat's crew that the rebel chief, Bacon, was a prisoner on board, a loud huzza burst simultaneously from twenty voices, among which Bacon distinctly recognised those of Ludwell and Beverly. Bitter indeed were his unavailing regrets that he had left his army, and thus fallen a prey to his most violent enemies. He now remembered, with not less regret, that he had strictly enjoined upon his temporary successor, not to march into Jamestown until he should rejoin the troops. This he saw would effectually prevent his present situation from becoming known to his friends, until, possibly it would be too late to render him any assistance.

The boat very soon returned in order to ascertain the Governor's pleasure with regard to his prisoner, and Bacon waited with the most intense anxiety for their return. His unavailing regrets were rapidly forgotten in a fierce and burning desire to be confronted with his enemies, alone and unsupported as he was. His noble mind could scarcely conceive of that malignity which could trample upon a solitary and defenceless individual, placed by accident in the hands of numerous personal enemies. He had yet to learn a bitter lesson in the study of human nature. His own impulses were all high and generous, and he naturally looked even upon his foes as to some extent capable of the like magnanimity. He imagined that Sir William Berkley, Ludwell, and Beverly would feel and acknowledge his indignant appeals to their honour and chivalry. How these youthful and sanguine expectations were realized will be seen in the sequel. The boat soon returned with orders from Sir William Berkley to detain the prisoner on board during the night, and to send him ashore as soon in the morning as it should be announced by a shot from a piece of ordnance, that the court had assembled. That he was to be tried by a court-martial had barely entered his imagination.

At dawn of day a gun from the shore announced the assembling of the court, and Bacon was brought upon deck by the orders of the Captain. He perceived that the ship's boat was already in the water, supported on each side by larger ones from the shore, filled with armed soldiers. However much he may have been surprised by these prudential preparations, he was still more surprised, and more fully began to realize his situation, when he perceived a man standing ready to secure his hands in irons. At first sight of this contemplated indignity, he shrank back instinctively with something of the natural feelings of youth, but the impression was only momentary; he shook it off and walked firmly to the smith, near whom stood Captain Gardiner, and a guard to do his bidding in case of necessity. As the youthful Chieftain approached, the hardy veteran of the seas was evidently embarrassed. He was reluctant to offer such a needless affront to one of so bold and manly a bearing. An indistinct apology was commenced, of which the only parts that Bacon distinguished or cared to learn was, that the precaution was taken by the orders of Sir William Berkley. "I doubt it not—I doubt it not, sir," he replied;

"Do your duty—I am in his power for the present, and must submit with the best grace I can; but a day of retribution is coming; and even should I be basely murdered upon these distant shores, as seems not unlikely from these preparations, and the tribunal of which I hear they are the precursors, my death will not go unavenged."

His hands were soon confined within the iron bands, connected by chains some two feet in length, and then, with the assistance of the Captain and crew, he was let down into the boat. He was not long in discovering that the military escort in the two outer boats was commanded by Mr. Philip Ludwell. No sign of recognition took place between them, notwithstanding they had moved in the same circles at the Capital before the irruption of the civil war. Bacon was too much of a soldier himself, and too well versed in the duties of a subordinate to throw any of the blame of his present condition upon his quondam acquaintance, and would readily have exchanged the courtesies due from one gentleman to another, had he not perceived a suppressed smile of triumph upon the countenance of Ludwell as he entered the boat. Whether the latter viewed him as rebel or patriot he felt indignant at his ungentlemanly conduct, and folding his chained arms upon his manly chest, took no farther notice of its author.

As they approached the shore, and the mists of early morning began to break away before the rising sun, Bacon recognised many landmarks which had not altogether been unknown to him in happier days. The house at which Sir William Berkley now exercised his vice-regal functions, surrounded by such of the Cavaliers as still adhered to his fortunes, became also visible. This Bacon recognised as the property of the officer in command of the guard surrounding his own person. The shore was covered with tents, marquées and soldiers, the latter being the English mercenaries, and marshalled for his reception in imposing array. Two lines were formed from the landing to the house, between which he was now marched in the centre of his guard.

When they arrived within the hall he found the martial tribunal ready assembled for his trial. A long table was placed in the centre of the room, upon which lay swords, caps, and feathers. At the farther end from the entrance sat Sir William Berkley, as president of the court, and on either side some eight or ten of his officers, all clad in the military costume of the day. Their gay doublets had been exchanged for buff coats, surmounted by the gorget alone, for the vambraces, with their concomitants, had been abandoned during the commonwealth. Some of the cavalry and pikemen, indeed, still wore head and back pieces, in the king's army,* but the Virginian officers were generally dressed at that time as we have described them.

* See statutes 13 and 14th Charles the 2d.

Among the number of officers now confronting the prisoner, sat Francis Beverly. He seemed perfectly calm and collected, and not in the least aware that there was any impropriety in his sitting in judgment upon the prisoner standing at the foot of the table.

Bacon drew himself up to his utmost height, as he again folded his arms and ran his indignant eye over his accusers and judges; as it rested in its course upon Beverly, a fierce indignation lighted up its clear hazle outlines, but it was only for an instant—his glance wandered on over the other members of the court, while his lip curled in a settled expression of scorn and contempt. The old Cavalier at the head of the board rose in visible agitation—his eyes flashed fire and his hands trembled as he took the paper from the scribe and read the charge against the prisoner.

The merest form of an impartial trial was indecently hastened through. Witnesses were not wanting indeed, and those too, who could testify to every thing the Governor desired, but no time had been allowed the prisoner to procure testimony in his own behalf, or prepare his defence.

The times were perhaps somewhat out of joint; but the state of the colony was by no means such as to require that a prominent citizen, standing high in the affection of his countrymen, should be deprived of those inestimable privileges secured by the laws of England, to every one under accusation of high crimes and misdemeanors; and these laws had been adopted and were in full force in the infant state. At the very outset of the trial, Gen. Bacon objected to the military character of the court, as well as to the indecent haste and the retired nature of the place in which it was held. He contended that his crime, if crime he had committed, was a civil offence, and ought to be tried by the civil tribunals of the country. All these weighty objections were answered by a waive of the president's hand, and the trial proceeded to its previously well known conclusion, without farther interruption.

Before the final vote was taken upon the question whether the prisoner was guilty of high treason or not, he was ordered to be removed from the court-room for a few moments, in order that their deliberations might be uninterrupted. As the guard marched the prisoner through the house into the back court of the establishment, his step still proud and his carriage elevated with the sense of conscious rectitude, he was at once brought to a stand by the sight of a spectacle which sent the blood, chilled with horror, back to his heart. This was a gibbet or gallows, erected in the very court to which they were conducting him, and upon it hung two of his own soldiers!* All evidence of vitality had long since departed, and their bodies swung round and round, under the impulse of the morning breeze, in horrible monotony. Bacon's

* See Sanguinary executions of Bacon's followers—without the legal forms of trial, in the Histories of the times.

first sensation was one of unmixed horror, but this was succeeded by indignation; not a thought for his own safety occurred to his mind while under the first impressions of the fearful spectacle. But as fierce indignation stirred up his torpid energies to thoughts of revenge, the means began to present themselves, and then it was that he shook the iron fetters which bound him, in savage and morose despair. Perhaps a chill from some more personal feeling ran through his veins, when he reflected how short had been the passage of his two humble followers from the sloop which had borne them across the bay on the preceding night, to eternity. They had evidently suffered some hours previous—perhaps during the night. They were the two subaltern officers—selected by himself for his expedition down the river, and chosen for their desperate bravery at the battle of Bloody Run. And now to see their manly proportions ignominiously exposed upon a gibbet, after having been most inhumanly murdered, was more than he could calmly bear. Bitter and unavailing were his reflections as he stood a spectator of this outrage, while his own life hung suspended by a hair.

He was not left long a spectator of this cruel scene; the guard was ordered to present the prisoner again before the court to receive sentence.

When Bacon stood once more at the foot of the table, surrounded by his unrelenting enemies, his countenance evinced a total change. When first he stood in the same place, he had not fully realized his situation; he was stupified with overwatching and fatigue. The young are always slow to apprehend the darker shadows in their own prospective, and instinctively cling to the brighter aspect of events and circumstances, until some sudden calamity or unexpected reverse in their own immediate career, opens their eyes to the stern reality. When such a change is brought immediately before the senses, then indeed the dreadful truth speaks direct to the apprehension. Few criminals at the moment of receiving sentence of death, realize more than a horrid and oppressive sense of present calamity—all hope has not yet entirely forsaken them. But could they see upon the spot a fellow criminal undergoing the last penalty of the law, they would at once realize the truth in all its terrors.

The sight of his unfortunate followers had thus opened the eyes of the youthful general, to the desperate character of his enemies, and the awful fate which immediately awaited him, but it was not fear which now revived his stupified powers to action. His look was bold and daring, while a preternatural brilliancy shot from his proud eye, as the president of the court, with an assumed calmness, pronounced upon him the sentence of death. As the last fatal word fell from the lips of the stern old knight, the prisoner's countenance was rigid, cold and deathlike for an instant, as he struggled to master his rebellious and scornful feelings into such a state of discipline as would enable him to express the little he had to say, with clearness and precision.

Although the usual question, "if he had any thing to say why sentence of death should not be pronounced against him," was not asked, he stepped boldly up to the end of the board, and notwithstanding the magisterial waive of the president's hand for silence, and a simultaneous order to the officer of the guard to remove him—gave utterance to his feelings in these words, and with a manner powerfully subdued, yet energetic; his voice issuing from between his rigidly set teeth like that of one under the influence of reckless desperation.

"If it may so please the president, and gentlemen of the court-martial, I will not tamely and silently submit myself to be butchered in cold blood, without raising my voice and protesting against the jurisdiction of the court—the time—the place—the manner of the trial—the persons who compose the court, and especially him who presides over your deliberations.

"Was it treason I committed, when I boldly and openly marched from Jamestown to Orapacks, at the head of the brave men who drove before them the savages by whom the dwellings of the Colony had been burned, and its women and children murdered. Did not the house of burgesses request the Governor to sign the commission, which the people had unanimously put into my hands? Did he not pledge his knightly word that the commissions should be ratified? Under the authority of that commission and that promise, have I not driven the enemies of civilized man before me, as I marched through the Peninsula? Have I not done what has never before been done? cut out a broad line of separation between the habitations of the white man and the savage? Have I not avenged the murders committed on the night of the massacre? Have I not avenged injuries committed against more than one member of this very court, by the bloody confederation? Have I not, with these hands, rescued the sister-in-law of the president of this very tribunal from the murderous tomahawk of the savages? True, it was only to die—but it was worthy of all my poor exertions to rescue her body from their unhallowed hands, that it might rest in consecrated ground. Have I not annihilated the confederation itself, cut to pieces the assembled tribes—rescued the prisoners, razed to the ground the fortifications at the falls, and made prisoners of the brave remnant of those misguided nations who erected it? If this be treason, then indeed am I a traitor!

"Why is it that this great and glorious country, opened to the oppressed and crowded nations of the old world by a kind and beneficent Providence, must so often become the theatre of struggles for personal aggrandizement and power? Why is it that our arms must be turned against ourselves in fratricidal conflict, when so many enemies have been swarming upon our frontiers, and devastating our settlements ? Must the great and evident designs of the Creator be thus constantly retarded? the great destinies of this vast land obscured in the dawn, by the petty struggles of contending chieftains? Who can tell how far to the mighty west the tide of civilization and emigration would have rolled their swelling waves, but for the scenes of personal rivalry and contention like the present, which have disgraced our annals ?

"The rosy tints of the morning dawn of destiny have scarcely risen in the east of this mighty continent—the boldest and the wildest imagination cannot soar into futurity, and predict its noonday glories, or count up the tides and floods of human beings, that shall be wafted to these shores, and thence roll in successive waves, to the dark and as yet unknown west.

"I have been but an humble instrument in the hands of the Great Mover of these mighty currents, and for this ye seek my life. But death to this frail body cannot arrest the great movement, in which I have been an actor. I have indeed been the first to point out the importance of drawing a broad line of separation between the European and the native, the first to show the necessity of rolling to the west the savage hordes, as the swelling numbers of our own countrymen increase upon our hands. Future emigration must advance westward in a semicircular wave—like a kindred billow of the watery ocean, sweeping all obstruction before it.

"If the natives flee before this rolling tide, and survive its destructive progress, well and happy will it be for them; but if they attempt to buffet the storm, ruin hangs upon their tardy footsteps. I confess that I have been the first to maintain the impossibility of the two species living together in peace, and to execute the primitive and opening step in this great revolution of nations. If this be treason, then am I a traitor. But if I fall, think not that the great movement shall fall with me. The Great Ruler of the universe has opened these fertile hills and dales to his oppressed creatures; and he has likewise pointed out the necessity of driving back them who make no use of these blessings, and who rise not from their idolatry and ignorance to a state fitted to render glory to their Creator. The tide will move on to the westward, in spite of such tribunals as this. If I am to die here in this insulated neck of land, by the hands of those who are themselves prisoners, so be it— I shall die contented in the knowledge that I have not lived in vain, and that future generations will rescue from oblivion the name of him who first opened an avenue to the mighty and unknown west, and however illegally my life may be taken, I will show you that I can die as becomes a soldier and a Cavalier. One request I would fain make, even of them whose actions I abhor and despise;

it is this; as you have tried and condemned me by a military tribunal, that you inflict upon me the death of a soldier. This is a request which I would alike make to a heathen or an infidel."

"Take him immediately to the gallows," shouted Sir William Berkley.

The officer of the guard approached with his myrmidons, and laid hold of the prisoner, in accordance with the mandate of the Governor; but three or four members of the court rose at once, and expressed their willingness to allow the prisoner until the succeeding day to prepare for execution.

"Away with him, away with him," again vociferated the president, at the same time, menacing the official who stood holding the prisoner, doubtful how to act, and apparently willing to listen to the more merciful suggestion. By this time the whole court was in confusion and uproar; every member was upon his feet, together with the president, each one endeavouring to be heard. A large majority of the members were for the longest time, and these now demanded of the Governor to submit the question to the court; but the old knight, having probably discovered that Ludwell and Beverly were his only supporters, clamorously persisted in ordering the prisoner to instant execution.

Bacon himself, during this time, at first stood with his arms folded and a bitter smile of contempt playing upon his features, until the turmoil growing louder and more protracted, he too attempted to obtain a hearing. "It is perfectly indifferent to me," said he, "whether I am murdered to-morrow, or at the next moment; let the hour come when it may, my blood be upon your skirts!"

His manly bearing served to reanimate those who contended for delay, and the strife continued to grow more noisy and turbulent, until, as if by magic, a side door of the apartment opened, and a new actor appeared upon the scene. The court was instantaneously hushed to silence, and Sir William Berkley stood as if he beheld an apparition, while Bacon bounded forward and clasped Virginia, who rushed into his outstretched (but fettered) arms.

When she first gently pushed open the door, not one of the court or of the attendants perceived her. She was clad in the loose folds of the sick chamber—her blond curls fell in unheeded ringlets over her brow, temples and shoulders—her face was pale as monumental marble, and her frame weak and trembling, while a preternatural excitement of the moment shot from her eyes, as she gazed through the partly opened door, to ascertain if her ears had not deceived her.

Not a word was uttered louder than a deep impassioned whisper, until Virginia perceived the chains upon his hands, when seizing the iron by the middle she stepped forward and boldly elevating her head, addressed Sir William —"Whence these chains, sir?—tell me quickly; tell me that they have not been put on by your orders—before

I curse the hour that united my destiny in any manner with yours!"

"Not only were they imposed by my orders, but they were so put on in preparation for a ceremony which shall alike cure you of your vagaries and release me from his hated presence for ever! Guard, lead her to her chamber, and the prisoner to execution!"

Scarcely had the words died upon his lips, ere she sprang from the grasp of the officer, and locked her hands around the neck of her lover, exclaiming, "Now you may shoot him through me—no ball enters his body but through mine. You may hack off my arms with your swords, but until then I will never leave him!"

The Governor and Beverly now came forward, and each of them seizing a hand, they tore her from his embrace, in the midst of a wild hysterical laugh, hot however before Bacon had imprinted a kiss upon her pale forehead, and uttered a brief and agonizing farewell. He then seated himself upon a chair, and covering his face with his hands, gave himself up to emotions which had not before been awakened during his trial.

As they were leading Virginia from the room, she suddenly recovered her composure, sprang from their grasp, and placing herself against the wall, between two of the officers of the court, who were still standing, clung to their arms while she thus addressed Frank Beverly—"And this is the method you have taken to win your way to my favour—this is the plan you have devised to rid yourself of a rival. And you too, his deadly enemy—to sit in judgment upon him, and mock justice by the cowardly device. Out upon you, sir, for a craven-hearted dastard. Is this the way you were to meet and conquer him in battle? Where are your trophies for my bridal turban, taken from the standards of his followers? You take trophies from Bacon in battle! One glance of his manly eye would drive the blood chilled to your craven heart, and wither the muscles of your coward arm."

Again she was seized, and dragged from the court-room by the Governor and Beverly. In a few moments the president returned, and found the court proceeding in his absence deliberately to take the question on granting the prisoner until the succeeding day to prepare for death, and allowing him the attendance of a clergyman. Sir William was fearful perhaps, that by resisting the will of the majority, he should defeat his purpose, and therefore acquiesced in what he could not prevent, with more amenity than might have been expected from his previous violence.

The prisoner had not so suddenly regained his equanimity; he was indeed making strenuous exertions to that end, but now and then a piercing scream from the upper chambers of the mansion thrilled through his nerves, and more than once he suddenly sprang to his feet, and made an attempt to rush past his vigilant keepers, but was as quickly reminded of his helplessness by the jarring sound of his fetters, and the ready grasp of the officials. After several such attempts, he at length folded his arms, and gave himself up to bitter reflections—a wretched smile flashing athwart his countenance indicating the violence of the internal struggle and the cruel pangs that rent his bosom.

The majority of the court having triumphed in the first matter, the question was again raised as to the manner of his death, and Bacon's countenance was actually lit up by a smile when he heard the decision of the court in favour of his own request, that he might die the death of a soldier. The guard were at the moment leading him from the court room to his prison house, and his step became more firm and elastic, and he could now look upon the wretched spectacle in the court, without the same degree of horror which he had before evinced.

When he had marched several paces in his progress round the mansion, he halted suddenly and wheeled round to survey the dormer windows peering through the roof, as was the fashion with the long low houses of the time. His eye rested from its piercing and steady gaze, in sadness and disappointment, and he threw down his chained hands with a violent motion, as he resumed his march between the soldiers. They conducted him to the door of a cellar at the end of the house, which was secured with double defences; in the next moment he was rudely thrust into a damp cellar, without a ray of light, and the door was closed and securely bolted.

CHAPTER X.

Bacon heard the rusty bolt shoot into its socket, and then the hasping and locking of the outside door, with a sensation of utter hopelessness. He wandered through the dark precincts of his prison, stumbling now over an old barrel, and anon against a meat block, until he came to some dry bundles of fodder, which seemed to have been spread out in one corner to answer the purpose of a bed. Before throwing himself upon this rude couch, he resolved to examine the structure of his cell. By passing his hands along the walls, he found that they were built of brick, well cemented by a long process of time--that the summit upon which the basement beams of the frame rested, were entirely out of his reach, and that in the present confined state of his hands, it would be impossible for him to make any impression on them, and he could distinctly hear the tramp of more than one sentinel, as they paced their monotonous rounds about that wing of the building. There was yet much of the day remaining, and he resolved to spend it in endeavouring to grind off the end of the rivets to the iron bands enclosing his wrists. By rubbing these against the bricks, he found that he could wear them away by a tedious and laborious process. Our hero was not one of those who surrender themselves up to despondency at the first appearance of insurmountable difficulties; decision of character was his most striking quality, and he knew that his devoted army only waited for him to lead them to avenge his wrongs. He felt the difficulties which lay between him and Jamestown, but he did not despair, however desperate his circumstances. For many hours he persevered in grinding the rivets against the bricks; with wrenching and great danger of dislocating his wrists, he at length succeeded in so wearing down the iron, that he could at any moment throw aside the manacles. Encouraged with this success, he moved the meat-block against the wall, and made all preparations for a breach, as soon as he should be satisfied that the darkness of night would cover his movements.

To while away the time usefully, he threw himself upon his rude bed, and was soon, from the effects of great previous mental excitement and bodily fatigue, wrapt in profound slumber.

The shadows of night had closed around this land in the midst of waters in sombre hues, and the prisoner still slept profoundly.

In the mean time circumstances were in progress on the bay, which had a most important bearing upon the fate of every one then at Accomac.

It has already been stated that Sir William Berkley had put in requisition such of the naval power as he could bring to bear upon his immediate designs and pressing necessities. But, after leaving the city in the precipitate manner which has been related, the citizens determined to summon to their aid, such of the ships and other vessels of war and merchandise, as yet remained in the river, within convenient distance of the city, and make the old knight a prisoner at Accomac.

The Governor had not long been gone before an armament superior to his own, was seen steering in the course which he had taken. This consisted of "one ship, a bark of four guns, a sloop and schooner." The expedition was under the joint command of Giles Bland and William Carver, both veteran and experienced seamen. On board of one of the vessels, and subordinate to the officers just mentioned, was Captain Larimore; he was one of the most devoted friends of Sir William Berkley, but his personal predilections and loyal principles were entirely unknown, either at Jamestown or on board the fleet. When this (at that time) formidable armament arrived in sight of the vessels at anchor, which had borne Sir William and his partisans to Accomac, it being now dark, (on the same evening in which Bacon lay sleeping in his dungeon,) Capt. Larimore proposed to his superior officers, that he would take one or two resolute tars, and, avoiding the hostile vessels, land and reconnoitre the position and forces of the Governor.

His proposition was promptly acceded to, and Larimore launched his boat, selected his men, and protected by the thickness of the fog and the darkness of the night, succeeded in effecting his landing unperceived by the vessels in the service of the Governor. If he had been aware of Bacon's imprisonment and condemnation, and disposed to do so, he might have rendered him the most important services; but whether disposed to hazard any thing in his cause or not, both he and his superiors were ignorant of Bacon's fate.

When the boat containing the adventurer and his two associates struck the shore, Larimore immediately sprang upon the beach and ordered his subordinates to push a few yards out into the bay, and remain within sound of his whistle. He proceeded directly towards the quarters of Sir William Berkley, until he was challenged by one of the sentinels with his carbine at his breast. Larimore desired the sentinel to lead him to the Governor. As soon as he had made himself known to his Excellency, he informed him of his disposition to advance the cause of the loyal party, and submitted the following proposition.

He requested the Governor to send one or two of his most daring and trusty officers, with one hundred rosolute men in boats or canoes, during that portion of the night when he should himself be in command of the watch—and promised that he would deliver the whole armament into the hands of the Governor. Sir William immediately summoned his officers and made the proposition known to them—requesting, at the same time that any gentleman who desired to be entrusted with the expedition would step forward. Philip Ludwell promptly acceded to the offer, and tendered his services, which were as promptly accepted. Ludwell having selected his supporters from the hardiest of the troops and sailors, he held himself in readiness to push off as soon as the appointed hour should arrive. Larimore giving the concerted signal, sprang into his boat and returned to those who sent him, with a very different account of Sir William's position and intentions from that we have just related.

All this time Bacon was sleeping as soundly upon his bed of corn blades, as if it was not to be his last sleep on earth. Criminals condemned to death generally do sleep soundly the night preceding their execution, and Bacon, whether criminal or not, was no exception to the rule.

It was some hours after the sun had gone down, and about the same time that Larimore put off to his vessel, when Bacon suddenly started up from his rude couch, under an oppressive sense of glaring light upon his eye balls. An aged and decrepid woman was leaning over him; she was resting upon her knees, in one hand holding the lamp and in the other the locket which had already exercised such an important influence upon his destiny. She had sprung the lid, during his sleep, and was now gazing upon the beautiful picture, with an interest and amazement not less intense than he had himself manifested on its first discovery in the Indian wigwam. So absorbed was her every faculty, that his sudden start from sleep scarcely attracted her attention. Her eyes were filled with water in the vain endeavour to decipher the outlines with convincing accuracy. When the date and the initials and the hair were submitted to a like scrutiny, conviction settled at once upon her mind. The feeling operated slowly at first, but as one doubt gave way after another, her pale and haggard features began perceptibly to assume the life and vigour of deep excitement. The locket fell from her grasp, and she clasped her hands—but suddenly throwing back the curling masses from his brow she exclaimed: "Tell me, my master, are you called Nathaniel Bacon?"

"I am! but tell me in your turn, why do you ask?"

She answered only by exclaiming, "O merciful Heaven! God be praised! Wonderful are the ways of Providence!" Bacon was on his knees also, his manacled hands laid upon her shoulders as he anxiously and hastily inquired, "Tell me, good mother, what do you know of Nathaniel Bacon?"

"More than he knows of himself, mayhap!"

"Speak it quickly—moments are more precious than diamonds—say, whence comes your knowledge? who are you? who am I? for God's sake tell me quickly!"

"You are the son of as worthy a gentleman as ever wore a sword. I knew him and your honoured mother well—that is, if you are the same mischievous boy whom I have mourned as drowned these many long and lonesome years."

The captive waited to hear no more, but springing upon his feet, paced wildly round the damp cellar like one in a delirium of joy. The old woman still maintained her humble posture, her hands again clasped, and her long wrinkled neck turning with difficulty to follow the strange movements of the prisoner. Suddenly, and as if stricken down by a cannon shot, he threw himself upon the earth his whole frame convulsed with thoughts of his present hopeless condition. "What matters it whether I am Nathaniel Bacon or not? What will it avail, this time to-morrow, when these limbs, now so full of life and vigour in the renewal of hope, will be still in the cold embrace of death?"

"Death!" the old woman screamed, rising from her knees, seizing the lamp and thrusting it in Bacon's face—"Death, did you say, my son? or did my old ears deceive me with the horrible word?"

"They did not,—truer words were never spoken or heard; to-morrow, before the sun has measured an hour in the heavens, the voice which now addresses you, will be silenced in the everlasting sleep of death!"

Horror struck his auditor dumb; her shrivelled lips moved with a tremulous motion, as if she desired to speak—but she spoke not. An ashy paleness overspread her features, and she staggered backward and would have fallen, had she not been caught in the arms of her long-lost foster son. A tumult of thoughts crowded upon her enfeebled mind, as she recovered, gasping with the unusual excitement, and her aged frame heaved as if it would burst in the effort. At length a ray of hope seemed to dawn upon her mental vision ; her eye sparkled with the thought, as she resumed the lamp which Bacon had taken from her hand, and placed upon the ground. "It must not, shall not be, my son. There is your coarse food, Heaven forgive me for not offering you better, but little did my thoughts turn upon such a godsend. I have a thousand things to ask and tell, but as you say, life—precious life—hangs upon every moment lost, so—"

At this moment the sentinel advanced directly before them, and taking the old woman rudely by the arm, said, "Come, old Tabby, the prisoner can find the way to his mouth without the light ; give him his bread and water, and be off ;" thrusting her up the steps, as he spoke, slamming the door, and once more turning the grating bolt upon the unfortunate prisoner.

Bacon's late reviving hopes almost died within him as he listened to the unwelcome sounds and the retreating footsteps of his visiters.

He threw himself once more upon his rude couch and abandoned himself to despair. But youthful hope never despairs utterly, however desperate the circumstances ; a few moments after saw him with his handcuffs thrown off, and busily engaged in piling the loosened bricks upon the floor. In less than an hour, he beheld the stars lightly twinkling in the Heavens, through the aperture created by the removal of a single brick, which he had taken from the outer layer before he was aware of his progress. Cautiously and intently he listened for the footsteps of the sentinel; strange sounds seemed to come from off the water, but all in his immediate vicinity was as quiet as the grave, except the tumultuous throbbing of his own heart. Again he proceeded cautiously in his work, until he had completed an aperture sufficiently large to admit the passage of his body. Then, bracing his nerves, he proceeded to effect his exit through the opening, and was vigorously struggling to free himself, when a musket ball whistled by his ear and buried itself in the wooden sill of the house. He sprang back into the cellar, and stood in confusion and amazement, until the short chuckling laugh of the sentinel roused him from his delusive dream of hope. He could distinctly hear the marksman who had exhibited such a dangercus proof of his skill, laughing and telling his comrade, who paced before the door at the end of the house, "how he had shaved the prisoner's head." The unfortunate captive now abandoned himself to despair in earnest. A thousand times he cursed his ill fated stars, for thus leading the old nurse into his cell to rouse his dormant hopes, and give a new impulse to his desires for freedom.

While these matters were in progress at the prison of our hero, the naval armament under the command of Bland, Carver and Larimore, belonging to and put in motion by his friends among the citizens, and which might have rendered him such effectual assistance had the two principal officers been aware of his situation, was itself about to perform its share in the contest. The expedition under Ludwell, as had been promised to the traitor Larimore, was sent out at the exact time specified, and with muffled oars skimmed along the surface of the tranquil lake, keeping under the shadow of the ships. As they approached, signals were exchanged, which satisfied Ludwell that Larimore was indeed in command of the watch, and still ready to betray his trust. Once or twice, indeed, a suspicion shot across his mind, that Larimore might only be an agent in the hands of Bland and Carver, and that his proposal was but a scheme laid to entrap himself and followers into the power of the rebels, as the Governor's party were pleased to call the patriots; but it was as speedily dissipated by the favourable train in which every thing seemed to lie, as the traitor had promised.

The loyal party under his command was in a very few minutes silently and stealthily climbing up the sides of the vessels. Having gained the decks, they proceeded at once to disarm and bind the sentinels. These unfortunate fellows had been induced by the traitor Larimore, to believe that the party under Ludwell were deserters from the ranks of Sir William Berkley, and were not undeceived until they found themselves bound hand and foot, and such other precautions taken that they could not alarm their sleeping comrades below. In less time than we have taken to record the transaction, the whole naval armament in the service of the patriots, together with the officers, crews and military stores, were delivered into the hands of Governor Berkley. The success of the enterprise was announced to the anxious expectants on shore, by a discharge of artillery, which was joyously answered on their part. Sir William Berkley was transported with delight—so lately abandoned by the majority of the citizens and soldiers of the capital, and compelled to desert the legitimate seat of government, he now saw himself in possession of a naval and military power, more than sufficient to command the obedience, if he could not win the affections of the rebellious citizens. He immediately called together his officers, and such of the cavalier gentry as had followed his fortunes to this remote corner of the colony, and imparted to them his determination to embark his land forces on board the ships brought over by himself, and those surrendered by Larimore, and sail within the hour for the capital.

It may be readily imagined that this sudden change in their fortunes was not received with murmurs and discontent; on the contrary preparations were eagerly and joyously commenced. The captured and betrayed patriots were divided

17*

among all the vessels, so as to preclude effectually any chance of their rising upon the Governor and his party. The soldiers, artillery and baggage were placed on board, and the signal given for the embarkation of the old knight and his staff—family and attendants.

Our gentle heroine was not forgotten—she too had been roused, not from her slumbers, for she had not slept, but from her restless and feverish pillow, and commanded to prepare for instant departure for the capital. The stern old Cavalier, her uncle, stood in the open plot in front of the house surrounded by his partisans, impatiently waiting her descent. At length she appeared, leaning upon the arm of Frank Beverly on one side, and that of her female attendant upon the other—her aunt following in evident dejection of spirits. Virginia's countenance was white as the spotless attire in which she was enveloped. Her eye wildly wandered over the faces crowding around, as she emerged from the house, but soon settled again in sullen composure as she perceived the absence of the one sought. The pine torches, borne by the negroes, shed a glaring and unsteady light on the objects around; the steady tramp of the soldiers, as they marched to and embarked on board the boats, were heard in the direction of the water, while other parties were seen in like manner provided with torches, floating in the barks already laden, toward the ships moored in the offing. As the party that had just emerged from the house was about to move in the same direction, Beverly spoke aloud to the Governor.

"Sir William, are you going to leave the prisoner in the cellar?"

"True—true, my boy," he replied, "I was so overjoyed at trapping so many of his compeers, that I had entirely forgotten his generalship; but we will care for his standing, and that right speedily. We will elevate him—I will not say above his desert—but certainly to a position to which he has long had eminent claims. Ho! Sir Hangman! Ludwell, order the hangman into our presence; we need a cast of his office before we set sail."

"It was customary with the Romans, you know, Sir William, to offer up a sacrifice before they embarked upon any important enterprise," said Beverly, laughing at his own wretched attempt at wit. But there was one countenance in the group upon which the first intimation of Beverly concerning the neglect of the prisoner, wrought a fearful change. Virginia threw her eyes wildly round, searching from face to face, for some small evidence of sympathy on which to cast her hopes, but they were all steeled in imperturbable apathy, or clad in more appalling smiles of derision. As her eye glanced around the circle, it fell at last upon the youth supporting her own enfeebled steps. Her knees were just sinking under her from weakness and dismay, but the sight of Frank Beverly's smiling countenance aroused her energies. Her muscles were instantly braced, her eye shot forth scorn and contempt, while she threw his arms from her, as she would have started from the touch of some loathsome reptile. The youth, with a grim smile, folded his arms in quiet serenity, to await the appearance of the prisoner, as if conscious that his hour of sweet revenge was near at hand.

Virginia threw herself at the feet, first of her uncle, and then of her aunt, and earnestly prayed for the life of her lover, as she heard the orders for bringing him forth, but from the first she received only a contemptuous glance, and from the latter silent tears. She was still kneeling upon the grass at the feet of the latter, her head fallen in despair and exhaustion upon her bosom, when the soldiers rushed out from the cellar, and proclaimed the escape of the prisoner. An electric stream poured into Virginia's sinking frame could not have more suddenly restored her to life and animation. She screamed, clasped her hands, sprang to her feet, and fell back into the arms of her aunt in a paroxysm of mingled joy and agitation.

Sir William Berkley gnashed his teeth, and swearing vengeance against the traitors who had permitted his enemy's escape, seized one of the pine torches and rushed into the cellar to satisfy himself that he was not concealed behind some of the rubbish of the apartment; but soon found convincing evidence of his escape, in the irons that lay upon the ground, and the aperture through which he had made his exit. The sentinels were all called up, who had at any time stood guard over the prisoner through the night. It appeared that the one who had discharged his piece so near to the head of the prisoner, had been some time since relieved, and that he had merely mentioned to his successor, the attempt of Bacon to escape, with his own amusement in showing him how near he could shoot to his head without wounding him.

"Would to God you had lodged the ball in his skull," exclaimed the enraged governor. The truth was, that the sentinel had supposed the prisoner still loaded with his irons when he appeared at the breach, having merely discovered one of the many evidences of dilapidation in the house, and had consequently left him in the care of his successor, with the full confidence that he would not make a second attempt. How he was induced to make that second attempt will appear in the sequel. The soldier on duty, at the time when he was supposed to have escaped, was immediately ordered to be put in irons.

Lady Berkley was about having her niece conveyed to the house, but her enraged husband harshly ordered those supporting her now prostrate form, to convey her to the vessel, which was accordingly done. The Governor, his suite and followers were soon also on board, and a roar of artillery announced their final departure from the "eastern shore."

When Bacon threw himself upon his couch, after his last unfortunate attempt to escape, every thought of once more gaining his liberty abandoned him. He very naturally supposed that his failure would only redouble the vigilance of his guards, and therefore resumed his irons, with the desperate resolution of throwing them off, when he should be led to execution on the following morning, and selling his life as dearly as he might.

He had lain for some hours in a state of mind that may be readily imagined from the late scenes through which he had passed, when at length he heard his own name softly whispered in his gloomy cell; the voice appeared to be in his immediate vicinity. He arose and followed the supposed direction of the sound, and again he heard it on the opposite side—proceeding from the still unclosed aperture in the wall. He answered in the same subdued whisper. "Come this way," said the voice of the old woman, the shadow of whose head he could now perceive darkening the partial light which broke through. "Come this way, Master Bacon. Tim Jones, the sentinel, has gone into my cabin to eat a chicken supper, and drink some aqua vitæ which I procured for him; his place is supplied by a soldier whom I engaged to be ready, as if by accident. He pretends to be asleep under the big tree yonder. Do you come forth and proceed round the opposite end of the house to that occupied by the other sentinel, until you come to the bushes at the end of the garden palings—there wait until I come to you—for your life do not stir, until I join you there."

Bacon succeeded in avoiding the notice of the

sentry and in gaining the spot indicated by the old woman, where he had scarcely concealed himself, before the discharge of artillery from the betrayed fleet startled him from his recumbent posture. He supposed that his own capture had been ascertained at Jamestown, and that vessels had been despatched to rescue him. This idea had scarcely entered his mind, before he sprang over the palings and was running at his utmost speed across the garden toward the bay, for the purpose of procuring a boat, but his attention was instantly arrested by the appearance of the Governor and his suite collecting in the yard in front of the house. He was on the point of running into the hands of the sentinel whose temporary absence had afforded him the chance of escape, and who now sat with his weapon ready for action, securely guarding, as he supposed, the person who stood just behind him. The man hailed him as soon as he heard the rustling among the shrubbery, but the liberated captive had seen and heard enough to induce him to seek his hiding-place once more.

CHAPTER XI.

When Sir William Berkley embarked on board the ships, he left a company of picked soldiers, commanded by an officer of tried fidelity, together with the smallest of the vessels and her crew, with orders to bring the fugitive to Jamestown, dead or alive. In a short time that portion of the eastern shore, lately so full of bustle and activity, was wrapped in profound repose, unbroken save by the monotonous tramp of the sentinel, pacing before the door of the mansion, now the solitary quarters of the sole remaining officer.

Bacon had perceived from his hiding-place, that some unusual commotion was in progress between the quarters of the Governor and the ships lying in the offing, and he was seized with the most eager desire to know what it foreboded. For the first half hour, he lay in momentary expectation of the commencement of a naval action ; at length he saw the glaring lights of the pine torches, skimming along the margin of the water, and dark shadows of moving crowds, as the boats floated to their destination. These movements he could not comprehend except by supposing that the crafty old knight had set on foot some secret expedition, for the capture of the newly arrived ships, the increased numbers of which he could easily perceive. But when the whole fleet set sail, with the exception of the small craft already mentioned, he was completely at fault. He was revolving these strange movements in his mind, when his kind preserver came again to his assistance. She was moving like an unearthly spirit along the garden palings, cautiously examining every bush, when he presented himself before her. She led him by a circuitous route, and one the farthest removed from the sentinel, to a lone cabin that stood some distance from the main building, and that had lately been occupied by the inferior officers attached to Sir William's cause; it had formerly been used as a negro cabin. After she had ushered him into the single room which it afforded, she pointed to a seat, and began stirring up the coals which had been left from the culinary operations of the late occupants. She was about sitting down to hear Bacon's account of himself, and doubtless of communicating her share of information for filling out the history, but recollecting that he had left his food untouched, she hastily covered the light, and went out, carefully securing the door on the outside, but soon returned with a remnant of Tim Jones' chicken supper, which she had no doubt preserved for her own use. This was speedily placed upon a rude table, and the fugitive urged to help himself in the midst of a torrent of questions.—Now she desired to know the fate of the Irishman—where they had landed after the shipwreck—who had so kindly nurtured and educated him—whether he knew any thing of his relations in England—if he remembered any thing of her features, or her home in the old country. What was his occupation. Why Sir William Berkley disliked him, in what position he stood with regard to the beautiful invalid, who had shown so much grief at the prospect of his immediate execution,—how he had managed to preserve the locket so faithfully—and a hundred other queries of like import, with the solution to which the reader is already acquainted, but which our hero answered with great impatience, interposing one of his own between every two of hers, and meanwhile doing ample justice to the provision she had set before him. The substance of the old woman's narrative was as follows :

"When Mrs. Fairfax, then Mrs. Whalley—"

"Merciful Heaven!" exclaimed Bacon, dropping his knife and fork—"was General Whalley her first husband? Then indeed he and the Recluse are the same person." The nurse stared at him a moment, but presently proceeded with her narrative.

"When Mrs. Fairfax, then Mrs. Whalley, left her infant son in my care, for the purpose of joining her husband, then an officer in the army of the commonwealth, I was entirely unacquainted with the opposition of her family to her marriage with General Whalley, and ignorant of the clandestine manner in which that ceremony had been performed, as well as the subsequent privacy of their movements, which they thought necessary for their safety.

"It was a long time after her departure from my house, and after the time of her promised return, before I received the least account of her, or the cause of her prolonged absence from her child. But when I did at length receive a letter from the unfortunate lady, the whole mystery was cleared up. In that letter she stated 'that while she was on her way to join her husband, she was overtaken in the highway, by a party of loyalist soldiers, commanded by her own brother. She was immediately recognised by him, and sent under a military escort to her father's house, not, however, before she had time to learn from one of the prisoners under the charge of the party, the death of her husband, who, he stated, had fallen by his side.' She made the promised remittances for the support of her infant, and every thing went on in the usual train, until the time arrived for the next promised letter, which indeed arrived, by the hands of a very different messenger from the one before employed. It was brought by the very brother who had arrested her in the road, and sent her a prisoner to her father's house. He presented the letter unopened, but stated that he was fully apprised of its contents, as well as of the existence of his sister's child, which she still supposed unknown to her family. He told me that his father was almost broken-hearted, on account of the disgraceful marriage which his sister had contracted, and that the sight of her infant in the house, or even the knowledge of its existence, would drive him to phrenzy ; that his brothers and himself had therefore determined to take effectual means, not only to remove the child from within the reach and knowledge of their father, but of its mother also. That they were determined to take it by force, a sufficient proof of which he showed me in a party of armed followers, (for they were all military men,) unless I would consent to a plan for the removal of the offensive little stranger, which would secure all their views, and be, at the same time, more satisfactory to himself and, he doubted not, to me. His proposition was, that I should remove with the child to a distant residence, the means for which he would amply provide ; and that I should then wait on Mrs. Whalley, his sister, and inform her that her child was dead. As an inducement for me to be guilty of this deception, he informed me that there was a young Cavalier, of good birth and connexions, who was enamoured of his sister, but if the child was permitted to absorb her affections, and remind her of her lost husband, they despaired of ever seeing her married to Mr. Fairfax, and consequently of wiping out the stigma upon their good name created by her first marriage. I was really attached to the little boy, and fearful that they would take him by force if I did not quietly yield, and being assured that I should watch over him wherever he went,

I consented to the plan. I waited on the mother, and with well dissembled sorrow, told her of the death of her darling boy. I thought at first that she would have gone distracted, but the necessity of keeping her secret from her father and brothers, roused her to the needful exertion. It was well that it was so, for I could not have endured her heart-rending distress five minutes longer. The next information I had of the unfortunate lady, was from the same young gentleman, her brother, who came to inform me of the success of their plans and thus relieve my conscience. His sister after a tedious delay had married Mr. Fairfax, and sailed for the Capes of Virginia. He assured me that the child should always be provided for, but that I must change his name from Charles Whalley to some other, which I might choose myself, so that he could never be able to trace his parentage. I was firmly resolved, however, that the innocent babe should some day know his real history. In the meantime I consented to all that the young gentleman desired, and he left the usual supply and departed. I never saw him again. The remittances for the support of the child were indeed kept up for some time, but they at length became irregular, and less frequent. My mind began to grow uneasy concerning the charge which I had thus by a crime brought upon myself, and which I considered but a just retribution for my evil deeds. Nor were my fears less anxious concerning the future prospects of my innocent nursling.

My health had well nigh sunk under the accumulating load of poverty and unavailing regrets for my wickedness, and I trust that I sincerely repented of the evil deed. Providence at length directed to my humble dwelling one who appeared indeed as one risen from the dead.

"It was none other than General Whalley himself; he had really been shot in the battle, but had recovered. Great God! what were my sensations, when the gigantic warrior, pale and worn with mental and bodily suffering, threw aside his disguise, and avowed himself to me. Notwithstanding the embarrassing position into which his being still alive was calculated to throw all parties, I fell upon my knees before him, and my Maker, and fully acknowledged my participation in the transactions which I have related. He had heard of the marriage of his wife to Mr. Fairfax, before he sought me out, but even at this comparatively remote period of time from her marriage, his huge frame shook, and he became like an effeminate being while he listened to my narrative. He told me that he was likewise about to sail for America; not that he desired or intended to make himself known to his wife, but because it was becoming unsafe for him to remain longer in the kingdom. I have no doubt in my own mind, that he was unconsciously indulging his desire to be near his still adored Emily, in his choice of a place of refuge, which he now informed me, was the same to which she had gone with her husband. He told me that it was his intention to live in the greatest seclusion, and that his very name should be unknown in his new abode. He proposed that I should follow him, after he should have established himself, and made arrangements for my comfortable reception, the time for which was specified. I felt myself impelled by an imperious sense of duty to repair, as far as lay within my power, the injury which I had helped to inflict upon him, and therefore consented to leave country and home with my little charge, now become so dear to me.

"After furnishing me with the necessary supplies for the long and dreaded voyage, together with particular directions as to the place of embarkation, and the course I was to pursue after arriving in Jamestown, General Whalley left me, and I have never seen or heard of him to the present hour. I did not consider that surprising, however, because he informed me that he would never more be known by the name of Whalley, and that I must school myself carefully before my departure for America, never to drop a hint that he had ever been more than he seemed to be in his new abode. But to proceed with my story. He had directed that I should sail with the boy after the lapse of one year from the time of his own departure. The most of this interval was employed in making my own little preparations for so long a voyage, and my final separation in this life, from all my kindred and friends. I had promised to keep my design as secret as possible, and every precaution was indeed taken to keep my intended departure a secret from all but my own immediate relations. But by some means unknown to me, my design became known to others, as I was apprised one day, by a visit from a gentleman named Bacon!"

The fugitive instantly dropped his knife and fork, which he had been occasionally using as the story of the nurse ran upon those events already known to him, but now a new name was introduced, and one which, it may be readily imagined, did not fail to command his undivided and breathless attention.

"Mr. Bacon informed me that he had heard of my intended expedition, and that I was to take out with me the tender boy then on my lap, and said he could readily surmise that the late unfortunate civil wars were in some way or other the cause of my undertaking so long and dangerous a voyage. As he saw my embarrassment from not knowing how to answer him, he hastened to assure me that he did not desire to pry into my secret. That he was placed in somewhat similar circumstances himself, to those which, as he supposed, operated on the parents of the boy. He informed me that his brother and himself had both been unfortunately in the army of the commonwealth, in which his brother had fallen, and that he had left an only son to his care, the mother of whom had died in giving him birth. 'Now my object in coming to you, my good woman,' said he, 'is to procure your assistance in conveying my ward to Virginia.'

"I readily undertook the task, and all necessary arrangements were made for the boy's comfortable passage. Some months before the time of embarkation, little master Bacon, or I may as well say yourself, was brought to me, in order that you might learn to know and love me before we set sail for this distant land. When I was on board the vessel, and had paid for my own passage as well as for those of my little charges, the money for which had been provided by the friends of each, I was startled to perceive that Mr. Bacon did not join me as had been agreed upon. My anxiety became more and more intense as the time approached for weighing anchor, for although I was amply provided with all necessary funds, my mind misgave me that some accident had befallen the unfortunate gentleman. He was indeed in disguise when he came to see me, and I doubt not, was a fugitive from the powers that then ruled our native land. My worst apprehensions were realized—Mr. Bacon was either made a prisoner, prevented from joining me by apprehension, or chose to deceive me in the whole business, but I have always religiously believed, since I have had time to reflect dispassionately on the subject, that his absence was not a matter of choice.

"We had a pleasant and prosperous voyage, until the first night after we came in sight of land, when such a storm arose, as it seemed to me that the whole world was coming to an end. Daylight found us a miserable company of forlorn wretches, hanging upon the wreck. The boats were already loaded to the water's edge. I prayed and entreated some of the good gentlemen to save my two precious boys, if they left me, but alas! every one was taking measures for his own safety. There was one poor, ignorant, but tender-hearted Irishman, who had been a soldier, that seemed to commiserate my helpless little charges, his name was Brian O'Reily—a talking, blundering, merry youth he was then. At length seeing some prospect of effecting a landing, he made a raft of parts of the wreck, and trusted himself and you to the mercy of the treacherous waves. That was the last I ever saw of the warm hearted Irishman, and of you, until I accidentally discovered, while you were asleep in the cellar, the identical locket containing your mother's likeness, which I had placed round your neck with my own hands. I saw the resemblance, too, which you bore to my lost boy, and was immediately satisfied that God had preserved you, in his own way and for his own wise purposes, and I determined also to save you, if I could, from the cruel punishment which I learned more fully from the sentinel, the Governor intended to inflict upon you in the morning. Thank God, I have succeeded. Now do tell me, what I have asked you so often, what became of the Irishman, and where you were landed and how preserved."

"First tell me, good nurse, how you escaped the wreck, and what became of your other ward. It is of immense importance for me to know. The liberty which you have given me is worth nothing, without a clear explanation of these points."

"That I can soon inform you of—the Captain, kind and generous man that he was, seeing the probable success of the Irishman's plan, adopted it himself, and after making a raft, with the help of some of his crew, placed all the females on it who chose to venture in preference to waiting for the return of the boats. Myself with my little remaining boy, and several other females who were steerage passengers, suffered ourselves to be lashed to the frail machine. For four dreadful hours we were tossed about at the mercy of the waves, the water for at least half the time dashing over us, and, as it seemed, carrying us half way to the bottom. At length, however, we landed upon the eastern side of this very neck of land, where I have remained ever since. I have never set my foot on board of any kind of water craft from that time to this. Together with another of the females mentioned and my little boy, the son of General Whalley, I wandered through swamps, and marshes, and sea-weeds, until we had entirely crossed the neck—never having eaten one mouthful until we arrived at this plantation. Here we were most kindly received by the widowed mother of the present proprietor, Mr. Philip Ludwell; but alas, my little boy had suffered too long and too severely from the combined effects of the night upon the wreck, the succeeding sufferings upon the raft, and the hunger endured before we came to this place. He sunk rapidly, notwithstanding the humane exertions of the good lady who had extended her kindness toward us. He died and was buried on this plantation—I have preserved his little clothes and trinkets to this day. Little did I think at that time that you had outlived him."

Bacon then performed his promise, and related all that he knew of his own and O'Reily's escape from the wreck—and likewise informed her that the latter had been on the "eastern shore" within the last two hours, but, he supposed had been taken as a prisoner to Jamestown by Sir William Berkley. "But tell me," he continued, "have you never seen or heard any thing of General Whalley, or Mrs. Fairfax, since you parted from them in England?"

"I have never heard a word of the General from that time to the present, though I have questioned every body that came from Jamestown. I knew that he intended to assume another name, and other habits, and I therefore described his person and manners, but no one had ever seen such a personage!"

The hasp flew from the pine log into which it had been inserted, and the door was driven back against the opposite wall. "Thou beholdest him now, woman! look at me!" and he pointed to his now haggard features, "and say whether I am that man!"

But his gigantic figure, never to be mistaken,

had scarcely darkened the doorway, before the person he addressed began to gasp for breath, and seized the arm of Bacon for protection—calling upon him for God's sake to save her—her eyes meantime immoveably fixed upon the intruder's countenance.

"Quail not, woman; there is no one here to harm thee, if thy own conscience condemns thee not. I have heard part of thy story, as I listened at the door, in order to find out how many of the Governor's minions I should have to slay before freeing the boy. Lay thy hand upon the Holy Evangelists, woman," and he drew his clasped Bible from his pouch and extended it across the table to her, "and swear that this boy is not my son, whom I entrusted to thy care."

With a trembling hand she touched the holy book, and said as distinctly as her fears would permit, "Before God and upon his word, I testify it as my firm and unwavering belief, that this young man who sits before me, is Nathaniel Bacon, and not your son."

"It was indeed my boy, then, whom thou buried upon this lone shore?" And without waiting for an answer he threw himself into one of the rude seats, leaned his head down upon the table, and gave himself up to uncontrolled emotion.

Bacon was moved to tears as he saw the stern Recluse thus overwhelmed with grief at the breaking up of the last tie that linked him to earth. He remembered, as he looked upon his agitated frame, how uncompromising had been the frowns of fortune upon this now solitary being. Once he was flushed with the joy of youth, and love, and hope, and fired with a military ardour like himself. But now (as he supposed) he was an outlaw, and an exile from his country—unconsciously abandoned by a doting wife—his only heir, and the sole stay and hope of his declining years dead and buried upon the very spot where he at last found the nurse to whom the child had been committed. He remembered also his unwavering kindness to himself, and his general benevolence and kindness of feeling toward his fellow men, and he unconsciously let fall the words which rose embodied to his tongue, as with swimming eyes he looked upon him, "'Tis a hard and cruel fate!"

"Rather say that retributive justice pursues and overtakes the guilty to the ends of the earth." answered the Recluse, raising his head erect from the table. "Oh God, how just and appropriate are thy punishments! How true and discriminating is thy retribution. Behold here a wretch who has fled three thousand miles from the scene of his crimes in the vain delusion that he could flee from himself and the mysterious all seeing eye above! Young man, there is a mysterious system of ethics which the world understands not—the reputed wise, subtleize it, and the vainly wicked contemn and despise it. It is comprised in the simple words justice—probity—and benevolence! There is a power of bringing about its own ends in the first which none but the wickedly wise know. Yea, and bringing it about by the very weapons used against its dictates, and if not upon the very scene of the crime, at least in a place peculiarly appropriate. Behold here before you this worn down remnant of humanity, summoned, as he supposed, to rescue the last of his race from the power of the oppressor; but in truth, only to weep over the grave of his real son, buried on this spot years ago. This hand once aided in severing the links between father and son,—a man as innocent and unoffending as his offspring was helpless. A royal line they were. Just heaven, how that crime has been avenged! How strangely and how justly! Probity and benevolence are mysteriously bringing about their own righteous purposes, as does justice her avenging decrees. The worldly wise look with contempt upon simple honesty, but the highest ultimatum of earthly wisdom and experience is to have the power and the knowledge of the wicked with the simple guide, that justice, probity and benevolence unerringly work out their own reward.

"The wickedly wise cunningly suppose that they are cheating their God and their fellow men; the last they may temporarily deceive, but the Great Political Economist of the universe so overrules their cunning, that their own hands are forging the chains of their future captivity, at the very moment when they suppose themselves constructing daggers for their neighbour's throats, and keys for their strong boxes. The mysterious power of which I speak is felt always in the latter end of human life, but can never be described to those just entering upon the scene. Thrice blessed is he, my son, who can fall before his Maker and say that justice, probity and benevolence have been his ruling motives of action—whether from the dictates of the heart or of the head. That thou art one of those I have long believed, and if thou art not the son of my loins, thou art of my affections. Come, my boat waits for thee; thy presence is even now needed in Jamestown. Thy troops are encamped but a few miles from the town, and are wondering at thy absence. The Governor has embarked for the city to perpetrate more wrong and oppression. By the will of Heaven this rusty weapon shall once more do battle in a holy cause."

As they were leaving the cabin, Bacon turned to the nurse and embracing her said, "I go hence, good Margaret, to battle in the cause of my country, and that right speedily. If I am successful, you will soon hear from me, and if not, you will have the consolation of knowing that your foster son died as became the son of a soldier. Before yon rising moon has twice performed her circuit, I will be either the conqueror of Jamestown or buried in its ruins."

With hasty strides he followed the Recluse, who was already half way to the little secluded inlet from which he had landed. As they approached the water, Bacon could perceive two slender masts dancing in the moonbeams, as the dark hull of a fishing smack pitched and tossed with the swelling billows. Stepping into a log canoe, (such as surround all water bound plantations in slave countries,) they were speedily on board the diminutive craft, where two lounging fishermen waited their approach. The wind was blowing fresh from off the sea across the neck of land they had just left, and they scudded before it at a rate, if not quite equal to the impatience of the more youthful voyager, at least with as much rapidity as could reasonably have been expected. The Recluse seemed as usual inclined for thoughtful silence, and as his companion leaned against the mast of the rocking vessel, he saw the workings of a mighty mind—wrecked, as he supposed, upon some unseen obstacle, as it was impetuously borne along by the resistless tide of youthful hopes and aspirations. He could not believe that the Recluse had ever been deliberately base or cruel, as he himself had more than hinted. "At least," said he, as he communed with himself, "he has paid tenfold penance for a single error."

The Recluse at length perceived that his companion was observing him, and arose from his half recumbent position, and stood beside him, his arms folded for an instant, and his attenuated countenance, as it reflected back the sickly rays of a hazy moon, settled in profound melancholy. He took the hand of the youth, and shook it some time in agitation before he could give utterance to his thoughts, but at length he said in a voice which betrayed the violence of his feelings,

"Nathaniel, canst thou forgive me for that cruel mistake at the chapel? Oh, couldst thou know what I suffered then, and since, both on thy account and my own, thou wouldst accept it as ample atonement for the unintended wrong. I saw, on that dreadful night, her who was the queen of my manhood's fondest dreams—who had basked with me in the sunshine of youth and hope—who had given me her young affections in return for my own, when life was in its bud, and who afterward blossomed into the rich fruition of maternal love and beauty in these arms—her who was torn from me by a base deception of her kindred, and married to another. I saw her face to face, for the first time in more than twenty years, when she was about to give the offspring of her second marriage as a wife to the offspring of her first, as I supposed. Oh, what human conception can realize the torrent that broke over my soul at that fearful moment? The shadowy remembrances which had been softening and fading in the lapse of years burst at once into life and being. Time and place were forgotten—the passions of youth rushed into the contest, and I stood as the frail mortal body shall stand at the final day, when its own spirit knocks for entrance. The buried ghosts of my own passions rose from their grave, the frail cloak of stoicism which had been woven round me, was blasted into shreds and patches, and I stood and quailed before a woman's eye like Belshazzar at his feast. Thou hast felt thy heart swelling and plunging against its bony prison, but thou hast never had it gorged and choked with the dammed up waters of bitterness, gathered through long and dreary years. Thou hast felt the words stick in thy throat, and refuse to leap into life, but thou wert never struck dumb with a judgment from Heaven, like a thunderbolt scorching and searing into the very citadel of thought and vitality! Thou hast writhed when stung by the scorpion tongue of calumny, but thou hast never been outlawed and abandoned of all human kind—condemned by thy own conscience—and given up of God!"

His eye shot forth vivid fires, and his arms, as they were flung abroad in violent gesticulation, cast giant shadows upon the moonlit waves of the Chesapeake.

"You do both yourself and your friends grievous wrong," said Bacon, after a painful pause.

"I have indeed wronged myself—most wretchedly wronged myself, but not now; the wrong which I did to others has recoiled ten-fold upon my own head. I know full well thy meaning—thou wouldst say that kindly feelings are not wholly dead within this seared heart! But thou hast made but little progress in analyzing our moral structure, if thou dost not know that crime committed by one whose nature would lead to good, is the true source of that misery which surpasseth speech.

"An intuitive villain, if there be such, or one become wholly corrupt, plunges from transgression to transgression, until his final ruin, without enduring any of that wretchedness which comes of a stain upon a tenderer conscience. Such a man has no conscience; it is seared or obliterated; but he of benevolent heart and virtuous impulses, wounds his guardian angel by the deed. The taint corrupts and sours the sweets of life into gall and bitterness. If that stain be but a single deed, and that, dark, damning and indelible, the perpetrator becomes as an angel of light in the companionship of hell. He may be likened to one who loses the power of sight, with all the other senses perfect. He hears what others see, but to him the grand medium of perception is dark and dismal, and the rhapsodies of others are his own damnation. There is but one hue to his atmosphere ; it is the fearful red which only the blood of man can dye. In his case the language of scripture is fulfilled before its time. The moon is turned to blood, and the morning beam dispelleth not the horrid hue."

Bacon thought any direction of his companion's thoughts preferable to his present mood, and therefore said "But she whom you supposed my mother—"

"I know it all, my son, interrupted the Recluse; I saw the marble features upon their last journey. For twenty years I have not envied mortal being, but I confess to thee, that there was something in the cessation from thought, suffering and action—and the sleep-like serenity of death for which I longed. Nevertheless, there is an awful mystery in that which seemeth so simple in itself. Mere lifeless clay, moulded by the hands of man into the same stamp, speaks not to man in the same language; it may indeed refresh the memory, but it stirreth not up the divinity within us. Who is he that looketh upon the features of the dead and looketh not up to the giver and recipient of life? I saw her mortal remains laid out in the midst of a camp, and the busy world faded away into indistinctness, while the God of the universe spoke in the person of the beautiful corse before me and said "Thus far shalt thou go and no farther."

As they steered their course uninterruptedly towards the source of the Powhatan, which they had entered as the sunbeams broke through the morning mists, Bacon threw himself down, and slept soundly, until he was aroused by the Recluse to inquire what direction their agents should give the vessel when they arrived within sight of the city.

He was roused to immediate thought and action by the question. He knew the danger of entering the capital, now that it was in the possession of Sir William Berkley, and therefore directed the boatmen to land him some miles above.

The Recluse, at his own request, was put on shore somewhat nearer the capital, but entirely out of reach of any precautions which the vigilance of the Governor might have instituted.

Bacon inquired eagerly, why he left him, after his promise to draw his sword in the cause of the people and the country, assuring him at the same time that he intended bringing the matter to immediate issue.

"I leave thee now, my son, to set my house in order. Trust in one who has never failed thee in need. I will be with thee in this last struggle—for there is something whispers me that it will be the last. Leave the event, therefore, with him who rules the destinies of battles." And with these words he sprang upon the shore and disappeared in the forest.

In a few hours more, Bacon was again at the head of his devoted troops, who were entirely ignorant of the cause of his protracted absence, but now that they knew its cause, were bursting with ardour to avenge his own and his country's wrongs.

CHAPTER XII.

General Bacon's ardour and decision of character were not in the least abated by his late perils and imprisonment; on the contrary, recent developments had relieved him from suspense and inspired him with new motives for action, to say nothing of the redress loudly demanded, by all classes of the citizens, for the Governor's increasing oppressions. Scarcely was sufficient time allowed for his devoted officers to shake him cordially by the hand, before his gallant band of patriots was marching towards Jamestown, without music or noise of any kind. There was a cool settled determination visible in the countenances of all, which was admirably evinced by the order and alacrity with which they obeyed the general's orders. Bacon's cause had now become personal with every man in the ranks, composed as they were principally of hardy planters and more chivalrous Cavaliers, who knew not at what moment they might themselves be subjected to like wrongs and indignities to those from which he had just escaped. As the chief had anticipated, the patriot army arrived on the heights of Jamestown, just as the shades of night were enclosing the forest. It was not his intention that Sir William Berkley should ascertain his arrival and position, until he had made suitable dispositions for his reception, should he feel disposed to pay him a visit. Accordingly, the whole army was immediately employed in digging an entrenchment, and erecting a barricade of fallen trees, for the protection of the troops, should it be found necessary in their future operations. These transactions took place, it will be remembered, on the evening of the same day in which Bacon parted from the Recluse, and landed upon the main shore.

Meanwhile, Sir William Berkley, his family, suite and followers, of high and low degree, had effected their landing without opposition at Jamestown. The same night that Bacon and his patriot followers were entrenching themselves on the heights, the Governor and his adherents were marshalling themselves in the city. Great numbers of the citizens, however, were decidedly opposed to Sir William and his measures; and his arrival and military preparations were no sooner perceived, then they betook themselves, with their families and property, under cover of night, to the privacy of the neighbouring plantations: numbers of them accidentally encountered the patriots at their work, and immediately sending on their families, joined their standard. Besides the land and naval forces now at the disposal of the Governor—and they already outnumbered his opponents—he offered every inducement to the worthless and dissolute loungers of the town to unite with his army; he did not even hesitate to promise largely of the plunder, and confiscated property of the rebels.

On the succeeding morning, the sun rose upon the ancient city, in unclouded splendour, for the last time it was destined ever to shine upon the earliest erected city in North America. It was the dreaded day to our heroine, appointed for her marriage. Her uncle had solemnly assured her upon their landing on the previous day, that the one which had now arrived, should see her the wife of Beverly. The latter, too, claimed the fulfilment of her solemn promise. The distressed and enfeebled girl knew not whither to turn for sympathy and succour; she was beset on all sides, and not a little oppressed with the shackles of her own promise. She did not dare to hope that her lover had already made his way from Accomac to her own vicinity. She remembered indeed, that the Recluse had charged her, in case of any sudden danger or emergency, to send him a memento of the bloody seal, but she likewise remembered, that he had since been the main cause of her separation from one to whom she was heart and soul devoted. She was also oppressed with unutterable sadness on account of her mother's death, the true account of which she had just heard,—the body having been sent by the patriots to the city for burial, immediately before her arrival. To her aunt she appealed, with touching pathos; but alas, she could do nothing, even had she been so disposed. Wyanokee had returned with the body of her mother, and by her devotion to the revered remains, revived all Virginia's former affection, but she was powerless, and withal a prisoner, and so wrapped up in her own gloomy meditations, that she looked more like one of the dumb idols of her own race, than a living maiden. When spoken to, she started up as one from a trance—and without speaking again, sought communion with her own ideal world.

The hour was a second time fast approaching for the celebration of the nuptials of our heroine. None of the fortunate occurrences or lucky accidents for which she had hoped, relieved the despair of the fleeting moments. Her uncle and Beverly had both repeatedly sent up to her apartments, and desired to be admitted to her presence, but on various pretences they had been as yet denied. Her aunt had again and again urged her to prepare for the ceremony, but hour after hour flew by, and she was still sitting in her *robe de chambre*, her neglected ringlets hanging in loose clusters over her forehead and neck, the former of which rested upon her hand, and it in its turn upon her knee—her head turned slightly to one side, where Wyanokee sat, straight as an Indian arrow, and silent and immoveable as death. At length she heard her uncle at the door, who swore that if she did not dress and descend immediately to the parlour, where the clergyman and Beverly were in waiting, he would have the door forced, and compel her to go through the ceremony even should her feet refuse to sustain her. Soon after he had retired, Lady Berkley again entered, when the distressed and bereaved maiden clasped her round the neck and wept bitterly. "Oh, dearest aunt," she exclaimed, "save me from this desecration--this perjury! Great and merciful God," she cried, loosing her hold, and clasping her hands, "how can I vow before Heaven to love, honour and obey a man that I abhor and detest?"

"You should have thought of that, my dear child, before you gave your solemn promise to Frank; it is too late now to retract."

"Is it even so? then I will swear when they come to ask me to pledge my vows, that my love never was mine to give away; that I learned its existence in another's possession. They shall not—they cannot force me to swear an untruth. They may lead me through the outward forms of a marriage ceremony, but racks and torments shall not make me in any way accessary to the deed. If I promised otherwise, it was the last despairing refuge of outraged nature. It was the instinct of preservation within me, and not my free and voluntary act." Influenced by this idea, she stood like an automaton, and suffered her women to deck her out in bridal array, and was then mechanically led from her room, accompanied by her aunt, Wyanokee, and her female dependants. She found Sir William Berkley and Frank Beverly waiting her approach in the entry. She shrunk back at the sight of the latter, but he, none the less bold, approached at the same time with her uncle, and together they led her toward the room where the clergyman waited, with many of the loyal Cavaliers. When they arrived at the door, and she saw the reverend gentleman in his robes, and the book open before him, her excited frame could bear the tension no longer, and she fell lifeless upon the floor. A loud roar from the brazen throat of a cannon at the same moment shook the windows like a peal of thunder, and was succeeded by the echoing blasts of the trumpet's charge, multiplying the bold challenge as it rolled from river to cliff. This plan of daring an opponent to battle, was strictly in accordance with the usages of the age, and was instantly understood by the Governor and his friends, all of whom flew to the windows, where they beheld a sight, which soon drove softer emotions from their hearts, if they had any. The former saw the smoke curling over Bacon's breastwork and entrenchments, and was struck dumb with amazement. But soon recovering his voice, and throwing up the sash, he shouted to the guard below, "to arms, to arms—for king and country."

Whatever were the faults of Sir William Berkley, and they will be considered many in this refined age and renovated country, cowardice was not one of them. In a very few moments he mounted his charger and, together with Beverly and Ludwell, galloped swiftly along his forming battalions rebuking the tardy and cheering on the brave. With his superior numbers and heavier appointments, he felt as sure of victory as if he already sat in judgment, or was pronouncing sentence upon the chief of the rebels. That Bacon was already at the head of his army never for a moment entered his imagination; but the knowledge would have made no change in his arrogant calculations, even had he possessed it.

So confident was he of an easy and speedy victory, that he scouted the idea of remaining within the palisade, and waiting for the attack of the patriots; and this was indeed becoming every moment more impracticable, for the cannon balls from the heights were even now tearing through the houses, riddling the ships and throwing his troops into confusion. No time therefore was to be lost. He ordered the vessels to draw off into the middle of the stream, threw open the gates, and sallied boldly out to meet the foe.

Virginia was borne to her apartment still senseless, and the physician was immediately sent for, but before his arrival, she had several times opened her eyes as her aunt with real but unavailing sorrow in her countenance applied the usual restoratives. At every discharge of the artillery she slightly moved; her excited imagination identified the sound with the fearful thunder that attended the former disastrous ceremony at the chapel.

But when her aunt explained to her the occasion of the uproar, she sprang up in the bed, clasped her hands, threw her eyes to Heaven, and exclaimed,—"Merciful God, I thank thee! Providence has indeed interposed for my preservation! Oh, if *he* could only be there ?—No, no, no, it is better, perhaps, as it is—for cruel as my uncle is, I could not bear to see him pierced by Bacon's sword, and he would assuredly seek his life. Merciful Father, thou orderest all things wisely. Aunt, let me prepare you for another turn of fortune! The patriots will be successful! my heart assures me they will. Young Dudley and Harrison are there, and they have lion hearts; but weep not, aunt, they are as generous as they are brave."

Sir William Berkley, with that blind, passionate, and impetuous courage for which he was distinguished, scarcely delayed to organize his troops effectually, but rushed with reckless fury against his enemies.

Bacon, from the moment that he perceived the marshalling of the troops outside the gate, silenced his cannon, and waited with coolness, and in profound silence, the approach of the opposing columns. Sir William began to calculate upon a bloodless and easy victory, and even contemplated sending in a flag with terms of capitulation. But dearly did he pay for his error, and terribly was he awakened from the momentary delusion.

Bacon had persisted in waiting the onset, notwithstanding the impetuous ardour of his troops, until he could make every shot effective; he knew his inferiority of numbers, and determined to compensate for his disparity of force by coolness and precision. "Wait until you see the white of their eyes, my fine fellows," was his often repeated answer to the suggestions and even entreaties of his impatient cannoniers ; but when at length he did give the word "fire!" most effectually was it echoed. The very heights seemed to the panic stricken troops of the Governor, to pour out red hot iron and smoke. They were speedily rallied and brought again to the charge—and again the same fearful reception awaited their farther progress, with the addition, at the second onset, of a volley of musketry. Dreadful was the havoc in the royal ranks, and terrible the dismay of the soldiery. The rabble which the Governor had hastily collected in the town, fairly took to their heels and fled to the protection of the fort. Again the valiant old knight rode among his troops, and cheered them to the onset, but at each succeeding attack, some more fatal reserve was brought into action. At length the patriot chief, standing upon his rude fortification, and looking down upon the dismayed and retreating loyalists, began to take counsel of his youthful ardour—he longed to measure swords with the officer whom he beheld riding so constantly by the side of the Governor. He saw the officers of the king, as they rode among their troops, some with tears in their eyes endeavouring to rally them, and others swearing and rebuking their cowardly followers; and he determined to permit them to rally and then bear down upon them with his own high spirited and ardent soldiers. He was quickly mounted, as were also Dudley, Harrison, and the brave band of youthful

Cavaliers who had adhered so long and so faithfully to his fortunes. When he announced this determination to his army, the welkin rung again with their joyous acclamations, and every heart throbbed in unison with his own, and assured him of victory.

"This night," said Bacon in a low voice to Dudley, as they rode over the entrenchment—"Jamestown shall be a heap of ashes!"

Dudley made no reply, but smote his clenched hand upon his harness with emphasis, returning the glance of his commander with one of cordial approval.

Sir William Berkley and his subordinates, seeing the movement of their opponents, were soon enabled to rally the disheartened troops, and as the patriot army marched down the hill, the royalists in turn, raised the cheering chorus.

The loyal army had not at any time during the engagement, presented so formidable an appearance, as they did at this moment, and they in their turn silently awaited the sortie of the enemy. As Bacon's followers debouched, they visibly accelerated their pace to double quick time, and the two bodies came together with a shock like the explosion of a magazine. Terrible was the *melee*, and dreadful the carnage which ensued. As they closed, Bacon raised his voice, and addressing Beverly by name, called upon him to sustain his late charges. Consternation was visible in the countenances both of Beverly and the Governor at the unexpected appearance of the patriot chief, but the former yielded to it only for an instant—in the next the youthful champions plunged the rowels into the flanks of their chargers, and rushed at each other like infuriated wild beasts. The fire flew from their swords, and their eyes flashed not less brightly, but at the first onset, Beverly's weapon snapped off short at the guard. Bacon raised himself in the stirrups, and was about to plunge his blade deep into the breast of his hated rival, but it fell harmless upon the mane of his charger, and he drew back to the command of his troops. Beverly wheeled his horse and rode slowly from the field, deeply wounded and mortified; as much perhaps at the contrast between Bacon's forbearance and his own late vote of condemnation, as at the disaster and defeat he had sustained.

As Bacon returned to reanimate his troops, he found that a new ally was doing battle in his cause. He saw near the right wing, the flourishes of a gigantic arm, which he had formerly seen do service. The Recluse was indeed there; how long since, Bacon knew not, but he seemed to be already in the thickest of the fight. He had lost his cap, and his bald head towered amid his fellows and brightly glistened in the sun. His right arm was bare to the shoulder, and dyed with blood to the finger ends. He seemed striving to throw his life away, and more than once thrust himself into the very ranks of the foe, but as often the terror-struck loyalists gave way before him. He seemed to be perfectly invulnerable, for not a wound had he yet received.

The consequences of the first repulse at the assault on Bacon's intrenchments could not be overcome by the now exhausted and dismayed loyalists. One column after another gave way, and fled into the town, until not more than half remained. These were the regular troops, which had throughout adhered so firmly to the person and fortunes of the Governor. His friends urged him to capitulate, but he was as obstinate in battle as he had before shown himself in council.

He was at length almost dragged from the field by his friends––as all his troops were flying in disorder and confusion into the town. The patriots rushed in, together with their flying foes. The Recluse had seized some flying charger, and, still bareheaded, was dealing death to those who came within the sweep of his terrific weapon. Bacon over and over again, offered quarter to the flying remnant, but they fought as they ran, keeping up something like an irregular action, the whole distance from the field of battle to the city.

At length both parties were within the walls, and the fight was renewed, but the loyalists were soon driven from the field. Some escaped by boats to the shipping—and among these, Sir William Berkley was forcibly dragged from the city as he had been from the field. In vain he pleaded the situation of his wife and niece ; he was assured by his friends of their safety in the hands of the victor, and still urged forward in his flight. Many poor fellows plunged into the river, and endeavoured to save themselves by swimming to the ships which still adhered to the loyal cause, but numbers perished in the attempt.

Bacon with difficulty restrained himself by a sense of duty, long enough to see the victory complete, before he leaped from his horse, and rushed up the stairs of the Governor's house, where, in a few moments, he was clasped in the arms of the amazed and delighted Virginia, notwithstanding the presence of Lady Berkley. He had no sooner exchanged those thousand little nameless but endearing questions and answers, that leap into life unbidden after such an absence and such a meeting, than he turned to Lady Berkley, and said. "Madam, a safe escort to convey you to your husband, waits your commands, at any moment you may choose to leave the city."

"But my niece—is she also free to go?"

"What says my Virginia—will she accept a soldier's protection?"

"With all my heart and soul," she answered.

While they discoursed thus, the bells were ringing, and huge columns of smoke shot up past the windows on every side, and burning timbers sparkled and cracked with increasing and startling rapidity. Bacon instantly understood the cause, and taking Virginia in his arms, and bidding Lady Berkley and Wyanokee, who till now had scarcely been noticed, to follow, he rushed into the street, and beheld Jamestown in flames. In a short time it was a pile of black and scorched ruins, as it has stood from that day to the present.

CHAPTER XIII.

After the battle and destruction of Jamestown, Sir William Berkley, accompanied by his now liberated Lady and his remaining followers, comprising the still loyal marine force, retired again to the shades of Accomac, where we will leave him and the remaining events of his life in the hands of the historian.

The political power of the colony was now in the possession of the victorious chief, so lately condemned to death. He was not long in surrendering it to a convention of the people, summoned to meet at Middle Plantations, (Williamsburg,) for that purpose, and in their hands we will leave the political affairs of the future mother of states. Our only remaining duty is to follow the fortunes of the principal characters of our narrative. The successful general, after attending to his military and political duties, accompanied his now betrothed bride from the ruins of Jamestown to the new seat of government. It was a delightful summer evening—the sun was just sinking beneath a horizon, where the darker blue of the distant landscape softened the shades of the azure sky, both merging in the indistinct prospect so as to form a magnificent back ground to a panorama, bathed in a flood of golden light. The youthful and happy pair instinctively reined up their horses, and gazed upon the enchanting scene, until their hearts were full of love and adoration.

Then by one impulse they turned their horses' heads, and gazed upon one far different, which they were leaving. The ruins of the first civilized settlement in North America were still sending up volumes of smoke, through which at intervals gleamed a lurid flash, as some more combustible materials fell into the mass of living embers below. But there were associations with this scene, to the hearts of our pilgrims, which no tongue or pen can describe; the melancholy treasures of memory collected through long forgotten years, came gushing back over their hearts in a resistless torrent. The scenes of their childhood—of all their romantic dreams, and those fairy and too unreal creations of young life—the graves of their relations and friends, were about to be surrendered up to the dominion of the thistle and the ivy, there to moulder through all future generations.* But this was not all that was saddening in the view before them. The Indian captives, some two hundred in number, were ascending the heights to the very spot which they occupied, on their way to the far west.

* The ivy capped ruins of the old church are all that remain to this day of the ancient city. We trust that no irreverent hands will ever be laid upon that venerable pile; but that it may be suffered to stand in its own melancholy grandeur, as long as its materials may cling together.

Poor and friendless beings they were! their worldly store they wore upon their backs, consisting for the most part of worn out leather garments, and a few worthless baubles carried in their wallets. They skirted along the brow of the hill in Indian file—their steps slow and melancholy. They too were about to leave the scenes of their long sojourn, the broad and fertile lands which they had inherited from the beginning of time—the honoured relics of their dead, and all the loved associations which cling to the heart of the rudest of mankind, when about to leave for ever the shades of home. They were just entering upon the wearisome pilgrimage of the exile, under a combination of the most cruel and unfortunate circumstances, and in a condition the worst calculated to subdue new countries, and battle with hostile tribes. As they passed in review before the youthful pair of another race, no sign of recognition manifested itself. They moved along with the gravity and solemnity of a funeral procession, until the last of the line stood before them. It was Wyanokee! She paused—attempted to pass on like her predecessors, but her feet refused to bear her from the spot, and turning to them she cried as if the words had burst irresistibly from her heart, "Oh cruel and treacherous is the white man! See you those braves, going down the path of yonder hill? So they have been going ever since Powhatan made the first peace with your race. May the Great Spirit who dwells beyond the clouds, shower mercies upon you both, equal to the wrongs which your people have visited upon ours." And having thus spoken she broke away, and ran swiftly down the hill in pursuit of her countrymen. She saw that Virginia was struggling with her emotions to speak, and she rushed away lest she should again be compelled to listen to a subject which was disagreeable to her. Virginia, before her own departure, had exhausted her persuasive powers in the vain effort to induce her to remain. A hope had till now lingered in her heart, that Wyanokee would follow her to Middle Plantations, and once more take up her abode in her house, but when she saw the last traces of her receding figure through the shadowy gloom of the forest, she knew that she looked upon the Indian maiden for the last time on earth.

With swimming eyes the lovers pursued their way across the narrow peninsula. Virginia sobbed aloud, until she had given vent to her overcharged heart. But an easy and gentle palfrey, and a devoted and obsequious lover, do not often fail to revive a lady's spirits, especially through such scenes as she now beheld, bathed as they were in the mellow glories of a summer twilight. "Hope told a flattering tale," and our hero and heroine would have been more or less than mortal, and wise beyond their years, had they not listened to it. Their laughter was not loud and joyous, it is true, they were far too happy for that; their frames trembled with the exquisite pleasure which words warm from and to the heart produc-ed. Sometimes they were silent indeed, but not for want of thoughts to interchange. Words had exhausted their power.

They had not proceeded many miles on their way, and the sun still hung as it were suspended beyond the purple glories of the horizon, when Ba-con pointed with his riding whip to an object before them which quickly changed the current of his companion's thoughts. Like human life, their short journey seemed destined to exhibit many dark and gloomy shadows. It was the Recluse; he was leaning against a tree, apparently waiting their approach, for as they rode up, he stepped out into the highway and saluted them. Virginia trembled upon her saddle with very different sensations from those to which we have just alluded, but her lover hastily unfolded to her his name and former delu-sion. "This, my young friends," said the Recluse, "is our last meeting on earth—and I have sought it that I might bless you both, before my departure from the land in which I have so long been a so-journer and an exile from the haunts of men."

"Whither are you going?" asked Bacon in astonishment. "You certainly will not leave us, now that the very time has arrived when you may dwell here in safety. I had even calculated upon having you as an inmate at my house."

"It cannot be," replied the Recluse. "My destiny calls me to a place far north of this, where some of my old comrades and now fellow sufferers, dwell in comparative peace and security. But it is only detaining you after night fall, to multiply words. May God of his infinite mercy bless and preserve you both," and thus speaking he also departed, and was seen no more.*

On a certain evening, not very long after the one just spoken of, General Bacon was married to Miss Virginia Fairfax, and at the same time and place Charles Dudley, Esq. led to the altar Miss Harriet Harrison.

After this happy announcement, it becomes our painful duty to cast a melancholy blemish upon the character of one who has figured in our narrative. On the two several occasions, namely, of his release from captivity by the storming and capture of Jamestown, and his master's marriage, Brian O'Reily was found hopelessly, helplessly drunk; or according to his own explanation, in that state in which a man feels upward for the earth.

* Our authority for assuming that one of the Regicides secluded himself for a time near Jamestown, may be found in Stiles' Judges, Chapter VI.

THE END

ADDENDA.

Should the author's humble labours continue to amuse his countrymen, he will very soon lay before them "The Tramontane Order; or the Knights of the Golden Horseshoe;"—an order of Knighthood in the Old Dominion, which first planted the British standard beyond the Blue Mountains.

A series of rep... American nove... portant to the study of American folklore, culture and literary history

THOMAS BAILEY ALDRICH
The Stillwater Tragedy

JAMES LANE ALLEN
A Kentucky Cardinal

GERTRUDE ATHERTON
Los Cerritos: A Romance of Modern Times
The Californians
Senator North
Aristocrats
The Splendid Idle Forties

ARLO BATES
The Puritans

OLIVER THOMAS BEARD
Bristling With Thorns

ALICE BROWN
Tiverton Tales
The County Road

FRANCIS H. BURNETT
Through One Administration

WILLIAM A. CARUTHERS
Kentuckian in New York, or the Adventures of Three Southerns
The Cavaliers of Virginia

CHARLES WADDELL CHESNUTT
The Conjure Woman
The Wife of His Youth; and Other Stories of the Colour Line
The House Behind the Cedars

KATE CHOPIN
Bayou Folk

JOHN ESTEN COOKE
The Virginia Comedians
Surry of Eagle's Nest
Mohun: or the Last Days of Lee and His Paladins
My Lady Pokahontas

ROSE TERRY COOKE
Rootbound and Other Sketches

MARGARET DELAND
John Ward, Preacher

THOMAS DIXON
The Leopard's Spots
The Clansman

EDWARD EGGLESTON
Roxy
The Faith Doctor

MARY HALLOCK FOOTE
The Led-Horse Claim

PAUL LEICESTER FORD
The Honorable Peter Stirling

HAROLD FREDERIC
Seth's Brother's Wife

MARY E. WILKINS FREEMAN
A New England Nun; and Other Stories
The Portion of Labor

HENRY B. FULLER
The Cliff Dwellers